Praise for A

The Pillars

The first book of th

"Bishop only adds luster to her

—*Booklist*

"Reads like a beautiful ballad. . . . Fans of romance and fantasy will delight in this engaging tale." —BookBrowser

"Fast-paced adventure, a winsome heroine, and a satisfying conclusion. . . . Entertaining." —*VOYA*

Shadows and Light
The second book of the *Tir Alainn Trilogy*

"A vivid fantasy world . . . with creatures from legends and myth. Beautiful." —BookBrowser

The Invisible Ring

"Entertaining otherworlds fantasy adventure. Fresh and interesting." —*Science Fiction Chronicle*

"A weird, but highly diverting and oddly heartwarming mix." —*Locus*

"A formidable talent, Ms. Bishop weaves another intense, emotional tale that sparkles with powerful and imaginative magic." —*Romantic Times*

"Plenty of adventure, romance, dazzling wizardly pyrotechnics, and [a] unique and fascinating hierarchical magic system. The author's overall sublime skill [blends] the darkly macabre with spine-tingling emotional intensity, mesmerizing magic, lush sensuality, and exciting action, all set in a thoroughly detailed, invented world of cultures in conflict. . . . It and its predecessors are genuine gems of fantasy much to be prized." —SF Site

continued . . .

Praise for the *Black Jewels Trilogy*

Daughter of the Blood

Heir to the Shadows

Queen of the Darkness

Also by Anne Bishop

The *Black Jewels* series

DAUGHTER OF THE BLOOD
HEIR TO THE SHADOWS
QUEEN OF THE DARKNESS

THE INVISIBLE RING

The *Tir Alainn* series

PILLARS OF THE WORLD
SHADOWS AND LIGHT

THE HOUSE
OF
GAIAN

Anne Bishop

A ROC BOOK

ROC

Published by New American Library, a division of
Penguin Group (USA) Inc., 375 Hudson Street,
New York, New York 10014, USA
Penguin Group (Canada), 90 Eglinton Avenue East, Suite 700, Toronto,
Ontario M4P 2Y3, Canada (a division of Pearson Penguin Canada Inc.)
Penguin Books Ltd., 80 Strand, London WC2R 0RL, England
Penguin Ireland, 25 St. Stephen's Green, Dublin 2,
Ireland (a division of Penguin Books Ltd.)
Penguin Group (Australia), 250 Camberwell Road, Camberwell, Victoria 3124,
Australia (a division of Pearson Australia Group Pty. Ltd.)
Penguin Books India Pvt. Ltd., 11 Community Centre, Panchsheel Park,
New Delhi - 110 017, India
Penguin Group (NZ), 67 Apollo Drive, Rosedale, North Shore 0632,
New Zealand (a division of Pearson New Zealand Ltd.)
Penguin Books (South Africa) (Pty.) Ltd., 24 Sturdee Avenue,
Rosebank, Johannesburg 2196, South Africa

Penguin Books Ltd., Registered Offices:
80 Strand, London WC2R 0RL, England

First published by Roc, an imprint of New American Library,
a division of Penguin Group (USA) Inc.

First Printing, October 2003
20 19 18 17 16 15 14 13

[ROC] REGISTERED TRADEMARK—MARCA REGISTRADA

Printed in the United States of America

for
Jennifer Jackson
and
Laura Anne Gilman

ACKNOWLEDGMENTS

My thanks to Blair Boone for continuing to be my first reader; Kandra and Debra Dixon for being beta readers; Nadine Fallacaro for information about things medical; Kristen Britain, Pat York, Paul Butler, Jim Hetley, Katherine Lawrence, Uriel, and Lisa Spangenberg for their thoughts and suggestions about weapons; and Pat and Bill Feidner for their continued support and encouragement.

Chapter 1

waning moon

Ashk, Bretonwood's Lady of the Woods, wandered the familiar woodland trails of her Clan's Old Place. Neall, distant kin to her despite his human face, walked beside her. She saw questions in his blue eyes, but he kept the silence she'd held since she came to his cottage early that morning and asked him to accompany her.

These trails knew her tread, both her human feet and the pads of the shadow hound that was her other form. And she knew the trails. She didn't want to leave Bretonwood, but she had to, had to keep her heart and mind on the task ahead. Whether or not she could do that depended on the young man who walked beside her.

At the end of the trail, she hesitated a moment before walking into the sunlit meadow. A favorite place. A special place where her grandfather had taken her to play and to learn to be a Lady of the Woods—and, later, although she wasn't aware of it at the time, to be the Green Lord . . . and the Hunter. He was buried in that meadow, right where he'd fallen after her arrow pierced his heart. A swift death that honored the old Lord of the Woods rather than the lingering, soul-wasting death that the nighthunter bites would have caused him. The Fae put up no markers like humans did, and Ari, Neall's wife and Bretonwood's witch, had worked her magic with care, so there was no mound of dirt, no disturbance in the grass and wildflowers. And yet, she could feel a lingering *something* when she was close to the spot, something she recognized as Kernos even though the Gatherer had taken his spirit to the Shadowed Veil so that he could go on to the Summerland.

What needs to be said and done today . . . it's fitting that it's done here, Ashk thought. *I miss you, Kernos. I miss your laughter and your wisdom. . . . And I hope with all that's in me that I have the strength and courage you believed me to have.*

She walked to the center of the meadow before she set her bow, canteen, and quiver of arrows on the ground. Her woodland eyes, a brown-flecked green, scanned the trees as she ruffled her ash-brown hair with her fingers. The cropped hair felt strange after letting it flow down her back for so many years, but she couldn't afford to have anything interfere with the smooth, swift movement of drawing an arrow from the quiver and nocking it to the bow. Not where she was going. Not with the enemy she was heading out to meet. It would be better to die a swift death than to fall into the Inquisitors' hands.

Neall set his things beside hers as he, too, scanned the trees. "I don't see any sign of the nighthunters."

"There are a few left, but not many," Ashk replied. "There's still a feeling of wrongness in the woods, but it's fainter now." She looked at Neall, who was still crouched beside their weapons. "You feel it, too."

"Yes."

Ashk nodded. He didn't understand yet what his being so attuned to the subtleties of the woods meant, but soon he would.

"Ashk." Neall rose to his feet. He took a deep breath, puffing his cheeks as he exhaled. "With everything that needs to be done, do you really think we should take the time for a lesson?"

For this one, Ashk thought, stepping away from the weapons. *Because of what needs to be done, it's time for this one.*

Neall followed a few steps behind her, his eyes and attention still on the trees. The nighthunters didn't like sunlight, and she and Neall were in the center of the large, sunlit meadow; but even during the daylight hours, the creatures the Inquisitors had created by twisting magic were a threat in the shadows of the woods.

He wasn't paying attention to her because he trusted her.

She turned, said, "Change," immediately shifted into her other form, and sprang at him, her fangs bared.

Even a month ago, he would have hesitated for that fatal moment that would have given her the advantage. Now he shifted in an instant, and the young stag leaped aside, pivoting as soon as he touched the ground, his head lowered, the tines of his antlers a weapon against her fangs.

She charged him again and again—and he met her, again and again, never giving her the opening to leap in and nip him in a place that, in a real attack, could disable him. He thought like a man, but he'd learned how to use that stag body that was his other form. Because he thought like a man, he didn't do the one thing a real stag would have done—he didn't run. There were times when she'd chased him around the meadow to build his endurance, to help him learn the stag body, but this lesson was a battle to confirm something for herself and to prove something to him.

Panting from the effort, she finally leaped away, putting some distance between them. Then she changed back to her human form.

"Enough," she said, walking slowly toward their gear.

He remained in stag form, pivoting to watch her.

She bent to pick up her canteen, winced a little as her muscles protested. It had been awhile since she'd worked that hard in her shadow hound form. She glanced at him, could feel his confusion and anger pulsing over the meadow. "Enough, Neall."

He hesitated a moment longer, then changed back to human form and strode toward her, his hands curled into fists.

"Mother's tits, Ashk! What was *that* about?"

"A lesson," she replied quietly. She opened the canteen and filled her mouth with water, savoring the cool wetness before she swallowed. "Kernos did it differently with me, but the lesson was the same."

He stared at her. As understanding filled his blue eyes, he shook his head in denial. "I'm not."

"You are."

"I *can't* become *the* Lord of the Woods. I'm not pure Fae. They would never accept it. Besides," he added, sounding a bit desperate, "*you're* the Hunter now, and I'm not about to challenge *you*."

Ashk took another sip of water before answering. "Do you accept that you are *a* Lord of the Woods?"

He shrugged, looking uncomfortable. "That's not the same thing."

"Do you accept what you are?"

"Yes," he said reluctantly.

Ashk nodded. "Yes. You're Fae, Neall. Looks alone are not what determines who is and isn't Fae. It's the gift of the other form, and our command of the animals in our world, that separates us from the humans and the wiccanfae. And you, my young stag, cannot deny that you have that gift."

"But . . ."

"Your mother was a witch, but she was born of a witch mother and a Fae father. And your father was born of human and Fae. Those matings made you what you are."

"Ashk . . ."

"As the Hunter, I command you, young Lord. And as the Hunter, I am telling you what I require of you."

Looking troubled, Neall stepped forward and fetched his own canteen.

Ashk took another mouthful of water, closed her canteen, and dropped it on the grass at her feet. She waited until he had slaked his thirst before speaking, keeping her eyes focused on the meadow, knowing intuitively that he'd listen with less protest if she wasn't looking directly at him.

"Padrick and I have talked," she said quietly, "and we've decided some things that concern you. I've told the Clan bard, so he'll stand as witness, but Padrick needs to do things the human way because of his estate and because he's a baron, so he's having his man of business draw up the papers naming you the guardian of Evan and Caitlin."

"Ashk—"

"It's necessary," she said sharply, cutting him off. "If something happens to Padrick, Evan becomes the next Baron of Breton. But he's still a child, and he'll need someone who can teach him what it means to be a good baron. You lived in a baron's house when you were growing up. You understand how to run an estate and what the people need. You can teach him those things." She took a deep breath to steady herself, feeling her stomach clench at the thought of having to say the next words. "And if something should happen to Evan, Padrick has named you his second heir."

"Ashk—"

"It's proper," she said, giving him a slashing look that silenced him. "It's customary for the title of baron to be passed from father to eldest son, but a baron can name anyone his heir, whether he has sons or not. Padrick has cousins, but none that he feels would rule Breton and this county the way it needs to be ruled, none who would understand the wants and needs of *all* the people who live here—the Fae, the humans, the wiccanfae, and the Small Folk, too." Watching him, she smiled at his discomfort. "The Small Folk have always been wary of the Fae, even here where we live in the world and walk the same woods, but they do talk to the Green Lady, and I've heard quite a bit about the young Lord of the

Woods and the witch who has taken him for her husband. 'Look here now, Lady Ashk'"—she lowered her voice to imitate one of the small men—" 'It's a fine thing for Lady Ari to be giving us a bit of cream or butter that's more than she has use for, and it's a fine thing for the young Lord to offer us a bit of beef. It's a treat to have them, so it is, but we're a wee bit worried that they're leaving their own table too lean, if you see what we're saying.' And I lie with an honest heart and assure them that I've never known the stew to be thin of meat or that either of you did without butter or cream," she finished in her own voice.

"We have enough," Neall muttered.

"And it harms no one if the stew is a little thin on meat every now and again. The fact is, the Small Folk feel easy with you and Ari, and that's not something to dismiss." Ashk hesitated, then sighed. "There's one other thing. If the fight comes to Breton, I want you to take Ari up to Tir Alainn. I want you to take Evan and Caitlin and the other children as well. And I want you to stay with them."

Temper flashed in Neall's eyes. "A baron's heir, when he's a grown man, doesn't run from a fight. Neither does a Lord of the Woods."

"It would be easier to stay," Ashk agreed. "I—and Padrick—need you to go."

"There are enough elders who stay in Tir Alainn who could look after the children."

"The Fae children, yes, but not the human ones. Tir Alainn will be strange to them, and they'll need someone they can look to who understands their way of looking at the world."

Neall stared at her.

Ashk huffed in exasperation. "If the fight comes here, it's not just the Fae at risk."

"You mean all the children, don't you?" Neall said slowly.

She nodded. "From the Clan, the village, the gentry homes, the tenant farms. Yes. All the children. And your horses."

"You can't protect things just because they're mine."

"I want Ari protected because she's a witch, one of the Mother's Daughters, and as she grows heavier with the babe, she won't be able to outrun an enemy if it comes to that. You have two of the finest Fae stallions anywhere in the west, not to mention the Fae mares that were bred by the Lord of the Horse himself. We can't count what has already been lost because of the Inquisitors coming to Sylvalan. We can't know what else will be lost before we're able to drive them out. But we can do our best to protect the people and things we'll need to rebuild our land and our lives. So you'll do what I need you to do. I can't look back, Neall. When I ride out of here, I need to go with an easy heart. And that is a burden I place on your shoulders."

Neall looked away. When he looked at her again, his eyes were years older. "I'll do what you need."

"Thank you."

Neall sighed. "This is just talk anyway. Nothing is going to happen to Padrick, and nothing is going to happen to you. You'll still be the Hunter when you're a wrinkled great-grandmother."

"No, I don't think so," Ashk replied quietly. "Power waxes and wanes, Neall, and it doesn't always follow the years. There are some who have ascended to command their particular gift and remained strong for decades, and there are others who have burned brightly for a few years before their power faded and another's power blazed. I was twenty when I became the Hunter. In a few more years, you'll be a seasoned man in your prime, and I'll be quite content to be nothing more than a Lady of the Woods playing with my grandchildren."

"You've got some years to go then," Neall said. "Evan's only eleven years old."

"And you're twenty-two and will soon be a father," Ashk replied. "There's a river of living between where he is in his life and where you are, but in another ten years, that river won't be as wide as you seem to think." She stepped up to him, cupped his face in her hands. "I hope you have a long Green Season. I hope when this is over, there will be years and years when you and Ari need to do nothing more than raise children and horses. I hope that with all my heart, for your sake and Ari's—and for my sake and Padrick's as well. But if that isn't to be, then know, here and now, that you're strong enough to be what you have to be." She kissed him lightly, then stepped away. "You'll do, Neall. You'll do just fine. Come along now. The others are waiting. Padrick wants to talk with all of us."

"If you're gone, how will I know how to be the Hunter?" Neall asked softly.

Ashk's hand froze over her gear for a moment. Then she settled her quiver comfortably on her back and picked up her bow and canteen. "The knowing is part of the gift. There are some things that aren't spoken of between the one whose power is fading and the one who ascends. But when that moment comes, the knowledge comes with it."

Including knowing why the Fae have good reason to be wary of the Hunter. But that's something you don't need to know until the time comes. That's something Kernos wouldn't tell me. If the Fae aren't careful, they'll discover they have a more vengeful enemy than the Inquisitors. The Inquisitors can only kill them. I can destroy them. I wonder if Aiden knew that when he came looking for the Hunter to help him convince the Fae to protect the witches and the Old Places against the Black Coats.

"Let's go, young Lord."

Morag, the Gatherer of Souls, leaned against a tree that gave her a clear view of one of the trails that led to the Bretonwood Clan house. Shivering, despite the warmth of the summer day, she wrapped her arms around herself. It didn't help.

"Are you cold?" Aiden asked quietly, coming to stand beside her.

In body and soul, she thought as she studied the black-haired, blue-eyed man who was the Bard, the Fae Lord of Song. "Why do bards and minstrels romanticize war? What is so glorious about men coming together at a certain place and time to die by the hundreds, by the thousands?"

"I don't know," Aiden replied. "The courage, perhaps, and to acknowledge that the presence of a few determines the outcome for so many."

"Will it, Aiden? If they have an army, and we have an army, will the battles between them really determine anything? If the eastern barons and Inquisitors lose, will they go away and let the rest of us go back to living the way we want to live? If we lose, will the people of Sylvalan just submit?"

"They submitted in the east. They watched the witches die. They watched the lives of their mothers and sisters and wives be torn apart. They stood aside and did nothing when the barons and Inquisitors ordered the . . . maiming . . . of all those women."

"I don't think they'll stand aside here," Morag said softly. "I think they'll fight on, village by village, until there's nothing and no one left to be crushed by the Witch's Hammer. If that's the case, will those thousands dying on a battlefield really matter?"

Aiden studied her for a long moment. "You could stay here with Ari and Neall. You don't have to go."

"Of course I do. I'm the Gatherer. I'm Death's Mistress. My place is on a battlefield." Morag sighed. "I should have killed the Master Inquisitor when I had the chance. Maybe things would be different now if I had."

"Maybe," Aiden agreed. "And maybe if you had, the battle would have come sooner, before we had any chance to meet it."

"I gave him a chance to leave, and to leave us be. I won't give him a second chance. I won't give any of them a second chance."

Aiden shifted uncomfortably.

None of the Fae—except Ashk—were comfortable with that aspect of her gift, but until last summer, it had been something that had been mentioned in old stories and songs. Unlike the other Fae whose gift made them Death's Servants, she could gather a spirit from one who was dying, not just from one who was already dead. And she could gather a spirit from someone who was very much among the living. She could ride through a village and leave nothing but corpses in her wake. It was one thing to know that was an aspect of the Gatherer's power; it was quite another to realize the person who wielded that gift was willing to use it.

And she would use it. *Had* used it. By the time she'd found the Witch's Hammer last summer, she had killed all of the Inquisitors he'd brought with him to Sylvalan. She'd hoped that would convince him to leave Sylvalan and never come back, but that had been a foolish, futile hope. So the Gatherer would follow the Hunter into battle, and Death would be her weapon.

Morag brushed her black hair away from her face. Ashk and Neall were coming down the trail, both looking solemn. She turned away and walked to the large outdoor table where Padrick waited—and she wondered if the Gatherer or the Hunter would be Death's true mistress in the days ahead.

Ashk studied the faces of the people sitting around the table. Padrick had asked to talk to just the Fae at this gathering since he would be meeting with the squires, magistrates, and captains of the guard at another time to plan the human defenses.

Good people, she thought as she studied them. *Strong-willed people.*

Aiden, the Bard, with his sharp mind and tongue and his passionate desire to protect the witches, the Daughters of the Great

Mother. Lyrra, the Muse, whose gift nurtured the poets and story-tellers. Morag, whose passion for life made her even more dangerous as Death's Mistress. Morphia, the Lady of Dreams and Morag's sister. Sheridan, the Clan's Lord of the Hawks, who had recently become Morphia's lover. Neall and Ari, who had changed the lives of many of the Fae around the table simply by being the people they were. And Padrick, Baron of Breton, gentry and Fae, Ashk's friend, lover, and husband.

Combined with the humans, would they be able to hold on to the things they held dear and to keep them safe?

Padrick unrolled a map of Sylvalan and placed a stone on each corner to hold it down.

"I've heard from two of the western barons," Padrick said. "Despite Baron Liam's absence for the vote at the barons' council a few weeks ago—or, perhaps, *because* of his absence after his impassioned speech—the vote went against all the decrees the eastern barons were trying to get accepted so that they would apply to all of Sylvalan. But there was no vote to demand that the eastern barons restore the rights of the women who live in their counties. Which leaves the people in those eastern counties at the mercy of the men who rule them."

"That is the human way, is it not?" Aiden asked.

Ashk could hear the effort he was making to keep his voice neutral.

"It is," Padrick said. "A baron can rule as he pleases and do what he pleases. The decrees provide a standard we're all expected to honor, but no one is naive enough to believe every man with power wields it in the same way. However, this has left the eastern barons who sold themselves to the Inquisitors twisting in the wind, especially after the news that an entire village of women chose death for themselves and their daughters rather than live with the constrictions that had been put on them. The fact that the news traveled so swiftly and couldn't be contained has also changed things. Any eastern baron who had considered bringing in the Black Coats won't do it now, at the risk of having his own people turn against him. Those men can't be counted as allies, but they aren't enemies. At least, not yet. That leaves the rest of Sylvalan standing against the eastern barons who are controlled by the Inquisitors."

"Stalemate," Aiden said.

Padrick shook his head. "I don't think so. If the Inquisitors had been willing to let us live as we choose, they never would have crossed the Una River. So I don't think a vote in the barons' council is going to stop them; it will just change the way they attack." He ran his finger down the eastern side of the map, from the north down to the southern coast. "They've been pushing steadily east and south, always pushing out from a place where a baron has reshaped his county to match the Inquisitors' demands. From what I can tell, since their return this spring, they've concentrated on destroying the witches to eliminate the magic in the Old Places. Or they did until Liam gave them another enemy to focus on."

"He wasn't the only baron the Black Coats focused on," Ashk said softly.

"No, he wasn't," Padrick replied grimly. "That was a mistake on their part. They may know of the Fae, but they don't *know* the Fae."

Ashk met Padrick's eyes for a long moment, then focused on the map. He was right. If the Black Coats had realized what kind of enemy they would awaken by attacking Breton and Breton-wood, they would have kept their distance.

"You think they're going to attack the baron you helped?" she asked.

Padrick hesitated. "I think if this Master Inquisitor is as intelligent and powerful as he seems, what he's going to focus on destroying is this." His finger landed heavily on the map.

"The Mother's Hills," Ashk whispered, feeling a chill go through her.

"As long as the House of Gaian rules the Mother's Hills, there will be witches. As long as there are witches, there will be vessels to embrace and channel the Great Mother's power and breathe magic into the world. As long as there is magic in Sylvalan, there will be the Small Folk—and the Fae. So, yes, once he realizes those hills are the wellspring of magic in Sylvalan because of who rules there, he'll throw everything he can at those witches until he destroys them—or until he and those who follow him are destroyed. And Liam, and the people of Willowsbrook, are standing squarely in his path."

Neall leaned closer to the map. "Those hills cover a lot of land, and I doubt the eastern barons can gather enough men to form an army big enough to take them."

"If the Inquisitors control the barons of Wolfram and Arktos, and it seems likely they do, they can gather an army that's strong enough to be a real threat," Padrick said.

"If they divide the army and have half swing below the hills to come up on the other side, they'll be attacking from both directions," Neall said.

"So we block the way," Ashk said. "Follow the curve of the hills to the south and north. If the barons who rule the counties there will stand against the Inquisitors with the help of the Clans in those areas, there would be no threat to the midlands or the western side of the hills, so the midland barons could send warriors to defend the gaps."

"Assuming you can get enough of the Fae to help," Aiden said with a trace of bitterness.

"If they want to spend time in the world, they can help defend the world," Ashk said coldly.

An uneasy silence settled around the table until Padrick finally cleared his throat. "There might be another problem with the Fae's presence in those southern counties. I've gathered that their ... manners ... haven't made the humans think well of them. The barons may not accept the Fae being among their people."

"They'd better accept it if they don't want to be outnumbered and crushed in a battle," Ashk snapped. Then she relented. She'd heard enough over the years about how the Fae dealt with humans in other parts of Sylvalan to understand why the humans wouldn't trust the Fae, even to fight a common enemy. "All right. We'll head for the southern end of the Mother's Hills first to convince the barons there to accept us as allies. Letters from you might ease things."

"You'll have them."

They talked for another hour, but it was more to confirm the things she and Padrick had already decided. A meeting of all the western barons would take place in Breton in a few days. Ashk had sent out the call to all the western Clans to have some of the huntsmen from each Clan join her. Now she'd divide those men, sending some to the northern end of the Mother's Hills and some to the south—and some would go to Willowsbrook. She hoped Baron Liam was as open-minded as Padrick thought. Based on what she knew about the Fae beyond the west, Liam and his people were about to meet something they hadn't seen before.

The meeting concluded, they'd all risen to stretch their legs and get something to eat when Ashk noticed the woman standing far enough away not to intrude on their discussion, but just as obviously waiting for her attention.

As Ashk walked over to meet her guest, tension tightened her shoulders.

"Blessings of the day to you, Lady Ashk," the woman said.

"Blessings of the day, Gwynith," Ashk replied. "Forgive my being blunt, but I've a long journey ahead of me and much to do before I go. What brings you here?"

"I'll be heading for the midlands myself come morning," Gwynith said. "I came down this way to tell you."

Ashk frowned. "A Lady of the Moon doesn't need to tell me her plans to travel."

"That's why I *had* to tell you. All the western Clans have heard the Hunter's call, and we've heard about the Black Coats, so I had to tell you because I don't know how this might change what you need to do."

"What are you talking about?"

"Dianna's power is waning." Gwynith frowned. "No, not waning, exactly, but there's a . . . challenger . . . and those of us who share the gift of the moon are being drawn together to find out who will ascend to become the new Lady of the Moon—and the Huntress."

Ashk said nothing for a moment. She didn't approve of Dianna or the Huntress's refusal to do anything to protect the witches and the Old Places, but at least she was a familiar adversary. A new Huntress . . . Gwynith was right. For good or ill, this *could* change things. "Then I wish you well."

Gwynith shook her head. "I'm not the one. I feel the call, so I go to bear witness, and to offer my pledge of loyalty to the one who commands my gift. But I wanted you to know, if I have to choose between the Huntress and the Hunter . . . You need only ask, and I'll do whatever you need."

Knowing Gwynith could be stripped of her power if she defied whoever became the Lady of the Moon, Ashk said, "Let's hope you don't have to make that choice."

Chapter 2

waning moon

"You don't have to do this."

Selena stopped packing the toiletries she'd set out on the dressing table to take with her on the journey, looked into the mirror, and met her younger sister's woodland eyes. "Yes, I do."

"You don't owe them anything."

Selena struggled not to smile. So fierce, so protective. Rhyann had always been that way, willing to hurl insults—or sticks and clods of dirt when words weren't sufficient—in defense of a sister who was different, who wasn't even a real sister by birth.

What she wouldn't tell this sister of the heart was that it was Rhyann's loyalty and love that was as much a spur to making this journey as her own needs.

"No, I don't owe them anything." Selena turned to face the young woman who had been a touchstone during the storms in her life. "I'm not doing this for the Fae, Rhyann. I'm doing it for myself. The moon calls. I can't escape its pull any more than the sea can. There's a power in me waiting to be released, filling me until it's become everything. I could celebrate that rising alone, but I think I need to do this by the Fae's customs. This time I need to stand among them."

"Why?" Rhyann asked, her voice worried and a little plaintive.

Selena sat on the dressing table stool, then waited for Rhyann to settle on the corner of the bed. "Do you believe what the storyteller, Skelly, told us when he came traveling this way? Do you believe there are men called Inquisitors who have made it their work to kill witches and destroy the magic in the Old Places?"

Rhyann nodded reluctantly. "It's hard to deny what he said when the wind tells the same tale. Every puff of air that comes from the east brings sorrow and anger and fear—and a feeling of malevolence that rejoices in the sorrow . . . and especially in the fear."

"Do you believe it was the Fae Lord of Song, the Bard himself, who brought that news and the warnings to Skelly's village?"

Rhyann shrugged. "That makes no difference."

"Yes, it does." Selena leaned forward. "It means there are some Fae who haven't forgotten who and what the House of Gaian is. It means there are some Fae who care about more than themselves. If *they* have finally been stirred to care, can we sit in our villages here in the Mother's Hills and do nothing?"

"No one has said we'll do nothing!" Rhyann snapped.

Selena stared at her sister, no longer really seeing her. "I've been having dreams since the Solstice. They've been getting stronger and stronger. I'm standing in a meadow I've never seen before, and there, in the center of it, the grass is greener, richer. Somehow, I float above it, and I can make out the shape of a stag. When I float back down, my bare feet touch that spot, and I feel the vibration of thousands of feet marching in step. I breathe in and choke on the stench of blood and death. I walk a little ways away and drink from a pool of clear water—and gag on the thick taste of gore that chokes the stream that feeds the pool. And I hear a heartbeat, slow and big, and I know that the woods has come alive. It hears. It sees. And it's coming toward the Mother's Hills. Then I'm surrounded by moonlight, filled with moonlight, and I know I can't stop whatever is in the woods from coming here, can't change its coming. But I *can* become strong enough to meet it."

Rhyann tipped her head to one side. "What happens then?"

"What?"

"In the dream. What happens?"

"I—" Selena pressed her lips together. Two shadow hound bitches racing through moon-bathed woods, racing toward a common enemy—a shadowy male figure standing in the center of a high, wide circle of female corpses. "I don't remember." She rubbed her hands over her face. Mother's mercy, she was tired. "I have to go, Rhyann. Succeed or fail, I have to try. This power inside me won't let me be unless I try."

"I'm going with you."

Selena let her hands fall into her lap. "No, you are not. I've already had this discussion with Father. I don't need an escort. It's better if I go alone."

"It's better if we travel together for a while. Father won't worry as much."

A chill ran through her, making her voice sharp. "What are you talking about? You're not going anywhere."

"I've reached my majority," Rhyann replied, equally sharp. "I can do whatever I want without asking anyone's permission." She sighed. "If we're willing to believe that the Bard cares for more than the Fae, isn't it possible that the Lady of Dreams also cares?"

"What do my dreams have to do with your leaving?" Rhyann couldn't leave. She *couldn't*. Father was simply going to have to do something about it. He'd always been the more successful parent when it came to dealing with Rhyann.

"Not because of your dreams," Rhyann said reluctantly. "Because of mine." After a long hesitation, she continued. "I dream of fire. Angry fire. Dreadful fire. I feel the heat of it, the pain of it. And then music is . . . silenced. Lost. Devoured by flame." She rested her head against the bedpost. "That's why I have to go. I don't think I can stop the fire, but I can prevent the music from being silenced."

Rhyann closed her right hand into a loose fist. When she opened her hand, a small ball of golden light filled her palm. "Dreams and will," she said softly. "Once upon a time, we made a whole world out of nothing more than dreams and will."

"And earth, water, fire, and air," Selena said, just as softly.

"Sunlight and moonbeams as the path between worlds. Do you remember the Crone whom Mother took us to see eight years ago, the summer I turned thirteen and was given my pentagram?"

Selena reached up and brushed her fingers across her own pentagram. She'd also gone through a ceremony that formally acknowledged the start of a girl's journey toward becoming a woman of power, a woman of the House of Gaian. And she remembered, at seventeen, standing with her mother and father while the Crones performed the ritual and presented the girls with the pentagrams that symbolized their bond to the Great Mother, that identified them as witches, as the Mother's Daughters. She couldn't say then, and couldn't say now, if she'd been prouder on the day when she'd received her pentagram or on the day when she'd watched Rhyann receive hers.

"I remember her," Selena said. "I remember what she taught us that summer."

"So do I.

Selena sighed. "Promise me you won't travel east of the Mother's Hills by yourself. Promise me that much."

"Will you promise the same?"

Her temper flashed, and she felt the heat of it under her skin, but she held back the scalding reply she wanted to make. Rhyann's temper could match hers any day, so what was the point of hot tempers now and hotter tears later when it was love holding the torch to the kindling?

"I promise the same."

Rhyann stared at her in surprise. Then she exhaled gustily and stood up. "Let's finish packing your saddlebags so I can take care of mine. We'll need to get an early start tomorrow."

Selena stared at the ceiling, seeing nothing in the night-dark room, her heart pounding too hard, too fast.

Just a dream, she thought as she crawled out of bed and stumbled toward the wash basin. Her hands shook as she poured water from the pitcher into the basin. *Just a dream, brought on because I know Rhyann isn't going to stay home where it's safe. Or as safe as any place can be these days.*

She stripped off her sweat-soaked nightgown, then twisted her hair to hold it back long enough to splash some water on her face. She dunked a washcloth in the basin, rung it out, and rubbed it over her body. The water didn't make her feel as chilly as the sweat drying on her skin, and she imagined washing off the scum of the dream along with the sweat.

Then she focused her thoughts and sent a flicker of the Mother's branch of fire to the candle sitting on the dressing table. The wick lit, and the single flame softened the dark into varying shades of gray.

Moving slowly, she went to the dressing table, sank down on the stool, and stared into the mirror.

The face that stared back at her wasn't human. Had never looked human. Her hair was a pure black, not the dark brown that was common, and her eyes were a gray-green instead of the brown-flecked green that was the dominant color among the people who came from the House of Gaian. Neither of those things would have drawn much attention to her, but the face . . . People looked at her and saw one of the Fae. And she was. May the Mother help her, she was as much Fae as she was witch, the product of an affair between a Fae lady and a feckless young man. The Fae lady hadn't wanted a child with a mixed heritage, and the feckless young man had turned to his married older brother for help with the babe the lady had left with him before disappearing from all of their lives. Just like the young man, who asked his brother's wife to watch the babe one afternoon and never came back. A year later, he sent a brief letter, letting his brother know he was well. He didn't ask about or mention the child, and they never heard from him again.

There had been times when other children had teased her unkindly about her pointed ears or the shape of her face, when she'd wanted to see the two people whose mating had produced her—to shout and rage and scream at them for being so careless and uncaring. In the end, it hadn't mattered. Not because of the man, her uncle by blood and father by heart, who had taught her to ride as well as to dance. Not because of the woman he'd married, who had shown her with hugs and scolds that she was a beloved daughter—and taught her what it meant to be a witch. In the end, it hadn't mattered because of Rhyann, the little sister who adored her. Rhyann, who had proudly come into her room one day to show her the triangle caps she'd made out of scraps of material and sewed together with clumsy, childish stitches so that she could have pointy ears, too. Rhyann who, the first time Selena had inadvertently changed into her other form, had carried her terrified, furry sister home—and then stayed with Selena for all the hours it had taken their parents to calm her down enough to find the key inside herself that changed her back into a child. And it was Rhyann, when needs seemed to tangle her up until she wasn't sure anymore who she was, who would always tell her fiercely, "You're a witch. You're always a witch, one of the Mother's Daughters."

Always, forever a witch. A rare and powerful witch, who could wield the power of the Mother's branches—earth, air, water, and fire—in equal measure. There were many in the Mother's Hills who were gifted with all four branches, but most of them had one primary branch and a lesser ability with the other three. But for her, all four were primary and flowed from her as easily as she breathed. In that, she and Rhyann were true sisters.

But she was also a Lady of the Moon, something she hadn't known until eight years ago. The Crone who had taught her and Rhyann some of the oldest magic known to the House of Gaian had recognized that part of her. The old woman had refused to say how she knew what she did about the Fae—and the Ladies of the Moon and *the* Lady of the Moon in particular—but that knowledge helped Selena understand the part of herself that had felt like a stranger living inside her skin.

Now that part of her heritage was rising, calling, commanding her to answer. So she would follow the call to the place where the other Ladies of the Moon would gather, and she would stand as a challenger to find out if she was strong enough to ascend and become *the* Lady of the Moon—and the Huntress.

She stood up, stepped away from the dressing table, and shifted into her other form. Then she put her front paws on the stool in order to look into the mirror again.

Shadow hound. A deadly predator the Ladies of the Moon used for their Wild Hunts.

Selena shifted again, stared into the mirror, her hands braced on the stool.

Two shadow hound bitches racing through moon-bathed woods, racing toward a common enemy.

Who was the second bitch? Was one of the Sleep Sisters just playing with her, haunting her with dreams to weaken her for the challenge ahead, or was this a gift from the Lady of Dreams herself, showing her an ally against a common foe? She would need an ally, especially if she won this challenge. Who was the second bitch?

Cold again, despite the warm summer night, Selena blew out the candle and returned to bed to huddle under the covers.

A shadowy male figure standing in the center of a high, wide circle of female corpses.

Yes, she needed an ally, because tonight, in that circle of corpses, she'd seen her mother—and Rhyann.

Chapter 3

waning moon

Breanna grumbled as she gathered up her bow and quiver of arrows from the corner of her wardrobe. She continued to grumble as she walked the corridors of her family's manor house to reach the kitchen door.

The trouble with men was that they saw the world in a way that was too rational to be wrong ... but also just wasn't quite right. And a man who was a baron as well as an older brother was the most stubborn, ornery creature in the world—especially when his argument that she should know how to handle weapons was supported by a Fae Lord who was *the* Lord of the Hawks.

"The featherheads," Breanna muttered as she opened the kitchen door and stood on the threshold. She looked down at Idjit, who was laying to one side of the doorway, busily gnawing on a soup bone Glynis, their housekeeper, must have given him. "They're both featherheads, even if only one of them has the ability to change into a form with actual feathers. And where are they? Tell me that. They're both so keen for me to interrupt *my* day, and then they don't even show up. They're probably off doing important man things—like molting in the case of the Fae featherhead. Or doing whatever barons do as an excuse for being late to an appointment *they made*."

The small black dog rolled his eyes, waved his tail, and kept gnawing on the soup bone.

"You're no help," Breanna said sourly. "Of course you're not. You're male, too."

She closed the kitchen door and headed across the extensive sweep of grass that was the manor house's back lawn. Since the cousins who had escaped from the eastern part of Sylvalan had arrived earlier that summer to stay with her family at Willowsbrook's Old Place, there were too many animals around the stables and paddocks and too many children running and playing on the back lawn to set up practice targets in those areas. So Clay, who was in charge of the horses, had set up bales of hay near the kitchen garden.

It wasn't that she objected to target practice. In truth, she often did it as a way to settle her thoughts and regain the balance between mind and body. What she objected to was the assumption that she *needed* target practice. Mother's tits! She could shoot as well as most men, had been bringing home game for several years now. Even Clay had told Liam and Falco that she didn't need to learn how to hit a target. Had the Baron of Willowsbrook and the Lord of the Hawks listened? No, they had not. The featherheads.

Breanna stopped and looked at the men and older boys who were cleaning out stables or grooming horses, looked at the women hanging wash on the lines, looked at the youngsters playing some kind of game on the lawn, looked beyond her kin to the woods that bordered the lawn and thought of the Small Folk who lived there. She pulled her shoulders back, trying to ease the tension in her chest.

"A copper for your thoughts."

Breanna turned toward the voice. Her cousin Fiona stood a few feet away, her hands filled with another bow and quiver of arrows.

"You're doing target practice too?" Breanna asked.

Fiona shrugged.

Breanna turned away, focusing on the woods again. "Do no harm," she said quietly. "That's the witch's creed. There are good reasons for that creed, good reasons why we should use the power within us only to help, to heal, to maintain the balance between the Great Mother and all the creatures who live on her bounty."

"And to protect?" Fiona suggested softly.

"And to protect." Breanna sighed. "I keep thinking that I don't need to learn to use weapons against other people, that I already have a weapon inside me more destructive than anything a man could create. Then I wonder if all the witches who have died at the hands of the Inquisitors had thought the same way and learned their error too late. Or had they been so hobbled by our creed that they hadn't even tried?"

"Could you kill a man, Breanna?"

She felt something settle inside her, something that had been haunting her sleep lately. She turned to face her cousin. "Yes, I could. If that's what it took to protect my family or the Old Place or the Small Folk . . . yes, I could." She lifted the hand that held the bow. "It would be easier to do that using a weapon made by human hands than break the creed I live by and use the power inside me to do harm. But I would do that, too, if there was no other choice."

"We're of one mind about this," Fiona said. "I've lost my mother and my grandmother. My father, too. And too many aunts and uncles. We're a large, sprawling family. Or we were. Sometimes I think we should have fought back, should have stood up to the baron when he started making decrees that took away so much. But we couldn't have done that without doing harm, and the elders held by the creed—and didn't understand the cost until it was too late for them to do anything but save those they could by sacrificing themselves."

"It was more complicated than that," Breanna said gently.

Fiona sighed. "I know. But some days it's easier to blame those I loved for dying to save the rest of us than to admit that breaking the creed wouldn't have made any difference. Not then. Not there. The Inquisitors already controlled the baron, and the baron controlled the people. What good would it have done to wither the crops in the fields or make the wells dry? All that would have done is hurt the common folk and prove witches are the evil creatures the Black Coats accuse us of being."

"You don't know the elders are dead."

"Breanna."

Fiona's voice held so much knowledge and pain. But not acceptance. If the Inquisitors rode into *this* Old Place, at least some of the witches here would use everything they could summon to fight back.

Breanna took a deep breath, let it out slowly. "My primary branch of the Great Mother is air. Yours is earth. It would help to have fire and water as well if it comes down to a fight here."

"Not everyone will break the creed. Even with what they know, with what they've seen."

"I know." Breanna tucked some strands of dark hair back into her loose braid. She looked at the bow in her hand. Even if they didn't use their power as a weapon, there were still ways for the witches to fight back. "Do you know how to use a bow?"

Fiona made a rude noise. "Of course I do."

"We might as well get some practice in before our 'instructors' show up to give us some practice."

Fiona laughed, but there was an edge to it. "I imagine Baron Liam and Lord Falco just want to be sure you're available and waiting so that you can protect them when they show up."

"Protect them from what?" Now that Fiona had said that, she realized Liam *did* tend to stay close to her when he visited, and when he wasn't with her, he spent his time with his mother Elinore, who, along with his little sister Brooke, was also living at Old Willowsbrook for the time being, or with her grandmother, Nuala. And Falco tended to head for any group of men if he couldn't be with her. What would two adult men need protection from that they would behave that way?

Breanna felt laughter bubbling up, threatening to burst free. It was the look on Fiona's face that made her force the laughter back. "Jean? You think they're going to that much effort to avoid *Jean?* Mother's tits, Fiona, the girl is only sixteen."

"And flirts outrageously with anything in trousers that has a handsome-enough face."

"All right," Breanna said, uncomfortable with the anger rising in Fiona, "she flirts."

"You make it sound as if she's too young to think of men and beds," Fiona said fiercely. "And perhaps she is too young to think of men in *that* way, but she's already become a predator where men are concerned. She wants, and expects, male adoration. She wants, and expects, men to fulfill her every wish and whim."

"Didn't we all want that at that age?" Breanna asked cautiously. The anger and contempt in Fiona's voice worried her as much as the word *predator.* "Didn't we all want the romance of being special?" *Don't we still want that?*

"You were never sixteen in that way. Neither was I. You never would have . . ." Fiona pressed her lips together until they were a thin, grim line. "She doesn't always live by the creed when she feels slighted by a man's lack of attention."

A chill raced up Breanna's spine. That spike of fear sharpened her voice. "What are you saying?"

"That Liam and Falco have a good reason to be wary of being alone with Jean—especially when it's clear to everyone but Jean that neither of them are comfortable with her interest and don't want to play the ardent lover."

"You can't be serious. You actually think she would use magic to harm them because they aren't interested in her?"

Fiona nodded slowly. "Because they aren't interested in her . . . and because they *are* interested in you."

Breanna stared at Fiona, too stunned to speak.

"Oh, not in the same way. I don't mean that," Fiona continued. "But you're the one they both inquire about first. You're the one they look to in order to understand our way of life. Jean resents your 'power' over them because she wants it for herself."

Breanna shook her head, not to deny what Fiona had said but because she still couldn't accept that Jean might be a danger to Liam and Falco. It was one thing to consider breaking the witches' creed in order to defend her family and home; it was quite another to break that creed and do harm simply because you *could* do it. "Have you any proof that Jean ever harmed a boy because he wasn't sufficiently attentive?"

"Proof? No. Suspicions? Oh, yes. But she always acted the darling around the elders, and they wouldn't believe sweet, pretty Jean has the heart of a cold-blooded bitch. There was nothing serious, you understand. Just little spiteful things that could have been easily explained as simple accidents if they hadn't occurred soon after a boy she wanted showed a preference for another girl." Fiona sighed. "I didn't want her to come with us. Even knowing what she would have faced if she'd stayed, I didn't want her to come with us. All during the journey, I was afraid she would do something that would call too much attention to us, make the guards in the villages we had to pass look too closely at where we were coming from. Make them look too closely at *us*."

"But she didn't do anything," Breanna said. "Perhaps, with Nuala keeping an eye on her . . ."

Fiona shook her head. "I told you, the elders only saw what Jean wanted them to see—and that's the face she shows to Nuala, too. Pretty, sometimes pouty in a teasing way, fluttery feminine Jean. She was fearful enough of the people the Inquisitors have turned against our kind to behave on the journey here, but the only reason she didn't do anything more damaging back home was because . . ."

"Because?" Breanna prodded.

Fiona looked uncomfortable. Finally, she said, "She was

afraid of Jennyfer. And she hasn't stirred up much trouble here because she's afraid of you."

"Me? Whatever for?"

"You and Jenny . . . you're . . . different . . . from the rest of us. I don't mean that in a bad way, but . . . there's a strength in both of you that runs so deep. A strength that comes from here." Fiona shifted the quiver to her bow hand in order to press a fist against her heart. "I remember the last time you came to visit the family and stayed for the summer. Do you remember?"

"I remember," Breanna said quietly.

"There was a brutal storm one night—wind fierce enough to uproot trees and rain that beat down hard enough to bruise skin. The rest of us huddled inside the house, but you and Jenny . . . I heard you sneak out of the room the three of us were sharing that summer. When I crept to the window and looked out, the two of you were outside in your nightgowns, dancing in that storm, celebrating it and . . . *changing* it. Air and water. You embraced that storm, took it into yourselves, made it part of your dance, gave it back as something gentler. You *tamed a storm,* Breanna. You and Jenny." Fiona smiled. "The look on your face right now. As if I've suddenly started speaking some strange, incomprehensible language."

"You are." Breanna shook her head. She remembered that night. Remembered extending her hand at the same moment Jenny extended hers so that they stepped out into that storm with their hands linked, feeling the Great Mother's power swirling around them, rushing into them while they danced. Yes, they had celebrated that storm, had acknowledged its strength, had connected to it in a way that had been so natural it had required no words, no thought. What was so strange about that?

They are deeply rooted in the Mother's Hills.

She remembered overhearing one of the elders say that the morning after the storm. Since she had kin in the hills, she hadn't thought it odd. But she also remembered that, while Fiona, Rory, and some of her other cousins had come here a few times to visit after that summer, she had never been invited back for a visit to their family homes. Except Jenny's.

Confused and self-conscious—and irritated with herself and Fiona for feeling those things—she shrugged dismissively. "Let's get some target practice." *I'm in the right mood to shoot something.*

Breanna had taken only a couple of steps toward the kitchen gardens when a hawk flew overhead, screaming a warning as it passed by her. At the same moment, a boy from one of the farm families who had escaped with Breanna's kin burst from the woods, running toward them as fast as he could.

"There's a man in the woods!" the boy shouted. "A man wearing a black coat! Coming this way."

"What were you doing in the woods?" Breanna snapped as soon as the boy stumbled to a halt in front of her. None of the children were supposed to go into the woods on their own. There were still some of those nighthunter creatures out there somewhere.

"Jean wanted to look for some plants," the boy said, panting. "She told me I had to come with her since we weren't supposed to go into the woods by ourselves and—" He glanced nervously at Breanna, then at Fiona. "And she didn't want to ask one of the other witches to go with her."

There wasn't time to consider what kinds of plants Jean was looking for that made her not want the company of another witch—or what she intended to do with the plants if she found them.

"Go—" Breanna looked toward the stables. The men, warned by the hawk's cries, were already in motion, saddling some horses, stabling others, gathering weapons that were always close at hand these days. "Go to the house. Warn Nuala. Go!"

As the boy raced for the house, Breanna and Fiona looked at each other.

"Get the children into the house," Breanna said.

Fiona started to protest. Then she noticed Clay and her brother Rory hurrying toward them—and the hawk flying ahead of them. Nodding, she ran toward the children, who had stopped playing and were now anxiously watching the adults.

Trusting Fiona to take care of the children, Breanna set her quiver on the ground and grabbed a handful of arrows. She pushed the heads of four of them into the ground in front of her to make them easy to snatch if they were needed. The fifth she nocked in her bow, keeping her fingers light on the bowstring. Facing the woodland trail, she waited.

Sensing movement on her left, she started to draw the bow and turn when she realized it was Falco. He had changed from hawk to man, but he'd forgotten to use the glamour to hide the pointed ears and feral quality of the Fae behind the mask of a human face. Or else he had a reason for not hiding what he was.

"Black Coat?" Breanna asked softly.

Falco shook his head.

That would have been reassuring if Falco hadn't looked uneasy, even nervous. Whoever was in the woods wasn't an Inquisitor, but also wasn't a friend.

She'd just turned back toward the trail when Jean ran out of the woods. The girl looked flustered, exhilarated. But not frightened.

When she was a few feet away from Breanna, Jean stopped running. She shook out her skirt, ran her hands over her hair to smooth it, licked her lips to wet them, and pinched her cheeks to bring more color to her face. "How do I look?"

Breanna stared at her. "Get in the house. There's an intruder in the woods. Possibly an Inquisitor."

"Is that what *he* told you?" Jean said, giving Falco a look that was equal parts pouty and scalding.

Any reservations Breanna had about Fiona's suspicions and feelings were destroyed by that look.

"It isn't an Inquisitor," Jean said. "It's a Fae Lord, and he's *so* handsome."

Breanna saw something cold and mean in Jean's eyes when she realized Falco didn't notice she now considered him an inferior specimen of a man.

"Breanna," Falco said quietly.

Looking at the trail, Breanna saw the man coming out of the woods. He *was* handsome, with his black hair and fair skin. He was too far away to see the color of his eyes.

"Jean, get in the house," she said quietly.

"So *you* can impress him?" Jean replied nastily. She gave the man a sweet smile of welcome.

The man stopped and gave Jean a long, considering look. When he resumed walking toward them, the look he gave Falco was as scalding as Jean's had been.

"So this is where you've hidden yourself," the man said harshly, stopping a few lengths away from them.

"This is where I live now," Falco replied.

"Where you *live*? Have you forgotten what you are? Have you forgotten your duty to your *Clan*?"

"I'm needed here."

"To do what? To be what? A witch's *pet*?" The man looked angry, disgusted. "When they told me you were down here, playing the tame Fae, I told them they were wrong. I told them Falco knew his duty to his Clan, and if he was cozying up to a witch here, it was only to seduce her into trusting him. Then he would persuade her to go back to Brightwood with him, and we would have a witch again to anchor the magic, to hold the shining road open. We would have a witch again who would perform the duty to the Fae she was meant to perform *and free my sister from the burden*. That's what I told them. Now I see they were right. You've abandoned your Clan, abandoned *your own kind*. For what? Does she even spread her legs for you, or are you so pale a man that you don't even demand that much for whatever favors you bestow here?"

Incensed, Breanna raised her bow, drew back the bowstring, and took aim at the center of the man's chest. "Who do you think you are?"

"Tell her," the man commanded, pointing a finger at Falco.

Falco hesitated. Then he said, "This is Lucian. The Lord of the Sun, the Lord of Fire. The Lightbringer."

Perhaps it was because the two men expected her to be intimidated, awed, maybe even frightened about confronting the male leader of the Fae that power rose in her as sharp, sizzling temper.

"Well, good for him," Breanna said. "*You* may see the Lord of Fire, but all *I* see is an intruder I'm going to shoot if he doesn't get off our land."

"Breanna." Falco sounded shocked, almost breathless.

"Breanna!" Jean said, sounding equally shocked. "How can you say such a thing to our guest?"

Mother's tits! She'd forgotten about Jean. "I told you to get back to the house," she said sternly. She didn't like the calculating look on Lucian's face, as if he were considering a filly he wanted to add to his stables.

"I'm not a child, Breanna," Jean snapped. "You can't—"

Breanna let power follow the path of temper. A wind suddenly whipped around Jean, turning the girl's hair into a tangled mess and blowing her skirt up. Shrieking in dismay, Jean grabbed the front of the skirt, holding her arms down to prevent the men from seeing everything she wore—or didn't wear—beneath her skirt.

Breanna drew the power back into herself. The wind died as quickly as it had appeared. "Get back to the house, Jean. *Now*."

"You'll pay for that, Breanna," Jean said before running to the house.

Breanna's arms were getting tired from keeping the bowstring drawn back for so long. But she didn't dare ease back, didn't dare give a moment's appearance of yielding in any way. Not when Lucian was watching Jean run back to the house.

If the girl had stopped and talked with him in the woods, it would have taken so little effort on his part to convince Jean to go with him. A promised visit to Tir Alainn? Oh, Jean would have loved that. And then what? If he got her to Brightwood and then abandoned her, what would happen to her? What would happen to anyone living near that Old Place who had to deal with her? No matter how you turned that stone, there was a sharp edge that would cut someone. So she had to get him to leave and not come back.

But how?

"Listen to me, Fae Lord, and listen well," Breanna said. "You aren't welcome here. If you ever come back and try to persuade any of my kin to go with you—"

"What will you do?" Lucian snapped. "Shoot me?"

She heard a horse galloping toward her. A muffled sound. There was only one horse she knew that sounded like his hooves barely touched the ground, and that was Oakdancer. Which meant Liam was riding toward her. Fast.

"You won't shoot me," Lucian said sneeringly. "Do no harm. Isn't that your creed?"

"That is our creed," Breanna agreed. "But we make exceptions."

That startled him. Unnerved him. He regained control quickly when he saw Liam rein in and dismount.

"This is no business of yours, *human*," Lucian said.

Liam strode toward Breanna, stopping beside her. "I may be gentry, and I may be a baron, but"—as he yanked one of the arrows out of the ground and held it up, the top half of it burst into flames—"I'm also a Son of the House of Gaian, so any intruder on my sister's land *is* my business."

"You threaten me, the Lord of Fire, with *fire*?" Lucian laughed nastily.

The man had a point. Liam's gift, which had come down to him through his mother, had awakened just recently. He could draw power from the branch of fire easily enough, but he still wasn't adept at controlling it or extinguishing what he'd created.

Before this could turn into a pissing contest that would, most likely, burn down part of the Old Place if it didn't kill someone outright, she lowered the bow, chose a new target, and released the arrow. Having an arrow go to ground between his feet startled Lucian.

Breanna took that moment to snatch the burning arrow out of Liam's hand. Using her own connection to the branch of fire, she banked the flames as she drove the arrow into the earth, doing it so smoothly that not so much as a blade of grass caught fire.

When she straightened up, she noticed how warily Lucian watched her.

Not so sure of yourself now, are you? she thought. Well, she'd give him more reason to think twice about her.

"The House of Gaian created Tir Alainn out of dreams and will. We created the shining roads that anchor that land to the human world. If you, or any other Fae, try to force or seduce or remove any of my kin from Willowsbrook, I will gather the rest of my kin, both here and in the Mother's Hills, and we will turn Tir Alainn into a wasteland. And then we will close the shining roads and leave you there."

Lucian paled, staggered back a step. There was fear in his eyes now. "You couldn't."

"Oh, but we could. As I *will* . . ." Breanna let the words hang in the air. "I suggest you go back to your own world, Fae Lord, and let us be."

"I'll make sure he gets there," Liam said quietly. Turning away, he mounted Oakdancer and waited.

Lucian stared at Falco, his expression cold and bitter. "You've made your choice, Falco. Don't come crawling back to us when she turns on you. Her kind will always turn on you."

He walked back into the woods, Liam following on Oakdancer.

Breanna watched them disappear into the trees. If the Lightbringer turned on Liam, would her brother be able to protect himself? Had she been a fool to make an enemy of so powerful a Fae Lord?

"Breanna?" Falco said softly. "Breanna, you're shaking."

"It's not every day I threaten the Lightbringer," Breanna snapped. "I'm entitled to shake." But facing down the Lord of

Fire wasn't the reason she was shaking. If something happened to Liam because of it, how could she expect Elinore to understand and forgive her? How would she be able to forgive herself?

Falco cautiously reached over and tugged the bow from her hand. "Come sit down on the bench under the tree. Can you walk that far?"

There was something queer and strained in Falco's voice, but she couldn't think about that yet. Her legs didn't feel like she had any bones left, and she really did need to sit down. She didn't argue when he cupped a hand under her elbow to help her walk.

"Do you want some water?" Falco asked once she was sitting on the bench.

Breanna studied him. He'd been nervous when the Lightbringer showed up. He looked terrified now. "What's wrong?"

"Breanna . . ." Falco looked away. A shudder went through him before he regained control and looked at her again. "Breanna, could you really do that?"

Breanna's attention was caught by seeing Clay and Rory. They'd been hurrying toward her before Liam galloped up to stand beside her. They'd probably held back to remain unnoticed while she held the Lightbringer's attention.

Clay lifted a hand and tipped his head toward the woods, turning the gesture into a question.

If she asked Clay or Rory to follow Liam, would she be putting another person she cared about in danger? She shook her head, then watched the two men head for the house to report to Nuala.

"Breanna? Could you do that?"

Confused by the question, she turned back to Falco. "Do what?"

"Could the witches really close the shining roads and leave the Fae trapped there? Could they really destroy Tir Alainn?"

"How should I know?"

Falco sat next to her. Puzzled, he studied her. "You were bluffing?"

"It was a good bluff," Breanna said defensively. "It got him to leave, didn't it?" *It was a good bluff only if Lucian doesn't retaliate by harming someone.* "Hasn't he ever met a witch before?"

Falco shifted uneasily. "Ari . . . Ari wasn't like you. She was . . . she wasn't like you."

You and Jenny . . . you're . . . different . . . from the rest of us.

"I need to talk to Nuala," Breanna said, pushing herself to her feet. When Falco remained seated, she hesitated, then said, "There isn't anyone here who could do what I told Lucian we could do." *But there may be some Mother's Daughters who live in the Mother's Hills who could do exactly that.*

He didn't respond, so she walked back to the house. Alone.

Liam followed the Fae Lord through the woods. He hadn't liked the man on sight, and he might have dismissed that feeling as nothing more than a brother's natural reaction to seeing his sister confronted by a stranger . . . except Oakdancer was making it plain that he didn't like the man either. It couldn't be because the stranger was Fae. The bay stallion had been bred and raised by Ahern, who had been *the* Fae Lord of the Horse before he was killed in a fight with some Inquisitors. So it had to be something about *this* man the horse was reacting to.

He saw the golden light through the trees and knew they were close to the shining road the Fae used to reach this Old Place. When Falco had shown the road to him, Clay, Rory, and Breanna, he and the other two men had seen nothing more than a wide band of sunlight that looked a little more golden than usual. If he'd ridden past it on his own, he never would have known what it was. Breanna, however, saw it as thick, golden air. Still translucent, but definitely recognizable as something created, in part, with elements of the natural world but not part of the natural world. Then again, she'd already known where to find the shining road.

The Lord of Fire stopped in front of the shining road and turned to face him.

"Your sister is a fool to challenge the Fae."

"My sister is many things, but a fool isn't one of them," Liam replied coldly. "If she drew a weapon against you, she had a reason. If she threatened you and your people, she had a reason. And *that* is reason enough for me to stand with her and stand against you."

"We are the Fae," the man said angrily. "We are the Mother's Children."

"The Mother's spoiled children," Liam snapped. "Mother's mercy! In the next few weeks, we will all, most likely, be embroiled in a war against the Inquisitors and the eastern barons they control, and many good people will die in the fighting. We don't have time for a race that sits above it all in their lofty world and only comes down to *our* world to play games and amuse themselves. We don't have time for the temper tantrums of spoiled, useless children. So go back to your world and stay there. And stay out of our way."

The man's expression changed, his face now full of understanding. He raised his hands in an open, giving gesture. "I understand how it feels to care for a sister. I understand how it feels to want her to be safe and happy." His voice was deep, smooth, soothing. "Don't you want your sister to be safe? If she came to Brightwood with me, she *would* be safe. The Fae would protect her from all harm. She would be cherished . . . and safe."

Liam swayed a little as he stared into the Fae Lord's gray eyes and that voice wrapped around him. Safe. Yes, he wanted Breanna to be safe. There were nights when he had nightmares, when he saw again the things he'd thought were fever dreams during the days when Padrick, the Baron of Breton, had helped him get home after the Inquisitors had tried to kill him. There were nights when the nightmares were the same except that the faces belonged to women he knew—Breanna, Nuala, Fiona. Even his mother, Elinore. Yes, he wanted them to be safe. Wanted . . . With a little help, the Fae Lord could take them someplace safe, someplace . . .

"Don't you want her to be safe?" the Fae Lord said in that so-persuasive voice.

Oakdancer suddenly reared. Thrown off balance, Liam struggled to keep his seat. He felt strange, as if the world had been muffled for a moment and now reappeared with painfully sharp intensity.

That persuasive voice was still talking about safety, still promising to keep Breanna safe.

Persuasive. *Persuasion.* Wasn't that one of the Fae's gifts, the ability to use persuasion magic to convince people to do what they might not do otherwise? That bastard was using it on *him* in order to have Breanna, was using his own fear for her safety as a hammer against his will.

Liam's temper flashed. Heat flooded through him beneath his skin. He knew what it was now, knew he was drawing power from the Great Mother's branch of fire. The heat cleared his head, burned clean in his heart. When he looked at the Fae Lord, that voice was no more persuasive than the eastern barons had been at the council meeting when they'd tried to convince the rest of them to follow their example and vote for the decrees that would turn all of Sylvalan into a horror for every woman who lived there.

"What happened to the other ones?" Liam asked, breaking the Fae Lord's repetitious assurance of safety.

The Fae Lord studied Liam's face and didn't seem pleased by what he saw. "The other ones?"

"If Brightwood is an Old Place, what happened to the witches who were there?"

The man hesitated a moment too long.

Liam leaned forward, the power filling him becoming uncomfortably hot. "Where were the Fae when the Inquisitors showed up at Brightwood the last time? Where was this protection in the other Old Places where witches have died? If it didn't inconvenience the precious Fae, you wouldn't give a damn if they died or not. No, Fae Lord, I wouldn't trust my sister to a man like you. So go back to Tir Alainn and stay away from us."

The man glared at him. Then he disappeared and a black horse, with flickers of fire in its mane and tail, reared, wheeled, and galloped up the shining road.

Liam took a deep breath and blew it out. He gathered the reins carefully, too aware that if he lost control of the power now, he could burn himself and Oakdancer. He didn't dare try to ground the power out here in the woods. He didn't have the skill yet to do it safely. Which meant doing it the only way he knew wouldn't harm anyone.

"Well," he said to Oakdancer as he turned the stallion and headed back to Breanna's house, "there are a lot of people living in the Old Place these days. Someone is bound to need hot water for *something*."

"What do you think?"

Perched on a stool in the pressing room, Breanna watched her grandmother fold camisoles and pantalettes, finding comfort in the familiar. Nuala always seemed to know when talking required her undivided attention and when giving hands a simple task made it easier to find the words. She'd taken one look at Breanna's face, led her to the pressing room, and shooed the girls who had been folding clothes out the door.

"About what?" Nuala asked, folding another camisole and

putting it in the stack. "You've given me a great deal to think about."

Too restless to be idle, Breanna plucked a camisole out of the basket. With so many people living in the house now, there was always laundry to be done—and plenty of hands to do the work. No one was idle in Nuala's house, and even the children had assigned chores. No one resented doing their share of the work.

Breanna's hands curled into tight fists.

Except Jean.

Nuala tugged the camisole out of Breanna's hands. "It's a good thing this one is yours. You can't complain about the creases in it since you made them."

Breanna shrugged. Nuala calmly continued folding clothes.

"Do I think you were wise to threaten a Fae Lord?" Nuala said. "I don't know. Based on what you told me, he looks at us and sees a surplus of witches in one Old Place and sees nothing wrong with selecting one or two to take elsewhere to suit his own purpose and the needs of his own family. While I sympathize with his desire to help his family, thinking of us as servants or tools for the Fae's use is unacceptable."

"You think my threat was excessive."

Nuala hesitated. "You frightened a powerful Fae Lord. What he will do with that fear is something we can't know. Did you act rashly? Yes. Did you act honestly?" She reached over and rested a hand against Breanna's face for a moment—and smiled. "I would have been surprised if you'd said anything more . . . tactful."

Breanna snorted softly, then reluctantly returned Nuala's smile.

"As for Jean," Nuala said, returning to her folding, "I'm not blind to the girl's faults. I can tell when sweetness is a deep well and when it's nothing more than surface water. So I'm troubled by Fiona's suspicions. More troubled by the fact that Jean was hunting for plants and didn't want any of us to know." She sighed quietly. "Her mother was a hedge witch, and that kind of magic is connected to plants and charms rather than the branches of the Great Mother. Like any gift, it can be used for good or ill. In Jean's case, she has enough connection with earth to draw some power from that branch of the Mother. That's a dangerous combination in someone who believes her every wish and whim should be indulged and becomes resentful when it isn't. Fiona's always been able to see people clearly, so her suspicions that Jean has used magic to cause mischievous harm can't be dismissed."

"Does she see me clearly?" Breanna asked, not sure if she wanted the answer.

Nuala folded clothes for a minute, saying nothing. Finally, she said, "We are not all the same, Breanna. We do not all have the same skills, the same abilities, the same strength. For some, the power we can draw from our branches of the Great Mother is no more than a trickle. For others, it is a small brook, or a deep stream, or a strong river. I am a deep stream, but you and Jenny . . . you are rivers, fast and strong. So, yes, you are different from our kin from the east—but you are not so different from many who live in the Mother's Hills. Power runs deep there, and it runs strong."

Thinking of Jenny, Breanna asked, "If Jenny and I are rivers, are there any witches who are the sea?"

Nuala hesitated. "If there are witches that strong, they would be very dangerous if provoked." She made a visible effort to push that thought aside. "Enough talk with me. Go on now and find out what's troubling Falco."

"The threat I made frightened him. That's what's troubling Falco."

"That is not the only thing."

"What else could be troubling him?"

Breanna squirmed as Nuala turned and gave her That Look.

"That," Nuala said, "is what you need to find out."

He was still sitting on the bench under the tree, looking lost and lonely.

As she walked toward him, Breanna wondered just how much he had given up in order to give whatever help and protection he could against the Inquisitors. She knew he'd been shunned by the Clan whose territory was anchored to Old Willowsbrook, but had he just forfeited his family as well?

When she sat down beside him, Falco said, "Liam returned. He said he needed to soak his hands in water."

Breanna sighed. "He needs more work in learning to ground the power."

"The women in the washhouse were glad to see him."

She let out a huff of laughter. "I'm sure they were. They'll have plenty of hot water for laundry without having to stoke fires and sweat. Still, it will be easier on him when he learns to ground his power in a more traditional way."

Falco smiled, but the smile faded quickly.

"What troubles you, Falco?" Breanna asked. "Do you miss your home?"

He shook his head. "It isn't a happy place. Hasn't been since . . ." He sighed. "Dianna resents having to live at Brightwood to anchor the magic."

"Dianna?"

"Lucian's sister."

"I see," Breanna said. But she didn't see, didn't understand. "She's from that Clan?"

Falco nodded. "There's something about her that allows her to anchor the magic in the Old Place to keep the shining road open—as long as enough Fae stay in the Old Place with her."

"So that Clan doesn't really need a witch."

He made a frustrated sound. "She's the Lady of the Moon, Breanna. *The* Lady of the Moon. The Huntress. She wants to live in Tir Alainn. She *doesn't* want to be burdened with staying in the human world."

"But she's doing this for her family."

He studied her, an odd expression on his face. "If it were your family, and you had to give up something special in order for the rest to have it, you would do it, wouldn't you?"

"Of course," Breanna said, puzzled. "They're family. I'm not saying it would be easy, or that there wouldn't be times when I would wish it could be otherwise, but, yes, I would do it."

"That's what makes you different from the Fae. One of the things, anyway."

"Falco—"

He shot to his feet, paced a few steps away from her, then returned to the bench. "I don't understand your ways." Frustration shimmered in his voice. "If this was a Clan, I would know what was expected of me, but I don't understand your ways."

"What don't you understand?"

"I don't know if you expect me . . . if your female kin expect me . . ." He slumped back down on the bench. "I don't like Jean. I don't want to bed Jean."

Breanna felt her jaw start to drop. "Whoever said you had to?"

"Since I'm visiting your . . . family . . . and you haven't said you want me for yourself, I'm obliged to . . . to . . ."

He was on his feet again, pacing in front of her.

"It's not that your female kin aren't fine women—most of them—but I—"

"Don't want to bed them."

"Yes!"

"You want to bed me."

"Yes!"

"Why?"

He stopped pacing and looked at her as if she'd just asked him to count every leaf on every tree in the Old Place.

"Because . . . you're you."

Breanna blew out a breath. What was she supposed to say to that?

"Breanna?"

She patted the bench. "Sit down, Falco."

He sat. Perched was a better word, since he looked like he was going to jump up again at any moment.

"When I was nineteen," Breanna said, "I visited my kin in the Mother's Hills during the celebration of the Summer Moon. A full moon, wine, lots of laughter and dancing. There was a young man there, older than me by a few years, who was staying with friends. We danced and talked and laughed . . . and when he asked me to go walking with him, I went. It was romantic and exciting, and he was experienced enough with women that I didn't regret him being my first lover. But in the morning . . . Well, he didn't seem quite so wonderful without the moonlight and the wine. I decided after that visit that I needed to like a man in the daylight before I gave in to the lure of moonlight."

"I see," Falco said thoughtfully. "Do you like me?"

"Yes, I like you," Breanna replied. "I like you very much. But I don't know you well enough yet to invite you to my bed."

Falco nodded. "What about kisses?"

He was persistent. "Kisses?"

"Do you like kisses?"

"Well . . . I . . . Yes."

Something about the way his gaze focused on her mouth before he raised his eyes to look into hers made her palms go suddenly damp. Watching her, he leaned forward slowly.

Just before his lips touched hers, she felt a prickle along her neck. She pulled back, turned her head.

Liam was leaning against the washhouse doorway, watching her.

Clay had his arms over the back of a gelding. He had a grooming brush in one hand, but he wasn't making any pretense of grooming the horse.

Looking around to see what had distracted her, Falco cleared his throat and eased back.

"Ah . . ." Breanna wasn't sure what to do. Go back in the house? Pretend nothing happened? Pick up her quiver of arrows, march over to the washhouse, and smack Liam over the head with it?

Quiver. Arrows. The bow leaning against the bench where Falco had set it after her confrontation with the Lightbringer.

"Target practice," she said, bouncing to her feet.

"What?" Falco blinked.

"You were supposed to help me with target practice." She brushed past him, picked up the quiver and bow. "Come along."

"You want target practice now?"

"The bales of hay are stacked as tall as I am," Breanna said patiently.

"So?" His puzzled expression turned to understanding. *"Oh."* He took the quiver from her and smiled.

As she and Falco started walking toward the kitchen garden and the bales of hay, Breanna glanced back at Liam. Which part of him would win the inner struggle—brother or man? She suspected she already knew, but she hoped the man would struggle long enough for her to try a kiss or two before the brother joined her and Falco for target practice.

Chapter 4

waning moon

Standing in the doorway of the Clan house, Ashk hesitated, wanting some excuse to delay. But everything was ready; the huntsmen who were going with her had already gone up the shining road to Tir Alainn, and her companions were waiting for her.

She studied them as they talked quietly among themselves, all of them carefully avoiding glances at the Clan house to allow her a private good-bye.

Aiden and Lyrra, the Bard and the Muse, were coming with her to record the events that would alter their world in one way or another and to use their gift of words to help her in whatever way they could. Sheridan, Bretonwood's Lord of the Hawks, was coming as one of her huntsmen—chosen from others because he was also Morphia's lover. As the Sleep Sister and Lady of Dreams, Morphia's ability to use sleep as a defensive weapon had proved useful when hunting down the nighthunters and when she had stopped two Inquisitors from hurting a family during the Black Coats' attack on Bretonwood, but there was no way to tell how effective that gift would be on a battlefield. Morphia was mainly coming with them in order to stay close to her sister, Morag.

And Morag . . .

The Gatherer had looked so pale and shaken when she'd joined them for the morning meal, Ashk hadn't dared ask what was wrong. They needed Morag, not just as mercy for the mortally wounded but as a warrior. Would she falter when she was needed most because of her passion for life?

No. Morag would do what needed to be done. And so would she.

"You're going now."

Ashk turned around. Padrick stood back from the doorway, not quite within arm's reach. "Yes. It's time."

Then she was in his arms, taking and giving a kiss that was as fierce as it was loving. She didn't want to leave him, didn't want to leave their children, didn't want to leave the Clan that had become her people. But they couldn't wait for the battle to come to them. Not if they wanted to survive.

Padrick broke the kiss, then buried his face against her neck. "Come back to me, Ashk. Just . . . come back to me."

Tears stung her eyes. As much as she wanted to, she couldn't promise him that. Instead, she whispered, "I will hold you in my heart. Always."

He stepped back slowly until they were no longer touching. "They're waiting for you."

She took a moment more to look at him before she walked out of the Clan house. When the others saw her, they mounted their horses. She swung into the saddle and turned her horse toward the forest trail that led to the shining road, her companions following behind her.

She didn't look back. Sylvalan didn't need Ashk, the Lady of the Woods and wife of the Baron of Breton. Sylvalan needed the Hunter. So she let them go—husband, children, family, and friends. By the time they rode up the shining road and were joined by the huntsmen waiting for them in Tir Alainn, all she was was the Hunter. It was all she allowed herself to be.

Chapter 5

waning moon

Jenny closed the iron grill gate of her new home and walked toward the sea. She could see it from some of the windows, could hear its song while she worked day after day cleaning more of the neglected rooms in the old house and getting them ready for her family. But standing at a window wasn't the same as standing on the cliff, where she could feel the warmth of the sun on her skin and taste the sea in the air—where she could look to the south, hoping to see the sails of a vessel large enough to be *Sweet Selkie*, her brother Mihail's ship.

Had he been gone long enough to have reached Seahaven? Surely, he'd been gone long enough. With a good wind, it didn't take that many days to sail the coastline of Sylvalan.

He'd stayed with her an extra day to help her get herself and their nephews, Guy and Kyle, settled into their new home—and to unload his ship and store the cargo in some of the empty first-floor rooms. Then he'd sailed away, intending to go to Seahaven and wait for Craig and any cargo their cousin could send by wagon from the family warehouses in Durham. And to wait for any other family members who had chosen to flee to a harbor town in the south rather than go to their kin near the Mother's Hills.

There wouldn't be many fleeing south. Mihail had gambled that he would be able to find a safe harbor in the western part of Sylvalan, had taken that gamble based on a conversation with Padrick, the Baron of Breton, whom he'd met when he'd gone to fetch Guy and Kyle at the western boarding school where they'd spent the past year. Because of that conversation, and because her branch of the Mother's power was water and her love was the sea, they *had* found a safe harbor here in the village of Sealand.

But there hadn't been any way to contact the family and tell them. They didn't dare send a letter that named a specific place.

If it was confiscated by any of the barons who had turned against witches or, worse, fell into the hands of one of the Inquisitors, they would forfeit the safety they had found. All Mihail could do was return to the port town that had been the agreed-upon meeting place and wait as long as he could.

What if he waited too long? What if his ship was confiscated? What if he and his men were imprisoned until they could be tested by the Inquisitors to see if they served the so-called Evil One? What if . . .

Jenny shook her head. No. Letting those thoughts grow only gave them power. She would focus her thoughts on this place, this safe harbor. She would focus on the house and the family who would live there with her soon. Soon.

As she turned away from the sea, she saw the ponycart coming up the road, heading for her house. She saw the woman beside the driver and guessed it was Cordell, the witch who lived on Ronat Isle. And she saw the two small, slumped figures sitting in the cart.

Guy and Kyle must have disobeyed her, again, and snuck down to the harbor to play with the young selkies. She didn't blame them for their fascination with the Fae, but she didn't like their confidence that they could disobey her whenever it suited them. She was their aunt, and their only kin here.

And might always be their only kin here. And they might be the only family I have left. Please, Great Mother, please don't let them be all that is left of the family.

Annoyed with herself, Jenny walked back to the house. How could she expect obedience from the boys when she couldn't obey herself? The Great Mother was the land, the air, the water. Ask for a sweet wind, and if you had the power and the will, you might get it. But compassion, kindness, tolerance . . . those things lived within people or they didn't. Magic couldn't change what was inside the heart.

But thinking of a sweet wind made her wonder if it might be possible to send a message after all. Not to Durham or Seahaven, but to Willowsbrook. Even if it was too risky to send a letter overland by human means, might one of the Fae be willing to travel through Tir Alainn and deliver a message?

She would have to ask Cordell. The Crone would know if such a thing were possible. She hoped so. Just the thought of writing a brief letter to Breanna—and, perhaps, getting a message back—lifted her spirits.

Chapter 6

waning moon

Adolfo, the Master Inquisitor, watched two of his Assistant In-quisitors tie the old witch to the chair, then dismissed them with a sharp wave of his right hand. As soon as they left the room, he locked the door, something he'd never done before while softening a witch to confess. It wasn't that he doubted his ability to contain her, despite his dead left arm, but he didn't want anyone walking in and disrupting his concentration at a critical moment. Besides, the trembling crone was dependent on his mercy now and wouldn't dare try to summon her power and use it against him.

He'd already taken her eyes, her ears, her tongue. He'd taken her hands and feet.

And still he heard whispers among the Inquisitors that Master Adolfo, the Witch's Hammer, had become soft, had become di-minished since he'd begun the extermination of the witches in Sylvalan. He drank too much. He'd ordered the witches recently captured to be brought to Wolfram, soiling the home country's land with the presence of those foul creatures.

Fools.

Even Ubel thought he'd grown soft, and that betrayal of un-questioning loyalty enraged him more than the whispers of the lesser Inquisitors. Ubel had been his finest warrior, his most trusted assistant in this war against magic and female power. He'd nurtured the hungry, beaten boy he'd found in a stinking alley one summer and had shaped him into an educated man with a great destiny.

Ubel could no longer be completely trusted, but there was no one else strong enough to lead, to do the things that must be done in order to win the coming war against Sylvalan.

Perhaps he did drink too much wine, but that hadn't clouded

his thinking or softened his determination to rid the world of witches and the power they wielded. It hadn't softened his determination to rid the world of magic in all its forms. When the witches were finally destroyed, the Fae and the Small Folk would be destroyed with them. Then men would rule the world as was their right—and the Inquisitors would rule the men.

Hearing a soft scrabbling coming from the wooden cage in the center of the room, Adolfo walked over to it and lifted a corner of the cloth that covered the cage. The squirrel froze for a moment before dashing for another corner in an attempt to hide.

Dropping the cloth, he turned to study the old woman.

Despite what Ubel and the other Inquisitors thought, he had not grown soft and he had not been idle last winter. He had thought, he had studied, he had prepared. But he hadn't had the one thing he'd needed to try his experiments. He hadn't had a witch.

He walked a circle around the cage, murmuring the words of the spell he'd created for just this purpose. The protective circle wasn't meant to keep anything out, it was meant to contain what went in.

When he was done, he positioned himself slightly behind and to the right of the woman's chair, then placed his right hand on her shoulder. It gave him an almost erotic pleasure to feel her shudder at his touch.

He closed his eyes. Breathed slowly, deeply, evenly. And began to draw power out of her, just as he'd drawn power out of the Old Places. He felt her resist, felt her pulling the power back into herself. Calmly, he slapped the side of her head, where the wound from the missing ear was still raw. While she gasped from the pain, he clamped his hand on her shoulder again and sucked her power into himself. Sucked it up and sucked it up . . . until he sucked her dry.

He raised his hand, pointing it at the covered cage. As he released the power, sending it toward the cage like an arrow shot from a bow, he said, "Twist and change. Change and twist. Become what I would make of thee. As I will, so mote it be."

The squirrel inside the cage shrieked as the power he unleashed struck it. Shrieked and shrieked . . . and then went silent.

Adolfo lowered his hand. His throat felt parched, his bones felt hollow. He wanted to close the circle and pull the cover off the wooden cage. But power still swirled, trapped within the protective circle. He could wait.

He looked at the woman. Her head lolled to one side. Drool dribbled from one corner of her mouth. With proper care and proper nourishment, she might recover enough to regain some of her power. But not enough to be useful to him. He would give her to the apprentices. One could not learn to use an Inquisitor's tools without practice.

Two hours later, Adolfo returned to the room.

There was no sound from the wooden cage.

He spent several minutes trying to sense any lingering power from the spell he'd cast. There was none. Even the power he'd used to create the protective circle had been absorbed.

Gingerly taking hold of a corner of the cloth, he stepped back as he pulled the cloth away. Then he studied what was inside the cage.

When his men used the Inquisitor's Gift to draw magic from an Old Place and release it again to twist the things it touched, there was no control over what was changed. It might cause a new well to go dry, or a cow might birth a two-headed calf, or a field of grain might whither and die overnight . . . or something living might be changed into something out of a nightmare. A flesh eater. A soul eater. A nighthunter. But there had been no way to control that twisted magic, no way to use it for a specific purpose.

Until now.

Even though he was certain the creature was dead, he approached the cage cautiously.

The squirrel had changed into a nighthunter. Almost. One hind leg, or what was left of it, was still furred. Unable to escape from the cage to hunt for other prey, the nighthunter had turned on the unchanged part of itself, ripping through flesh, snapping bone . . . devouring while it bled to death.

Excitement shivered through Adolfo. There hadn't been enough power left in the old witch to complete the change. He would have to soften the next one faster so that her body was still ripe enough with power to provide what he needed.

Despite the creature's incomplete transformation, the experiment had worked. Before, it had been chance and the strength and number of Inquisitors drawing power from an Old Place that determined the creation of nighthunters.

Now he could create them whenever he chose.

The remains would have to be burned. He wasn't ready to share this with his Inquisitors yet. Which meant giving the task to someone he could trust to remain silent for the time being.

Ubel.

Yes. He'd have Ubel take care of it.

"And then, my fine Inquisitor," Adolfo said quietly, "once you've seen what's in this room, look me in the eyes and tell me I've gone soft."

Chapter 7

dark of the moon

Selena and Rhyann rode into the Old Place, reining in a few steps after crossing the boundary they recognized by the slightly different feel of the land.

"This is it." Selena rested a hand on Mistrunner's neck to keep the gray stallion quiet. "This is where the Ladies of the Moon will gather tomorrow night to see who will become the Huntress."

"Are you sure?" Rhyann asked, looking around. "It doesn't feel any different than the other Old Places we've seen on the way here."

"I'm sure," Selena replied. Power thrummed through the land, but it wasn't the power from the Great Mother's four branches. This was power from the Fae side of her heritage, seeking a way to fill her. *It's not time yet. Not quite yet.*

She raised her arm, and her hand swung like a compass needle until it was aligned with the core of that power. "Somewhere in that direction. That's where the Fae will gather. That's where the power is gathering."

Rhyann frowned at her. "What does it feel like?"

Selena lowered her arm. "Heavy. Full."

"And how do you feel?"

Ripe. Juicy. Swollen with desire. For what, I'm not even sure. The power calls me. I have to answer.

"Selena?"

She saw the fierce concern in Rhyann's eyes. They had lived in the same house, had argued and laughed and cried together for years. In another day or two, they would separate to follow their own life journeys, and things would never be the same again. "I'm going to miss you, little sister."

"We have some time left," Rhyann said quietly. "Tonight is still the dark of the moon."

Selena shook her head. "Endings and beginnings. Tomorrow the new moon rises, and the Fae will gather for whatever will come."

"These tests or challenges or whatever they're called always happen at the full moon. That's the way it goes in the stories we've heard about the Fae."

"Not this time. The power will rise with the new moon. I feel it." Selena sighed. She was nervous, even a little frightened. Her face and her ability to change into another form were all she had in common with the Fae, all that made her one of them. She didn't know the ceremonies or rituals that were used for these tests of power. The Fae would surely realize that, resent that. And yet, if she *did* become *the* Lady of the Moon, the Fae would be hers to command—and their strength, combined with human and witch, might be enough to save all of Sylvalan's people from destruction.

It always came down to that need, to defend the Great Mother and protect all Her children from those who would destroy and devour. So she would find her courage, swallow her fear, and meet the Fae tomorrow night. Besides, she wasn't sure if the power that had drawn her there would let her walk away.

"Come on," she said, gathering the reins. "Let's pay our respects to the Daughters who live here and beg some hospitality."

Before Rhyann could reply, Mistrunner snorted softly and Fox, Rhyann's dark horse, stamped a foot as if in agreement.

The women looked at each other and shrugged. Both horses were almost too intelligent for comfort, as well as stubborn when something wasn't to their liking, but those traits had been the reason why Selena had been able to talk her father out of hiring men to escort them on this journey.

As long as those two are under you, you'll be safe enough, her father had said. *There's nothing that can outrun them, and they won't take you anyplace that's not to their liking.*

The two horses swung into an easy trot, apparently having decided their riders had tarried long enough. They moved silently on the wide trail through the woods, their hooves making no sound.

How did two witches end up with Fae horses? Selena wondered, not for the first time. Fox had shown up late last autumn, taken one look at Rhyann and tried to follow her into the house. He wouldn't leave and wouldn't let anyone else near him until she loudly announced that he belonged to her. After that, the dark horse with lethal hooves acted like a docile pet.

Mistrunner . . . She still wasn't sure about Mistrunner. She'd been out in a clearing three years ago, celebrating the Great Mother and the full moon, playing with the power that swirled inside her. She'd braided the strength of the earth to moonlight, dazzled it with air and drops of water, warmed it with the heat of fire. When she was done, she'd stared at the glittering path that rose from the land and disappeared into the night sky, uncertain if she was delighted or uneasy about what she had done.

And then she heard the desperate, terrified scream, and shouted, "Here!"

A heavy mist poured out of the sky, obscuring the top end of her glittering path. A gray yearling burst out of that mist, galloping down the path she'd created as if it were a solid road, stumbling a little when his hooves touched firm earth. He raced past her, getting as far away from the path as he could without leaving the clearing.

Unnerved that something had come down a path she'd thought led nowhere and had no real substance, she'd unraveled the magic and grounded the power—and her glittering path disappeared. Which left her with a terrified young animal that had decided she was the only safe thing in a strange world. So she ended up taking him home with her and naming him Mistrunner.

She suspected he had come from Tir Alainn, but she still didn't know what had terrified him or how he'd found her glittering path and recognized it as a way to reach the world . . . and safety. She never tried to find out who he belonged to—and she admitted to herself that part of her apprehension in meeting the Fae was that someone would recognize him and want him back.

"We're here," Rhyann said.

Selena blinked. "Where?"

"Where your body has been but you haven't," Rhyann replied testily. She leaned toward Selena. "We aren't home anymore. You can't get so lost in thought you're not aware of the world. You don't know what's out there. Or who is out there."

Feeling her shoulders start to hunch at the justified scolding, Selena straightened in the saddle. "You're right. I shouldn't let my thoughts wander so far. I'm just . . . I guess I'm nervous."

"You don't have to do this."

"You wouldn't say that if the power was pulling at you the way it's pulling at me."

"Well, it won't impress the Fae if you're knocked out of the saddle on the way to this gathering because you weren't paying attention to the low-hanging branch in front of your face."

What an embarrassing picture *that* made.

As she brushed her heels against Mistrunner's sides to give him the signal to move forward toward the buildings up ahead, she said in her best long-suffering, big-sister tone of voice, "Mother, grant me the patience needed to deal with a younger sister."

"The Great Mother doesn't care about such things."

"She would if she had a younger sister," Selena replied sourly.

"Maybe the moon is Her younger sister," Rhyann said, a mischievous light in her eyes. "Maybe that's why they play this constant game of catch-me-if-you-can."

"It's possible. The younger sister is always playing with the tides while the elder moves sedately through the seasons."

"Sedately? *Phuuu.*"

"Brat."

"Mouse breath."

Selena's mouth fell open. "Mouse breath?"

"Remember the time Mother found you in the barn with half a mouse?" Rhyann said primly.

"I was still getting used to changing into a puppy!" And had been learning, usually the hard way, to curb the instincts of a shadow hound that had hunted down its prey.

"And Mother wouldn't let you change back until she was sure the mouse bits had gone through you—one way or another."

She remembered the scolding that had followed the discovery—and the flat-handed whack on the head she'd received when she'd snarled at her mother for taking the rest of the mouse away.

"I only did it once," Selena muttered.

"Which is one time more than *I* ever did it," Rhyann said. Then she raised her hand in greeting to the man who stepped out of the cottage, followed by two women. "Blessings of the day to you."

Faced with three strangers, Selena gave up the idea of leaning over and giving Rhyann's braid a hard yank and worked to compose her expression into something more suitably adult. "Blessings of the day to you."

The man stepped forward, nerves and temper plain on his face. "And what would the Fair Folk be wanting with the likes of us?"

"Chad," the younger of the two women said, placing a restraining hand on the man's arm. She studied Rhyann for a moment, then Selena. "What can we offer you, Ladies?"

"Your hospitality for the night, if you're willing," Selena said coolly. They'd been met with wariness and suspicion at almost every Old Place they'd been to since leaving home—because of her. Because she looked Fae, and the Fae, for reasons none of the witches in those Old Places understood, were keeping watch in a way that made the witches and the Small Folk uneasy.

"But . . . wouldn't you be more comfortable in Tir Alainn?" the woman asked.

"I don't know," Selena said. "I've never been there. I am Fae because that was my mother's legacy to me. But I am first, and always, a Daughter of the House of Gaian."

That startled them.

The older woman, the crone of the family judging by her looks, said hesitantly, "You're a witch *and* Fae?"

"Yes."

A look passed between the two women, while the man watched them anxiously.

"Would you be a Lady of the Moon?" the crone asked.

"I am," Selena replied.

"You're gathering with the others to see who will become the Huntress?"

"Yes."

The crone smiled. "Come in and be welcome, Ladies. Oh, yes, you are welcome."

As Selena and Rhyann dismounted, the man, who introduced himself as Chad, said, "If you're easy about it, I can take your horses to the barn and give them a light feed."

"Is there somewhere they could graze for now?" Rhyann asked.

"Aye, there's a pasture by the barn. We've been keeping the animals close since—" He stopped, his lips pressing together in a tight line.

Since the Fae started arriving, Selena finished. There was anger here, and she was going to find out why. It was becoming clear that the Fae were distrusted and disliked, even feared, and nothing short of desperation was going to make the humans and witches welcome their presence.

"We'll go with you to the barn," Selena said. "It will help these two settle in better."

Chad turned his head, and called, "Parker. Come help with the horses."

A boy appeared in the doorway. He hesitated for a moment before joining his father. His eyes were wide, his face filled with awed delight.

"Oh, they're beauties!" Parker said.

Both horses snorted and laid their ears back tight to their heads.

"He was talking about you, not me," Selena said dryly, resting a hand on Mistrunner's neck.

The boy said hastily, "Oh, you're pretty too." He gave his father an anxious look.

Rhyann burst out laughing. "Let it go, laddy-boy, and just show us where to put these two." She stepped around Fox until she was facing the dark horse. "Behave. If you act like the gentleman I know you can be, perhaps the boy can be coaxed into giving you a treat."

Both horses swung their ears forward.

Selena pressed her lips together to keep from laughing.

Chad cleared his throat, and muttered, "This way."

They followed father and son to the barn. The horses were unsaddled and given a quick rubdown before being escorted to the barn door that led to the fenced pasture.

Keeping her eyes on the boy, who had continued into the pasture with the horses, Selena said quietly, "Now. Tell me why you're angry with the Fae."

"It's nothing to do with you, Lady, and I'm sorry we didn't give you the welcome guests deserve."

A flash of anger sizzled under her skin. She struggled to bank the branch of fire that wanted to answer the heat of her feelings. "Do you know what's been happening in the east? Do you understand that Sylvalan is at risk?"

"I understand well enough," Chad replied. He kept his voice low, but it was edged with temper. "I understand well enough that more than trouble could be heading our way. Mother's tits, woman! The minstrels have been singing songs about the Black Coats and their evil for months now. And a few days ago, the baron who rules this county came to the Old Place to pay his respects. The *baron*. A responsible man, one who looks after his own, but he's never come *here*. Came near to scaring my Ella out of her wits when he showed up with the squire and a handful of guards."

"What did he want?" Rhyann asked.

"Said the last barons' council made him realize he'd been neglectful of some of his duties. Said the Old Place wasn't part of the land he ruled."

"It wouldn't be," Selena said. "The Old Places belong to the Mother's Daughters."

Chad nodded. "He wanted us to know that it was his intention to be a good neighbor, and if we needed help from his people, we need only ask." He smiled. "He meant well, but this isn't his home village and he doesn't spend more than a couple of days here each year to make sure the squire and the magistrate are keeping things right and proper, so he didn't know how things stand with us here."

"And how do things stand?"

"The squire is my father's cousin, and one of the guards who came with the baron that day is the brother of my older brother's wife. Ella's brother is the village blacksmith. So, you see, we've already got ties to the 'baron's people.' Doesn't matter if those Black Coats come here or come to the village. We'll stand together."

"I'm glad to hear it, but you haven't answered my question about the Fae," Selena said.

Chad's expression hardened. He was silent for a long time, watching Parker's slow return to the barn. "They aren't good neighbors. Oh, I know they all live in their grand Tir Alainn, but that's no excuse for—" He blew out a breath. "If they want to go riding, there's plenty of open land. There's no reason to ride down a man's crops, spoiling the harvest he needs to feed his family or sell at the market. They've no right to steal chickens from the tenant farms. They've plenty of coins in their pockets. They can buy a chicken in the market same as other folks. And they've no business seducing young girls and leaving them with babes in their bellies. I'm not saying it's all the man's fault, but if he sires a child, he should do right by that child."

"The Fae aren't the only ones who walk away from their children," Selena said flatly.

He gave her a measuring look. "No, they're not. And that's not right, whether they're human or Fae. But you asked about the Fae, so I've told you how it is." He rubbed the back of his neck. "And to be fair, we don't see much of them, and there were a handful of Ladies who rode up the other day to pay their respects. They gave Ella some gifts as thanks for letting them gather in the Old Place. Ella said they seemed . . . embarrassed . . . by the way the other Fae were acting."

As Parker reached the barn door, a high, young voice behind them said, "Papa?"

Chad turned. "Yes, Hayley-girl?"

"Mama wants to know if you're going to keep our guests in the barn all day. She says the food's ready for the table, and Gran's gone back to her cottage to fetch Grandpapa to come eat with us, and the Ladies might like to wash up a bit before we eat."

Chad grinned. "She said all that, did she?"

"She said more, but she told me to fetch you." Hayley looked disapprovingly at her brother. "And Parker has to wash his hands before he touches the bread. He's dirty."

"Am not," Parker said.

"Are too."

"We'll all go in and wash up before we sit at your mother's table," Chad said firmly.

Rhyann slipped her arm through Selena's as they followed Chad and the children back to the cottage. "Younger sisters," she said sweetly. "Aren't they wonderful?"

"*Phuuu,*" Selena said.

Dianna gazed hungrily at the beautiful gardens and terraces she could see from her window in the Clan house. She took a deep breath and let it out in a luxurious sigh.

She was back in Tir Alainn. Finally, she was back in Tir Alainn after all those weeks of being chained to Brightwood in order to anchor her Clan's piece of the Fair Land, living in that miserable cottage crammed with other Fae, hearing the muttered complaints about where she rode her pale mare, what she ate, where she sat, as if she hadn't been forced to give up *everything* for *their* sake. And now there was a challenge to her position as *the* Lady of the Moon.

She wouldn't have been challenged if she hadn't been chained to Brightwood, if she'd still been free to travel through Tir Alainn and visit the other Clans the same way her twin, Lucian, could do.

Well, it wasn't going to happen. She would meet the challenger and show that upstart she was still *the* Lady of the Moon, still the Huntress. And after her rival yielded, she would spare the bitch's life in exchange for a small service. Her rival would have to return with her to Brightwood and become the anchor for the Old Place's magic. Her rival would have to live in that cottage and listen to the complaints. Her rival could spend sleepless nights looking out on land that demanded sweat and hard work. Her rival would live in the human world—and she would be free to return to Tir Alainn.

Dianna turned away from the window to stare blindly at the tastefully decorated room.

No smells from a chamberpot. No stains on the bedcovers. No chipped vases or cracked mirrors.

If she lost this challenge . . . if her rival was actually strong enough to ascend and steal her place as the Lady of the Moon . . .

She would end up back in Brightwood, back in that cottage, trapped forever as the seasons changed, summer giving way to autumn and autumn yielding to unforgiving winter. Even the thought of having to spend a whole winter in the human world was more than she could bear.

Lyrra did it last year. They aren't even her Clan or kin, but she stayed in the cottage with the cold and the winds driving in storms from the sea.

That was Lyrra, whose refusal to accommodate the Lady of the Moon and remain at Brightwood had forced that duty on her.

No matter. She might even forgive the Muse someday—once her rival was settled into that cottage at Brightwood.

So she had to win. She had to. Because after she returned from the Old Place where the challenge would occur, she had no intention of leaving Tir Alainn.

Selena felt Rhyann shift, pause, then roll over to face her.

"Can't sleep?" Rhyann asked sleepily.

"No," Selena replied. "Too many thoughts, too many feelings."

"Mmm. You always think too much."

"Did you notice how excited Ella and Mildred were about me standing with the Fae for this gathering?"

"You're one of their own. Why shouldn't they be pleased?"

"The way they fussed over the dress to make sure all the creases and wrinkles were out of it, you would think I was preparing for my wedding."

"Oh," Rhyann said, yawning, "they wouldn't have fussed over you half as much if you were just getting married. Hundreds of women get married every year. But there's only one Lady of the Moon at any time."

"Thank you for being so comforting."

"Welcome," Rhyann mumbled.

"Rhyann?"

"Erf?"

"What if I lose?" Selena made a noise that sounded terrifyingly like a laugh changing into a whimper. "Mother's mercy, what if I win?"

"You get to be the Lady of the Moon."

"I'll be expected to give orders to people I know almost nothing about."

"That shouldn't bother you. You're always bossy."

Selena just sighed. Nothing would be gained by pointing out that Rhyann could be equally bossy.

When she thought her sister had fallen back asleep, Selena whispered, "I'm afraid I'll change."

Rhyann stirred. Propped herself up on one elbow. "The moon waxes and wanes. The tides ebb and flow. The seasons turn, each in their own time. Ever changing, never changing. Of course you'll change. The dance of life spirals, remember? Even when you return to a point, you're not in the same place. The dance would have changed you, whether you'd come here or stayed home." She leaned over and kissed Selena's forehead before laying back down. "Don't worry. If you start to act too much like them, I'll still be nearby to help you remember who you are."

Selena smiled in the dark, Rhyann's sleepy reassurance giving her more comfort than anything else could have.

"Good night, little sister," she said softly, feeling love swell inside her.

"Good night, mouse breath."

Chapter 8

new moon

Aiden sat in the shade of one of the Clan's courtyards and plucked idle notes on the harp, letting his mind wander just as idly, drifting on the sound. He looked up when a boot quietly scuffed the paving stones.

"Are you working on a new song?" Taihg asked. The Clan's bard looked ready to retreat if the Bard wanted privacy—and also looked hopeful that he could sit in the courtyard and listen to a song come into being.

"No, just thinking," Aiden replied, smiling when he noticed the whistle tucked into Taihg's belt. "Why don't you sit down, and we'll see what two bards can do?"

Taihg pulled the whistle from his belt and hurried over.

For the first few minutes, harp and whistle played idle notes that twined around each other. Then Taihg slid into a gentle tune, and Aiden let the harp follow and fill in, absorbing the whole of the tune as easily as he breathed.

When the song ended, Aiden stilled the harp strings. "You wrote that?"

"Yes," Taihg said.

"Did you write a harp accompaniment as well as the whistle melody?"

"No, I think you just did that."

They grinned at each other. Then Aiden looked away.

He'd met Taihg a few weeks ago, when he and Lyrra had stopped at this Clan house while searching for the Hunter. He had threatened to strip the bard of the gift of music when the man refused to tell him what the western Clans knew about witches—and had been stunned when Taihg said he'd prefer to lose his gift rather than his home and Clan.

If I'd been fool enough to strip him of his gift, the loss of his music would have been on my head.

He'd backed down, and Taihg had yielded enough to send him and Lyrra to Ashk, Bretonwood's Lady of the Woods. And there they had found the Hunter, who was not what they had expected . . . and more terrifying than he could have imagined.

Needing a rest from troubling thoughts, he gave his attention back to the music, and said, "Let's try it again to make sure it's set in the hands and the heart."

They went through it twice more before Aiden nodded, satisfied. "Can you get the part for the harp written in with what you've got for the whistle?"

"I-I haven't written anything down. It was just a little tune I—" Taihg swallowed hard as Aiden's blue eyes flashed with annoyance.

"Write it down," Aiden said. "Lyrra will need the music to learn the whistle part."

"Learn the— You actually want to play it outside of the Clan here?"

You'd think I'd just asked him to jump off a cliff. Maybe I have. "Yes, I want to play it. I want it heard. I want other bards to take it up and send it on." He began plucking idle notes again. "And I do want you to go with me for part of the journey."

"Me?" Taihg's voice rose close to a squeak. "Why?"

"The Ladies of the Moon are gathering somewhere in the midlands," Aiden said quietly, "but there's something not quite . . . right . . . about this. Dianna's power isn't waning, no one has come forward as the challenger who wants to try to take her place as *the* Lady of the Moon, and this isn't the phase of the moon when these challenges take place."

"There may not be a challenger, as such," Taihg said hesitantly.

"Meaning?"

"There's a saying in the west: The gift commands, and the gift chooses. That's why the Fae in the west haven't traveled to these gatherings much. It's really just a formality, a ritual so that the new leader can be acknowledged. If the gift chooses someone, that person will ascend no matter where he or she is."

"If that's the case," Aiden said grimly, "let's hope whoever ascends is in that Old Place tonight."

"Why?"

Aiden set his harp aside and turned on the bench to look at Taihg. "If Dianna loses, we need to know who the new Huntress is. We need to know if she's going to be like Dianna and refuse to do anything to help in the fight against the Inquisitors or if, the Great Mother willing, we might have another ally in the fight that's coming. When we leave here in the morning, we'll have a few days before Ashk has to decide if we're heading for the southern end of the Mother's Hills or going straight to Willowsbrook. I want you to travel with us until we get word about who the new Lady of the Moon is. Then you'll come back to the west and make sure all the bards and minstrels have all the information we can glean about her."

"Ashk will be getting that information, too, and she'll send word back to the west."

"How the Hunter and the Bard interpret that information may not be the same. Ashk needs to consider it from the view of protecting Sylvalan. I'll consider it with the view of deciding whether or not the minstrels and bards will support the female leader of the Fae, whomever she might be."

Taihg stared at him. "If you ridicule the Lady of the Moon in a song, the Clans won't have anything to do with you in fear of offending *her*."

"Does that include the Clans in the west?"

Taihg hesitated, then shook his head. "No. Unless, of course, the Hunter takes offense."

"Then I've nothing to lose," Aiden replied. "The Clans beyond the west already disapprove of me."

Before Taihg could reply, an annoyed male voice beyond the courtyard said, "Mother's tits! Considering how far I've traveled, I'm going to talk to *someone*."

Aiden couldn't hear a reply, but a moment later, a man strode into the courtyard. He had sable hair that fell to his shoulders and dark eyes full of sharp intelligence—and more than a little annoyance. A tall man, with a honed body that moved with sleek grace, yet gave the impression of suppressed violence, like the sea on the edge of a storm.

The man was definitely Fae, but Aiden felt uneasy the moment he saw him. He rose to face the stranger.

"Who are you?" the stranger demanded.

"Aiden. The Lord of Song."

"The Bard, is it? I'm Murtagh, the Lord of the Selkies. I was looking for the Hunter, but you'll do for now."

"Will I?"

Murtagh flashed a feral smile that made Aiden wish for a large knife and the skill to use it. He had the feeling Murtagh possessed both.

"When you've the time, Bard, I'd appreciate it if you'd come by Selkie Island and give the minstrels there a bit of encouragement. We've a handful of them on the island, and there's not one of them that will lift his ass to fart let alone learn a new song. Don't any of you write anything new?"

"Occasionally," Aiden said dryly.

Murtagh eyed Taihg. "If you're too busy, you could send another bard."

"I get seasick," Taihg said quickly.

Murtagh sighed. "Well, see what you can do. I've been hearing the same songs since I was a boy. I'd throw the lot of them into the sea, but they're selkies, too, so it wouldn't gain me anything."

"I'll keep it in mind," Aiden said, "but there are other concerns right now."

"True enough." Murtagh raked a hand through his hair. "There's talk, Bard, and I don't like what I'm hearing."

"What have you heard?"

"That witches are being killed by men called Black Coats. That the Old Places are being taken over by humans, and the Small Folk are being driven out."

"It's true."

"Well . . . Mother's tits! Why aren't the Mother's Daughters going up the shining roads to escape and letting the Fae deal with the bastards?"

"The Fae in the east of Sylvalan refused to do anything to help the witches—and now the Fae are lost as well, trapped in their Clan territories in Tir Alainn after the shining roads closed. If they're surviving at all."

Murtagh stared at him. Then he swore softly. "If that's the case, they've gotten what they deserve."

Aiden studied Murtagh with more interest. "Would you allow a witch into your Clan's piece of Tir Alainn?"

Murtagh's dark eyes flashed with temper before he smiled ruefully. "My gran's a witch whose gift of water is best suited to the sea. She's fit and spry for a woman her age, but cold, damp weather is hard on old bones, so I bundle her and the other elders up every year when the autumn winds take on the edge of winter and tuck them in the Clan house in Tir Alainn. Not that she'll *stay* there. She misses the moods of the sea, so she'll come back down and spend a few days before she'll let me bundle her back up." He paused. "I've heard a young witch with a love of the sea has recently come to Sealand."

"I've heard that, too," Aiden said cautiously.

Murtagh shook his head. "I saw that ship pass. If I'd known there was a witch in the hold, I would have persuaded the captain to put in at one of our ports for a day or two."

"The witch is content where she is," Ashk said, stepping into the courtyard with Morag beside her.

Murtagh gave both women a long look and a small but courteous bow. "And I wouldn't have held her if she wasn't willing to stay. Just saying I would have liked an introduction before the lady decided on where to settle. We can offer as good a harbor as Ronat Isle."

Ashk's eyes searched his. "You would have offered her family safe harbor?"

"There's more of them?"

Aiden winced, wishing Murtagh's question didn't sound like he was ready to scoop up any witch that crossed his path, especially when Morag said, "Answer the question," in a voice that held a hint of the grave.

He saw Ashk shift her weight slightly and wondered what she thought she could do against the Gatherer if Morag decided to kill the Lord of the Selkies. Unfortunately, Morag had been withdrawn since they left Bretonwood, and not even Morphia had been able to discover why. But that dark turn of mood had made the rest of them cautious about dealing with the Gatherer of Souls.

Finally, Murtagh said, "I would have offered her safe harbor—and anyone she cared to bring with her. And I'll offer it now to any witch looking for a place away from those bastard Black Coats and the Sylvalan barons who have lost their balls—or sold them in order to put more gold in their purses." He looked away for a moment before focusing on Ashk again. "You're the Hunter, aren't you?"

"I am."

"You're gathering the Fae to put a stop to the slaughter?"

"Yes."

Murtagh nodded. "The Hunter rules the woods. The Lord of the Selkies rules the sea. So. How can I and mine help you? Fae whose other form is suited to water are of little use to you on land, but we control the sea around our island, right to the shore of the mainland."

"What do the barons on the coast say about that?" Aiden asked.

Murtagh smiled sharply. "A few years ago, when I first became the Lord of the Selkies, one of the coastal barons came to the island. He wasn't pleased that our boats were fishing the same waters as his villagers since he got a share from every boat as well as what he made from his tenant farmers. Well, he came over and told me that since there was no baron ruling the island, he was taking it for his own. I explained to him that we didn't need a baron, and I would rule my own people. He didn't take kindly to that."

"What did you do?" Ashk asked.

"Sank his ship. We rescued the people on board, but it was close to a fortnight before the baron set foot on ground he could call his own, and he learned a few things about how a baron's power compares to that of a Fae Lord. He drowned a couple of years later. Wasn't my doing, but no one mourned his passing, especially once people found out he'd made a deal with the sea thieves who had been making things difficult for merchant ships. His son was barely old enough to take up the title, but he's done well for his people, and he and I have an understanding that suits us both. So if there are ships coming that need safe harbor, they'll have it." Murtagh paused. "And if there are ships that need to sleep at the bottom of the sea, and their crew with them, I'll see it done."

No one spoke.

Finally, Ashk asked, "Do you still have trouble with sea thieves?"

That sharp smile flashed again. "Not in my waters."

"I would consider it a kindness if you would keep watch for one ship. It's called *Sweet Selkie*, and Mihail is her captain. If you see her brother safely home, I think he'll oblige you with an introduction to the new witch at Sealand. But I can't tell you about other ships."

"I understand, Hunter. I'm honored to have finally met you . . . and the Gatherer of Souls."

Morag just stared at him before turning and walking away.

"Blessings of the day to you," Ashk said quietly before she, too, walked out of the courtyard.

Aiden took a deep breath, then blew it out slowly. Out of the corner of his eye, he saw Taihg slump on the bench, as if exhausted. So, his weren't the only nerves stretched by this encounter.

Murtagh watched the courtyard entrance a moment longer before turning to Aiden. "They're a pair, aren't they?"

"Yes," Aiden said softly, "they're a pair." And he wasn't sure he'd sleep easy tonight if he started thinking about the journey he was about to make with two women who embraced Death, each in her own, but equally deadly, way. He gave himself a mental shake. They were exactly what Sylvalan needed for the fight ahead.

"Well, then," Murtagh said.

Aiden shifted his foot and nudged Taihg's boot. The other bard jerked, stared at him blankly for a moment, then jumped to his feet.

"My Clan would be pleased to have you guest with us tonight," Taihg said.

Murtagh smiled and shook his head. "You just want another target available in case either of those two become annoyed about something."

"True," Aiden said, pitching his voice over Taihg's stammered protest. "But if you decide to stay, I can promise you'll hear a new song or two."

Murtagh laughed. "You set a mean bargain, Bard, but it's not one I'll refuse."

Good, Aiden thought, picking up his harp. Of course, he fully intended to hear a few of the songs Murtagh knew, since he suspected many of those "old" songs had never been heard beyond Selkie Island, but there was no reason to mention that.

It hunted. Vicious. Almost mindless. Hungry. It hunted.

She raced through the trees at Bretonwood, desperate to find It before . . .

The rattle of a ponycart's wheels on a forest trail. A baby wailing in fear. She saw Ari looking back, terror turning the young witch's face into an almost unrecognizable mask.

Flesh. Blood. Souls. Food. It hunted.

She ran. Ran and ran and ran . . . and still couldn't find the enemy. How could she get between It and the ponycart if she couldn't find It?

Closer. Closer. It could hear the female's raspy breathing, even over the baby's cries.

She ran faster. The enemy was too close to those she loved. Too close.

A stag hidden among the trees leaped out, landing in the center of the forest trail.

For a moment, she thought he was the old stag, thought this was the memory of that terrible leap that had saved a boy from the nighthunters. But this stag was younger, blue-eyed, the build not yet as mature and powerful as it would one day be, the rack of antlers smaller than the one she remembered.

Food!

The stag charged, fought with antlers and hooves. Screamed in pain as claws sank into shoulder muscles, ripping, tearing. Screamed as sharp teeth pierced the throat, and It gulped the blood gushing from the wound. More. More. It wanted more. Its insatiable hunger always wanted more. First the blood. Then It would devour the soul.

No!

She stood on the forest trail. She couldn't see the enemy. All she could see was the stag crumpled in front of her, dying. She watched as the stag changed back into a man. As the blue eyes dimmed, Neall gasped one word: "Morag."

Gasping for air, Morag flung herself out of bed and stumbled to the window, clawing at the shutters to get them open. She sank to her knees, clinging to the windowsill as she worked to steady her breathing. Her heart pounded in her chest, racing ahead of the fear that threatened to consume her.

It was the third time she'd had this dream. The first time had been the night before she left Bretonwood with Ashk. She'd lain awake the rest of that night, too frightened of what might be waiting for her if she fell asleep again.

The next morning, as they were getting ready to leave Bretonwood, she'd almost asked Morphia if she had sent the dream.

But the Sleep Sister wouldn't have shaped a dream like that and sent it to someone she cared about, and certainly not to her own sister.

Unless it was a true dream, a warning of danger.

But how could she protect Neall and Ari when she didn't know what the enemy looked like? How could she recognize what she couldn't see?

Feeling brittle, Morag pushed herself to her feet, then staggered over to the wash basin. She poured water into the basin, dipped her hands into the soothing coolness, and splashed her face. When she felt steadier, she straightened up, letting the water drip down her face and neck.

After that first time, she had almost convinced herself that it had been nothing more than a bad dream conjured up from the depths of her mind and cobbled together with images of some of the frightful things she'd seen since the Inquisitors came to Sylvalan last summer. If it had come to her only that one night, she might have dismissed it as nothing more than that. But . . . three times. No, she couldn't dismiss a dream that returned to haunt her.

So. Danger was coming. Something that terrified Ari. Something that would kill Neall if she couldn't stop it. But there was the babe in the ponycart to consider. Ari still had several more weeks before the babe was due. There was time to continue the journey with Ashk and give the Hunter whatever help she could before she turned back and returned to Bretonwood.

Morag went back to bed and sank into restless, but dreamless, sleep.

Chapter 9

new moon

Liam rubbed his hands over his face, then leaned back in his chair to stare at the sheet of paper on his desk.

No matter how he tried to look at the situation, it always came out the same: Willowsbrook had six guards who served under the village magistrate. Six men who were trained in weapons and fighting to protect the village and surrounding farms. Six.

His father had thought it extravagant to have so many guards for a village the size of Willowsbrook. In a way, the old baron had been right. It did seem an excessive number of men to handle the occasional drunken brawl on market day and to make sure arguments between neighbors were brought before the magistrate instead of having something small escalate through acts of petty vengeance into violence. Now . . .

How could he protect his people with only six guards? If he added his gamekeeper and the two men under him, that gave him three more men who were skilled with a bow. Not enough. Not nearly enough if the Inquisitors gathered an army to crush the barons who wouldn't yield to their view of the world.

He could ask Breanna's kin to stand with his people. The men now living in the Old Place who were skilled with a bow would double the fighting force, and a couple of them even had some skill with a sword. But that would leave the Old Place, and the women there, vulnerable if the enemy had enough men to split their forces, one half keeping his fighters occupied while the other went to devastate the Old Place.

He could command the magistrates in every village in the county he ruled to send him half their compliment of guards. That would swell the ranks of fighters, but it also would leave those villages with little protection, and the additional men still

wouldn't be enough, not when every baron who supported the Inquisitors could gather as many men and combine them into an
army.

*Great Mother, what am I supposed to do? How can I protect
my people, my friends, my family? How can I—*

A footman burst into the room. "There's a rider coming!
Coming fast. Sloane thinks it's Squire Thurston's son."

Liam bolted from the room and rushed to the open front door,
where Sloane, his butler, watched the rider galloping toward the
manor house. Squire Thurston's oldest son was one of the gentry
youths who were riding the roads these days to keep watch
around the village and outlying farms. They'd all been given
strict orders not to approach any strangers. If they saw anyone,
they were to ride to the nearest home and give a warning before
riding on to warn the magistrate.

He stepped outside, Sloane following him. If Thurston's son
was heading here, that meant the manor was the closest house.
And *that* meant . . .

The youth galloped up to them and reined in hard, setting his
horse on its haunches.

"Riders coming!" he shouted, despite being almost on top of
Liam.

"How many?" Liam asked, trying to ignore the heat that
washed through his body.

"I counted twenty men and two coaches."

"Any idea which way they came from?"

"The village . . . I think."

Which meant the magistrate was already aware of the
strangers and would summon the guards. Not that they would arrive in time to do anything but bury the dead.

"Should I tell my father?" the youth asked.

Liam hesitated a moment, then shook his head. "Ride to the
Old Place. Warn them. If we're attacked here, they'll be next."

"Yes, sir." The youth applied his heels, and his horse galloped
off in the direction of the bridge that crossed Willow's Brook.

Liam turned to Sloane. "Have the bucket of wood brought
out. And send one of the footmen to find the gamekeeper and tell
him he's needed at the house—and tell him to come armed."

"Yes, Baron."

As Sloane hurried into the house to relay orders, Liam saw

Flint, his stable master, striding toward him, the man's face flushed with anger.

"Saddle as many horses as you can," Liam said as soon as Flint got close enough to hear him. "Get the horses hitched to the farm wagon as well. Make sure one of the grooms stays with the wagon to drive it."

If his servants had to run, they had a better chance to escape on horseback and reach the Old Place than they would on foot. Most of his footmen could sit a horse, even if none of them rode well. Each one could take a maid up behind him. The older servants and the young ones could go in the wagon.

Flint didn't stop and return to the stable to follow orders. Instead, he kept coming toward Liam, finally stopping when there was a man's length between them. His hands were clenched, and the look on his face was close to hatred.

"This is your doing," Flint said harshly. "The baron wouldn't have put us in danger this way."

"*I* am the baron."

"You've got the title, but you're not half the man your father was. You never will be. You're nothing but a witch's brat that she tricked the baron into believing was his."

Liam stared at Flint, who had been, and always would be, his father's man. The urge to strike Flint for the slurs against his mother was strong, but the heat beneath his skin was getting more intense, warning him that he'd unthinkingly drawn too much power from the branch of fire and he couldn't be sure, if he raised his hand now, that he could control what he'd summoned.

"Get off my land," Liam said quietly, fiercely. "I don't want you near my family. I don't want you near my people. Get out."

"And go where now that you've brought the enemy down on us?" Flint demanded, fear now coating his anger.

"You can obey my orders and stay until it's safe to leave, or you can leave now."

"Bastard!"

Liam nodded. "Which should prove to you that I truly am my father's son."

Flint looked stunned for a moment.

Liam saw the first riders turn off the main road onto the long drive that led to the manor house. "Make your choice, Flint. They're coming."

Flint's breathing became harsh as he watched more riders turning onto the drive. Then he ran back to the stables.

A footman came out of the house, grunting a little as he placed the large brass bucket next to Liam. Normally, the bucket sat on the drawing room hearth, filled with kindling. Now it was filled with chunks of wood and thick sticks long enough to be used as torches.

"Get back in the house," Liam said, watching the riders approach.

The footman didn't have to be told a second time.

Horses feared fire. If he threw burning pieces of wood at them, they might bolt, might even throw their riders, might buy him enough time for the servants to get away before one of the men put an arrow into him—or, he added honestly, before he set himself on fire.

Four guards rode in front of five men who wore gentry clothing. The rest of the guards rode to the side and behind the two coaches. The road dust kicked up by the horses' hooves made it difficult to identify the men until the front guards swung their horses to the side, and Liam found himself facing Baron Donovan. The baron was an acquaintance, someone whose company he had occasionally enjoyed when they'd attended the same parties or dined together at the club.

What made Liam's heart sink was that Donovan had been the only other baron besides Padrick who had given him any acknowledgment after his impassioned speech at the barons' council in Durham—the speech that set the Inquisitors against him.

Why was the other baron here?

Donovan dismounted. So did the other four gentry men and half the guards. Liam recognized the four men as barons he'd seen in the council chambers, but he couldn't remember their names or what counties they ruled.

"Baron Liam," Donovan said, his voice courteous yet wary.

"Baron Donovan," Liam replied. "To what do I owe the pleasure of this visit?"

"You left Durham in a hurry." Donovan watched Liam intently.

"I had reasons." None he was willing to share until he knew why Donovan was here.

The door of the first coach opened. Liam saw one of the guards hastily extend a hand as a hooded figure stepped down.

A flicker of—fear?—swept over Donovan's face as the hooded figure came forward. Then his face became hard, his expression determined.

"Answer one question so I'll know if we're wasting our time," Donovan said. "Where witches are concerned, where do you stand?"

The heat under his skin was intolerable. He wanted a few minutes to quietly focus in order to try to bank the power he had raised. Since he wasn't going to get those few minutes . . .

He raised his hand, releasing the power as he pointed at the wood.

Flames roared out of the bucket, shooting up to twice his height before settling back down to something closer to a normal fire.

While the men fought to get the horses under control, the hooded figure seemed to stare at him. Liam was trying to think of something to say when Breanna galloped around the corner of the house and reined in. Her eyes took in the men and nervous horses, then settled on the hooded figure for a moment before she flung herself out of the saddle and strode forward, her eyes now focused on the barons.

When she stopped, she pointed a finger at Donovan. "If you raise so much as a finger here to do harm, I will summon a wind that will knock you all into the sea!"

Strong female hands suddenly flung the hood back, revealing an attractive woman who glared at Breanna. "If you knock us into the sea, then *I'll* summon the sea and send a wave back here that will turn this place into a lake!"

Tension buzzed around the women for several seconds—seconds when no one, not even the horses, dared move. Then they grinned at each other.

"Where are you from?" Breanna asked.

"The midlands, on the northwest side of the Mother's Hills," the woman replied.

"Do you have kin in the hills?"

"I do. And you?"

"I do."

"I'm water."

"I'm air. And he's"— Breanna glanced at Liam before looking at the bucket of burning wood—"learning."

The woman's lips twitched. "So I see."

Now that his heart seemed able to get some blood back up to his brain, Liam noticed how pale the other barons were—and the stunned expression on Donovan's face.

"Since Liam's being a featherhead, I'll pretend I live here and offer you some refreshments."

The woman gave Liam an uneasy look. "You don't live here?"

"Why would I?" Breanna asked, surprised.

"Then, perhaps . . ."

"It will be fine. Since Liam's mother and sister—"

"Youngest sister," Liam cut in, bristling.

Breanna rolled her eyes. "Since they're staying at the Old Place with us, Sloane is quite happy to take household instructions from any sensible person."

"I'm sensible!" Liam said.

"Of course you are."

"Refreshments sound lovely," the woman said quickly.

"This way," Breanna said, leading the way into the house. "Where are your kin in the Mother's Hills?"

Liam didn't hear the answer since the door had closed behind the two women.

He and Donovan eyed each other.

"She's . . . ?" Donovan asked.

"My sister," Liam replied. He gestured toward where the other woman had stood. "And she's . . . ?"

"My wife."

The door opened again, and two junior footmen came out with buckets of water.

"Mistress Breanna said we should douse the fire," one of them said.

"Unless you want the ladies to summon a bit of a cloud to rain on it," the other added.

They looked so disappointed when he sighed and told them to just douse the damn fire. They all watched the water quench the fire—except for one chunk of wood at the top, which stubbornly kept burning despite being watersoaked.

"She's right, you know," Donovan said blandly.

"About what?" Liam asked.

"You are still learning."

Liam just shook his head. "Gentlemen, why don't we join the

ladies for some refreshments? Then you can tell me why you're here."

Donovan looked back at the guard captain. The man said, "We'd prefer to stay out here, if it's all the same to you."

Liam nodded. "Go on to the stables. You can feed and water the horses if you like." He led the barons into the house while some of the guards took up a position in front of the house to watch the drive and the others took the horses and coaches to the stables.

The refreshments were being set on a low table when the men entered the room. Now that the immediate crisis had passed, he realized he was still scared to the bone—and he knew why. So after inviting his guests to help themselves, he hustled Breanna out of the room, closing the door behind them.

"Could you do that?" Liam asked urgently.

"Leave guests to serve themselves?" Breanna replied. "Apparently, I can."

"No. Not that. Could you really summon a wind that could reach the sea?"

She stared at him as if he'd just stripped off his clothes and started dancing on top of the refreshments. "Are you *daft*? Do you know how *far* that is?"

Of course he did. That's why it had scared him. "So what was that? A witch's version of a pissing contest?"

She pondered that before nodding. "Yes."

He closed his eyes.

"Did you get the fire put out?" Breanna asked.

"Most of it."

"That's fine then. Come and have some tea. You look like you could use it."

Personally, he thought the men, at least, could all use a healthy dose of whiskey. Ah, well. He could serve *that* kind of refreshment later.

"You did the right thing," Donovan said two hours later, after Liam had told the other men how he'd been poisoned at his club, and how Padrick had intervened, not only saving him from the men who had been sent to kill him once the poison made him vulnerable but also getting him out of Durham—and getting him home. After he told them the contents of the letter his mother's cousin had sent to her, revealing the truth about the "procedure" the eastern barons wanted performed on all women, the level of whiskey in the decanter dropped considerably.

Liam shifted in his chair. The dining room didn't have the most comfortable chairs, but it had the accommodation of the table that made it easier for the men to see each other as they talked. Besides, any other room would have made this conversation feel too informal.

"I regret not being there for the vote," Liam said, running a finger around the rim of his glass.

Donovan shook his head. "Your absence—and Padrick's—served better than your presence could have. Those two empty seats made too many barons nervous, especially after Hirstun said you must be too ashamed to show your face for the vote. Mother's tits! Anyone slightly acquainted with you knew you'd show up for the vote after that speech you made, and if you didn't, there would be a reason for it. When Padrick didn't show up"—he shrugged, but he looked uncomfortable—"that told the rest of us how the western barons would vote, and we all knew we were no longer voting on the proposed decrees. East and west were now on opposing sides, and when the rest of us voted, we were indicating which side we were standing with."

Liam studied the other five men. "You all voted against the decrees."

"We wouldn't be here if we hadn't," Donovan replied sharply. He raked his fingers through his hair, the gesture full of frustration. "All the midland barons voted against the decrees. So did most of the northern barons. The southern barons were almost equally divided. That isn't the point."

"Then what is the point?"

"The point is we're going to war. The eastern barons are going to combine forces and gather arms and men, and it's a good bet they'll be supported by arms and men from Wolfram since that's where the Inquisitors came from. The barons from Arktos might send even more men against us if the Black Coats have control of them as well. What have we got? Even if we use every guard from every village, it won't be enough. Not if the eastern barons have Wolfram and Arktos fighting with them. Liam"—Donovan raked his fingers through his hair again—"things can be said on a journey that are confidential, and I'm not asking you to break another man's trust. What I am asking . . . There has to be a reason why the other western barons defer to Padrick. If you know why, please tell us. By allying with the west, we've placed the welfare of our people in his hands."

Liam refilled his glass, then took a sip of whiskey, stalling for enough time to think, to consider. There were things he knew about Padrick that he wouldn't reveal. But there were other things he could say. He just didn't know if the other men sitting at this table would find those things reassuring.

"He knows the Fae," Liam said quietly.

Silence filled the room before one of the other barons snorted. "There are plenty of farmers' daughters who have known the Fae—and there are plenty of young men who have had an encounter with one of the Fair Folk, for good or ill."

Liam shook his head. "That's not what I mean. Padrick *knows* the Fae. He told me the barons weren't the only ones who ruled in the west, and they weren't the most powerful."

Another long silence.

Donovan leaned back in his chair and stared at Liam. "Are you saying he can actually convince the Fae to stand with him against the Inquisitors and their army?"

"I don't think it's a matter of convincing them," Liam said cautiously. "It seemed more like a matter of not getting between them and anyone they decided was an enemy."

"Mother's mercy," Donovan whispered. "If we had that kind of help here . . . But we don't, do we?"

Liam shook his head.

Donovan studied the whiskey inside his glass. "There's one other place we can look for allies . . . if we dare." He drained the glass, then set it on the table with deliberate care. "There's a story in my family about the man who was my great-great-uncle. He went out riding one moonlit night and met a lady, a woman like he'd never seen before. He fell in love with her and continued to ride out to meet her for a full turn of the moon. He gave her gifts, which she sneered at, but he was a younger son and could afford nothing finer. One night they argued, and she left him, never to return. But after that night, he felt compelled to write poetry. Every morning, when he woke, he rushed to his desk for paper and pen and spent agonizing hours, sometimes weeping in frustration, as he tried to write another excruciating poem. And just as he was compelled to write them, he was equally compelled to read them to guests who came to the house—or family if there were no guests, or even the servants if he could find no one else.

"It was like a sickness inside him, because once he managed to get the words down on paper, he was fine for the rest of the day. But it was destroying him, and his family feared for his sanity. It was speculated that the lady he'd met had been the Muse, or one of the ladies who shared that gift of words, and she had cursed him by forcing this need upon a man whose joy came from the land and who had no gift for words.

"One autumn, he disappeared. The family didn't see him again until spring, when he returned. He wouldn't say where he had been, but the family could tell he was different. He had a slender wand made of oak that he carried with him. He was still compelled to write a poem every day, but he no longer wrote on paper. He used that wand to write words in the grass, in the creek, in the air. The compulsion no longer tortured him. He would simply write some little poem, then, with the compulsion satisfied for the day, he would go on with his work.

"The one thing he did when he came home was to urge his brother, who was the baron, to pay his respects to the Ladies who lived in the Old Place. He was quite insistent that the baron had to make sure their basic needs were met, that they had wood for the fires, fabric for clothes, enough food to eat, that their home was kept in good repair. When the baron asked why, he promised to tell his brother in one year's time if his brother helped look after the witches.

"So the baron kept his promise, and found it no hardship to do so. His wife invited them to small dinner parties or musical evenings, and slowly the witches, who had kept to themselves because they'd believed they wouldn't be accepted, became part of the community, and they repaid the friendship they'd found by using their gifts to help the farmers and villagers.

"During that year, whenever the baron asked his brother about why the man had insisted on helping the witches, the only answer was, 'We must never forget who calls them kin.'

"One year after the baron paid his first courtesy call to the Ladies in the Old Place, his brother handed him a sheet of paper with a poem written on it. It was the only poem he had written on paper since he'd returned home. It was the last one he ever put to paper."

Donovan refilled his glass with whiskey, then sighed. "That poem has been handed down to the heirs in my family since that day. The original paper has been carefully preserved, and is brought out long enough for the heir to make a careful copy in his own hand, which the ruling baron checks against the original to be sure no word is lost or changed." He hesitated. "I married Gwenn because I fell in love with her and wanted to be her husband. Before her family consented to the marriage, we made a journey, and I learned what my great-great-uncle meant about never forgetting who calls my lady wife kin."

As he sipped his whiskey, Liam noticed the slight tremble in Donovan's hand.

"Gentlemen," Donovan said in a hushed voice, "I tell you plainly, the eastern barons are fools to have allowed the Inquisitors into our land. They are fools to have done so much harm. Even if they gather an army and defeat us, they will lose. Because the day will come when they kill the wrong witch, and then . . . And then may the Great Mother have mercy on us all."

No one spoke while whiskey glasses were refilled again.

Perhaps it was because he was no longer quite sober that Liam asked, "What does the poem say?"

Donovan stared at some distant point the rest of them couldn't see. Finally, he recited:

"Do not wake the Mother's Hills.
Do not break the quiet dreaming of
The ones who walk there.
If roused, their wrath can
Shake the world,
And men will not see the
Light of day again."

"Mother's mercy," Liam whispered just as someone rapped softly on the dining room door.

Breanna entered, followed by Gwenn.

"Please pardon the intrusion, gentlemen," Breanna said, "but I—"

"You said it was a pissing contest," Liam said. "But are there witches in the Mother's Hills who really could summon a wind like that or bring the sea so far inland?" *You're drunk, laddy-boy.* But he sobered up second by second as he saw both women go absolutely still.

"Not among my kin, no," Breanna said carefully. "At least . . . I don't think so."

"There are some questions it is best not to ask about the House of Gaian," Gwenn whispered.

Donovan slowly rose to his feet. "Gwenn?"

She shook her head, then began rubbing her hands over her upper arms, as if suddenly chilled.

"There are Crones," Gwenn said reluctantly, "who know the old magic. Things the rest of us never learn. They are very powerful. You didn't meet any of them."

Liam glanced over at Donovan and saw him swallow hard. Mother's mercy. Donovan had obviously been awed by those he *had* met—and now Gwenn was telling him there were others even more powerful?

"Mostly they teach," Gwenn continued. "They teach the strongest and the best, the ones whose hearts embrace our creed. The ones who also have the temper to use that power if it's needed."

"We need allies, Gwenn," Donovan said softly. "I don't think my people can stop the Inquisitors. Not alone."

"That's why Gwenn needs to come to the Old Place this evening," Breanna said. She held up a small piece of paper. "Rory brought this a short while ago. It's from my cousin Skelly. He says something is happening tonight, and we need to stay aware for whatever might be written on water, whispered on the wind."

"What's tonight?" Liam asked.

"The new moon rises," Gwenn replied, still rubbing her arms.

"Whatever it is, the House of Gaian is paying heed," Breanna added. "So whatever happens tonight could change everything."

Liam rose, then walked slowly to the door. "Let me see if the cook has the means of providing a meal for all of us. Then we can ride out to the Old Place."

Breanna nodded.

As he stepped into the hallway, he heard Gwenn say quietly, "I met two of them a few years ago, when I studied for a while in the Mother's Hills. Two who were being instructed by the Crones. They are too strongly trained in the creed, as the most powerful of us must be, to ever strike first, but may the Mother have mercy on anyone foolish enough to provoke Selena or Rhyann into striking back."

Chapter 10

new moon

Selena stopped fiddling with the saddlebags already tied to Mistrunner's saddle, took a deep breath, then turned to face the people watching her. Their hopeful smiles scraped her raw nerves. Ella and Mildred had spent the day fussing over her; washing and pressing the slim white trousers and the split overdress; preparing a bath for her; helping her wash and dry her long black hair; urging her to rest and eat and rest some more. Chad and Parker had cleaned all her tack and then brushed Mistrunner until his coat gleamed. And all through the day were the excited murmurs spoken not quite out of her hearing about how there would finally be a Huntress who was one of them, who would stand by the witches and be the protector she was meant to be— and had been once a long time ago.

But nothing she heard indicated that Ella or Mildred understood *why* the Huntress was the protector. If witches who lived beyond the Mother's Hills no longer remembered why the Ladies of the Moon were connected to the Mother's Daughters, had the Fae forgotten as well?

And what will they say when I tell them why they're standing in that clearing tonight? Should I tell them? If they had known before, would they have stood back and watched a part of Sylvalan die under pain and fear and hatred? How will they react to an outsider telling them a truth I doubt they want to hear? How can they deny it when the truth is in their own blood and bones?

Rhyann stepped forward and placed her hands on Selena's shoulders. As she kissed her sister's cheek, she whispered, "You're thinking too much. Just go to the dance. Celebrate the gift that wants to rise in you."

"I don't know if I'll be able to come back here afterward," Selena whispered, her arms going around Rhyann and holding her close.

"You won't be coming back. You'll have to deal with the Fae—and give them a chance to understand what it means to deal with *you.*"

Selena leaned back. "What does *that* mean?"

Rhyann just grinned.

She tried, but she couldn't return Rhyann's grin. "Where will you go tomorrow? Will you try to find the source of your dream?"

Rhyann shook her head. "South . . . and west. It's pulling me now. I feel like I'm a key. If I can find the door . . ."

"Remember your promise to father—and to me. Don't travel alone south or east of the midlands."

"I'll remember if you will."

Selena hugged Rhyann, reluctant to let go.

"The dance waits," Rhyann said softly.

"I know." Selena drew back until they were no longer touching. "Merry meet . . ."

". . . and merry part . . ."

". . . and merry meet again." Selena looked at Ella and her family. "Thank you . . . for everything."

Ella linked arms with her husband and mother. "Blessings of the day to you, Lady Selena."

Mistrunner stamped his foot, jingled the bridle.

Selena mounted. Her white overdress, split at the waist to make riding easy, flowed down Mistrunner's sides. Since the horse had been impatient about *her* delay, she felt annoyed at the way the gray stallion stood still while Rhyann twitched folds of the overdress into place until she was satisfied with the way it looked.

When Rhyann stepped back, Mistrunner turned in the direction of the clearing where the Ladies of the Moon would gather. As he cantered across the meadow to the forest trail that would take her to the clearing, Selena put aside her worries and fears and surrendered to the power that was calling her to the dance.

Dianna rode her pale mare to the edge of the circle of women. Dozens of women, Ladies of the Moon, had come to witness this challenge to her authority, to her *power.* She'd spent the day studying her potential rivals and had seen no one who could meet her in a test of power. But *someone* had challenged. *Someone's* gift was ascending in a way that required challenge. She'd wondered about the five women who had come from the western Clans, then had dismissed them. Except Gwynith. That one had power. Not enough to defeat her, but enough power that, if it grew any stronger, she might be a serious rival. Perhaps, after she'd reestablished her dominance over all the other Ladies of the Moon, she would strip the gift from Gwynith, just to avoid another challenge in a year or two. After all, it was her right to do so.

If there was no challenger, why had they been drawn here by the feel of power ready to ascend? And why here? *She* should have chosen the Old Place where the challenger would meet her. The place was always decided by the one who ruled a particular gift. If *she* hadn't made the choice, who had?

She dismounted, handing her pale mare over to one of her escorts to lead back to the edge of the clearing. She strode past the other women, who hurriedly stepped aside. She took two steps into the circle before she stopped, frozen by a rush of jagged fear.

Power filled the very center of the clearing, pulsing with the need to be released. So much power. But there was something . . . not quite right . . . about it. It was almost as if the *power* was the challenger, daring any of them to find a way to take it without being consumed by it.

But that wasn't right. *Couldn't* be right. The challenge to ascend and rule a gift always came from another Fae, not the gift itself.

She took six more steps toward the center of the clearing and what waited there, then stopped, unable to force herself to go any closer.

"Who challenges me?" she shouted. As she turned slowly to look at all the women gathered in the circle, they averted their eyes. Or, like the ones from the western Clans, they stared apprehensively at the center of the clearing.

"Who challenges the Lady of the Moon for the right to lead the Fae?"

No answer. No one stepped forward to test their power against hers.

Then she saw a glow among the trees, coming toward the clearing. As it came out of the trees, it took shape as a woman riding a gray horse.

Two Fae males stepped forward to intercept the intruder, took a long look at the woman's face, then hastily stepped back, bowing respectfully.

The woman dismounted, rested a hand on her horse's neck, then walked to the circle. The Ladies of the Moon stepped aside to make room for her, but she walked past them into the clearing until she stopped a few lengths from the center, her face lifted as if she were looking at something hovering above the ground.

The glow on the woman's dress, on her skin . . . It was as if the moon itself had walked into the clearing.

Jagged fear slashed through Dianna again. No. There was nothing special about this woman who had intruded into one of the Fae's private gatherings. There wasn't. It was just a trick of the starlight. The woman was just an intruder, while she, Dianna, was *the* Lady of the Moon. How dare this stranger ignore her? This time, when she asked the question, her voice rose in a scream. *"Who challenges me?"*

Selena heard the words, but they had no meaning. Nothing in the clearing had meaning . . . except that glory in its center. She felt the pull of it, the hunger of it, and she felt the jagged need *within* it.

It should have been glorious. And it was. But it was also dangerous. Why had these women raised power like this and then never used it? Why hadn't they released it back into the world, or grounded it to merge with the rest of the magic that lived in the Great Mother? It had the flavor of something that had been done over and over again. They'd taken what they'd needed and had ignored the rest. Now that power was no longer willing to be taken . . . or ignored. It was going to release tonight. Whether it became something wonderful or something devastating would depend on how it was shaped by those who could channel it.

She glanced at the women around the circle. Why weren't they coming forward to start the dance? Couldn't they feel the urgency? What were they waiting for?

Her eyes rested briefly on the woman standing opposite her, inside the circle. Was this the current Lady of the Moon? She could see the glow of their magic, could see the waxing and waning of the gift within each woman, just as they could surely see it in her while they stood together in this place. There was strength in the woman standing on the other side of that globe of power, strength that was anchored to earth. But . . . She looked at the woman directly to her right. That woman also was anchored to earth, and while she wasn't quite as strong as the woman inside the circle, her power was richer.

Puzzled, Selena turned slowly to look at the other women. More of them had power anchored to air or fire than earth or water. Neither air nor fire could channel the power that had been raised—at least, not without careful, extensive training—but they could have supported earth and water. Why hadn't they?

And what were they waiting for?

She looked at the woman inside the circle, looked at the clenched hands and a face now hardened by hatred.

The test. Wasn't there supposed to be some kind of test to see who would ascend to be *the* Lady of the Moon, the Huntress? When would it start? How was she to indicate she wanted to be part of that test? How . . .

The test, the Fae . . . everything had to wait. Because the point had been reached when the dance *wouldn't* wait.

She walked forward, felt the air grow thick and heavy as she moved to the very center of the clearing, the very center of the power.

She didn't know the dance for the moon. She knew the spiral dance and other ritual dances, but she'd always danced for the moon in her own way, for her own pleasure.

She looked at the other women. No one moved.

They don't know how to do this. They don't know how to dance to draw power into themselves and send it back out into the world. All right. A spiral dance, but not one that draws power to the center before being released. The power has already been gathered, so the spiral has to go outward, giving the power a clear path to follow. So, a dance for the moon. Never changing, ever changing. Dancing around her older sister while the Great Mother moves through the seasons. Waxing moon. Waning moon. Full moon to dark of the moon. Merry meet, and merry part, and merry meet again . . . little sister.

Smiling, Selena raised her arms and tilted her head back. The strength of the earth rose up through the soles of her feet, filling her slowly as it anchored her to the land. Within that strength was a hint of fire, the warmth of the summer sun. Above her was air . . . and water in the clouds that had slowly covered the night sky, turning it a pearly white.

As she lowered her arms, she brought her hands together, forming a cup out of them. Within her cupped hands, the power in the clearing began to glow—a ball of delicate, glittering moonlight. She shifted the ball of moonlight into her right hand, leaving the left open and free.

Holding her right hand close to her body, she turned in a slow circle. As she turned, a streamer of moonlight from the ball followed the movement. With each circle, she extended her hand a little farther. By the time her arm was fully extended, the air around her glowed. The power in the clearing, having been given a gentle channel of magic, constantly refilled the glowing ball in her hand.

Then she began to dance, her steps circling, spiraling out from the center. She let her movements represent the tides and the phases of the moon, while streamers of moonlight followed in her wake. She extended her left hand out in invitation, letting the other women know they were welcome to join her in the dance.

Blank faces. Wary faces. And the sullen anger from the woman standing inside the circle.

For a moment, her temper flashed, and she felt the power she was drawing from the branches of the Great Mother as well as the power in the clearing hesitate for just that moment, trembling on the edge of following this new channel.

Then, as she circled again, she saw the face of the woman she'd noticed before, the one with the richer strength. *Her* face was filled with wonder and delight—and a yearning.

Selena extended her left hand.

The woman took a step forward, but her companions held her back and whispered urgently. Regret shadowed the delight in the woman's face, and she stayed with her companions instead of joining the dance.

So Selena danced alone, ignoring most of the Fae present, focused on keeping the raw power in the clearing benevolent. But she continued to notice the woman and her four companions—and she realized the other four had stopped the woman because they were afraid to disrupt the dance, afraid it would end if they stepped forward now.

So she danced alone, spiraling out until she reached the edge of that globe of power. When she finally stopped, she stood almost where she'd stood when she'd first walked toward that power. The whole center of the clearing was now streamers of moonlight in motion, following the spiral of the dance.

There was still too much power here. If the other women had joined her in the dance, they would have absorbed some of it, renewing their own strength in the process. They still needed to do that. There were enough of them that, once they'd taken in the power they could, the rest could be shaped into something harmless or gently grounded through the branches of the Great Mother. But how to tell them that?

She couldn't. She doubted they would listen to her. So how to do what needed to be done?

She looked at the glowing ball of moonlight in her hand, then tossed it skyward as high as she could, sending a small breath of the branch of air with it. The ball burst over their heads, arcing in all directions, coming down on the women who made the circle.

She watched the glow of their power brighten. When their gift had been renewed, the power flowed harmlessly into the earth, filling the whole clearing with gentle light.

Tired now, she took a careful step back, breaking her connection to the spiral. Her limbs trembled with the need to ground the power she'd raised from the branches of the Great Mother, but she would need a few minutes of quiet and focus to do that safely, so it would have to wait a little longer. But not too much longer. Her emotions were raw. The joy she'd felt in the dance had constantly been pricked at the edges by the Fae's resistance to what she had done here, forming little jagged slices of anger inside her that she needed to smooth out.

That, too, had to be done soon because as conflicting emotions washed through her, she saw the power in all of those women flicker. It didn't matter how the Fae usually decided who ascended to control a gift. The power itself had issued the challenge—and she had met it. She controlled the gift now. Their lives were in her hands.

Mother's mercy, if I lose control now . . . Please, Mother, please let me get out of this circle and find someplace quiet for a few minutes.

She looked at the woman on the edge of the circle, who was now smiling at her shyly, hesitantly, as if waiting for some signal. But she didn't know the signal, didn't know—

"Who are you?" a harsh voice, bordering on hysteria, demanded.

The woman who had been inside the circle with her strode forward a few steps.

"Who are you?" the woman demanded again.

"I am Selena. And now I am *the* Lady of the Moon."

The woman stared at her, wide-eyed, as if she had just been slapped. Then her eyes narrowed, and an ugly anger filled her face. *"What are you?"*

The sneering anger in the woman's voice made those jagged slices of anger inside her rip a little more.

"I am Fae," Selena answered coldly. "But I am first, and always, a Daughter of the House of Gaian."

"A witch?" The woman's voice rose to a shriek. "A half-breed wiccanfae has dared intrude on one of our ceremonies, has dared try to pretend she could be one of us, has dared think she can control the power that belongs to *us*?"

"I pretend nothing. I *do* command the gift now." Power was spiking inside her, painful little flashes of lightning along her nerves.

"You command *nothing,* you *bitch!*"

Her body reacted to the word before she realized what she was doing. One moment she was facing the former Lady of the Moon; the next, she was a shadow hound racing across the distance between them, a snarl of fury filling her throat. The woman didn't have time to scream before she leaped, her forelegs hitting the woman in the chest hard enough to knock her rival to the ground. Then she pinned her enemy, her fangs a mere handspan away from the vulnerable throat as the woman screamed and flailed and screamed again.

She realized her enemy's flailing had a purpose when she heard flesh slap boot leather, saw the flash of moonlight on metal. She whipped her head around, her fangs slashing the woman's right forearm before the knife found its mark. Blood—and the taste of flesh, of prey—filled her mouth. She fought against the shadow hound instinct to rip and tear. This was prey. This was—

Blood sprayed over both of them as the woman flailed again—and the knife flashed again.

Her jaws closed unforgivingly over the torn forearm until teeth met bone. One fast, hard twist of her head—and bone snapped.

The knife fell to the ground. The woman screamed. Screamed and screamed.

She released the arm, turned her head so that she and the woman stared at each other. Blood dripped from her fangs onto the woman's face. She snarled.

"I yield!" the woman screamed. "I yield I yield *I yield*!"

The throat. So vulnerable. So rich with hot blood. So . . .

Selena carefully backed away from the woman, her paws leaving bloody prints in the grass. With the scent of blood in the air and the taste of it in her mouth, it took fierce effort to change back to her human form.

She could still taste the blood.

The woman stared up at her, her face pale with shock. "W-what are you?"

Selena looked down at her rival. "What you should have been and never were. The Queen of the Witches."

She walked away, striding toward the center of the clearing. Too much power churned inside her. Too much. She couldn't ground it, not until she'd dealt with these Fae, but if she didn't release some of it and it got away from her . . .

When she reached the center of the clearing, she raised her voice. "To make sure you understand who you now must deal with . . ."

She gave her anger to fire, forming it into a circle behind the circle of women. She held on to it long enough so that flames a finger-length high shot up from the ground, giving the women enough warning to step forward before the fire roared straight up as high as a man, forming a burning wall.

She formed another circle an arm's length from the fire and summoned air and water. Wind whipped around that circle with enough force to knock several women off their feet. It rose into the sky, twisting through the clouds overhead, gathering them until they turned dark and heavy with rain.

Thunder rumbled, loud enough to make the ground shake. Lightning flashed.

She gave her power to the storm, letting her temper and raw feelings be its channel.

The clouds released their burden, and torrents of rain pounded the clearing and the women inside the circle. In the pauses between thunderclaps, she heard horses neighing in fear, she heard the Fae men shouting, she heard women wailing—and she heard the angry, distressed bugling of one other horse.

Then she heard nothing. She fed the storm. The storm fed her. The Fae didn't want to accept her because she wasn't *exactly* what they were? So be it. Let them see exactly what she *could* be. Let them—

She saw the woman and her four companions. The woman, whose face had been filled with joy and delight while watching the dance, now looked at her with terror-filled eyes.

Do no harm.

For a moment, her mind went blank, her feelings went numb. In that moment, she felt something flowing from the land, something that had been striving to reach her through the fury of the storm.

Joy. Celebration. Love.

Rhyann.

Do no harm.

She heard the horse's angry bugling and turned to see Mistrunner rearing on the other side of the wall of fire. He wheeled, galloped away from the fire, wheeled again, and charged toward the flames. He stopped short of the flames, then wheeled again to make another charge.

"No," she whispered. The breeding or training that instilled in him a need to protect his rider would soon override his instinctive fear of fire. He would try to leap that wall of flames in order to reach her and—

Fire burns.

Do no harm.

Moonlight swirled with the rain and wind. She whipped her hand in a circle, drawing that moonlight to her until it formed a large ball around her hand. She flung it toward the fire. It hit the ground a man's-length from the flames, burst upward, and arched over the fire, forming a glittering bridge. She summoned the strength of earth to anchor it. She channeled some of the power from all four branches of the Great Mother to give the bridge strength. It still looked as insubstantial as moonlight, but it was as solid as the land.

She barely had time to make it strong enough to hold him before Mistrunner charged over the bridge and into the storm, trotting toward her.

Tears stung her eyes as he came up to her, whickering softly, snuffling her chest for the reassurance of her scent.

"Silly boy," she said as she rested a hand against his cheek. "Silly, silly boy. You know better than to try to leap over a wall of fire."

His presence helped her regain emotional control. Her anger at the Fae turned to ash. They would never be her people, but she wasn't planning to stay among them forever. Just long enough to drive the Inquisitors out of Sylvalan once and for all. Then she could go home.

Men rushed over the bridge she'd created. They hesitated when they realized she was watching, but when she did nothing to stop them, they hurried toward the Ladies they had escorted to this place—the five women who were somehow different from the others.

Her legs trembled with fatigue. It felt good to lean against Mistrunner. But she had to deal with the storm. Wind still whipped the rain with blinding fury. Since she had contained the storm's release to the circle within the clearing, she suddenly realized she was standing in ankle-deep water that was swiftly rising.

She tried to get a sense of the size of the storm . . . and almost whimpered.

If she released it, it would devastate this Old Place, drown the crops for miles around, flood the creeks and cause even more damage.

Start with the simplest thing first.

Stepping away from Mistrunner, she banked the wall of fire until it was nothing more than a smoldering circle. Then she pushed the circle holding the storm outward just beyond the fire circle. The ground sizzled and steam rose as the rain and standing water rushed to fill the larger space.

As soon as the fire was out, other Fae men rushed into the storm to reach the Ladies of the Moon.

She ignored them as she gathered the wind in the clearing, shaped it into a wide wedge, and sent it flying toward the farthest edge of the storm. It sheared the cloud bank, driving the clouds before it, heading east.

Broken off from the rest of the storm—and the magic that had prevented it from releasing anywhere but in the clearing—the rain poured down.

Selena flinched when she saw the flash of lightning, but she shaped another wedge of wind and used it to slice off another piece of the storm and send it eastward.

The third time she sliced off a piece of the storm, she felt another power brush against hers, another wind grab the storm, pulling it further apart, draining some of its energy and sending it back in a way that would keep some of the storm restrained as it was sent on so that not all of it would fall here.

Rhyann, playing with air and water in a way that would spread the storm farther and farther, diluting it in the process.

Selena's heart lifted. She worked to slice the storm into pieces, trusting that Rhyann would catch those pieces and send them on, driven by fast winds.

The storm would keep spreading out, driven east by the winds. Other witches who could command the branches of air or water would catch the storm when it came to them and continue to send it on. It would fly over the Mother's Hills, softened by the many witches who commanded those branches of the Great Mother. Perhaps it would go even further east, but it would diminish to a soft rain, a farmer's rain that would nourish the crops instead of destroying them.

She worked the storm. She didn't know how long it took. It might have been hours. If felt like days before she sent the last clouds toward Rhyann and the rain in the clearing finally stopped. Overhead, the clear night sky was filled with stars.

Shivering from exhaustion as much as the chill in the air, Selena slowly grounded the power that held the circle in the clearing. The standing water poured out, spreading itself through the woods.

She walked back to Mistrunner, wondering if she had the strength left to mount—and wondering if he would be able to find his way back to Ella's house.

As she rested her forehead against his neck, someone said hesitantly, "Huntress?"

She looked up and saw the woman standing nearby, watching her anxiously. She said nothing. She simply waited.

The woman came forward slowly, then went down on one knee. "I, Gwynith, here and now pledge my loyalty and service to you, Selena, the Lady of the Moon . . . and the Huntress."

Since she didn't know the correct response to this part of the ritual, Selena said nothing.

Gwynith looked at her. "Do you accept?"

"I accept."

A look of relief that was almost brutal to see filled Gwynith's face. She rose and stepped aside.

Her four companions immediately stepped forward and made the same pledge of loyalty and service. The rest of the women came forward more slowly, more warily, but they made the same pledge. While they did, Selena noticed the intense, whispered conversation between Gwynith, her companions, and some of the men who were with them.

When the last woman stepped aside, one man came forward. "Huntress . . . Lady Dianna is badly hurt and needs a healer to look at that arm as soon as it can be done."

Dianna. So that was the name of the woman who had denied her right to be *the* Lady of the Moon after the power had already accepted her as such.

"It is your right to deny her access to any Clan territory where you are present, especially after . . . after she shamed her Clan by acting as she did."

"Is there a healer in the Clan who is connected to this Old Place?" Selena asked.

"There is, Huntress."

"Then take her there to get the care she needs."

He bowed. "Thank you. She will not disturb you while she is there." He hesitated, looking uncomfortable. "It is within your right to strip her of her gift. But, Lady, there is no witch in the Old Place that anchors our Clan's piece of Tir Alainn. There hasn't been since the Black Coats came and she was . . . lost. We don't know why it is so, but Dianna's gift can anchor the Old Place's magic and hold our piece of Tir Alainn. Without her gift . . ."

They don't know why it is so. Mother's mercy. "I have no wish to harm your Clan. I will not take what your people need."

"We are grateful for your mercy, Huntress." He started to turn away, then turned back. "Tonight was the first time Dianna acknowledged that witches were the House of Gaian. Up until tonight, she has denied there was any connection."

Selena stared at him, puzzled. "We have always been the House of Gaian. Why would she deny it?"

He gave her an odd look, started to say something, then

changed his mind and hurried back to the other men kneeling beside Dianna, who was still on the ground.

She saw Gwynith approach her at the same time three men stepped up.

"We"—one of the men gestured to the other two—"are bards from different Clans. We are here as witnesses . . . and to send the news out to the rest of the Clans. May we ask, Lady Selena, what Clan you are from?"

"That can wait," Gwynith said firmly. "The Lady is wet and tired and needs dry clothes and warm food. Your questions can wait until we're back in Tir Alainn and she has been looked after properly."

Gwynith sounded so much like Rhyann, Selena had to bite her lip to keep from laughing. "I think I have the strength to answer one question." Before Gwynith could protest, Selena turned back to the bards. "I don't come from a Clan."

The bards' spokesman looked puzzled. "Then . . . where *do* you come from?"

"I come from the Mother's Hills."

Instant silence as even Gwynith stared at her. She could hear the raindrops dripping from the leaves of the nearby trees.

"Mother's mercy," the bard whispered.

She didn't want to terrify these people any more than she'd already done, but they needed to understand how much her presence among them, and her power over them, was going to change their lives. She said gently, "I think you will find, good bard, that if the wrath of the House of Gaian looks in your direction, the Mother will have no mercy."

All three men glanced up at the clear night sky and turned deathly pale.

"Enough," Gwynith said.

"In a moment," Selena said. "Now I have a question. Do you know the Bard?"

The bards' spokesman nodded warily.

"Do you know where to find him?"

The man looked even more wary. "Not at present, Lady. He is . . . traveling. But we could send a message through the Clans," he added hurriedly.

"Then tell the Bard that the new Lady of the Moon would like to speak with him, if he would so oblige me."

"We'll send the message, Lady." They moved away, hurrying toward their horses.

Selena looked at Gwynith. "It is not that I don't appreciate your assistance, but I'm wondering why you're offering it so freely."

"Two reasons," Gwynith replied after a long pause. "First, I have pledged my loyalty and service to you, and I think you are not familiar with Tir Alainn or riding the shining roads."

"I have no experience with either."

"You have no reason to trust any of us, but I swear to you I will do nothing that would harm you in any way. I—I can't say with any certainty that will be true of the others here tonight . . . or other Fae who weren't here tonight."

"Understood. Your second reason?"

Gwynith hesitated, obviously struggling with how to say enough without saying too much. "Lady Ashk did not approve of Dianna and the way she was leading the Fae. But I think . . . I think Lady Ashk would approve of you."

And that's very important to you, isn't it? "Who is Lady Ashk?"

"She's the Lady of the Woods at Bretonwood, a Clan in the west."

Lady of the Woods.

A shiver went through Selena. The woods coming alive. Coming toward her. "What is her other form?"

Gwynith gave her an odd, searching look. "She is like you, Huntress. She is a shadow hound."

Two shadow hound bitches racing through the woods, racing through the moonlight, united against a common enemy.

"How far away is Bretonwood?" Selena asked, feeling lightheaded.

"It's— Well, she isn't there right now. She's traveling east to a place called Willowsbrook." Gwynith touched Selena's arm. "Lady, please. Let's get some food and get warm. Then we can talk about whatever you wish."

Selena nodded. A few minutes later she was riding beside Gwynith, the escorts who had come with Gwynith riding ahead and behind them, followed by Gwynith's four companions with their escorts.

As they reached the clearing that held the shining road that led to Tir Alainn, Selena said, "I think I'd like to meet Lady Ashk."

Gwynith replied softly, "I know she'll want to meet you."

Chapter 11

new moon

As night gave way to dawn, Breanna watched the storm swiftly coming toward them over the Mother's Hills. She rose from the bench beside the kitchen door and stretched her stiff muscles, listening for any sound that didn't belong. When the sun went down yesterday, she and Gwenn had spent an hour arguing with Liam and Donovan about needing to be outside in order to receive whatever message might come through the Great Mother's branches. Neither she nor Gwenn had been able to explain well enough that the message wasn't carried *on* the elements, it was *in* the elements—something felt on the skin, breathed into the body, tasted. They *had* to be outside to read it properly.

An open kitchen door and the bench beside it were as much of a compromise as either man—and Falco—was willing to make, since there were still nighthunters in the Old Place. They hadn't seen any of the creatures, but they had found more rotting, half-eaten animals beneath dead trees. So the men led the animals to pastures in the morning and led them back to the small pasture near the stables every evening, the children were confined to the house once the sun set, and some of her kin, armed with bows and crossbows, kept watch each night—and she and Gwenn had had to promise they wouldn't step more than a few paces away from the house until the sun rose.

Hearing quiet sounds in the kitchen, she turned toward the door. Liam stepped out, rubbing his neck.

"Gwenn's put the kettle on for tea and is muttering about toasting some bread," he said quietly. He leaned toward her and added, "I gathered she doesn't greet the morning cheerfully under any circumstances."

"Did you get any sleep?" Breanna asked, studying him. "You

look a bit rumpled." Which wasn't surprising since he'd kept watch with her until after midnight, when Falco took his place.

"A couple of hours," Liam replied, still rubbing his neck. "Which is more than you got, unless you dozed off out here. And since you so kindly pointed out my rumpledness, I'll point out that you're looking a bit disheveled yourself."

Breanna looked away, hoping the dawn light was still pale enough to hide her blush. Sleep had been the last thing on her mind while Falco was keeping watch with her. But she didn't think her older-brother-the-baron wanted to know that.

She ran her fingers up between her breasts, checking to make sure she'd retied the tunic laces Falco had untied last night.

"Where is Falco?" Liam asked.

Breanna jolted and tried not to look guilty. There was no reason to feel guilty. She was a grown woman and could take a lover if she chose to. Why shouldn't it be Falco? Until she'd gotten to know him, she hadn't met a man who made her feel ripe and . . . juicy. The feel of his hands as he caressed her breasts and the way his mouth—

"Breanna?"

"Hmm?"

"Falco?"

"Mmm, yes."

"Where. Is. He?"

Mother's tits! Her mind had drifted, and now Liam was giving her that narrow-eyed brotherly stare.

"Is there anything you'd like to tell me?" Liam asked.

She really didn't think so. "About what?"

"About Falco."

"He went over to the stables to check on the men standing watch. Storm's coming," she added, changing the subject.

"Maybe more than one," Liam replied not quite cryptically enough.

Breanna crossed her arms over her chest. Gran wasn't making a fuss about Falco's interest. Why should Liam?

The thought of her grandmother brought other uneasy thoughts. "Liam?"

He was watching the storm. "Hmm?"

"Do you think Gran's becoming ill?"

That got his full attention. "Why do you ask?"

Breanna shrugged. "Fiona said Gran didn't eat much at dinner last night and she went to bed shortly after we came back here."

"She was tired. That's all."

"She's never tired."

Liam walked over to her, put his arm around her shoulders, and kissed the top of her head. "This has been a trying time for her, Breanna. So many people looking to her to make wise decisions, so much uncertainty about what's going to happen. I'm not surprised she's tired. Even *my* mother dozed off last night while we were still talking, and she's a generation younger than Nuala. Don't worry over something a good night's sleep will set right."

She and Liam turned as a boot scuffed the kitchen threshold.

"Here," Donovan said as he walked toward them, balancing two plates of buttered toast and two cups of tea. "Tuck into that. It will take a while for us all to get a proper breakfast."

"I see Gwenn is teaching you how to make yourself useful," Liam said. He released Breanna in order to take the plate and mug that Donovan held out to him.

Donovan just snorted.

"Does your staff make a fuss over Gwenn knowing her way around the kitchen?" Breanna asked, thinking about how their housekeeper, Glynis, was always arguing with her about what was and wasn't proper work for a lady.

Donovan grinned. "The first time Gwenn wandered into the kitchen to make herself a cup of tea, they were appalled. My cook, housekeeper, and butler cornered me and told me I simply had to explain to my lady wife that gentry ladies didn't do that."

Breanna leaned forward. "What did you say?"

"I told them I'd just married her. If they wanted her out of the kitchen, *they* could explain it to her."

"So what happened?" Breanna said when it didn't seem like Donovan was going to say anything else.

"She still wanders down to the kitchen to make her own tea when it suits her, so what do you think happened?"

Gwenn came out of the kitchen with two more plates and mugs, so Breanna held her tongue and ate her toast while she watched the storm come in.

"It's moving fast," Gwenn said.

Breanna just nodded. The edge of the storm was in the Old Place now. She watched the lightning, heard the thunder. As the first breath of wind flying before the storm reached her, she shiv-

ered. "It must go from one end of the Mother's Hills to the
other."

"If it's still this strong, it must have been a mean bitch of a
storm wherever it started," Gwenn said.

Breanna noticed the way Donovan frowned at his wife's
choice of words, but she wasn't sure if he disapproved of the language or if he was considering what it might mean for Gwenn to
refer to a storm in that way.

She set her mug and plate on the ground and stepped forward.
Gwenn did the same thing before looking back at Donovan. "You
should go inside. You'll get wet out here."

"Will you go inside?" Donovan asked.

Gwenn shook her head. "The storm is out here. The message
is out here."

"Then I'm staying."

Breanna glanced at Liam, saw the stubborn look in his eyes,
and didn't waste the effort to persuade him to do what they both
knew he wouldn't do. Besides, the storm required her attention
now.

She watched the wall of rain come toward her, tasted it on the
wind. Tasted the power still entwined with it. She shivered. "This
wasn't a natural storm."

"No, it wasn't," Gwenn agreed.

"What do you mean it wasn't natural?" Liam said.

Breanna half turned toward him. "It didn't form on its own.
Someone created it—and released it."

"Mother's mercy," Donovan whispered.

"It wasn't formed in the Mother's Hills," Gwenn said
thoughtfully. "Somewhere in the midlands, I think."

"Why would someone do that?" Donovan said, his voice
sharp and worried.

Neither woman answered him. They stepped forward together
as the rain came across the lawn and finally reached them.

A message written on water, whispered on the wind.

This wasn't a whisper. Despite how far the storm had traveled, she could still taste the anger that had summoned that wind
and sent it flying.

Yes, something had definitely changed.

She watched Gwenn cup her hands and sip the rain that collected there. And she watched Gwenn turn pale.

"Do you have what you need?" Breanna asked.

Gwenn nodded.

Breanna walked to the center of the lawn and began to dance, channeling the wind through her body and sending it back to shred the clouds, spreading them out even further. A hand clasped hers . . . and Gwenn circled with her, taking in the strength from water and sending it out again to hold back some of the rain.

As they broke apart, Fiona stepped forward to join them.

Breanna felt the power in the dance, felt the way Fiona's presence kept grounding that power in the branch of earth, spreading it through the land.

Acknowledging, celebrating, taming. Isn't that what Fiona said she and Jenny had done once before?

When the last cloud passed over them, she stopped the dance. All three women were soaked to the skin and shivering from exhaustion.

As she pushed her wet hair away from her face, she noticed Liam and Donovan standing side by side, their expressions watchful . . . and a little wary. Standing near them were Clay, Rory, and Falco, their expressions equally watchful, equally wary.

We are what we are, Breanna thought wearily as she walked back to the house.

When they reached the men, Donovan slipped an arm around Gwenn's waist to lead her the rest of the way to the house. Rory and Clay took Fiona's arms to support her.

Liam put his arm around her shoulders, and said tightly, "You're going to get dry and go to bed before you get some kind of lung fever."

"It's summer," she muttered. "It's warm." But now that the dance was done, her muscles wouldn't stop shaking.

Nuala stood in the kitchen doorway, a shawl around her shoulders. She stepped back as Donovan led Gwenn inside and pointed to the large kitchen table. "The kettle's boiled. Let her sit there for a minute and have something hot to drink." She raised her hand, cutting off Donovan's protest before he could say the first word.

Liam, Clay, and Rory didn't argue. They pulled out chairs for Breanna and Fiona, then stood back while Nuala took a seat and Glynis set hot mugs of tea in front of the women.

Breanna felt a pang of regret when she saw the way Falco hurried through the kitchen without saying anything to her. She felt puzzled confusion when he returned with three blankets. He gave one to Donovan, another to Clay, and wrapped the third one around her, his hands resting on her shoulders for a moment in a way that was as comforting as Liam's arm had been.

"Now," Nuala said quietly. "What was the message?"

Breanna looked at Gwenn, who nodded to indicate Breanna should go first. "Something definitely changed. Something that, I think, preceded the storm. Something that will change things for all of us—witches, humans, the Small Folk."

"The Fae, too?" Falco asked quietly.

Breanna thought about the feel of the wind and nodded. "Yes, the Fae, too. But I can't tell you more than that."

"I can," Gwenn said. She shivered. "I told you I'd studied in the Mother's Hills a few years ago and met some of the other witches who were being trained by the Crones. I think . . . I think this was Selena. It's hard to tell. There's been so many who have touched that storm, but at the core of it, I think it was Selena. Her power had a different feel to it because"—She hesitated, then looked at Falco—"Because Selena is a very powerful witch, but she's also Fae."

Breanna felt Falco's hand come down on her shoulder, but she didn't think it was meant as comfort to her as much as for the support he needed at that moment.

"What does that have to do with the storm?" he asked in a strained voice.

Gwenn kept looking at him, and there was something close to pity in her eyes. "I think someone was foolish enough to provoke Selena into striking back—and the storm was her answer."

Chapter 12

waxing moon

Adolfo stared out the window, watching the storm continue east into Wolfram. Not much of a storm now—and still too much. Far too much.

He shuddered.

"Master?"

Adolfo turned away from the window. Ubel had been reporting on the number and position of the men marching toward the western border under the family crests of Wolfram's barons, the fleet of warships standing ready in the harbor, the messages sent by the Arktos barons to confirm their readiness to wage righteous war against the Sylvalan barons who couldn't see with a clear eye what honorable, decent men needed to do to cleanse their land.

He'd heard nothing from the moment he'd opened the window to let some rain-cleaned air into the stuffy room. One of the things that had helped him become the Master Inquisitor, the Witch's Hammer, was his ability to scent magic. It was how he detected witches—the *real* witches—and it was how he recognized men who had the Inquisitor's Gift. He trained those men, honing them into weapons. The ignorant might call the Inquisitor's Gift a kind of magic, but he wouldn't permit such blasphemy to be spoken out loud. He didn't like his Inquisitors wondering about magic, except as a thing to be destroyed.

"Master?"

"The rain stinks of magic," Adolfo said heavily, half turning to watch the raindrops roll down the outside of the window. "Do you know what this rain will do, Ubel?"

"I—I'm not sure, Master Adolfo."

Ubel wasn't sure of much lately. His fault? Perhaps he should have been gentler when his Assistant Inquisitor had returned from the west, even though he had failed to destroy Baron Padrick's family and had lost the other five Inquisitors who had gone with him. Yes, perhaps Ubel had heard too much of the reprimand in his voice.

"What does rain do, Ubel?" Adolfo asked gently.

Ubel watched him warily for a moment, then licked his dry lips. "It falls from the sky to the ground."

Adolfo nodded encouragingly. "And then?" He sighed before Ubel could answer, not out of impatience but out of the dread that had begun filling him as soon as he realized what *this* storm could do. "It soaks into the ground, Ubel. It soaks deep into the soil, into the fields and forests. It fills the brooks and streams and rivers."

"Yes, Master. I suppose it does."

"This storm . . . this rain stinks of magic."

Adolfo waited patiently, watching as understanding paled Ubel's fair skin and filled the blue eyes with horror.

"Yes," Adolfo said heavily.

"But— But the magic in Wolfram's Old Places is *dead*. We destroyed it when we destroyed the witches."

He shook his head. "As long as there is *any* left, magic never fully dies. You can bleed it out of a place so that the place *feels* dead, but it's like creatures that bury themselves deep in the mud when a brook dries up. You think they're gone, destroyed. Then the rain comes and renews the brook—and they come back with it to live and breed again."

"No," Ubel whispered.

"Yes. A puddle of magic, hidden so deep even the Small Folk can't feel it . . . This rain will feed it . . . and it will rise again. A small piece of woods will suddenly have enough magic for the Small Folk to live in it. And once they return and take root, no man will be able to set foot there and hope to come out again. This rain will make a few women forget their proper place in the world, and they will remember things they hadn't known they'd forgotten . . . and men will no longer rule the land. How can men rule when a *female* can flood the fields, or hold back the rain so that crops wither and die, or command the land itself to remain barren? How can a man's toil fight against that?"

"Then we have to stay here and fight," Ubel said. "We have to stay and protect our own country."

"How do we protect it from rain, Ubel? How do we protect

Wolfram when every storm that crosses the Una River from Sylvalan is filthy with magic?"

"We have to do *something*," Ubel insisted.

"We will. And we are." Adolfo walked over to the table and looked at the papers filled with Ubel's neat handwriting, scattered over a map of Sylvalan. "The only way to keep Wolfram clean is to wade through the muck of Sylvalan until it, too, is clean."

"Within the next phase of the moon, we'll have most of our—"

"We can't wait." Adolfo took a deep breath, then let it out slowly. *Don't remind him of his failures. He needs to believe nothing can stand against him. Afterward . . . Afterward I will have to consider carefully whether or not Ubel has been too mired in Sylvalan's filth to be trusted.* "We must strike now. We must strike fiercely . . . and without mercy. Any Sylvalan baron who does not support us in our fight against the Evil One and its servants must be destroyed. We must bring the battle into Sylvalan before those creatures, those *witches,* can do more harm to Wolfram."

"What do you want me to do, Master Adolfo?"

Ubel still looked pale, but there was a fire in his eyes now. He wouldn't run away from the fight *this* time, not when his homeland was at risk of being contaminated by the magic spawned by their enemies.

Adolfo pushed the papers aside until he uncovered the western part of the map of Sylvalan. "You will take our ten largest warships and fill them with Wolfram warriors. Those ships and men are yours to command. Check the ports at Seahaven and Wellingsford as you head west. There may be witches and their kin trying to find transport to the witch-loving barons further up the coast. But do not linger. We must not give them time to gather an army against us." He pointed to a spot on the western coast. "That looks like a small harbor, opposite those islands. From there, it doesn't look to be more than a day's march to Breton—two at the most."

"There is a harbor town south of Breton," Ubel said.

"But you would have to march inland and then north to reach Breton. That gives the western barons more warning and more time to gather men to stand against you."

"I was told there wasn't a harbor town near Breton."

Disliking the shakiness he heard in Ubel's voice, Adolfo continued softly but firmly. "You don't need a harbor town. A small fishing village will suffice. *Anywhere* you can bring the ships in close enough to land your men will suffice. The more swiftly you move, the less resistance they can bring against you. After thinking about your report on the barons' council, it is now clear to me that Padrick, the Baron of Breton, controls the other western barons. Therefore, it is no longer enough to punish him for helping Liam after that whelp spoke out against us in the barons' council. Padrick must be destroyed. Completely. His home, his family, his fields, his livestock. You must leave nothing but corpses and ashes, Ubel. Without him to lead, the western barons will need time to regain their balance, and while the west is in turmoil, the Arktos barons will lead their men to the northern part of Sylvalan, along with the northeastern barons who already support our cause. Our Sylvalan barons in the southern part of the land will march to here." Adolfo pointed to another spot on the map. "They'll come up to the southern end of the Mother's Hills, blocking the midland barons if they attempt to enter the fight."

"What about the Fae?" Ubel asked in a strained voice.

What about the Gatherer? is what he's really asking. Adolfo suppressed a shudder. He would never forget that black-haired woman riding her dark horse. He would never forget that she'd killed his Inquisitors. And he would never forget what she did to *him*. His left arm dead, just from touching her. And the dreams lately . . . No. No one could know about the dreams.

"You must strike swiftly," Adolfo said again, "before a warning can be sounded. Swiftly, Ubel. And then you must leave just as swiftly. I do not want to lose my finest Inquisitor. When Padrick is dead, bring the ships and men back to Wellingsford. From there you can keep any ships from sailing out of the west—and destroy any ships trying to sail *to* the west."

"Yes, Master." Ubel hesitated. "And what will Wolfram's army be doing?"

You mean, what will I be doing? Perhaps it was an attempt at arrogance, but Adolfo thought the question sounded more like a young boy's plea for reassurance.

"I will lead the Wolfram army, and the rest of the Sylvalan barons who are decent men, as straight as an arrow to Willowsbrook. And after we crush the bastard Liam . . ." He turned to look at the sun coming out, shining through the last wisps of the storm. "After we crush Liam, the three prongs of our great army will march into the Mother's Hills and destroy everything that lives there."

"Will the magic die completely then?" Ubel asked.

Turning back, Adolfo laid his right hand on Ubel's shoulder, and said softly, "I told you, Ubel. It never dies completely once it's taken root in a place. But if you destroy all the creatures who have the ability to reach it, then it's as good as dead."

Chapter 13

waxing moon

*S*he was a child again. Seven years old, maybe eight. The village wasn't the one she'd grown up in, but she knew it was supposed to be home. Behind her, the Mother's Hills rose, looking comforting and close but still a day's journey away. In front of her, all around her . . .

The village burned. The fields burned. Animals screamed as they were slaughtered. Women screamed, in anger and in pain. Men roared, in fury and despair.

Confusion and slaughter all around her. She saw the black-coated men riding into the village. The warriors with them spread out as the people in the village rushed to meet the attack. Her father and two of his friends ran past her, armed with bows and knives. The two friends fell a moment later, pierced by enemy arrows. Her father ran on to where the black-coated enemies waited for him.

She heard a woman scream. "Mother?" She turned, frantically trying to see through the smoke.

Another field. But it wasn't crops the Black Coats were burning. Women and wood. The stench of burning flesh. The screams of agony.

One woman burst through the piled wood, fire eating her legs, turning them black as she tried to run.

"Mother!"

The woman looked at her, pointed to something behind her.

The Mother's Hills. She would be safe if she could reach the Mother's Hills.

A black-coated man swung something at the woman's head, turning her face into a red smear. Still she screamed in defiance until the fire devoured her.

"Mama! MAMA!"

She spun around as the other child cried out. Rhyann. So small, so young, and still so fierce. She had to save Rhyann.

She grabbed her sister's hand, pulling Rhyann with her. "We have to run. We have to reach the Mother's Hills."

"Mama! Papa!"

"Come on, Rhyann! Run!"

They ran and ran but couldn't get beyond the burning fields and the knots of men fighting, bleeding, dying.

When Rhyann stumbled, Selena picked her up, staggering under the weight as she kept walking forward, her eyes on the hills. She had to get Rhyann to a safe place. She had to.

Her legs burned from the effort of carrying her sister. Her arms ached. Her breath came in painful gasps. She heard a distant roll of thunder, but the sky was so smoke-darkened now she couldn't tell if a storm was coming.

She had to rest, had to find a safe place for them to hide for a little while.

Then she saw them, astride their beautiful, strong horses. The Fae.

"Help me!" she cried. "Please, help me. I have to take my sister someplace safe."

They stared at her out of cold, cold eyes. They smiled as a shadow fell over her.

A man stood in front of her, blocking the road to the Mother's Hills. A tall, large man with a lean face that was too deeply shadowed for her to see any details. Around him were dark, winged creatures with needle-sharp teeth.

"Leave her alone," she said, putting Rhyann down and pushing her sister behind her. "She's just a little girl."

He smiled at her.

"Let her go. Take me instead."

"Oh, I will take you," he said gently. "But I will punish you for being what you are by making you watch your sister die."

"No." She looked at the Fae. "Please, take her," she begged them. "Please."

They just watched her out of cold, cold eyes. Then they turned their horses and rode off into the woods, which were suddenly so close and yet so painfully out of reach.

Thunder rumbled again, closer now.

"Yes," the man said, "you will watch your sister die. My pets will tear her flesh and drink her blood."

"No."

"And then they will devour her soul."

"NOOOOO!"

Someone pounded on the door.

"Huntress? Huntress!"

Shaking, gasping with the effort to breathe, Selena pushed herself halfway to a sitting position.

"What is it?" she said hoarsely.

The door opened and closed. Gwynith rushed to the bed. "What's wrong? Are you all right?"

"A dream," Selena muttered, kicking at the tangled covers to free her legs. "Just a dream."

As Gwynith helped her get free of the covers, Selena wondered if it really was "just a dream." There were Fae whose gift controlled sleep and dreams. Had one of them sent this nightmare to exhaust her, weaken her? Or had this dream come from the Sleep Sister herself as a warning? Right now, it didn't matter. Right now, she needed earth and air and water.

"I'm going riding," Selena said, surprised at how unsteady her legs felt as she got up and walked to the basin and pitcher of water. "I want to see a bit of Tir Alainn before I leave."

"Leave?" Gwynith said, sounding alarmed. "Where are you going?"

Anywhere, as long as it wasn't Tir Alainn.

She poured water into the basin, then sent a glimmer of fire through her fingers as she put them in the cold water, which warmed quickly. After stripping off her nightgown, she pulled the basin that served as a catchall from the shelf beneath the wash table and stepped into it. It would take a real bath to completely clean the smell of sour sweat off her skin, but she didn't want to take the time for it. The sponge bath would have to do.

"Would you like company on your ride?" Gwynith asked hesitantly.

"Are you asking because you'd like to go riding or because you're afraid some of the Fae here might try to throw me into the mist at the edge of the world?" She'd meant it as a biting tease—until Gwynith's silence filled the room. The sponge dribbled water down her belly as she turned to face the other woman. "You think that's possible, don't you?"

Gwynith linked her fingers and twisted them. "Many of the

Fae are upset that Dianna lost the challenge. Especially to someone who isn't pure Fae."

"Like Dianna," Selena said, knowing by the puzzled look in Gwynith's eyes that the woman didn't understand why that was so amusing. "I'd be pleased to have your company on the ride."

Gwynith hurried to the door and opened it just enough to stick her head out.

As Selena finished her quick wash, she heard a quiet rumble of a male voice responding to Gwynith's murmurs.

"They'll bring the horses," Gwynith said, closing the door. "What do you want to wear?"

"The white outfit," Selena replied as she dried herself. The Ladies of the Hearth had done a good job of cleaning the white trousers and overdress yesterday while she'd spent the day trying to get to know the other Ladies of the Moon as well as learn the ways of the Fae.

Cold, cold eyes.

Selena shivered.

Just a dream. She was no longer a child. Neither was Rhyann.

She had to get away from this Clan house. Had to meet the land. That was for herself. But she also wanted to understand why Tir Alainn felt so . . . strange.

By the time she had dressed and they reached one of the outer doors of the Clan house, Gwynith's four escorts were waiting with the horses. Of course. She should have realized the men would be coming, too.

As she approached Mistrunner, the stallion snorted to let her know he didn't approve of having his reins held by a strange man.

The escort, giving the horse a wary glance, touched two fingers to his temple in greeting, and said, "Blessings of the day to you, Lady."

Surprised by the greeting, Selena looked at the man more carefully. He seemed tense, uncertain. "Blessings of the day," she replied—and saw him visibly relax. "Did you check Mistrunner's tack?" She regretted asking. The tension in the man returned, and his mouth was a grim line.

"I did," he said.

Would you have checked it if it was Dianna going out for a ride? Selena wondered as she mounted Mistrunner. She didn't think he would have, not because Dianna would have been in no danger from other Fae but because he wouldn't have cared what happened to the former Lady of the Moon. Which made her wonder why these western Fae were so determined to look after her.

With effort, she pushed all thoughts aside and focused on the feel of Mistrunner beneath her—and the feel of the land as he lifted into his easy canter. As they left the Clan house behind, his little snorts, tail flicks, and head tosses told her plainly that he didn't like it here, didn't like the feel of this ground beneath his hooves, didn't like grass that looked healthy and green but wasn't good to eat.

Why was she so certain the grass wasn't good to eat? Was it because her own belly had still rumbled with hunger even after she'd eaten a large meal at the Clan house?

She reined in and dismounted, walked a few steps away from her companions, then crouched to put her hands on the ground. A few moments later, Gwynith crouched beside her.

"Lady Selena?" Gwynith said.

Mother's mercy. Were they all so blind that they couldn't see what was in front of them? "Is all of Tir Alainn like this?"

"Like this?" Gwynith looked around. "The Clan territories all look a little different, depending on what part of Sylvalan they're anchored to."

"How does this place look to you?" Selena asked impatiently.

Gwynith frowned. She considered the question for several seconds before she said, "It feels . . . pale. That's not the right way to say it, but . . ."

"It's a good way to say it. How does it compare to your Clan's territory?"

"It's . . . pale." Gwynith shrugged. "I don't spend much time in our piece of Tir Alainn, but I don't remember feeling hungry all the time when I *was* there. The food here has little taste. At home, you can't tell the difference between what was grown in Tir Alainn and what was grown in the fields we tend in our Old Place. Well"—she smiled—"you won't find a worm in an apple that came from Tir Alainn."

Selena didn't smile back. She stood and brushed off her hands.

Gwynith studied her. "If I may ask, what is it *you* see here?"

"A beautiful land ruined by ignorance and blind arrogance," Selena said sharply. "Let's get back to the Clan house. There are things to be done before I leave."

"But . . . where are you going?"

Home. She wasn't sure anymore. "You said Lady Ashk was on her way to Willowsbrook?"

"Yes."

"Then that's where I'll be going." Selena hesitated. "Do you know where it is?"

"It's on the other side of the Mother's Hills. I think." Gwynith looked at the escorts. "We could find out for you."

"I would be grateful." She returned to Mistrunner and mounted, then waited for Gwynith to mount and move up beside her.

"It would be a long journey from here, no matter which direction you went," Gwynith said.

"Direction?"

"There aren't any long bridges between the midland Clans and the Clans on the eastern side of the hills. You'd have to go north or south to swing round the hills."

"There is one other possibility," Selena said, smiling. "I can simply ride straight through the hills."

"But you *can't*," Gwynith protested.

"Whyever not?"

"Because the Fae . . . Because we don't . . ."

"Maybe the Fae don't, but as one of the Mother's Daughters, I certainly do."

"I forgot," Gwynith said faintly. "I forgot that's where you come from."

Because she truly liked this woman, Selena leaned in the saddle and lightly touched Gwynith's arm. "Moon sister, that is something you should never forget about me."

Tonight, I'll be back in the real world, guesting with Ella's family. Mother's mercy, a meal of soup and day-old bread will be a feast compared to what I've eaten here. Would Gwynith be willing to come with me? There's so much I need to understand about the Fae. So much they need to understand about themselves.

Selena let the words of the Clan's matriarchs drift over her. She'd requested the presence of the Ladies of the Moon who hadn't already left for their home Clans, as well as the bards and storytellers who had come to this Clan's territory to bear witness to the ascendance of the next Huntress. Since she *hadn't* said other Fae couldn't join them, the matriarchs had made themselves

comfortable around the large round table in one of the outer
courtyards that overlooked some of the gardens and the rolling
land beyond. She'd tried to listen to the older women out of respect, as she would have listened to the Crones. Unlike the
Crones, these women weren't willing to listen to her, and used
brittle courtesy and sly remarks to say what they wouldn't say directly to her face: she wasn't welcome, she wasn't accepted. She
would *never* be welcome or accepted.

Cold, cold eyes.

They would be capable of watching a child die simply because the child wasn't like them.

"Dianna left this morning," one of the old women said, sniff-
ing. "She didn't want to remain any longer, despite the pain traveling will cause her."

"I expect she's anxious to return to her Clan, since they need
her," Selena replied politely.

"That's not why she left," the woman snapped.

"Now, now," one of the other matriarch's said, patting her
friend's hand while giving Selena a sly look. "Perhaps the new
Lady of the Moon can use her power to help the Brightwood
Clan."

"How so?" For a moment, Selena thought it was the sun on
her skin that made her feel overheated. Then she realized it was
temper bubbling *under* the skin that made her feel too warm. She
gritted her teeth as she made the effort to bank the branch of fire.

"Since your loyalty is to the Fae now, and since you know
how to deal with witches . . . Well, we'd heard there are more
witches than *we* need in the Old Place here. You could command
one of them to go to Brightwood and assume her rightful duties."

"And what duties might those be?"

"To anchor the magic that keeps Brightwood's shining road
open, of course. It's the least you could do after cheating Dianna
out of—"

"I cheated Dianna out of nothing," Selena said sharply, feeling the heat rise inside her. "I ascended because I could meet the
gift on its own terms, because *I* was what it needed. The witches
who live in the Old Place that anchors your Clan's territory *are a
family*. I would have thought even the Fae could understand that
bond. They have no desire to leave their home or their land, and
if any of them did, she would go to a place of her own choosing.
The Fae have no right to dictate what one of the Mother's Daugh-

ters does or doesn't do. You have no say except among your own people. And you obviously have no understanding of why the Huntress came into being."

The old woman's face reddened with anger. "And you're going to tell us?"

"The Huntress is the Queen of the Witches because she is their protector. So if you think I'll use my power to force a witch to live someplace against her will for your convenience, you'd better think again. And if *you* try to force a witch against her will, I won't be going after her. I'll be hunting *you*."

Gwynith, who was sitting beside her, gasped.

The matriarchs muttered angrily under their breath. The one who faced Selena looked ready to explode. "It is because of creatures like you that we leave half-breed spawn in the human world."

Selena burst out laughing. "You must have missed a few."

Hearing Gwynith's stifled moan, she tried to rein in her amusement, mostly because she could feel sharp bitterness and anger under the laughter. The dream came back, swelling her temper. She stood up abruptly, needing to get away from these people before she lashed out at them.

As she stepped away from the table, a man strode into the courtyard. Combined with his black hair and gray eyes, he had a face and body that would make a woman's pulse jump under other circumstances. Now she just looked at him and wondered how many women he had seduced and how many half-breed spawns *he* had abandoned in the human world.

"Mother's mercy," Gwynith whispered.

One of the matriarch's looked over and said with a note of triumph in her voice, "Lucian! Come meet the new Lady of the Moon."

He strode over until he faced her, with barely an arm's length between them.

"What sort of witch tricks did you use to steal my sister's rightful place?" he demanded.

Her temper spiked, barely held in check now. "Be very careful, Fae Lord," she said softly.

"Careful? A wiccanfae bitch usurps the power of one of the Fae, and you're telling *me* to be careful? Do you know who I am?"

"I don't really care as long as you get out of my way—and stay out of my way."

"I am the Lord of the Sun, the Lord of Fire. I am the Light-bringer. And I lead the Fae."

"Then I fail to see why my presence is such a terrible insult," Selena snapped.

"The wiccanfae have no place among us—and they have no place in Tir Alainn."

"Then you should leave."

Lucian stared at her until her control frayed to the breaking point.

"I am Fae," Selena said, "and I am a Daughter of the House of Gaian. So that would make me one of the wiccanfae. But if I am wiccanfae, Lord of *Fire*, what did you think *you* are?"

"What?"

"Fire is a branch of the Great Mother. It isn't a Fae gift. The only way you could command fire is if you're a descendant of at least one person who was from the House of Gaian."

"You lie!" Lucian shouted. "I. Am. Fae!"

"Wiccanfae," Selena shouted back. "You *can't* be pure Fae and have the power you have. *No* Lord of Fire can have that power and be anything *but* wiccanfae. What did you think you were?" She shook her head and turned enough to look at Gwynith, feeling a pang of regret that she couldn't ease into the truth as she'd intended when she'd asked the Ladies of the Moon, the bards, and storytellers to gather. "What did you think *you* were?"

Gwynith stared at her.

Selena pointed a finger at Gwynith. "Earth." She pointed to the other Ladies of the Moon. "Water. Water. Air. Air. Earth. Water. Air." She looked at Gwynith again. "Did you think I couldn't feel what branch anchors you? That I wouldn't be able to tell?"

"You're bluffing," Lucian snarled. "You're just trying to justify taking Dianna's place."

She turned back to face him. "I don't have to justify anything, Lightbringer. Least of all to you."

He raised his hand. "You need to learn who you're dealing with."

"I'm connected to the Mother in ways you will *never* be. So don't play fire games with *me* unless you want to see Tir Alainn burn."

Lucian paled, but his eyes still flashed with temper. "You're not in your world anymore. There's nothing *you* can do in Tir Alainn."

"Really?"

She flung out one hand, giving earth the temper building inside her.

A moment later, a clap of thunder boomed overhead. The ground shook. The Clan house shook. Someone screamed.

The land ripped apart, zigzagging as if following a lightning bolt.

Selena poured more of her power into the land, holding it now, giving it strength to fight against the first lash of power she'd flung out.

The rip continued, speeding through the land, becoming narrower and narrower until it ended as a crack between Lucian's and Selena's feet.

It had happened, and ended, so quickly, the Fae hadn't had time to get up from the table, let alone run.

"That is what I can do in Tir Alainn, Lightbringer," Selena said quietly.

His arrogance was gone. Standing in front of her was a shaking, terrified man.

"You bards and storytellers," Selena said, not taking her eyes off Lucian. "You Ladies of the Moon. Listen carefully. The House of Gaian made Tir Alainn out of dreams and will. It is our power that made the shining roads to anchor this place to the world and keep it alive. What we gave we can take back. Or destroy. I have no wish to harm those who have done no harm, but I will not leave an enemy at my back when all of Sylvalan is at risk. So I will give the Fae this choice: The rest of Sylvalan is going to war against the Inquisitors and the barons they control. You will either fight with us, and earn your place in the world, or you will stay here."

Lucian brushed the sleeve of his coat with a shaking hand. "At least you're being sensible about this."

"You misunderstand, Lightbringer." Selena waited until he looked at her. "If you choose to stay in Tir Alainn, then here is where you will stay. Forever. We will close the shining roads. Oh, we won't destroy them as the Black Coats did when they slaughtered the witches. We will simply turn the shining roads into ropes. They will still anchor your Fair Land . . . but there isn't any one of you who will be able to get down that rope to the human world. You will have your Tir Alainn—and that is all you will have. Forever."

She looked back at the other Fae, sitting pale and silent, too frightened now to dare speak. "Send that message to all the Clans, and send it swiftly. You have until the full moon to decide. If you do not decide then, we will decide for you."

"D-do no harm," Lucian stammered. "That's your creed. We're the Fae, the Mother's Children. You can't harm us."

At that moment, he looked more like a terrified child desperately seeking reassurance than a grown man.

"Please, take her. Please."

Cold, cold eyes.

"My pets will tear her flesh and drink her blood. . . . And then they will devour her soul."

"Lightbringer," Selena said with terrible gentleness, "anyone who makes the mistake of trying to use our creed as a weapon against us does not understand the House of Gaian . . . or the ones who live in the Mother's Hills."

As she walked back into the Clan house to pack her saddlebags, she heard someone hurrying to catch up to her.

"Lady," Gwynith said shakily. "Huntress? Oh, Selena, please listen!"

Selena stopped and waited. "Come up to my room. We can talk while I pack."

Gwynith managed to keep silent until they'd reached Selena's room and the door was closed. Then the words spilled out.

"Selena . . . Lady . . . if some of the Clans refuse to help, you won't punish *all* of the Fae, will you? You won't close *all* of Tir Alainn away from the world, will you?"

Selena removed her saddlebags from the wardrobe, walked around Gwynith, and put them on the bed. "You said you don't live in Tir Alainn. Why would it matter?"

"I *don't* live there. Most of the Clan only goes there a few days each season to rest. But our *elders* live there. The weather is milder and the work is easier. Don't they deserve some ease in their autumn years? And . . . and anyone in the Clan who is seriously ill or injured is taken to Tir Alainn to heal. If you close off all the Clan territories, our elders will be alone."

Selena retrieved her clothes from the wardrobe, folded them carefully, and filled one saddlebag. "Do the witches ever go to Tir Alainn?"

Gwynith linked her fingers and twisted them so hard Selena expected to hear a bone snap at any second.

"Sometimes," Gwynith said cautiously. "They need to rest from the labors of the world, too. And one time, when my cousin's mother got lung fever during a bad winter, she stayed at the Clan house in Tir Alainn for a month to make sure she had recovered. The Clan matriarchs invite her to spend a turn of the moon with them in Tir Alainn every winter to help her stay strong and healthy."

And that kindness is why your piece of Tir Alainn remains strong and healthy. A witch's roots are in the real world. She would draw in the strength from the Mother's branches and breathe it out again. As Tir Alainn gives her the peace to renew body and heart, she renews Tir Alainn.

Selena walked around Gwynith again to reach the dressing table. She could have asked Gwynith to move, since the woman had chosen to stand in the one spot in the room that put her in the way no matter what Selena was trying to reach, but Gwynith was so distressed right now, even a simple request might bring on a collapse.

"You said the western Clans are willing to defend Sylvalan?" Selena asked as she began packing her toiletries in the other saddlebag.

"They were gathering at the Hunter's command when I left to come to this Old Place."

The Hunter. Did the Fae remember who the Hunter was, or were the Crones in the Mother's Hills the only ones who still knew the old stories and passed them down to be remembered?

"The Hunter is in the west?" Selena asked carefully. She went back to the dressing table for her comb and brush. She stayed there, moving her hand idly to look occupied while she watched Gwynith in the mirror.

"The Hunter is traveling east," Gwynith said.

"With Lady Ashk?"

A hesitation. Too long a hesitation.

Selena liked Gwynith, but how much she trusted her now depended on this answer.

"Lady Ashk *is* the Hunter," Gwynith said reluctantly. She glanced over, her eyes meeting Selena's in the mirror.

Selena sat on the dressing table stool and turned to face Gwynith. "The Green Lord is a *woman?*"

"The Green Lady," Gwynith said, bristling.

Quick to defend her, aren't you? Selena thought. *And proud of her—and wary of her as well. As you should be.*

"I imagine that twisted the Fae's tail in a knot when she ascended and took the old Lord's place."

"The Fae outside the west don't know," Gwynith said quickly. "If they had known, the Lords of the Woods outside the west would have refused to accept that she'd ascended and would have kept challenging her. And after she'd married Baron Padrick and was heavy with their first child, she couldn't safely accept a challenge, could she? So she stayed in the west, and . . . the Clans in the west listen to Ashk."

Selena held up a hand to stop Gwynith. "Wait. The Hunter is a woman who, somehow, hid the fact that she was a woman from the rest of the Fae because she married a gentry baron and had his child?"

"Children," Gwynith said, sounding sulky. "They have two. And it's not as strange as it sounds because Baron Padrick is also Fae."

Selena laughed. She couldn't help it. "I'm sorry," she gasped between giggles. "I'm sorry. I don't mean to offend, but . . . Mother's tits, Gwynith, even a storyteller couldn't come up with something like that and expect to be believed."

Gwynith tried to look offended, but ended up smiling. "I know."

Selena realized she no longer felt any heat beneath her skin. Good. The laughter had banked the last bit of temper. Now she could deal with the rest. "What happens to the Fae will be decided at the full moon. But I don't think the western Clans need to worry. However, it might be in everyone's best interest if the Hunter and I can meet before then."

"I'm not sure if she was headed straight to Willowsbrook," Gwynith said. "But one of the escorts may have been told her direction since she would want news about the Lady of the Moon. I could send an escort with a letter, asking her to meet you at Willowsbrook before the full moon, if that is acceptable to you."

"That is acceptable." Selena walked over to the bed, tucked

her comb and brush in the saddlebag, and secured the straps. She reached to lift the saddlebags, then let her hand drop. "Didn't the Fae in the west disapprove of the Hunter taking a gentry baron for a mate, even if he is Fae?"

Gwynith gave her an odd look. "No, we didn't disapprove. But then, we know Ashk."

The bards, storytellers, the Ladies of the Moon, and their escorts stood between Selena and the stables where Mistrunner pawed the ground. Any moment now, he would charge through the people to reach her.

"Easy," she said.

His only response was an angry snort, but he stopped pawing the ground.

The three bards took a step forward, more pale and frightened than when she'd summoned the storm.

"Huntress," one bard said, raising his hand in a plea. "You're leaving Tir Alainn?"

"I am," Selena replied.

"But . . . how will we let you know that the Clans have obeyed your command? How will we send word? And . . . when the huntsmen come down to the human world, *where are they supposed to go?*"

"And where is the Bard supposed to meet you?" another bard asked. "We've already sent word that you want to see him, but we couldn't tell him where."

Wondering how coherent a message three frightened bards could shape, Selena said, "He can find me at the Old Place closest to Willowsbrook. As for the huntsmen . . ." She thought a moment. There would be losses when the Inquisitors' army marched across Sylvalan. Villages would burn. People would die. She wasn't going to be able to prevent all of it. She wasn't going to be able to prevent the deaths of any witches in the path of that army. But if she could block the Black Coats enough, she could force them onto a battleground that could not only be defended but could defend itself. There were reasons why no one with intent to do harm dared enter the Mother's Hills. "The Fae huntsmen should gather at the northern and southern ends of the Mother's Hills, blocking the way into the midlands. Hold those roads and we can keep them out."

"Block the roads and it's easy enough to go cross-country," one of Gwynith's escorts said.

"Easy for the Fae," Selena agreed. "But the Inquisitors and the eastern barons will have a human army. They'll use the roads. It's too easy to get lost in unfamiliar land. And angry land can be quite dangerous to travel through," she added softly.

She felt the tension crackle in the air as the people in front of her realized once again that the earth magic they'd thought of as useful but harmless could be deadly.

"The western coast is already being protected," she continued, looking at Gwynith, who nodded. "The Clans nearest the midland coastline should be on guard for any ships that enter the harbors there. If the Inquisitors can't come in by land, they may try to come in by sea."

One of the other western Ladies lifted her hand. "I come from a Clan near the coast, almost at the border between the midlands and the west. Any ships trying to reach the west would have to pass between the mainland and Selkie Island. If the Lord of the Selkies was warned . . . Well, it's been said that no ship passes Selkie Island unless it pleases Lord Murtagh to allow it to pass."

"Will you send the message to him?" Selena asked.

"I will, Lady."

"Huntress," Gwynith's escort said, "if the coast is blocked as well as the north and south . . . Well, I'd try to drive an army right through the center."

"Exactly," Selena agreed.

"But . . . the Mother's Hills would be in the way."

"Yes, the Mother's Hills—and the House of Gaian—would be in the way."

They all stared at her.

"You would send the Black Coats' army against your own people?" Gwynith asked, sounding horrified.

Selena smiled. "They have to reach the Mother's Hills first."

"Roads," Gwynith's escort said.

Selena opened the branch of water, found the well near the stables, and called a thin stream of water to her. The water found its way up through the earth near her left foot. "Earth and water. Mud." Calling air and earth, she circled her right hand until a swirling wind picked up some earth and rose waist high. "Earth and air."

She wanted to laugh at the way they stared at her little dust whirl. When they were children, she and Rhyann used to make these little whirls and have races—until the day the dust whirls got away from them and collided with the laundry their mother had just hung out to dry.

She banked the connection with water so the water would remain in the well. She slowly banked the wind until the earth it had gathered once more rested with the rest of the land.

"You all have tasks to perform," she said. "And so do I."

Before Gwynith could join the other western Ladies, Selena touched her arm to indicate she wanted to speak to her and walked far enough away to keep the conversation private from the other Fae.

"Where will you go now?" Selena asked.

"Home," Gwynith replied.

"Are you needed there right now?"

Gwynith gave her a wary look. "I hope I always have something to offer my Clan."

"I wasn't questioning your value to your Clan." Selena looked away. Sometimes pride could chafe. "I'd like you to travel with me for a while."

Gwynith's eyes widened in surprise. "Travel with you? Me? Why?"

"Because you understand the Fae, you understand how to travel in Tir Alainn—and because I'm comfortable with you."

A gleam came into Gwynith's eyes. "If I go with you, would you teach me the moon dance?"

Selena smiled. "I can try. Come on, then. Let's get your saddlebags packed. I want to leave as soon as possible." She heard a loud snort. "And I'd better explain to Mistrunner that he needs to be patient a bit longer."

"If you want to stay with him, I'll run back to the Clan house and pack."

Snort. Stamp.

"That's probably wise," Selena said dryly.

Gwynith rushed toward the Clan house, then rushed back. "Huntress?"

"Selena."

Gwynith smiled. "Selena. I'm really wiccanfae?"

"Yes, you're really wiccanfae." Selena shrugged. "Perhaps in other parts of Sylvalan, the word no longer means the same thing as it does in the Mother's Hills."

"And Dianna and Lucian are wiccanfae?"

"Yes. She anchors to the branch of earth, and he obviously can draw power from the branch of fire. Having another form is what distinguishes the Fae from the rest of Sylvalan's people, regardless of what other talents that person has. Being connected to a branch of the Great Mother is the heritage of the House of Gaian. Long ago, people who had another form *and* that connection to the Mother were called wiccanfae—the wise Fae."

"By the fields, full and fallow." Gwynith shook her head. "Last summer, when the Bard was trying to find out anything he could about the wiccanfae, he guested with Lucian and Dianna's Clan. I wonder what he'll say when he finds out he was dining with the very thing he was searching for and didn't know it."

Chapter 14

waxing moon

Ashk made herself as comfortable as possible on the stone bench that ran along the terrace wall. Tomorrow, or the day after, she would have to drop the glamour of appearing male so that she could spend a few quiet hours in the women's communal room at the Clan house where they would guest.

She was glad she'd made the decision to make her first appearance as male, however. The Clans had been startled, and uneasy, about the Hunter's sudden reappearance—especially when the Hunter rode into their Clan territory with the Gatherer, the Bard, the Muse, the Sleep Sister, and fifty huntsmen from the western Clans who had come with her to be her personal guard and fighters. Despite their uneasiness, the midland Clans had been resistant to her command that the Fae go down to the human world and join forces with the witches and the humans to defend Sylvalan from the Inquisitors' army. Resistant and surly, each Clan insisting that *their* Clan was safe and they were keeping a close watch on the witches as the Lightbringer had told them to do, so there was no danger for *them*—and no reason to soil themselves with further contact with witches, let alone humans.

There wasn't time to argue, so she and her companions traveled through the Clan territories with as much speed as possible. When necessary, they stopped to rest themselves and the horses for a few hours, or left the others to rest while Ashk and a few escorts went down the shining roads to deliver the letters Padrick had written to particular barons he thought would join them in the fight.

Soon, though, she would stand in a Clan's territory and issue one command that would be sent to *all* the Fae. They would either obey that command . . . or discover how much power the Hunter truly had over them.

But there were other concerns tonight. A bard had ridden in a short while ago and had been terribly relieved to find Aiden guesting at this Clan. Perhaps now they would finally have some news about whether or not Dianna was still *the* Lady of the Moon. *Something* must be going on, because Aiden and the bard had been standing in the garden far too long, and the bard delivering the message seemed too agitated for the news to be a simple announcement.

Aiden would bring the news to them when he was ready. Since there was nothing she could do except wait, she turned her thoughts to her biggest concern—to the woman standing a few feet away from her, watching Aiden with dark, troubled eyes.

With every day they traveled, Morag became edgier, moodier, more unpredictable and volatile. *That's* why Ashk had stopped arguing with the Clans about sending fighters down to the human world. The last "discussion" had become heated, and when an arrogant Fae Lord had insisted that witches were the Fae's servants, Morag had turned on him and would have ripped out his soul if Ashk and Morphia hadn't intervened.

Morag understood death so well. That was why she revered life so much. For her to strike out with her gift . . . Mother's mercy. She could ride through a Clan or a human village and leave nothing but corpses in her wake.

"Morag?" Ashk asked quietly. She waited until Morag looked at her. "Why don't you sit down and rest? I think Aiden will be a while yet."

Morag hesitated, then sat on the stone bench near Ashk, twisting around to continue watching Aiden.

"What's wrong, Morag?" Ashk said.

"Nothing," Morag said flatly.

Ashk suppressed a spark of temper. "How can anyone help if you won't confide in anyone?"

"There's nothing to confide."

Ashk let her breath out in a huff. "Then at least accept Morphia's offer to help you get a decent night's sleep."

"*No.*"

She might have given up if she'd hadn't heard a quiver of fear beneath the sharp denial. "I thought we were friends."

"And you'd do anything for a friend?"

"Yes, I would."

Morag looked at her. Really looked at her. Then turned away

again to watch Aiden. But after several moments' silence, she said very softly, "I've had dreams. Terrible dreams."

"Will you tell me what they're about?" Uneasy about what kind of dreams could have affected Morag so much, Ashk worked to keep her voice low and soothing.

"Insatiable hunger," Morag whispered, shuddering. Then, "Shadows and light. Isn't that what all dreams are about in the end?"

Shadows and light. Death and life. Why would those be terrible for the Gatherer of Souls?

"I'll let Morphia give me a dreamless night if you'll make a promise to me," Morag said abruptly.

"What is the promise?"

"If I can't stop this . . . If I fail . . . Promise me, Hunter, that you will do what needs to be done."

Ashk stared at Morag.

Hunter. Morag wasn't asking for a promise from her friend Ashk. The Gatherer was asking the Hunter. Considering who they both were, Ashk understood quite well what might be asked of her.

She held out her hand. "I will do what needs to be done. This I promise."

Morag hesitated, then took Ashk's hand.

"Come along, now." Ashk stood up, tugged Morag's hand until Morag stood beside her.

"But . . . Aiden . . ."

"He'll tell you everything in the morning. Now you need to rest." Ashk looked over at Morphia, who was standing with Sheridan and Lyrra at the other end of the terrace. When she nodded, Morphia hurried over to meet them as Ashk and Morag walked into the Clan house.

Despite Morphia being the Lady of Dreams and Ashk's continued assurances that she would do what needed to be done, it was an hour before Morag finally sank into a deep, peaceful sleep.

I will do what needs to be done, Ashk thought as she and Morphia returned to the terrace. *Shadows and light. Morag . . . what have I promised you?*

There wasn't time to think about that because Aiden was sitting on one of the benches with Lyrra. Sheridan stood nearby.

When Lyrra saw them, she gestured impatiently. "Aiden's been waiting for you."

"If you'd wanted the news sooner, you could have joined the others in the common room to hear the bard's announcement," Aiden said testily.

Not good. The Bard and the Muse rarely snapped at each other. Ashk understood Lyrra's impatience—they'd all been waiting for some word about what had happened among the Ladies of the Moon—but she wished Lyrra would pay more attention to the distress in Aiden's eyes.

"I'm here now," Ashk said calmly, coming to stand before Aiden. "What is the news, Bard?"

"Where's Morag?" Aiden asked, looking from her to Morphia.

"Sleeping. You can tell her the news in the morning."

Aiden nodded. He took a deep breath, then let it out slowly. "Dianna lost the challenge. We have a new Lady of the Moon. A new Huntress."

Ashk watched Aiden carefully. Had she imagined his slight emphasis on the word *Huntress*? No. She hadn't imagined anything. Which meant he considered *that* part of her title to be the more critical change in power.

"Who is she?" Lyrra said. "What Clan is she from?"

Aiden didn't look at his wife. He kept his blue eyes fixed on Ashk. "Her name is Selena. She isn't from a Clan."

Since Lyrra looked ready to debate the reliability of the information, Ashk said firmly, "Let him speak, Muse."

Lyrra glared at her but kept silent.

"Her name is Selena," Aiden said again. "She *is* Fae, but she is first, and always, a Daughter of the House of Gaian." He hesitated. "She comes from the Mother's Hills."

Ashk felt the muscles in her legs go suddenly limp, and she wondered if she was going to sink to the terrace floor. She was no stranger to the Mother's Daughters, but even for her, thinking of the Mother's Hills produced a shiver up her spine.

A reflex, a reaction that had no basis in fact. There was no reason to think the witches who lived in the Mother's Hills were different from the witches who lived in the Old Places throughout Sylvalan. They all had the same roots. Their gifts all came from the four branches of the Great Mother. They all lived by the same creed.

Didn't they?

That was the crux of it, wasn't it? No one really knew much about the witches who ruled the Mother's Hills. But Padrick had met a few of them when he'd traveled through the hills after seeing Baron Liam of Willowsbrook safely home. And Aiden and Lyrra had gone through the hills to head west in search of the Hunter. None of the travelers had come to harm, and yet . . .

She had to be strong. She had to stand and be strong. Now more than ever.

"The new Huntress is a *witch*?" Lyrra asked, her voice full of disbelief. *"How?"*

"She's a Fae Lady of the Moon as well as a witch," Aiden said sharply. "The gift accepted her." He laid a hand on Lyrra's arm. "I know you're annoyed with me for not telling you before the others. Most likely, I would have felt the same way. But, please, Lyrra. Please listen."

Lyrra looked down at his hand. "You're shaking. Why are you shaking?" She studied his face closely, the Muse's annoyance with the Bard forgotten.

"The new Huntress wants to see the Bard—and I'm afraid."

Ashk felt her heart leap against her chest. "What haven't you told us yet, Aiden?" She knelt in front of him, took his other hand. "You went through the Mother's Hills. You met some of the witches there."

Aiden closed his eyes. His fingers curled tightly around Ashk's hand. "Not like her."

They all waited, no longer impatient for news.

Finally, Ashk asked softly, "What happened to Dianna?"

Aiden made a sound that might have been a bitter laugh. "Oh. Well. Dianna. She refused to accept a half-breed witch as her successor, despite it being clear that Selena was so much more powerful than Dianna could ever dream of being. Everything was fine until Dianna challenged Selena *after* Selena ascended and became *the* Lady of the Moon. It . . . provoked . . . the new Huntress into showing the Fae who now rules them." He opened his eyes and looked at Ashk. "She summoned a storm. She summoned fire. And when her horse tried to get through the wall of fire to reach her, she created a bridge out of moonlight for him."

"Mother's mercy," Ashk said, sinking back on her heels.

"Were the other Ladies of the Moon harmed?" *Gwynith*. Why hadn't she heard from Gwynith?

"I don't think so. The bards who were witnesses at the clearing sent out the news as fast as they could, and I don't think they conveyed everything they knew."

"If she wants to see you, where are you supposed to meet her?" Lyrra asked worriedly.

"I don't know. I know where the Ladies had gathered, but I don't know if the Huntress remained with the Clan connected to that Old Place."

"Can it wait a few more days?" Ashk asked. "I still have to ride to the southern part of the Mother's Hills to give Padrick's letters to the barons who live near there. I was going to go on to Willowsbrook from there, but if it makes you easier, I'll go with you to meet the new Huntress." Ashk forced herself to smile. "And I admit to being curious about her other form."

"Shadow hound," Aiden whispered. "She's a shadow hound."

Ashk's smile faded. Being one herself, she knew better than the rest of them how dangerous that form could be. "Then let's hope the Lightbringer and the Huntress don't cross paths anytime soon. We can't afford to have Lucian do something that would turn the Huntress against the Fae." She gently pulled her hand out of Aiden's and stood up. "We should retire now. I want to get an early start in the morning. I'd like to reach Willowsbrook before the full moon, which means we have a lot of traveling to do. Bard, I'll have one of my men inform the bards of your direction. It will make it easier to find you if there are other messages."

Aiden nodded, getting to his feet slowly.

Ashk led them into the Clan house and saw them all to their rooms before slipping into Morag's room to check on her. Satisfied that Morag would get a good night's rest, she went to her own room and stared out the window for a long time.

A Daughter of the House of Gaian as the Lady of the Moon. A shadow hound as the Huntress.

Great Mother, let me hear from Gwynith soon. She'll tell me more of what I need to know than all the bards put together. Because Selena will either be a very good friend for the battles ahead . . . or a very dangerous enemy.

Chapter 15

waxing moon

Jenny stood at the bow of the small ship and watched Selkie Island grow larger. Perhaps she was being foolish to come here. Cordell had told her the Lord of the Selkies and his people on the island were keeping a sharp eye on any ships sailing north to the western coast of Sylvalan. But as each day passed without word from Mihail, she became more fearful. Was he waiting at sea somewhere, hoping other ships that belonged to the family made it to open water? Had he tried to go back to Durham for any family members who were unable to find a way out of the city?

What about the ones who were going overland to Willowsbrook? Had they arrived safely? Were they still safe?

"Not as fine a harbor as we've got at Sealand," the ship's captain said as he came to stand beside her. "But it suits them here."

She heard pride, and a touch of apprehension, in his voice. Being a selkie himself, he didn't want to speak ill of the man who ruled the Fae with his particular gift, but he'd made enough comments on the journey for her to understand he was hoping Lord Murtagh's virility wouldn't sway her into remaining on Selkie Island.

At another time, she might have been amused by the verbal tug-of-war the captain was engaged in—approving of the way Murtagh ruled the selkies and dealt with the human gentry in one breath and in the next giving warning hints that many a young lady had been lured into a lover's arms by moonlight and the sea, and while a lover could stir the blood, his appeal could fade with the turning of the moon while love rooted in family was forever.

Since she doubted anything she said would reassure the man, she just smiled and turned her attention to the sea.

As they got closer to the island, she saw six small fishing boats—and she saw a man from each boat dive into the water.

When she heard the captain order the mainsail lowered, she
stared at him in surprise.

He shrugged. "Best to go easy in these waters. Take a look."
He pointed down.

Jenny caught the flash of a sleek brown head before it disappeared under the water again.

Two selkies surfaced near the bow of the ship. Four others
surfaced a little farther out.

"Merry meet!" the captain called. "I'm bringing Lady Jen-
nyfer to the island to meet with Lord Murtagh!"

The selkies bobbed their heads, then raced away. Jenny
watched two of them head for the harbor while the other four
swam back to the fishing boats.

"You can bet a bag of gold coins that there's an archer in each
of those boats," the captain said quietly. "Now that they know
why we're coming to the island, they won't fire on us."

"I thought they were out fishing." Jenny narrowed her eyes a
little to study the boats more carefully.

"Oh, they are. But the Fae have always been protective of
these waters, and these days . . . well." He pointed at the sky.
"There's plenty of *them* who aren't looking for fish."

"Sea hawks?"

The captain didn't answer, and Jenny didn't wonder why. This
wasn't a harbor for the inexperienced or unwary. But an enemy
trying to land wouldn't know which channels through the sen-
tinel stones were deep enough to give safe passage into the harbor itself and which had unseen rocks that would rip the bottom
out of a ship.

No, an enemy wouldn't know, but neither would a merchant
who was being pursued and needed a safe harbor.

She wouldn't think of that. She wouldn't.

Safe harbor. Oh, Mihail, come back to safe harbor.

They were expected. As the last sails were lowered and the
anchor dropped to bring the ship gently to the long dock, Jenny
saw the men on the stony beach. Many held crossbows. Others
held the hooks used to gaff big fish.

She waited in the bow while the lines were secured and the
gangplank lowered, studying the men. Studying the *man*. He
didn't look that different from the other men on the beach, but
there was something about Lord Murtagh that made him stand
out. An arrogance in his stance perhaps. Or just a sense of power.

She wasn't sure. She'd never met any Fae until coming to Sealand, and she'd never met one of the Fae who ruled a gift.

Perhaps this hadn't been such a good idea after all.

Breanna wouldn't falter, Jenny thought. *Breanna wouldn't back away from meeting a Fae Lord if that's what it took to get what she needed. Mother's tits. Breanna would yell at the Lightbringer himself if she got riled enough.*

Thinking about Breanna produced an ache around her heart, but she felt calmer when the ship's captain carefully escorted her down the gangplank to the dock where the Lord of the Selkies now waited for her.

After the ship's captain introduced them, Murtagh smiled at her. "What brings Sealand's water witch to Selkie Island?"

"I have a favor to ask," Jenny replied.

Murtagh looked down at her feet. "You're wearing sensible boots. Good. Let's take a walk." He held out his hand.

She hesitated for a moment before taking his hand.

He seemed amused by that, which annoyed her enough to match his stride as he led her off the dock to a set of steps carved into the cliff. The steps were wide enough for two people, and only the first few steps put a person at risk of taking a fall onto the beach. At the first landing, the steps angled away from the beach and were protected by the cliff on both sides. Another landing and another flight of steps brought them to the top of the cliff.

After leading her a little ways away from the edge, Murtagh released her hand.

Jenny looked around. A footpath followed the cliff. Another, wider path led to the stone cottages. Bright splashes of color indicated flower beds. She guessed the low stone walls she could see behind some cottages were the kitchen gardens. Not so different from Sealand, but a much, much smaller village.

"This is your Clan?" Jenny asked hesitantly.

"Some of it," Murtagh replied. Then he laughed. "There are little villages scattered all over the island. All together, they make up the Clan here at Selkie Island. Why crowd everyone into one place? And while everyone here chooses to live on the island, not everyone's heart belongs to the sea."

"Oh. I—I don't know much about the Fae yet." Did that sound lame? That sounded lame.

"You'll learn." Murtagh smiled at her. "Let's walk."

After a few minutes, warmed by the sun and the exercise, Jenny pulled off her cloak. Murtagh took it from her and slung it over his shoulder.

Since Murtagh didn't seem inclined to break the silence, Jenny asked, "You have no witches on the island?"

"We have a few. This whole island is an Old Place, so some have found their way here over the years. There's two hedge witches—sisters—who grow herbs and make medicines for the healers. There's my sister—"

"Your *sister*?"

"—who lives in a dell at the center of the island because the sea can't compete with the feel of earth beneath her hands. And there's my grandmother, who has danced with the sea since she was a young maid who was lured here by a selkie Lord. His affection was about as constant as the tide, but I've always suspected she knew that and the island was more of a lure for her than he was. Of course, she might have returned to the mainland after a while if another selkie Lord hadn't been waiting for a chance to take his rival's place."

"How convenient," Jenny muttered, understanding much better the ship captain's comments about maids being lured by moonlight and the sea.

"I think so," Murtagh replied. "A persistent lover can be a powerful force in the world, and he was everything his rival was not."

"And how long did *he* stay?"

"They were together until a few years ago, when one of Death's Servants took his spirit to the Shadowed Veil."

"Was your father as constant?" She was sorry she'd asked, because he stopped walking and just stared at the sea.

"It's hard to say," Murtagh finally said. "Even for a selkie, there are dangers in the sea. He went out one day and never came back. Now my mother was another story. She was from a southern Clan. He must have cared for her, because he stayed with her—and stayed away from the sea—until my sister was born two years after I was. The southern Fae don't allow half-breeds in their precious pieces of Tir Alainn. She didn't know my father wasn't pure Fae until my sister was born—a babe who didn't look Fae. She demanded that my father take the two of us down to the human world and abandon us. Instead he abandoned her and brought us back here. He disappeared a few months later. My grandparents raised me and my sister."

"Why did you tell me this?" Jenny asked softly.

Murtagh turned away from the sea and looked at her. "So you would know I understand about family. I'm keeping watch for your brother's ship."

"I know. Cordell said you would. But . . ."

"What favor do you want from the Lord of the Selkies?"

"I'd like to stay here for a few days." Jenny raised her hands, then let them fall to her sides. "Foolish, I know, but—"

"But once he passes this island, he'll have clear sailing back to Sealand . . . and safe harbor. The sooner you know that, the easier you'll feel."

"Yes."

"Then stay. Gran will be pleased to have company."

"Gran?"

Murtagh grinned. "You're welcome to stay with me, but I think you'd be more comfortable guesting with my grand-mother."

"Yes," Jenny murmured, feeling flustered. She didn't want to stay with him. She really didn't. But she hadn't expected him to anticipate that and provide the solution.

His expression serious now, Murtagh brushed his fingertips down one side of her face. "You're easy on the eyes, Lady Jen-nyfer, and if times were different, I would have given consider-able thought to courting you by moonlight and the songs of the sea. But I think, right now, you need a friend more than a lover. So I'm offering a friend's hand rather than a lover's kiss. Is that all right with you?"

She clasped the hand he held out to her. "Yes."

He studied her. "Is there something else?"

"I wish—" She pressed her lips together.

"You wish . . .?"

She shook her head. "It's nothing. It's foolish."

Keeping her hand in his, he started walking back to the har-bor. "Wishes may not be granted, but they're never foolish. What is it you wish?"

"I have kin who live near the Mother's Hills. Some of the family was heading there overland so that not all of us would be together in case . . . in case we couldn't get past the eastern barons. My cousin Breanna . . . I wish I could send her a letter, letting her know where I am."

"She holds a special place in your heart," Murtagh said after a small silence.

"Yes." Jenny smiled, remembering a summer when the two of them had changed a storm by celebrating it.

"Then write your letter."

Her smile faded. "I couldn't risk it. If the letter was confiscated by a baron or magistrate controlled by the Inquisitors, they would know about her, know where to find her—and my other kin as well."

Murtagh snorted. "This is an Old Place, and you're among the Fae. I'll send your letter by messenger. He'll travel through Tir Alainn. Your letter will get to your cousin safely, that I can promise you." He smiled at her as he led her toward the cottage closest to the sea. "You see? It wasn't such a foolish wish after all."

Chapter 16

waxing moon

"**B**ut I thought we were going north!" Gwynith almost wailed as she hastily closed her canteen.

"We were. Now we're not." Selena attached her own canteen to Mistrunner's saddle and mounted. While Gwynith and the two escorts who had remained with them scrambled to mount their horses, she studied the Mother's Hills rising up in the distance. A hard day's ride would take them to the foothills. By midday tomorrow, she would reach her destination.

Written on water. Whispered on the wind. How long had the Crones been sending the messages? Should she take the time to call up a wind and send back an answer? No. Best to get there as quickly as she could.

Written on water. Whispered on the wind. But not in Tir Alainn. Barren air. Barren water. Barren earth in another generation if the Fae didn't come to understand the reality of their land hidden above the world.

She shouldn't have gone back to the Fair Land after she went down to the Old Place and guested with Ella's family overnight. She shouldn't have listened to Gwynith's argument that they could travel north faster by using the bridges between the Clan territories—and also that it would be wise to let other Clans meet the new Huntress. Had Gwynith known staying in Tir Alainn would isolate her, would keep her from the information she could draw from the Mother's four branches?

She looked at the woman anxiously waiting beside her. No, Gwynith hadn't known, and her arguments for continuing to travel through Tir Alainn had been sound. Hopefully the Crones would see it the same way.

"Huntress?" There was a hint of wariness in Gwynith's voice. "If we're not going north, where *are* we going?"

Selena pointed. "There." She looked back and saw the tension in the escorts' faces. She looked at Gwynith and noticed how pale the other woman had become.

"We're— We're going into the Mother's Hills?" Gwynith asked, her voice barely above a whisper.

"That's where I have to go," Selena replied. "It's not something you have to do." She didn't understand the Fae's reaction to the Mother's Hills, but she'd quickly realized *where* she came from had frightened the Clans who had been her reluctant hosts as much as what she could do. "It's just land," she added soothingly. Which wasn't quite true. Not after so many generations of witches had lived there, loved there, danced there, taken their last breaths there.

"It's the House of Gaian," Gwynith said.

"Yes, it is. Why does that bother you? You live with witches in your own Old Place."

"Not so many. And—" Gwynith faltered. "What if they object to Fae being in their land?"

"Do no harm, and you'll come to no harm." Selena gathered Mistrunner's reins. His ears pricked. "I have to go, Gwynith. When the Grandmothers send a message, a Granddaughter does *not* ignore it."

Gwynith's eyes widened. "But you're *the* Lady of the Moon now. You're the Queen of the Witches."

Selena laughed and felt her own tension drain away. "That might impress them long enough to cool a cup of tea. After that, I'm just a Granddaughter again." She smiled at Gwynith. "You don't have to come. You can go north, or you can go home if that's what you'd rather do."

Gwynith studied the Mother's Hills, then took a deep breath and let it out slowly. "We'll go with you."

Selena wondered, and not for the first time, if Gwynith was being so helpful to help *her* or to be able to send reports to the Hunter about the new Lady of the Moon. Right now, it didn't matter. "Then let's ride."

Chapter 17

waxing moon

L iam leaned back in his chair and looked at the other five
barons, who were once more gathered around his dining
room table. He found it a strange twist of events that the Inquisitors' attempt to kill him after the barons' council earlier that summer had resulted in this delegation of midland barons arriving at
Willowsbrook to find out why he, and Padrick, had left Durham
so hastily. Because of that, the fate of Sylvalan would be decided
here. "That's it, then."

"That's it," Donovan agreed, while the other barons nodded.
"The midland barons will gather men from their counties and
march north and south to block the roads to the midlands, using
the Mother's Hills as a natural barrier. The barons nearest the
western bay will send men there to keep the Inquisitors' army
from coming in by sea. We'll assume Baron Padrick will lead the
western barons in defending the west coastline." He raked a hand
through his hair. "And if he truly does have the Fae as allies, he's
got a stronger fighting force than the rest of us put together. If
you'll write a letter to him, telling him our intentions, I'll send a
courier to Breton as soon as I return home. We can't afford to
have our plans fall into the hands of the Black Coats, so I'll feel
easier about handing the letter over to a rider once I'm back in
the midlands."

"I'll write the letter this evening," Liam said.

Donovan started tracing circles on the table with his forefin-
ger. "There's nothing we can do about harbors like Wellingsford
unless some of the southern barons side with us." He shook his
head. "There's not a lot we can do about a good many things. We
don't have enough fighting men. That's what it comes down to.
If it was just the eastern barons, I think we'd win. But if the

barons in Arktos and Wolfram send men to swell the eastern army . . . I envy Padrick's ability to ask the Fae for help."

From the comments Falco had made to him, Liam didn't think help from the Fae was something they could hope for. And if they asked for help from the House of Gaian . . . He could tell by Donovan's carefully neutral expression the other man was thinking the same thing. If they asked for help, and got it, would the price be more than they would want to pay? One storm created by one witch had made the roads impassable for days, which was why the barons were still staying with him at Willowsbrook. If one witch could do that much, what could a hundred witches do? A thousand? Could fear of a thousand witches change to hatred of a single witch? Would a village kill one witch or a family of witches to avoid having to live near that kind of power? Was that how it started in Arktos and Wolfram? Had the Inquisitors started out as protectors and defenders, only to become the next power to be feared?

He thought of Breanna and Gwenn and Fiona. Temper and laughter. Passion and compassion. And power balanced by a creed they'd been taught from the cradle.

"Liam?"

He smiled ruefully at Donovan. "Sorry. My mind wandered." He was about to suggest that they adjourn from the dining room to let the servants set the table for the midday meal when Sloane opened the door after a brief knock.

"A messenger, Baron Liam," Sloane said. "From Old Willowsbrook."

The announcement was swiftly followed by one of Donovan's guards, who had a firm grip on a flushed, excited boy.

"There's men in the woods!" the boy said. "Armed men. On horses. Clay sent me to warn you."

Liam leaped to his feet. His mother and little sister were still living at the Old Place with Breanna and her kin. And Donovan's wife, Gwenn, was there as well, visiting.

"How many men?" Donovan demanded.

"Lots!" the boy replied.

That doesn't help much, Liam thought, as he ran to the stables, shouting for the grooms to get the horses saddled. Donovan ran with him, followed by the other barons.

"Liam," one of the barons said, puffing. "We"—he gestured

to the other four barons—"aren't fighters, but our guards are good men, skilled with weapons. They'll go with you."

Before Liam could agree, Donovan said, "Two from each of you would be welcome." He turned to Liam. "You can't leave this place completely undefended."

In case those men weren't heading for the manor house in the Old Place but were coming to deal with the upstart young baron who had spoiled the eastern barons' chance to get the votes they needed for the decrees they wanted passed. And he couldn't leave four barons who now carried the weight of being leaders in the coming fight for Sylvalan's survival to the mercy of whoever might be out there.

"Agreed," he said, swinging into his gelding's saddle. He wished Oakdancer was there, then decided the stallion was better at the Old Place. The horse could carry two riders. If it came to that, he could toss Breanna and his little sister Brooke onto Oakdancer's back and tell the horse to run to the Mother's Hills—and the stallion would run until it killed him if that's what it took. "Send someone to Squire Thurston's estate. He'll rouse the villagers and the farms."

He put his heels into the gelding, sending the animal bolting out of the stableyard and up the lane that would lead to the stone bridge. A few moments later, Donovan caught up to him, the guards strung out behind them as each man finished saddling his mount and followed.

They slowed when they reached the bridge. Pointless to damage a horse going over the stones carelessly—and he remembered the other reason why it was prudent to approach slowly when he saw a small flash of movement near the bank.

"There are men in the woods," he said, raising his voice. "I beg of you, if they come this way, give what warning you can."

"Liam," Donovan said sharply. "What are you playing . . ." His words died as six water sprites rose from their hiding places.

"These are yours?" one of the water sprites asked, looking at Liam.

"Yes," he answered.

"If they throw a copper in the water each time they cross into the Old Place, they will come to no harm," the water sprite said.

"Why a copper?" Liam shifted in the saddle. They were wasting time!

The sprite smiled in a way that chilled him. "Because then we will know they are yours, and we will let them pass."

Donovan stood up in the stirrups, shoved a hand in his pocket, and came up with a few coins. "I don't have enough coppers for all of us. Will you accept a silver coin this time?"

"We will."

Donovan tossed the coin in the water, then he and Liam crossed the bridge. As their horses stepped onto the land that was the Old Place, the water sprite shouted, "We saw you kissing Gwenn. We like the way you kiss her. So does she."

Liam heard several splashes as the water sprites dove into the brook.

"Mother's tits," Donovan muttered.

At another time, Liam would have cheerfully teased Donovan about taking care when he indulged in a romantic walk with his wife. But he didn't feel like teasing as they galloped toward Breanna's house.

When they reached the arch, he turned left, galloping across the lawn, swearing under his breath. Donovan was swearing, too, with good reason. Standing in front of the men armed with whatever weapons had easily come to hand were Breanna, Gwenn, and Fiona.

He reined in hard enough to set the gelding back on its haunches and was out of the saddle and pushing through the men to reach his impossibly stubborn sister, who was standing right out in the open with her hair piled up on her head and an arrow nocked in her bow. Fiona also had a bow, and Gwenn was holding a fireplace poker. All three of them were wearing nothing above their skirts except camisoles which covered skin but didn't exactly hide anything.

After giving the woods a quick scan and detecting no movement, he allowed himself a moment to consider what Breanna wasn't wearing.

"Why are you dressed like that?" he asked at the same moment Donovan asked, "Gwenn, why are you out here holding a poker?"

"Because it's hot," Breanna snapped.

"Because I still can't hit a target with an arrow," Gwenn said testily.

We could be fighting for our lives in another minute, and I'm embroiled in a farce, Liam thought, keeping his eyes focused on the woods. He noticed the guards, after a swift, appreciative glance, were also keeping their eyes on the woods as they moved to stand in front of the women.

One of the guards glanced back at Donovan. "The ladies should go into the house. It will be safer there."

A hawk's scream distracted the women before any of them gave the man her opinion. A few moments later, Falco joined them.

"Breanna—" He stopped, stared at her, then asked, "Why are you dressed like that?"

"I will shoot the next man who asks me that," Breanna said. "Looks like we've got company."

"We do," Falco said hurriedly as the riders approached on their silent horses. "Breanna, don't get mad at me for what I say." He winced. "At least . . . don't hurt me."

The riders came out of the trees, spreading out in a double line. Twenty grim men armed with bows or crossbows. They stared at the armed men facing them. Then their faces changed, freed of the glamour that gave them a human mask.

Before Liam—or Falco—could stop her, Breanna pushed past the guards in front of her and drew back her bow. Falco pushed through to stand behind her, and Liam followed him, forcing the guards to step back.

"You're trespassing," Breanna said coldly. "I told your Lightbringer he wasn't welcome here. I'm telling you the same thing."

Nerves. Fear. That's what Liam saw in these men.

One of the Fae urged his horse forward a step. "Falco?"

"Varden," Falco replied.

"We would speak with you."

"He has nothing to say to you," Breanna snapped. Wind suddenly gusted around her.

Falco placed a hand lightly on her shoulder. "Breanna, love, it will do no harm to let Lord Varden speak."

She lowered the bow, easing back the tension on the bowstring before giving Falco a look that would make a man break out in a cold sweat.

Liam watched the Fae. Falco's familiarity with a witch didn't reassure them. If anything, it made them more nervous and fearful. But why?

"Can he fly?" Breanna asked.

"No, Varden is a wolf in his other form," Falco replied.

"Then he won't like getting tossed up to the treetops if he's mean to you, will he?"

"I wouldn't like getting tossed up to the treetops, and I *can* fly," Falco muttered.

"May we speak?" Varden asked.

"I'd like to hear what he has to say," Liam said quietly.

Varden gave him an assessing look before dismounting and taking a few steps toward them. "We've come to help."

"Why?" Liam asked. "You've never shown any concern for the people I rule or the Mother's Daughters who live here. You shunned Lord Falco because he did want to help. Why have you come now? Won't your Lightbringer be displeased?"

"Things have changed." Varden gave Breanna a nervous glance. "And it hardly matters if Lucian's displeased since he's afraid—" He stopped, hesitated, then focused on Falco. "Perhaps you've heard there's a new Lady of the Moon, a new Huntress."

Falco shook his head. "I've heard nothing about the Clans since I left Tir Alainn. So, Dianna was challenged and lost."

Varden nodded. "The new Huntress is not only a Lady of the Moon, she is a Daughter of the House of Gaian. From the Mother's Hills. She has said that if the Fae do not help the humans defend Sylvalan, she will close the shining roads in a way that will not destroy Tir Alainn but also will not allow us to come down to the human world. Forever."

Breanna's arm went limp. The bow and arrow dropped to the ground.

"Mother's mercy!" Gwenn pushed her way through the men. She and Breanna stared at each other, then turned to stare at the Fae. "So *you're* what got Selena so riled up."

Varden flinched. "Not our Clan." His eyes flicked toward them, then away. "You know the Huntress?"

"Not well," Gwenn said. "But well enough to know Selena will do what she says she'll do."

"Since you don't want to be a part of the world, why is this so important to you?" Liam asked.

Falco made a disparaging sound. "Because the game that fills the tables in Tir Alainn comes from the human world. Because we keep few animals except our horses and the shadow hounds. Some chickens for eggs, a few cows for milk. But not enough, if that's all there was. Perhaps enough to survive, but not live easily . . . or well. So it comes down to the Fae once again looking out for themselves."

"To someone else's benefit as well," Varden said angrily.

"Have you—any of you—seen what the Inquisitors do to witches?" Liam asked softly.

Varden hesitated, then shook his head.

"I have. Some nights, what I saw in those Old Places comes back in dreams that are almost more than I can stand. So I don't care why you're here, Fae Lord. I'll take the help. I'll take whatever skills your people have that will help us stop the pain and the slaughter and drive the Inquisitors out of our land. Saving our world is the only way you'll save your own."

Varden said nothing. Then, "There's a rumor that the Hunter has reappeared and is heading east . . . with the Gatherer. If that rumor is true, I tell you this, gentry Lord. I would rather face these Black Coats than the Hunter." He hesitated before adding, "With your permission—and yours, Lady—we will ride out now to become more familiar with the land."

Since Breanna still seemed stunned by the news that a witch could actually do what she'd bluffed the Lightbringer into believing a witch could do, Liam nodded his assent.

After the Fae rode off, Donovan whistled softly. "Mother be merciful, Liam. Even if we only get help from a few of the Clans, we stand a better chance than we did an hour ago."

"I know." Now that the Fae were gone, he noticed how pale Falco looked. Couldn't blame the man. He hadn't been sleeping easy after learning there were witches out there more powerful than Breanna and Gwenn, who he thought were quite powerful enough. Since Falco would have to work through his own feelings, Liam rested a hand on Breanna's shoulder. "Are you all right?"

She just blinked at him, as if she were trying to get the world back into focus. Then she blew out a breath and bent to pick up her bow and arrow. When she straightened, she looked at the woods. "The Huntress, the Hunter, and the Gatherer."

"Sounds like the title of a play the Muse would create, doesn't it?" Gwenn let out a little grunt as Donovan finally wrestled the fireplace poker out of her hand.

"Yes, it does," Breanna replied. "If they do come together, at least we won't be sitting in the front row."

Chapter 18

waxing moon

Smiling, Adolfo watched through the bars of the locked door. The largest of the three nighthunters in the cage had been trying to figure out the simple lock on the cage door for an hour now. Its incentive was close enough to make it fiercely hungry but was still out of reach. Yes, there was a feast waiting for his creatures if they could get free of the cage: the two old witches he had drained of power in order to try this experiment—and the apprentice Inquisitor he'd used to assist him. The youth had been a good choice, an open channel for power but too weak to use it himself. Useless as an Inquisitor because of it, but he'd taken the youth because it was better to control a weak vessel than to have it controlled by someone else. Besides, even the useless had their uses—and it had quieted the doubt that had plagued him since the Gatherer had left him with a dead arm to weave the Inquisitor's Gift of persuasion around the apprentice, to chain another person so completely with nothing but that Gift flowing through his voice.

He looked at the corner of the room where the apprentice lay, staring at him with terrified, pleading eyes. While his voice had rolled over the youth, the apprentice had taken the knife Adolfo handed him and cut out his own tongue—and then opened his own belly with a deep slash of the blade. Now the apprentice lay on the floor, his face smeared with blood, a little more of his guts spilling onto the floor with every effort to move.

The witches were crawling around on the floor, sensing there was danger nearby, but unable to see it, hear it, or scream out of fear of it. No feet to walk on, no hands to guide them. They always thought they were so powerful, but they were nothing more than meat.

He heard a *click*, saw the cage door swing open. For a few

heartbeats, the nighthunters stared at the opening. Then they spilled out, flinging themselves on the blood and fresh meat that flailed desperately to escape the sharp teeth and claws.

Adolfo watched for another minute or two before closing the wooden door over the bars and latching it.

It was a pity he had to leave the nighthunters locked in that cellar room to die, but they were too dangerous to take with him. No matter. Now that he'd mastered how to twist the magic in a specific way, he could create the nighthunters when and where he needed them.

He'd succeeded beyond his expectations—but not beyond his hopes. The successful transformation of this new host creature into a nighthunter gave him a far more terrifying, and deadly, predator than the animals in the woods. *This* is what he would unleash on Sylvalan as punishment for defying him, for refusing to put women in their proper place, for helping the females whose power continued to seep into the world.

He was ready. Everything was ready. Even now, the army from Arktos was marching toward the northern border of Sylvalan to join the eastern barons he'd commanded to take the roads north of the Mother's Hills, cutting off any help from the midlands. The southern barons that he controlled, along with more of the eastern barons, were doing a forced march to cut off the roads between the southern end of the Mother's Hills and the coastline. Their orders were clear, and there were enough Inquisitors going with both armies to make sure the orders were carried out. They would kill any baron who tried to stand against them. They would kill his wife, his children. They would kill the squires and magistrates, leaving the villagers and farmers with no leaders to follow. They would take whatever food and supplies they needed, then burn the fields. Starving people had little strength for defiance. They would lay waste to the enemy's lands until there were no enemies.

Ubel was already on his way with a fleet of ships packed with fighting men. A quick stop at Seahaven and Wellingsford to make sure there weren't any ships trying to hide witches among their cargo, then up the west coastline to the small harbor that was a day's hard march away from Breton.

By tomorrow night, he, the Master Inquisitor, would cross the Una River to lead the Wolfram army and the remaining eastern barons under his control straight to Willowsbrook. He wouldn't kill Baron Liam, not right away. He would take the time to soften Liam and his family. Liam's last act would be to offer himself as meat to the gifts that would be left behind to haunt his people for years to come.

The Sylvalan barons who defied him had no chance. He had the strength of Wolfram and Arktos to throw into the fight, as well as the eastern barons he controlled, while his enemies would have to splinter whatever strength they could gather in order to meet the three arms of his army as well as Ubel's attack in the west.

No, Adolfo thought as he left the cellar and went up to his room, the Sylvalan barons had no chance. And once *they* were eliminated, his armies would come together and crush the Mother's Hills, destroying the wellspring of magic forever.

Chapter 19

waxing moon

The air was fresh, invigorating, rich with scents. The water tasted sweet and cool. The ground beneath Mistrunner's hooves hummed with energy and life. She was home. Not her family's land or the village she grew up in, but as soon as she entered the Mother's Hills, she was home.

Almost giddy with the pleasure of being back, Selena looked over her shoulder to see her companion's reaction to being in the land that belonged to the House of Gaian. After a moment, she returned her attention to the trail in front of her; her pleasure dimmed.

Gwynith and the escorts were obviously uneasy about traveling through the hills. They rode with their shoulders hunched, as if they expected to be attacked at any moment.

The trail forked. Selena took the wider branch, then gestured for Gwynith to come up and ride beside her.

"Why are you so uneasy?" Selena asked. "You live in an Old Place. This can't be that much different."

"It is," Gwynith said, her voice just above a whisper as she glanced fearfully at the trees around them. "There is power in the Old Places. You can feel the difference in the land and the air the moment you cross the boundary and ride out on land that belongs to the humans. But this place . . . It's so *potent,* Selena. I feel reluctant to touch the land or drink the water for fear I might offend someone—or some*thing*—here."

Selena looked around. "I suppose it is potent," she said after some consideration. "There are so many of us who live here, so many generations who have served as the Great Mother's vessels, taking in that power and giving it back again. I felt the lack of it when I traveled into the midlands, but I never realized other people would fear what they felt here."

Gwynith gave her a pale smile. "In a way, it's not so different from standing before one of the more powerful Fae. One just gives one's manners an extra polish."

"You can still go back," Selena said gently. She studied the other woman. "Or is staying with me in order to send reports to the Hunter important enough that you'll ride your fear to the end of the road?"

"Oh, that's not the only—" Gwynith looked away, her face losing all color. "I truly did want to help you."

"I know. That's why you're still with me." She waited until Gwynith looked at her. "It must be difficult to have your loyalty divided."

"It would have been . . . if I'd had to make a choice. But you and the Hunter want the same thing, so I haven't had to make a choice after all."

They didn't talk after that, simply rode until the trail came to one of the main roads. It was tempting to turn south toward friends and family. She hadn't been gone that long, but she yearned to be a daughter again, just for a day, to regain the sense of who she was and where she came from before resuming the challenge of shaking the Fae out of their complacent way of life.

Instead, she turned north. The Crones had summoned her.

An hour later, she and her companions cantered down the lane that led to the sprawl of buildings and gardens where she and Rhyann had spent a summer in order to learn from the Crones, the Grandmothers of the House of Gaian.

One of them was waiting for her at the edge of the open courtyard, resting lightly on the cane Selena suspected was still carried so that it would be easily at hand if a difficult student needed a whack on the rump to understand a point that was being made.

"Blessings of the day to you, Grandmother," Selena said.

"Blessings of the day, Granddaughter," the Crone replied. "You've brought guests."

"I have."

The Crone studied the Fae. Then she lifted her cane and pointed to the two young men who had hurried toward them from the stableyard. "The boys will see to the horses and have your saddlebags brought up to your rooms. Come in and be welcome."

Working to hide her relief—she *hadn't* been sure the Crones would welcome the Fae here—Selena dismounted. Mistrunner snorted, sat back on his heels in a way that indicated he was going to be stubborn, and laid his ears back in warning.

"Ah, now," one of the grooms said, holding out a hand. "We've got good grain and cool water, and a soft rain came by the other day to sweeten the grass. But if you'd rather stand here wearing a saddle in the hot sun . . ."

Selena wasn't sure how much Mistrunner understood beyond *grain, water, grass,* and *hot,* but apparently those words were enough. His ears pricked, and the next snort sounded thoughtful.

"Go on, then," she said, stepping forward to hand the reins to the groom. "You deserve a bit of pampering. And I'll be with the Grandmothers, so I'll be perfectly fine." *Unless one of them decides I deserve a whack on the rump. Now that would certainly convince the Fae I'm a power to be reckoned with, wouldn't it?*

She felt a little stab of envy that the Fae's horses didn't show any obstinance about being led away. She wondered, again, why she'd ended up with a horse who thought for himself too much of the time.

As the Crone led them to a shady part of the courtyard, Selena noticed the way Gwynith and the escorts were looking around, wide-eyed.

"It looks like a Clan house," Gwynith said quietly.

"Or perhaps Clans houses look like this," the Crone said, settling herself on a cushioned bench.

No cushions for the guests, Selena noted as she sat on the hard wooden bench to the left of the Crone's bench. Never any cushions for the students. Some things hadn't changed. Gwynith sat down beside her. The escorts chose to stand. Selena wished she could do that without giving offense. The bench felt doubly hard after days in the saddle.

"So, Granddaughter, you have brought one of the wiccanfae to visit us."

"I have." Selena slanted a look at Gwynith.

"I-I am pleased to meet you," Gwynith stammered.

The Crone smiled. "No, you're not. But if you do no harm, you'll come to no harm." She looked at Selena, her woodland eyes taking measure with some invisible yardstick before she nodded, apparently satisfied. "And you, Granddaughter. You've become *the* Lady of the Moon. The Huntress and protectress."

"I have," Selena replied carefully.

Silence. Then, softly, "Was there no joy in it for you?"

Selena closed her eyes. "The dance was glorious—and there *was* joy in it."

"There was no joy in the storm you shaped and sent into the world."

"No." She swallowed hard. "That was fury . . . and hurt."

"Who hurt you?"

Was there something under the mildly spoken question? Oh, yes. In this place, she needed to choose her words with care.

She opened her eyes, letting the Crone see beyond the words. "The former Lady of the Moon took offense at being replaced by a witch. I lost my temper."

"She challenged you after you ascended," Gwynith said fiercely. "She had no right to do that. And you still gave her a chance to yield. If she hadn't pulled the knife on you, you wouldn't have hurt her."

Selena looked down and watched her hands curl into fists. "There was too much at stake and too much power in that clearing. Anger gave that power form."

"And mercy tempered that anger," the Crone said quietly. "You did what you could to ease the nature of that storm."

"If Rhyann hadn't been in the Old Place to help me, it could have harmed a great many people."

"Yes, it could have. But it didn't. There will be other storms, Selena. The path you have chosen—or that has chosen you—will not be an easy one. The Huntress does not have the luxury of doing no harm. She is justice . . . and she is vengeance. Perhaps the Fae needed to be reminded of that as well as being reminded of their place in the world."

Gwynith stiffened. "We know our place."

"Do you?" the Crone asked.

"I've given the Fae a choice," Selena said. "They can be a part of the world or they can remain apart from the world. If they choose to remain apart, I said I would close the shining roads in a way that wouldn't destroy Tir Alainn but would prevent the Fae from coming down to Sylvalan."

"You would do that?"

Selena looked at the woman who had first taught her that she was a Lady of the Moon, had helped her understand the Fae half of her heritage. "Yes, I would."

The Crone studied her. "What does the Hunter say about this?"

Selena smiled grimly. "I don't know. The Hunter is heading east to a place called Willowsbrook. I expect, when we meet there, I'll find out."

"What about you?" Gwynith asked, the words bursting out of her. "Why hasn't the House of Gaian done anything to help the witches and save the Old Places?"

"The wiccanfae did not ask for our help," the Crone replied mildly. She used her cane to trace the shapes of the courtyard's stone floor. "Do you understand who and what the House of Gaian is? Do you understand what we are in the world—and what we can do *to* the world? We are the Mother's Sons and Daughters. We are the vessels for Her joy and celebration—and we are the vessels for Her terrible justice. We are the rich fields that feed Her children, and we are the storms that can destroy those fields, leaving starvation and death in our wake. Are you sure you want us to walk in the world again?"

Gwynith shivered. The escorts shifted their feet uneasily.

"I'm sure," Selena said. "The Black Coats will never destroy the magic in the world as long as the House of Gaian stands in the Mother's Hills. Sooner or later, they will come here, and sooner or later, we will fight."

"Yes, we will," the Crone agreed.

"Then let it be sooner. Let the power of what we are sing in the world again before the Inquisitors leave villages in ruins and—" She swallowed hard against a sudden wave of sickness. "And children are slaughtered."

Silence shrouded the courtyard until the Crone said, "As you will, Huntress, so mote it be."

Selena pressed her lips together and nodded, not daring to speak yet.

The Crone leaned over and laid one hand on top of Selena's clenched ones. "You can only do what you can, Granddaughter. It is the Hunter who will make the final choice for the Fae. You understand that?"

Selena nodded again.

Gwynith frowned. "The Lightbringer and the Huntress lead the Fae. What does the Hunter have to decide?"

The Crone stood up. "The Lightbringer and the Huntress may lead the Fae, but it is the Hunter who *rules* the Fae. That was true in the beginning, and it is true now."

Gwynith shifted on the bench. "I don't understand."

"Don't you? Then the Fae have stayed away too long and forgotten too much. Come. First we will enjoy the midday meal and take a walk in the gardens. And then I will tell you a story."

Chapter 20

waxing moon

"I can't travel any more today," Dianna said, slumping in the saddle as if exhausted. She peeked through her lashes at Connor, her Clan's Lord of the Deer and her senior escort on this twice-cursed journey, and felt uneasy when his expression became grimmer, harder. It was bad enough that she'd lost her place as *the* Lady of the Moon to that half-breed bitch and was savagely injured in the bargain, but her escorts' lack of sympathy on the way back to Brightwood hurt as much as her physical pain.

Connor waved on the other three escorts, who rode a few more lengths before reining in. Then he looked her over, his grim expression never changing. "There's still plenty of day left to travel, and the bridge to the next Clan's territory is a short one. We can stop there until morning."

True enough, but going on to the next Clan meant they were a hard day's ride from Brightwood—and she didn't want to get back to Brightwood until she figured out how to get someone else to act as the anchor for the Old Place's magic. "I tell you I *can't* travel any more today. I need rest if my arm is ever going to heal."

"You traveled well enough while we were still in the midlands," Connor said suspiciously. "You had no complaints about a full day's travel then. You didn't start whining about your arm until we reached the southern Clans and were closer to home."

"I endured the pain because I felt it was important to leave the midlands," Dianna replied coldly, pride making her sit up straight in the saddle. "It would have been awkward if *she* showed up at a Clan house where I was staying. No Clan is going to accept *her* as the Lady of the Moon while I'm present."

Connor let out a short, harsh laugh. "It's time you looked at the world as it is and not how you want it to be. No Fae is going to defy the new Huntress. *No one,* Dianna, is going to want to face her wrath because of some foolish show of defiance."

"She's a half-breed witch who shouldn't have been there in the first place," Dianna snapped.

"Since she was drawn to the place where the Ladies of the Moon were gathered, I'd say she was meant to be there."

"Meant? *Meant?*" Dianna's voice rose to a shriek. "She knows *nothing* about the Fae."

"That is true, but she understands more about the world than you ever did. And I'm thinking that maybe that's why she ascended. Maybe we need someone who can remind us of our place in the world."

"We. Are. The. Fae. *That* is our place in the world!" Why couldn't he see that? How could he have forgotten that?

Connor looked at her with open dislike. "You and Lucian both did well enough as leaders when you only had to deal with the Fae, but you played with the Brightwood witch as if her life were a casual amusement, and what came of that? The Blacks Coats. That's what came of it. And the only one who tried to help her was the Lord of the Horse."

"And it killed him."

"It killed him because he was the only one in the fight."

Dianna stared at him. "You're blaming Lucian . . . and *me* . . . for that?"

Connor looked away. Stared hard at the Clan house in the distance. Finally, reluctantly, "No, I'm not blaming you and Lucian for that. We all share the blame, and the shame, of having lost the witch. If we'd made the effort to know her before last summer, maybe it would have made a difference. And I'm thinking that if we'd listened to the Bard and the Gatherer a year ago, some of the Clans that have disappeared since spring would still be with us, would still be able to do something to change things."

"You think too much," Dianna said, but a ball of sickness started forming in her belly.

"A man has plenty of time to think on long winter nights."

She shuddered. She was *not* going to spend a winter in the cottage at Brightwood. She wasn't.

Connor continued to stare at the Clan house. "But you wouldn't know about that. You wouldn't know about the struggle to build a mean little place to live that doesn't quite keep out the cold sea winds. You wouldn't know about not having quite enough to eat or making do with blankets that are fine in Tir Alainn but aren't warm enough in the human world. No, you stayed away and let Lyrra learn those things."

"I was the Lady of the Moon and had duties to *all* the Fae. It was Lyrra's selfishness—"

"Lyrra wasn't from our Clan. She didn't have to stay as long as she did. She didn't have to stay at all. And as the Muse, she had duties to all the Fae, too. If she'd left us during the winter, we wouldn't have blamed her. We didn't blame her when she *did* leave this spring. At least, none of us at Brightwood. But I've been hearing plenty on this journey, Dianna. Hearing about how you twisted the way of things—"

"I twisted nothing!"

"—to put Lyrra in the wrong for leaving, hearing how the Clans wouldn't give her or the Bard any help because the only reason she left was to keep Aiden's bed warm so he wouldn't look elsewhere for company. Selfish? Aye, there's been selfishness in all of this, but it hasn't been Aiden's or Lyrra's doing."

Dianna's heart pounded, causing her wounded arm to throb. "You wouldn't be saying *any* of this if that bitch hadn't tricked the power into believing she could be *the* Lady of the Moon!"

Connor finally looked at her. "Tricked, is it?"

"I wouldn't have lost the challenge if my strength hadn't been drained by anchoring the magic at Brightwood!" She had to believe that. *Needed* to believe that.

He shook his head, looking weary and sad. "I was your escort when you ascended to become the Lady of the Moon. Since it wasn't that many years ago, I remember it well. So I'm telling you, Dianna—you never were what she is. You don't know what she knows. Mother's tits, woman! She *danced* with the *moon*! She created a bridge out of moonlight. What she did in that clearing before . . . before things went sour . . . was something the Bard should have witnessed and set to music."

Dianna felt her lips quiver, felt the sting of tears. "You like her better than me."

"I think she's the Huntress we need in the days ahead."

Anger, hot and bitter, welled up inside her. "If that's what you think, then get *her* to find an anchor for Brightwood because I am not going back to a place that won't appreciate the sacrifice I made by using my power that way."

A long pause. Then Connor said quietly, "You weren't going back anyway, were you? That's what all the delays and complaints have been about since we reached the southern Clans. You've been trying to find someone who would yield to your pleas to help you anchor the magic while your arm healed. But if someone else agreed to help, you would have stayed in Tir Alainn to recover and never set foot in Brightwood, expecting *us* to make that person enough of a captive that she wouldn't be able to leave. That would have suited you quite well, wouldn't it have, Dianna?"

Yes, that would have suited her. Was there anyone in the Clan who *wouldn't* be trying to do the same thing if they were in her place?

"So I'll tell you this now," Connor continued quietly. "We've been talking to the squire, since he's the leader of the humans left around Ridgeley. They're mostly farmers and a few craftsmen. They've been afraid to rebuild the village. Don't really want to rebuild on the same ground. They say some of them feel the presence of too many ghosts there. But they're also afraid to buy supplies from the nearby villages to the east, especially since there're rumors that things are turning bad at Seahaven. They don't want the Black Coats looking at Ridgeley again."

It was hard to swallow, hard to breathe. "What does that have to do with the Fae?"

"We've worked out a barter. We'll act as traders to get the supplies from villages in this part of the south and sell them to the humans in exchange for supplying some of the food and grains we need, as well as helping us build sturdier cottages to live in."

"You're going to sweat and toil like humans? How will you face the other Fae?"

"I'm thinking they're going to learn a bit about sweat and toil themselves. And if the Black Coats come in force, they'll learn about bleeding and dying as well." He let out a gusty sigh. "So here's your choice. We're going on to the next Clan territory. We want to get home. You can come back with us and be the anchor we need to hold the Old Place's magic—or you can stay here in Tir Alainn."

A giddy excitement filled her. He wasn't being unreasonable after all. "I can stay?"

Connor nodded. "But if you stay, you will no longer be welcome in the Clan's piece of the Fair Land."

The excitement turned dark and brittle. "What do you mean I won't be welcome? That's my *Clan*. They won't shun *me*."

"Oh, we won't shun you. We'll throw you over the back of a horse and take you back over a bridge to another Clan's territory. We'll bear them no hard feelings if they welcome you, but we'll not have you with us. It's your choice, Dianna. What will it be?"

"I have to decide *now*?"

"Now."

"I don't believe it. *You* may think you can make ultimatums, but I'm sure the Clan elders have something to say about it!"

There was pity in the way he looked at her, as if he suddenly remembered the days when they'd all been so proud of her. "That *is* what the elders say about it."

Tears filled her eyes. Her Clan was betraying her, abandoning her. All because that bitch had stolen her place as the Lady of the Moon. They wouldn't have done this if she were still the female leader of the Fae. "But I suppose Lucian will still receive a warm welcome," she said bitterly. He'd backed down. That's what was being whispered in the Clans. Instead of insisting that Selena yield to a Lady who was *really* Fae, when the Huntress had done a bit of her thunder-rumble witch magic, he'd backed down. Her brother. Her *twin*. Even he had abandoned her.

"The Clan will still welcome Lucian," Connor said quietly. "But I'm thinking that he won't find many who will listen to the manure he spews about witches being servants and the Fae being above the concerns of the world. And I'm thinking that, now that the minstrels and bards are looking hard for Aiden, when he shows up again, we're all going to be listening a lot more carefully to what the Bard has to say." He paused. "What will it be, Dianna?"

"I can't ride any more today," she said, her voice breaking.

Connor gathered his reins. "Good luck to you, then." Giving his horse the signal to move on, he cantered off, passing the other escorts, who glanced back at her before urging their horses forward to catch up to him.

Dianna stared at them. They wouldn't leave her. Not really. Connor was just trying to make her do what *he* wanted. And who was he, anyway? The Lord of the Deer. The leader of the Clan's huntsmen. Someone nowhere near as important as a Lady of the

Moon . . . who would have no status at all if her own Clan
wouldn't acknowledge her.

She waited for them to stop, to come back for her, to cajole
her into going back to Brightwood.

She waited—and then kicked her mare into a gallop to catch
up to them. They'd stop at the Clan house for a bit of a rest and
a bite to eat. Surely they would. That would give them the chance
to tell her how important she was to the Clan. That would give
Connor a chance to apologize for the harsh things he'd said.
Surely they would stop.

She was still too far away to catch up to them when she saw
Connor lift a hand in greeting as he passed the stableyard and
continued on to the bridge that would take him and the other escorts to the next Clan territory.

She slowed the mare to a walk, letting the animal make its
own way to the stableyard. She couldn't see well enough to guide
it since her eyes kept filling with tears.

The mare stopped. A hand lightly touched hers.

"Lady Dianna?"

Sniffling, she looked at that Clan's Lord of the Horse—and
suddenly remembered that no one had ascended to become *the*
Lord of the Horse after Ahern died.

"Your escorts rode by a little while ago," he said, studying
her.

"I couldn't ride anymore today. My arm." She lifted the heavily bandaged arm—and thought she still saw doubt in his eyes. "I
told them to go on since the Brightwood Clan will be eager for
the news."

"The news has traveled fast," he said with a hint of grimness.
"I expect they already know."

What could they possibly know without hearing *her* side of it?

He held up both hands. "Here. I'll help you dismount and take
you over to the Clan house. Things are a bit . . . scrambled . . .
right now, but someone will see that you have a meal and a place
to rest."

Dianna waited until he was leading her to the Clan house before asking, "Scrambled? Why are things scrambled?"

"As I said, news travels fast. The men who have the skill and
training to defend the Old Place are preparing to do so. And the
elders are selecting gifts to bring to the witches."

Bitterness filled Dianna's throat. "So you're going to dance to the Huntress's tune, is that it?"

"Yes, that's it. We don't want to be closed off from the human world—and if the Black Coats defeat the humans in Sylvalan, there might not be any place for us in the world. So we're going down to defend the Old Place and the witches who live there."

"I'll only be staying tonight, so I won't inconvenience you for too long," Dianna said, holding on to her battered pride.

"That's fine."

It wasn't the reply she wanted, but, she discovered as she stayed in her room and felt the hours drag by, it had been the only reply she'd received from any of them.

If that's the way they wanted it, so be it. Let them scramble to please the new Huntress. Let them see what it was like to live day after day in the human world.

Let that bitch Huntress deal with the Black Coats. They deserved one another.

Chapter 21

waxing moon

*I*t hungered. It hunted.

The man had been a fine meal, but the feast was still up ahead. Running. Trying to escape, trying to hide. The woman couldn't hide the feast, but it was amusing to let her try.

It looked down at the man, at the torn flesh and the blood seeping into the forest trail. His spirit had been strong, delicious. Had whetted Its appetite for more.

The woman would eventually stop running and fight to protect. No matter. It would have the woman—flesh, blood, and spirit—and then enjoy the feast of sweet young flesh and a spirit still so new in the world.

It hungered.

With a last look at the man who had been a young Lord of the Woods, It ran up the forest trail, following the path of the witch . . . and the feast.

Pulled out of her own hazy dreams, Ashk rolled out of bed, approached the bed where Morag thrashed and moaned, and placed a hand on her friend's shoulder.

Morag screamed, dove off the bed, and came up in a crouch, her teeth bared. Her dark eyes looked wild and held no recognition of the person standing before her.

Ashk slowly raised her hands in a placating gesture, and said firmly, "Morag. It's Ashk. You were dreaming. *Morag.*"

Slowly—too slowly—understanding seeped into Morag's eyes.

Ashk stayed perfectly still. The Gatherer wasn't a woman to startle when she wasn't quite in her right mind.

A second later, Ashk's heart jumped when someone pounded

on the door, and a male voice yelled, "Hunter! Hunter! Are you all right?"

A quick glance at Morag, who was now staring at the door with deadly intent.

"We're all right!" Ashk yelled. "We're all right," she said quietly, looking at Morag, hoping the woman understood.

Her sharp hearing made out a low, intense argument on the other side of the door. Not the words, but the tone.

Stay out, she thought fiercely as the door opened enough for Morphia to start to slip into the room.

Ashk shook her head. Morphia looked at Morag, then at Ashk before withdrawing and closing the door behind her.

Ashk stepped back until her knees bumped against her bed. She sat down and studied Morag, who was slumped over the other bed.

"Bad dream?" Ashk asked quietly.

Morag nodded.

"The same dream?"

Pushing her hair away from her face, Morag shifted until she sat back on her heels. "Not quite the same. Worse in some ways."

"Is that why you wanted to share a room with me? So you wouldn't be alone at night?"

Morag nodded. "And because you . . . understand the shadows."

She didn't like these dreams Morag kept having. She didn't like knowing the Gatherer of Souls was walking a knife edge of self-control. She didn't like seeing a friend suffer night after night. Morag wouldn't talk about the dreams, and without knowing even a little of the content, even Morphia, the Sleep Sister, couldn't understand what was haunting her sister.

"Perhaps you should turn back," Ashk said gently. "Perhaps you should go back to Bretonwood."

"No," Morag said, her voice rough. "I have to go on. It's deadly, Ashk. I have to find it before it kills everyone I—" Her teeth clicked together as she bit off the words. "I have to go on."

"All right." Ashk rose. "Come on, then. Best to meet the joys of the day." When Morag just looked at her, she smiled grimly. "I spent yesterday afternoon in the women's room, so the fact that I'm female is no longer a secret from the Fae beyond the west. And there's been enough time for that news to travel, so I expect any Lord of the Woods within a few hours' ride of this Clan house will have arrived by now."

Morag frowned. "You think someone will challenge you because you're a woman?"

"A challenge can be issued anytime two people with the same gift are in the same place. It doesn't usually happen unless the power is waning in the one who rules the gift since the challenger can lose a great deal more than the challenge." Ashk shrugged. "But I expect there will be a young Lord among those gathered outside the Clan house who will be foolish enough to issue a challenge. A tool for the lesson, I suppose."

Morag rose, her eyes now filled with uneasiness and concern. "Ashk?"

Ashk shook her head. She wanted a quick bath to start the day clean. It wasn't likely it would end clean. "As you said, Morag. I understand the shadows."

The dreams haunted her. Ashk scared her.

As she followed Ashk to the grassy, open ground near the Clan house where dozens of the Fae had gathered around a handful of young men, Morag decided it was good for the Gatherer of Souls to feel wary of the power of another Fae. The Gatherer's gift could overshadow anything the Hunter commanded—after all, Death embraced everything sooner or later—but there was something about Ashk herself that made it easier to face the dreams.

She would lean on that strength, using her own to pursue a deadly enemy that hunted in her dreams.

As they reached the open ground, Aiden, Lyrra, Morphia, and Sheridan joined them. The huntsmen riding with Ashk formed a broken half circle behind them, leaving an open path directly behind where Ashk stood.

A way to escape? Morag wondered. A step to the side, and the men in the front row would block the path. As she glanced back, she caught a glimpse of arrows loosely nocked in bows among the men in the second row of the half circle. One step to the side, and the front row of men would give their comrades the opening needed to fire on the enemy.

Except the only other people here were also Fae.

She opened herself to her gift—and heard Death whisper.
Ashk?

She thought she'd spoken out loud, but she couldn't be sure. She was certain Ashk hadn't heard her, since the Hunter kept moving forward to stand alone and face the young Lords of the Woods, who were backed by their own half circle of Fae from the residing Clan.

As one of the Lords of the Woods stepped forward in challenge, Morphia gasped, "Cullan."

Morag clamped down on her temper. Cullan had been Morphia's lover last summer. Her lover, but he didn't *love* her. She would have been his excuse to leave his home Clan, who disapproved of going down to the human world more than was necessary. Not an easy Clan for a Lord of the Woods, since there were no woods in Tir Alainn.

Not that it mattered anymore. She'd been there when the shining road had closed, and she, Morphia, Cullan, and a few other Fae she'd been able to force down the road with her had escaped before the road closed completely, trapping the rest of the Fae in the mist that had rolled in to shroud that Clan's piece of Tir Alainn.

Because of Cullan, Sheridan had worked hard to convince Morphia that he wanted to be more than a mere bed-warmer.

Now she looked at Cullan's angry face. A tool for the lesson? *Mother's mercy, Ashk. What kind of lesson?*

Death whispered.

"I am the Hunter." Ashk's voice rang clearly in the morning air.

"A deceiver!" Cullan spat out the words.

Ashk smiled.

Morag shivered.

"Did I deceive the Lords of the Woods into believing I was male?" Ashk said mildly. "Yes, I did. But the time for that deception is over. Did I deceive you into believing I'm the Hunter?" She shook her head. "Oh, no, young Lord. I *am* the Hunter. The gift is mine, and I command the woods and all that lives there. Wherever the woods resides."

"Perhaps you were able to wrest the power from the old Lord of the Woods all those years ago, but you should have offered a time for challenge after that so that a man worthy of commanding the gift could ascend."

"Like you?" Ashk said softly. "There are Ladies of the Woods. They command the gift just as well as the Lords."

"But none of *them* had the audacity to pretend to be the Lord of the Woods."

"I pretend nothing. My sex doesn't matter. Whether I'm the Green Lord or the Green Lady doesn't matter. What matters is I am the Hunter."

"A title gained through deception!"

Ashk shook her head slowly. "Kernos knew who I was, and what I was, and what I *am*. That is why he trained me."

A ripple of uneasiness went through the Fae who stood behind the Lords of the Woods—and among the Lords as well. Except Cullan, who was now red-faced with anger.

Ashk asked quietly, "Do you understand who the Hunter is, young Lord? *What* the Hunter is? Do you understand what I can do?"

Cullan stared at her defiantly. "What can you do?"

"Destroy the Fae."

Silence.

"I am the Green Lord and the Hunter. I command, I rule, I harvest . . . wherever the woods resides." Ashk smiled gently. "You still don't understand." She removed the hunting horn from its place on her belt, raised it to her lips, and blew one soft, long note.

Morag felt a queer tickle in her chest.

Ashk blew another note, louder this time, more commanding.

The tickle became a fluttering. A desperate fluttering of wings, as if the raven, which was her other form, was trying to break free of her to answer the command in that one note.

Looking around to see if she was the only one who felt it, she saw Aiden with his fists pressed against his chest as if he were trying to hold something in, a look of understanding and horror on his face. Lyrra was curled up on the ground, weeping.

Morag stared at Ashk. *Wherever the woods resides.* Mother's mercy!

Morphia was hunched over, her arms crossed over her chest, panting. Sheridan supported her, looking grim.

Morag looked to her left, at the western huntsmen. Hard eyes. Grim faces. Every one of them standing tall with a weapon ready in his hands.

They know. They've always known what she is and what she can do.

"Ashk." Her voice broke on the plea, but it was enough.

Ashk lowered the horn and turned slightly to look at her.

An enraged cry. Shouts of warning.

Ashk dove for the ground as Cullan's hunting knife flew toward her. But it was paws, not hands, that touched the ground. Before the knife impaled the earth behind her, the shadow hound pivoted and raced toward her prey.

Cullan froze for a second before changing into a stag and trying to leap away from the shadow hound.

That lost second was all Ashk needed to close the distance between them.

Jaws closed on a hind leg. Fangs ripped through flesh and tendons.

Cullan staggered, still tried to run on three legs. Ashk danced around him, nipping his flanks, forcing him to keep trying to run. When he finally turned at bay, she sprang—and changed again in midair.

Her left hand caught an antler below the points and jerked his head back. Her right hand reached for her boot as she came down hard on his back, straddling him. His hind legs buckled. The hunting knife in her right hand slashed deep across his throat.

Blood pumped from the wound. His forelegs scrabbled desperately as his eyes began to glaze.

Death howled.

Still holding his head back, Ashk leaned forward, and said, "*This* is why *I* am the Hunter."

She released the antler. Cullan collapsed, blood still pouring from the wound, but not for much longer. Stepping behind him, she cleaned her knife on his still-trembling flank, sheathed it, and walked toward her men.

Morag stared at her, afraid to move. She didn't know this hard-eyed woman who walked toward her. Wasn't sure she wanted to.

Ashk picked up the hunting horn and turned to face the Clan who now stared at her with terror in their eyes.

"I am the Hunter. Each Clan will send no less than twenty fighters down to Sylvalan. They will go to the southern end of the Mother's Hills or the northern end, the midland coast, or to a place called Willowsbrook on the eastern side of the hills. The Clans closest to those places will be expected to defend those places. We are the Fae, and it is the Fae who are the protectors of the Old Places and the woods—and everything that lives within them. Either you are Fae or you are not. If you do not defend the land from an enemy who will wipe it clean of magic, then I will take back the gift that came from the spirit of the woods. That is your choice. If you do not make it soon, I will make it for you. I do not have to be here. I don't even have to be in Tir Alainn. I am the Hunter. I command the woods . . . wherever it resides."

Ashk turned toward her men. "Get ready to ride. We have some ground to cover today." Then she looked at Aiden. "Will you write a song about this, Bard?"

Seeing the flash of pain in Aiden's eyes broke the chains of fear that had kept Morag silent. "Ashk, that was cruel."

Ashk turned to look at her. "Cruelty resides in the shadows. Didn't you know that, Morag?" She looked at the ground. "But, sometimes, so does mercy." Taking a deep breath, she turned back to Aiden. "My apologies, Bard."

"Accepted, Hunter."

Just as Morag breathed a sigh of relief, a huntsman, deathly pale and trembling, approached them.

"Hunter?" he said.

What now? Morag thought wearily. The day had barely begun, and she suspected Ashk would set a grueling pace the rest of the day.

Ashk studied him. "You're one of Gwynith's escorts."

"I am, Hunter. She entrusted me to find you and deliver this." He reached into his leather, thigh-length vest, withdrew a folded piece of paper, and held it out to her.

Ashk took it, then asked, "Will you be returning to Gwynith?"

He shook his head. "She has other messages for me to deliver."

Aiden stepped forward. "If you meet up with a bard or minstrel who is coming east with messages, perhaps you could exchange them. That way each of you would have less of a journey."

The huntsman tipped his head. "I thank you for the suggestion, Bard. I would like to return to Lady Gwynith as soon as possible."

"She is well?" Ashk asked.

"She is well, Hunter." He hesitated. "She rides with the Lady of the Moon."

"I see. Safe journey, huntsman."

As the huntsman followed Ashk's men to the stables, the

Hunter walked away from all of them, then broke the seal on the letter and began to read.

With shaking hands, Aiden helped Lyrra to her feet.

"Mother's mercy, Aiden," she said, clinging to him. "Did you know any of this when you decided to find the Hunter?"

"No."

"Would you have still searched if you knew?"

"I don't know." Aiden led her to a bench near the edge of the open ground. "It wouldn't have mattered. The Black Coats attacked her Clan, her family. She would have come east to gather the Fae whether we'd found her or not."

But we wouldn't have been riding with her, probably wouldn't have been at this Clan house on this day to experience what she could do. The Inquisitors were a vicious threat to all of Sylvalan, but for the Fae personally, the Hunter was more terrifying.

Sinking down on the bench beside Lyrra, he rubbed his chest. He'd always felt embarrassed that his other form was a tiny whoo-it owl, and he seldom changed to that form to enjoy the gliding flight through woods and over fields except when he was alone—or with Lyrra, who ran beneath him, her red fox coat shining in moonlight. Knowing how easily it could be taken away from him, he didn't think he'd ever feel embarrassed about his other form again. He didn't want to lose it, didn't want to lose a vital part of what made him Fae.

Ashk would have come east anyway. And some foolish Lord of the Woods would have challenged her because she was female—and the Fae would have learned why they should fear her.

"He challenged her," Lyrra said, her voice sounding shaky. "It was within her rights to kill him."

"I know." He felt Lyrra shudder.

"Bard?"

He looked over at the young, terrified minstrel who stood a man's length away from the bench.

"I'm the Bard."

"W-what are we supposed to do?" The minstrel began to cry. *"What are we supposed to do?"*

Aiden was up and leading the youth to the bench. He hugged him, kissed his forehead to soothe as he would a frightened child. "We do as the Hunter commands."

"But we *can't*," the minstrel wailed. "If we don't obey the Huntress, she'll be angry with us."

A chill swept through Aiden. "You have a message for me about the Huntress?"

The minstrel nodded, his head resting on Aiden's shoulder.

"What is it?" Aiden asked, working to keep his voice gentle.

The minstrel sniffed, then pulled a wax-sealed paper out of the inner pocket of his traveling vest.

With a comforting squeeze, Aiden withdrew enough to break the seal and read the message.

He read it twice—and then a third time.

"Aiden?"

He closed his eyes and savored the warmth of Lyrra's hand on his arm. He didn't want to give the words power by speaking them out loud. Not yet.

He handed the paper to her. With his eyes closed, the world faded to the sound of the minstrel's quiet sniffles and Lyrra's ragged breathing.

At least they didn't have to choose, Aiden thought. Which was something the young minstrel didn't fully understand or was too frightened right now to realize. Between Ashk's demonstration and Selena's threat, the minstrel had good reason to be frightened.

"Mother's mercy," Lyrra finally said.

"You have news, Bard?"

He opened his eyes and looked at Ashk, standing before him, with Morag beside her. He licked his lips. "The Huntress has sent a message to all the Clans. They have until the full moon to send fighters down to Sylvalan to defend it against the Inquisitors' army. If they don't defend Sylvalan, she will close the shining roads in a way that won't destroy Tir Alainn but will lock the Fae out of the human world. Forever." He glanced at the paper she held in one hand. "And you, Hunter? Have you also had news?"

"The same," Ashk replied. "With two additions. Having personally witnessed the power the new Lady of the Moon wields, Gwynith believes Selena can do exactly what she says she can do."

"It's fortunate the Fae don't have to choose which of you to obey, since you're both commanding them to do the same thing," Morag murmured, echoing Aiden's thoughts.

"Yes, it is fortunate," Ashk agreed.

Aiden watched Ashk, a sick feeling in his belly. "What's the second addition?"

"The Huntress wants to meet me before the full moon. At Willowsbrook."

Breanna. Mother be merciful. He could imagine how Breanna was going to react to Fae pouring into the Old Place.

"I hope Baron Liam's brief encounter with the Fae was sufficient to educate him." Ashk smiled with grim amusement. "It would seem he's about to have a houseful of unexpected guests."

Chapter 22

waxing moon

Ubel strode down Seahaven's waterfront with two hundred of his warriors behind him. They broke off in companies led by captains to swiftly search the warehouses and the ships. Buckets, used as chamberpots, were being emptied over the side in the darkest hours of night. The stench was strong. Ship captains might be able to sneak people into the cargo holds and hide them, but they couldn't hide the *evidence* of those people.

In the end, it would be simple. Loyal merchant captains and fishermen would keep their ships—and would prosper since they would have fewer rivals for their business and could set a higher price for their goods. They would need that income to pay for the license each ship would be required to carry in order to prove that loyalty—income that would build ships, as Wolfram had done, to keep the harbors and seaports clean of unsuitable traders or visitors. Income that would finance an estate for the Inquisitors who would have to remain here to keep the barons under control and continue the search for escaped witches.

Right now, however, his goal was to flush out the witches and witch sympathizers who had fled from Durham and the southern counties of Sylvalan, flooding into Seahaven in the hope of finding any kind of seaworthy craft that would take them away from the Inquisitors' justice. Rats and witches. Both vermin. Both plague carriers in their own way. He'd find plenty of both on this waterfront. And when he was done cleansing Seahaven, only the rats would remain.

Right now, his eyes were on that merchant ship at the far end of the docks—a ship, according to the harbor master, that had slipped in and out of Seahaven several times in the past few days, taking on some cargo, but nothing like the usual amounts. And having nothing to unload to speak of. Most unusual, the harbor master had said, since the ship was one of several belonging to a well-to-do merchant family.

A merchant family that was also a filthy nest of witches and men so ensnared by the bitches that they pumped good seed into foul wombs to produce more filth. Oh, plenty of those vermin had already been eliminated, burned in their very ships or taken by the Inquisitors and the barons to be questioned and exterminated. But that nest was being rebuilt somewhere by the witches who had escaped, and he suspected the captain of that ship would be able to tell him the exact spot—after he'd softened the man sufficiently.

"Why do you accost me this way?" said a loud, panicked voice. "I've done nothing. Nothing! I'm an honest merchant just trying to catch the evening tide to take my goods to Wellingsford!"

Ubel hesitated. Stopped. Finally, with a last look at the merchant ship at the end of the docks, he motioned the guards to continue on as he turned toward the commotion behind him.

"You shouldn't have come back," Craig whispered fiercely, his tone a mixture of gratitude and anger. "You shouldn't have waited for me."

"You're family," Mihail replied. *And we've already lost too many.* He shifted a little, easing the strain of leg muscles that had been in a crouch position too long. Something was happening at one of the other docks, but he couldn't quite see around the crates he and Craig were hiding behind.

Craig was right. He shouldn't have made this last trip, shouldn't have waited one more day for one man when his cargo hold was filled with people—strangers who had offered him their last coins for standing room in the holds of his ship. But among them was a woman, with her daughter, who had lived close to Durham. So he'd stayed one more day, hoping Craig had gotten out of Durham, too, and had managed to reach Seahaven.

If he'd left yesterday evening, he'd be out in the open sea right now, and *Sweet Selkie's* sails would be full of a Mother-blessed wind that would take him back to Sealand, back to Jenny and the boys, back to safe harbor.

If he'd left yesterday . . . before the Inquisitors' ships had sailed into the harbor and the harbor master had sent bellringers to make the announcement that no ship was permitted to leave

Seahaven until it had been inspected by the Inquisitors and duly licensed as a ship loyal to the barons.

Barons. Bah. Inquisitor puppets. Puppets or not, it wasn't going to be easy to get *Sweet Selkie* out of the harbor, and he couldn't afford to let her be boarded. Not with the living cargo he was carrying.

"You shouldn't have stayed," Craig said again. "She's the last ship, Mihail. *The last one.*"

"I know it." He just couldn't think about it. His brothers gone. His father gone. Had his wife and daughter gotten to Willows-brook safely, or were they gone, too? How long would it be before he knew? Would he ever know?

Couldn't think of it. Couldn't think that way. He needed to think of the sea, of the strong tide drawing *Sweet Selkie* away from the dock, giving her room to run, to flee fast enough to get past the Inquisitors' ships and out to the open sea. He could out-run them in the open. Had to outrun them.

First, he and Craig had to get to the ship.

"You—"

"You stayed," Mihail snapped.

Craig said nothing. What could he say? He'd stayed in Durham, pretending he didn't see the danger coming closer and closer as he sold off what he could, drained the assets to get as much gold and silver to family members as he could, quietly burned the business records that would have told the enemy where to look for other branches of the family. In the end, he'd escaped by setting the warehouse on fire just ahead of the guards breaking down the door to bring him in for questioning.

That commotion at the other end of the docks sounded like it was heating up. Mihail straightened up enough to peer over the top of the crates. Warriors forming a circle around someone. A buzz of angry voices—a low sound slowing gaining in volume as more sailors and dock workers moved closer to whatever was happening.

Mihail crouched again, shifting the heavy leather satchel slung over one shoulder—a twin to the one on Craig's shoulder. How had the man managed to walk to Seahaven carrying both satchels? "I never realized ledgers were so heavy," he muttered.

For a moment, a smile eased Craig's grim expression. "There's only one ledger in that bag. One that's any use to the family anyway. The other three are hollowed out and filled with the last of the gold and silver I had in the family coffers at the warehouse. That's why it's so heavy."

Mihail rested his forehead against the crates. "Mother's tits. Did you think to bring a clean shirt and another pair of socks?"

"They're in this bag. Isn't my fault you grabbed the heavier one."

Mihail just shook his head, then turned a little to study the dock where *Sweet Selkie* was moored. The docking ropes were untied. Two of his men stood at the bow, playing out rope that had been slipped through a dock ring, letting the ship ease back with the tide. His orders to his first mate had been clear. They sailed with the tide, with or without him. The gangplank had been withdrawn. Now only a board wide enough for a nimble man's feet was being balanced by another member of his crew so that it wouldn't scrape on the dock and draw someone's attention.

He noticed the way the men kept glancing around, searching for some sign of him while trying not to look like they were searching for someone. And he noticed the sea hawk perched on the end of the dock, watching his ship.

Another one glided low over the water and looked at the stern, as if trying to read the ship's name under the mud he'd smeared over it to hide it.

But hawks couldn't read.

Unless they weren't hawks.

A shiver went through him. Hope. Fear. He wasn't sure.

"The tide's going out," he said. "We have to go now while we can."

"The guards will spot us."

"No choice. Come on."

They stood up in time to see a merchant captain break free of the circle of warriors and run for his ship.

"I'm an honest merchant!"

Ubel stared at the sweating, shaking man. "If that is true, you'll have no objection to my warriors searching your ship to confirm that."

"I-I carry nothing that would interest the Inquisitors."

"That is for me to decide. Search the ship." Ubel nodded to two archers as several warriors turned toward the ship's gangplank. From a special pouch, the archers carefully withdrew a thick shaft of wood with the glass ball secured to the end. They fitted the shafts into their bowstrings and looked at him, waiting for the signal.

"No!" The merchant captain broke through the warriors and ran for his ship, his crew shouting now, panicked as other archers nocked arrows in their bows and took aim.

Ubel waited until the captain had reached the gangplank, gave the man that moment to think he'd escaped. "Now."

Arrows flew, finding their mark in the captain's back. He teetered on the gangplank, his hands reaching for the hands his crew held out to him. More arrows flew, and the men who had tried to help were felled. The captain tumbled off the gangplank and into the water.

"Now," Ubel said again.

The archers with the glass-balled arrows took aim. As the glass balls hit the mast and deck, they exploded, spraying a liquid that burst into flames, burning men, burning wood.

"The ship's on fire!" someone screamed.

Two more glass-balled arrows flew, and more liquid fire washed across the deck, caught the sails.

People rushed on deck now—women, children, old men, young men. Some jumped into the water. Men, mostly. The women were too burdened with long skirts and arms full of children. They knew they had no chance in the water, so they ran down the gangplank to the dock, as terrified and mindless as rats, uncomprehending that there was nowhere to go, no way to escape.

And his archers exterminated them as efficiently as they would any other vermin.

A howl of rage suddenly filled the waterfront. Ubel spun around as sailors, armed with boot knives or clubs, and dock workers, with sharp hooks, threw themselves at the warriors, turning an extermination into an ugly fight.

Suddenly surrounded by screaming, fighting men, Ubel pushed his way to a clear space on the dock, falling to his hands and knees as he tripped over a dying woman crawling away from the other bodies.

He'd miscalculated. He should have used the Inquisitor's Gift of persuasion to quiet that merchant captain, should have handled the extermination more carefully. He should have realized that the sailors had helped sneak people onto the ships, that the dock workers had looked the other way when supplies in the warehouses had gone missing. Should have realized that some of them might have family or friends hidden on the ship.

As he got to his feet, he noticed two men walking swiftly toward the last dock. The ship he knew belonged to a witch-loving merchant family was already quietly slipping back with the tide.

"Stop those men!"

The warriors who had gone ahead of him and had turned back to join their comrades couldn't have heard him. But they must have seen his urgent hand gestures and, looking in the direction he was pointing, spotted the easier prey.

"Fire the ships!"

The Wolfram captains riding anchor in the harbor couldn't hear him either. No matter. They already had their orders. They knew what to do. Even if that witch-loving bastard captain managed to reach his ship, he wasn't going to escape.

The tone of the fight behind him changed. The sailors were no longer fighting the warriors, exactly. Now they were fighting to reach the ships, the smaller fishing boats, anything that would get them away from the docks.

As if they actually believed they could get out of the harbor.

"You there!" someone shouted.

Glancing back, Mihail saw the warriors moving toward them. "Run," he said, grabbing Craig's arm.

No need to say it twice, not when the two sea hawks perched on the dock near his ship suddenly screamed and took flight.

They ran for the end of the dock. The sailor dropped the wooden plank. It scraped along the dock as *Sweet Selkie* began following the tide to open water.

Just one chance. Two other men stood by on board, ready to throw ropes that would keep him and Craig from tumbling into the sea.

"Go!" Mihail said, pushing Craig toward the plank as his men threw the ropes. Craig grabbed one and hurried up the bucking, bowing plank as fast as he could.

As soon as his men grabbed Craig's arms to pull him on board, Mihail rushed up the plank. He was knocked aside by Craig before both feet touched the deck.

Glass shattered. Craig screamed. Mihail felt a sudden burning along his left shoulder and down his back.

More screams.

Mihail twisted—and stared.

The right side of Craig's face was on fire. Fire burned down his neck, down his arm. The satchel he was still holding burned.

Someone beat Mihail's left shoulder and back, and he cried out in pain.

"You're on fire!" a crewman shouted.

Fire. "Water!" he shouted, putting his heart into the command, the plea.

Two barrels of fresh water burst open as he grabbed Craig, still staggering and screaming, and pulled him down on the deck. The water arched as if following a bridge of air and came down in a waterfall on both of them.

Gasping for air, he blinked water from his eyes—and saw the archers with odd-looking arrows take aim at his ship.

Fire. Not just flaming arrows, but something else. Something filled with fire.

"Get us away from this dock!"

He tried to get to his feet, but a woman, bent low to make herself a smaller target, bumped into him, sending him to his hands and knees.

Get to the wheel. He had to get to the wheel. But they couldn't raise sails while those archers could shoot those arrows and set the canvas ablaze.

The arrows struck the deck. Glass shattered. Liquid sprayed—and turned into fire.

Before he could shout, the flames vanished. Wood smoldered.

Someone touched his shoulder, making him gasp. He looked at the woman kneeling on the deck in front of him.

"I have no place to ground it," she said with effort. "I have to ground it or let the fire go."

"Can . . . you send it elsewhere?"

She was breathing hard, fighting to hold something she could barely contain. "Not far."

"The dock. Give it to the wood in the dock."

He forced himself up on his knees, aware of female voices quietly murmuring, calling water, calling air. Aware that *Sweet Selkie* was away from the dock, swinging round to face the entrance to the harbor . . . and the Inquisitor ships were raising anchors and sails to close off the harbor and block her escape.

The dock burst into flame. Glass-balled arrows shattered, spraying the archers with their own liquid fire.

"Raise the sails!" Mihail shouted.

Women's voices murmuring.

He watched wind fill the sails, felt the power of it as *Sweet Selkie* leaped forward, racing toward the enemy ships and the freedom that lay beyond them.

Denying the pain in his back and shoulder, he got to his feet and looked back at Craig. The woman who had bumped into him knelt beside his cousin.

"Do what you can for him," he said.

She nodded, and he made his way to the wheel, telling himself he had to be content with doing just that. His duty was to get them all to the open sea.

Behind him, the dock burned—and men burned. Behind him, a handful of smaller ships and fishing boats were following in *Sweet Selkie*'s wake, having made good use of the fights and distractions to make their own escape. And no doubt following in his wake because there was wind in his ship's sails—and the enemy ships had none.

But they had men and oars, and two of those ships were moving to cut him off from the mouth of the harbor. They didn't need to reach him, just get close enough to fire on his ship. And if those ships carried more of that liquid fire . . .

Ignoring pain and fear, pushing desperation aside, he guided *Sweet Selkie*, using every bit of his skill, every breath of his connection with the sea to guide her—already knowing they wouldn't get out of the harbor.

Take care of the boys, Jenny. And don't grieve too long. Remember us by building a life full of love and laughter. Just remember us.

"Captain?"

Mihail glanced over, then gave his attention back to the sails and the sea. The young man had begged for passage to anywhere. His family was gone. Lost. He'd had a couple of pieces of jewelry in his pocket, little more than trinkets really, that he'd offered in exchange for passage. Mihail had declined the jewelry and found him a place in the cargo hold.

"Whatever's on your mind, be quick about it," Mihail said.

The young man hesitated, then said in a rush, "If I set fire to those two ships, you'll be able to get past them?"

Mihail glanced over. Then his head snapped around for a longer look.

The same young man he'd brought aboard—but not the same now that the glamour had been dropped, revealing the face behind the human mask.

"You're Fae."

"Yes. A Lord of Fire. The . . . witch could quiet the fire. I can't do that. But I can call it—and send it."

Mihail focused on the two ships slowly moving to close the gap. If he tried to swing around them on either side, the other ships could attack him. That gap was their only chance now.

"You didn't mention this before. Why? Afraid I'd throw you overboard if I found out?"

"Yes."

That answer sliced his heart. "You don't know much about us, do you?"

"No."

What would the Fae Lord learn about them now?

"Captain?"

Do no harm. If he gave the order . . . Burning ships. Burning men. Most would jump into the harbor to escape the fire. Could they swim? Could they manage to stay afloat long enough for their comrades in the other ships to rescue them? How many of them had wives, children, families? If he gave the order, would he be any different than the Inquisitor who had killed that other captain and set fire to the man's ship? Would he?

Do no harm. Not just his ship and the people on board her at stake. Those other ships following in his wake . . . They wouldn't survive, either.

Great Mother, forgive me. "Fire the ships."

The Fae Lord turned to face the ships, staggering a little to keep his balance as *Sweet Selkie* ran with the wind.

Fire bloomed in the two ships' lufting sails. It burst from the wood in the bows. Oars caught the moment they were lifted from the water.

They burned so fast.

Close enough to hear shouts. Screams. Close enough to see men leaping from the ships, slapping the water in an awkward attempt to swim toward him.

He sailed between the burning ships, offering no lifeline, no rope, no help.

A burning mast cracked, fell. More screams.

Come on, darling. Come on. Get us past before those ships sink.

Sweet Selkie lifted as even more wind filled her sails, felt almost as if she were skimming the water.

The harbor mouth. The open sea.

He dared to look back. The smaller ships that followed him had made it, too, safely beyond the pull of the sea as the two Inquisitor ships sank to the bottom of the harbor.

Safe. Safe, for now, in the open sea.

The ship suddenly bucked. He clenched the wheel, but it burned. Something burned. He couldn't seem to find the wind. He had to find the wind.

The last thing he saw was his first mate and two crewmen running across the deck toward him as his legs buckled. The last thing he heard was his first mate saying he'd take the wheel, it would be all right.

The last thing he remembered was someone grabbing his left shoulder as his mind spun down into the deep cradle of the sea.

Ubel stood in the bow of his ship and pounded his fist on his thigh as his captain hastily prepared to sail after their fleeing prey.

That filthy, witch-loving bastard had cost him good men and two fine ships! Master Adolfo would accept the loss as part of the cost of cleansing this filthy land—but *not* if that bastard captain managed to escape.

No matter. He, Ubel, had the best ships—Wolfram ships. He had the best warriors. And if warriors weren't enough, he had his fellow Inquisitors. *No one* could defeat men trained by the Witch's Hammer. *No one.*

That bastard captain thought he was getting away, but he was just leading the Inquisitors to the new lair. And when Ubel found him . . .

He wouldn't kill the bastard. Not right away. He'd punish him first for the trouble he'd caused, punish him for the deaths of Wolfram warriors—and the two Inquisitors who were on those ships when they burned. And after the bastard had received the initial punishment, he would take whatever bitch was dearest to the bastard's heart and sharpen his knives against her bones.

And she would still be alive while he did it.

Chapter 23

waxing moon

Since Keely was assigning garden chores to a handful of children and didn't need her help, Breanna walked between the rows of crops until she reached the wooden water bucket resting on the kitchen garden's stone wall. The water, after sitting in the sun all morning, was too warm to drink. She didn't have to take a sip to know that. She could feel the heat in it.

Resting her hand against the bucket, she quietly drew the heat of fire out of the water, through the wood, and, finally, into the stones. When she was done, she picked up the dipper resting in the bucket and drank. Cool. Delicious. She drank another dipperful, refilled it, then handed it to Keely when the other woman joined her.

"The Mother has been bountiful," Keely said, sipping the water while studying the garden with a sharp eye.

These moments were the only ones when Keely sounded like the adult woman she was, the only moments when the emotional scars that had frozen her forever in a mental childhood receded. The only moments Breanna glimpsed the woman her mother might have been if the old baron, Liam's father, hadn't raped Keely when she was still a girl on the cusp of womanhood. Those moments hurt, but Breanna held on to them fiercely, determined to remember them when Keely acted more like her little sister than her mother.

"The harvest will be good," Breanna agreed. But would there be enough? Oh, there would be plenty for the table during the harvest season. The plants were producing more than they'd ever done, and already there were vegetables to be picked for cooking. But would there be enough to feed all of them and still preserve what would be needed to see them through the winter? There had to be enough.

But for how many? If the fighting came to Willowsbrook and other families lost kitchen gardens or farmers lost entire crops, would there be enough to share so that *everyone* got through the winter?

Everyone who survived. The thought made Breanna shiver, so she pushed it aside. Not so easy to push aside the feeling that had been growing throughout the morning.

There was a storm coming. Something dark and violent.

She looked to the west, studying the blue summer sky and the puffy clouds that leisurely floated through it. She looked to the east and saw the same.

But *something* had shivered on the wind that morning, waking her suddenly out of a sound sleep when the air from her open window brushed against her skin. She'd realized then how foolish it had been not to fasten the shutters and make do with the air through the slats. There were still some nighthunters out in the woods, somewhere. They hadn't seen any recently, but there had been signs of them. Dead trees. Half-eaten animals. The Fae who had taken on the task of riding the boundaries of the Old Place rode in pairs—and rode cautiously.

She still wasn't sure she liked the Fae being around so much, still wasn't sure she liked the Fae—with a few exceptions.

Remembering Fiona's offer to find another place to sleep if she wanted her bedroom to herself so that she could have some private time with Falco made her face hot. She refused to think about that. She was hot enough as it was, and thinking about his kisses and the way his hands caressed her through her clothes whenever they found a few minutes to be alone wasn't going to make her feel cooler.

It would have been easier if they could have taken a moonlit ride, found a clearing that pleased them, and explored in private the intimacy of becoming lovers. But it wasn't safe to go into the woods after dark. Not with nighthunters around.

Maybe she should take Fiona up on that offer after all.

"I don't like Jean," Keely said suddenly, sounding like a girl again. "She's sneaky."

Breanna sighed. Jean had become a thorn in all their sides. "What's she done now?"

"She *knows* children aren't supposed to be in the pantry."

"She's not a child, Keely."

Keely ignored that. "She *knows* we're supposed to ask if we want something to eat." She dropped the dipper back into the bucket, then curled her arms around her body as if giving herself a comforting hug. "When Brooke and I saw her and *told* her she wasn't supposed to be there, she—" Keely bit her lip.

"She what?" Breanna's stomach tightened.

"She said she'd make us sorry if we told anyone she'd been in the pantry. She said it was her own business and none of ours. But she's sneaky, and she's mean, and I don't like her. Why can't she stay with Liam? He's got a big house."

That's precisely what Jean would like to do. Stay in Liam's house. Be waited on by Liam's servants. Have Liam in her bed until he felt obliged to do the honorable thing and offer her marriage so that she'd always live in a big house with servants to wait on her. There was no point telling Jean that gentry men didn't feel obliged to wed a woman they'd bedded, especially if the woman wasn't from a gentry family. There was no point telling Jean that Liam was more touchy about making a child out of wedlock than any man she knew, so he'd think hard about being a lover to any woman he wouldn't be willing to marry, and trying to force him with some kind of love charm would kindle hatred rather than love. And there was no point telling Jean that, while the Fae Lords looked at Fiona with cautious interest, she'd seen something ugly slip into their eyes whenever Jean appeared.

When she'd pointed out to Falco that the Fae's habit of using persuasion magic to seduce a human woman wasn't really any different than Jean making her love charms, he'd surprised her by not defending the Fae or insisting there was a difference. Instead, he'd pointed out the Clan was too nervous about giving offense to any of the Mother's Daughters to be able to shrug off getting caught by a love charm's magic. And he'd added brutally that *no* man would want to endure Jean any longer than it took to have her.

"She can't stay with Liam," Breanna said. "Besides, he's letting Lord Varden's men use his home as a resting place since we've no room for them here." And having Jean among those men would be begging for trouble—especially when Liam and Falco were cautiously introducing some of the Fae Lords to the human gentry in Willowsbrook so that both sides would recognize the other as an ally. And Varden and Donovan, with Gwenn's help, were working out a way to send messages from one side of the Mother's Hills to the other by using the bridges in

Tir Alainn to shorten the time required to travel from one place to another and Gwenn's connection to kin in the Mother's Hills to give messengers a route through the hills instead of having to go around them.

Breanna sighed. She was glad to have their help and their company, but Gwenn and Donovan should have left with the other midland barons who had come to Willowsbrook. A war was coming, and their own people needed them. But Gwenn had insisted that she needed to stay, that there was something she needed to do here before she could go home. She couldn't explain it, wasn't even sure what it was—but she was certain it had something to do with Selena.

A common enemy hadn't brought human and Fae together to make a determined effort to work together. A witch, powerful enough to shake the Fae's world and threaten their way of life, had frightened them into coming down from Tir Alainn and making their presence felt in the world. Because of Selena, the world would never be the same—for humans or the Fae.

"Of course, we went and told Elinore and Mother right away," Keely said, pulling Breanna back to the conversation she didn't want to have. "That's why Jean had to help Glynis with the washing."

And that explained the new lock that Clay had put on the pantry door.

"Gran didn't mention it," Breanna murmured, trying not to feel hurt at being excluded by her grandmother from something that affected her home.

"Elinore said they should tell you, but Mother said she'd tell you later," Keely said. "She said she and Elinore could deal with the household—both households, since they have to take care of things for Liam, too—but you were shouldering the burdens of dealing with the world beyond the Old Place and didn't need the burdens of the household added to it."

"What burdens do I have?"

Keely chewed on her lower lip. "The Fae," she said thoughtfully. "Every time Liam makes a suggestion to them, they want to know if you approve of it. They're afraid of you, so they won't do anything if they think it will make you angry with them."

Breanna's mouth fell open. "Why would they be afraid of me?"

Keely gave her a look that was both childlike and wise. "You were going to shoot them."

Suddenly feeling uncomfortable, she shrugged. "Yes. Well."

"And you made that Lightbringer man go away, and he's very powerful. So they don't want you mad at them."

She wasn't sure she liked being feared. After all, she'd only done and said those things to protect her home and family. And while the information was certainly useful, she was going to have to talk to Nuala about Keely's sudden habit of listening to conversations Breanna doubted she was meant to hear.

"Is Mother sick?" Keely asked abruptly.

Tension slammed into Breanna, tightening muscles until she had to work to breathe. "Why do you think that?"

"She gets tired so much. She never used to get tired until nighttime."

The tension turned cold, shivered through muscles. She'd noticed the same thing, and Liam's reassurance that Nuala's fatigue was a reasonable reaction to the strain had dulled the worry but hadn't relieved it. Her grandmother had been her emotional anchor, had provided the practical wisdom that had taught her how to be a witch and a woman. *Was* Nuala ill and hiding it? Or was it simply a need for more rest to deal with the turmoil? Had Elinore noticed anything?

Gran would deny whatever she didn't want to reveal, but Elinore . . . Surely Elinore would tell her if there was anything to tell. And Gran was more likely to confide in Elinore, who was only a generation younger and a mother herself. Yes, she needed to talk with Elinore at the first opportunity. And she'd keep a sharper eye on Jean. Fiona would help her with that.

"I'm sure there's nothing wrong with Gran that a good rest won't cure," Breanna told Keely with an assurance she didn't feel.

Keely nodded. "I'd better check on my helpers." She narrowed her eyes and stared past Breanna's shoulder. "Liam's coming."

Turning, Breanna watched Liam, Donovan, Gwenn, and Varden striding toward the kitchen garden. Not wanting to waste time walking to one of the gates, she swung herself over the garden wall and hurried to meet them.

Gwenn looked pale. The three men looked grim.

"What is it?" she asked as soon as they met.

"It's begun," Donovan said. "Thanks to Varden's assistance, we're hearing about it sooner than we would have otherwise."

"What?" Breanna demanded, her heart now thumping against her chest.

Liam took her hand. "The barons of Arktos have crossed the border with an army. They've joined up with some of Sylvalan's eastern barons." His fingers tightened around hers. "They're fighting in the north."

Breanna tightened her own hold on his hand, finding comfort in his strength.

Do no harm.

The creed had shaped her life. Now it felt like a cherished luxury she had to wrap up and put away. The pang of regret was sharp enough to cut, and she hoped with all her heart that before too many seasons passed, she would be able to wrap herself in that creed again.

"Come along then," she said. "We'd better tell the others and make sure we're as prepared as we can be for whatever the Inquisitors are aiming at us."

As she released Liam's hand and walked toward the house, she suddenly realized Liam and Varden were following her, intent on listening carefully to what she was sensing, feeling, seeing in the world around her.

She watched Falco glide toward the house, land, and change into his human form.

Witches were the bridge between Fae and human. They'd always been the bridge, even if none of them had realized it. But *she* was the link here because her brother was a baron and the man who would soon be her lover was Fae—and because the Small Folk and the other witches in this Old Place would obey her commands.

Nuala had been right. She carried a burden that went beyond her home and the Old Place in her family's care. And now, as she reached the kitchen doorway, she felt the entire weight of that burden.

Chapter 24

waxing moon

Selena shifted restlessly, tangling the covers as the dream tangled her mind.

The ground trembled. Not a disturbance that rose up from the land, but a force upon it. Rhythmic. Steady. Something that would be familiar if it weren't so strong.

Rhythmic. Steady.

One-two. One-two.

She recognized it now. Thousands of feet marching, striking the ground at the same time, making it tremble.

Turning around, she saw the small waterfall and pool that was in one of the gardens at the school where the Grandmothers taught young witches. Now a small willow tree grew beside it. As she watched the play of sunlight and shadow on the leaves, she noticed a pink tinge to the water falling over stone. A pink tinge that deepened into bright red. The water thickened, splashing the willow's leaves. Staining them red. Clots plopped on stone, slithered to the edge and clung there before falling into the pool that looked so dark it was almost black, hiding the things she sensed floating just beneath the surface.

And the ground trembled.

Stumbling out of bed, Selena half fell across the other narrow bed in the room, and gave Gwynith a hard shake.

"Wha'?" Gwynith mumbled.

"Get up," Selena said. She held a finger near the bedside candle. Fire leaped to the wick. Satisfied, she pulled off her nightgown, rolled it into a ball, then stuffed it into her saddlebags. Cursing softly, she pulled it out again to reach the clean underclothes.

After pulling on her underclothes, she paused long enough to give Gwynith another hard shake. "Get up. *Now*."

Gwynith raised her head off the pillow. "Still dark," she complained.

"Fine. Then I'll ride out without you. You can catch up when you can."

That roused Gwynith enough to prop herself on one elbow. "What's wrong?"

"I had a dream." Out loud, it sounded foolish, but being thought foolish wasn't going to stop her from packing, rousing the inn's landlord to provide whatever food could be hastily assembled, and riding out *now*.

"What kind of dream?"

Selena paused, then finished pulling her tunic over her head. "A bloody one."

Gwynith shot out of bed. "I'll tell the men we're leaving." She was out the door and pounding on the door across the hall before Selena had time to reply.

A murmured conversation. The other door closing with more haste than courtesy, loud enough to wake the rest of the inn's guests.

As Gwynith rushed back into their room to start her own frenzy of dressing and packing, Selena continued stuffing her belongings into the saddlebags.

Another day of hard riding to reach the village where Skelly, the storyteller, lived. How long to reach Willowsbrook after that? Skelly would know. Wasn't he kin to the Willowsbrook witches? Surely he'd know the fastest way from his village to that Old Place.

So. Two days at the least. She couldn't do it in less time. Fae horses had endurance far beyond ordinary horses, but even Mistrunner was wearing down after so many days of hard riding. Reaching Skelly's village was as much as she could do today.

She closed her eyes and thought of the willow tree in her dream, stained with blood.

Two days.

Would she get to Willowsbrook in time—or get there too late?

Chapter 25

waxing moon

Aiden hurried toward the Clan house, anxious to locate the Clan's bard or minstrel and find out if there was any news or messages. Once the Fae here realized the Hunter had arrived in their piece of Tir Alainn, it would take hours to get a coherent sentence out of anyone who could provide information. The Clan house would be in an uproar while people scrambled to figure out how to feed and provide beds for Ashk, her companions, and the hundred men who now rode with her.

Ashk's ultimatum to the Fae had raced ahead of her, and the Clans had offered a wary welcome when she arrived in their territory to rest for a few hours before moving on again. Among the Clans who had already been staggered by the *Huntress's* ultimatum, the Hunter was considered the lesser threat. At least Ashk was one of them, even if she did come from a western Clan. The new Lady of the Moon, a witch from the Mother's Hills, was so far outside their experience they didn't know what to do—except fear her and, out of fear, obey.

So the ranks of Ashk's fighting men had swelled as the Clans, anxious to prove their sincere intentions of helping drive the Black Coats out of Sylvalan, simply sent the required number of men with her. After all, the Huntress couldn't fault the Clans if the men were in the Hunter's company and obeying *her* orders.

Privately, Aiden suspected the Fae were hoping a conflict between the Hunter and the Huntress would end with the death of one or both of them. Regardless of the outcome, the meeting of *this* Hunter and Huntress would be sung by every bard and minstrel for years to come.

He couldn't honestly say he was looking forward to witnessing it.

Preoccupied with his thoughts, he hurried across a courtyard—then stopped abruptly as a door opened and the last person he wanted to meet walked toward him.

"Lightbringer," Aiden said uneasily.

Lucian smiled. "Aiden! Well met!"

Wary now, Aiden approached Lucian. "That's not what you said the last time we guested at the same Clan house."

Lucian's smile faded. "I know. That was not well done on my part. I was angry and—" He stiffened.

Hearing the quiet scuff of feet on stone, Aiden knew who now claimed the Lightbringer's attention.

Turning toward him, Lucian said softly, hurriedly, "We need to talk privately before you leave here."

"I'm not sure—"

"Please, Aiden."

There was an eloquent plea in Lucian's gray eyes that Aiden couldn't refuse. Despite their clashes over the past year, they *were* still kin on their fathers' side. "All right. After the evening meal. Things should be settled down by then." *Or as settled as they are going to be,* he added silently as he turned toward Ashk and the others. He noted Lyrra's apprehension as she glanced from Morag to Lucian.

Mother's mercy. Morag, with her unpredictable moods of late, wasn't someone he wanted near Lucian any longer than necessary.

"Hunter," Aiden said quickly, "may I present Lucian, the Lightbringer. Lucian, this is Ashk."

Lucian made a slight bow, keeping his eyes on Ashk. "Well met, Hunter. I've heard a great deal about you lately. After so many years of silence, you've made your presence felt in Tir Alainn."

"As you have made your presence felt, Lightbringer," Ashk replied. "Your denial of what's happening in Sylvalan has cost so many people suffering and sorrow, if not outright death. Because *you* are the Lord of the Sun, more witches have died since last summer, more Clans have been lost. That's what *your* presence has done for the Fae and the other peoples of Sylvalan."

Lucian stared at her. "You're blaming *me* for what the Black Coats have done?"

"I'm blaming you for not protecting, not defending, not doing anything while the Inquisitors have continued their slaughter of witches and their mutilation of other women's bodies and spirits.

I'm blaming you for being so blindly selfish that even when you understood the cost, you chose to ignore that the Fae have a duty to the world. We've *always* had a duty to the world. Now, instead of fighting against a few barons and Inquisitors, we have armies marching toward us, intent on snuffing out all magic in the world. And that means the Fae as well as the witches and Small Folk. So, yes, Lightbringer, I do blame you for what the Black Coats have done. Without your willful insistence that the Fae didn't have to do anything to protect Sylvalan, the Inquisitors couldn't have destroyed so much, couldn't have killed so many."

Lucian paled. "How dare you!"

"Look at the bodies of those who have died, and you won't have to ask how I dare," Ashk said. "Look at the women whose lives have been crushed by the Inquisitors' words and a physician's knife, and you won't have to ask. Look at the Old Places that are gone—and the Clans that are gone with them."

"So your solution is to threaten your own kind."

"The world was not made to supply the Fae with amusements and treats. It's time they were reminded of that. It's time they remembered the world is made of shadows as well as light."

Lucian and Ashk stared at each other. Aiden held his breath. Lucian had challenged the new Huntress—and lost that confrontation. He couldn't be foolish enough to push Ashk into a challenge, could he?

Finally, Lucian said, "I hope you're right, Hunter. I hope forcing the Fae into this conflict truly is the right thing to do. If it's not, the only thing the surviving Fae will remember about you is that you destroyed us." He turned and walked back into the Clan house.

Aiden let out a gusty sigh of relief. One evening. One uncomfortable evening in the same Clan house. Surely they could get through a few hours without fighting with each other.

Then he looked at Morag, saw a bleak fury in her dark eyes, and felt something wash through him that was so cold it bit down to the bone. Before he could decide if he should say something, Ashk linked arms with the Gatherer and walked toward the Clan house.

Someone touched his arm.

"Aiden?" Lyrra said, her eyes filled with concern.

He put his arms around her, needing her warmth. Would Ashk

be angry with him for meeting privately with Lucian? Would Morag?

But this wasn't about the Lightbringer and the Bard. This was a meeting between two men who were kin. Surely they would understand that—and appreciate the difference.

Nevertheless, he would keep his meeting with Lucian as private as possible—and hope Ashk and Morag didn't find out about it until they were all long gone from this place.

"They're bitches, both of them," Lucian said, staring fiercely at the wood carefully arranged in the fireplace.

That was true enough, Aiden thought wearily, since Ashk and Selena were shadow hounds in their other form. At another time, he might have tried to play with words to make *bitch* mean other than what Lucian intended. But the truth was, he was exhausted. The Clan, taking courage from the Lightbringer's presence, hadn't quite told Ashk that they wouldn't heed her command to send huntsmen down to Sylvalan to help in the fight that was coming; they'd simply insisted that they were keeping careful watch on the witches to make sure the women came to no harm. He would never know how Ashk would have responded because Morag had stood up then and said in a voice that was far too calm and too quiet that if anything happened to the witches, the Fae had better hope that the shining road closed quickly, because if there was any way for her to reach them, there would be no one left but the dead.

There was no argument Ashk could make after that, even after Morphia led her sister from the room. He didn't know what was pushing Morag to the edge of sanity, but he was certain he didn't want to be around her when she finally lost control.

And now, having pushed Lyrra out of their room with no more explanation than a request for an hour's privacy, he was sitting on the bed listening to Lucian's complaints.

"They're going to destroy the Fae, you know that, don't you?" Lucian said, still staring at the fireplace. "Maybe I am selfish, but I've *never* terrified my people into obedience. That's what they're doing, Aiden. One threatens our home, the other threatens an essential part of our nature. They're ruthless, cruel bitches who used tricks to gain the power they have, and now the rest of us will have to pay for it."

"You didn't help matters by doing nothing this past year,"

Aiden said quietly. "You not only gave the Clans the excuses they wanted to justify doing nothing to protect Sylvalan, you continued to encourage those excuses, even though you knew who the witches were. You were the one who insisted the Daughters of the House of Gaian were no more than servants whose purpose was to serve, and service, the Fae."

"It's so easy for you, isn't it?" Lucian said bitterly as he turned to face Aiden. "You're not alone, are you, Bard? You have the woman who matters to you. You can hold her, talk to her, feel the pleasure of her under you at night. You don't have the anger of grief and the guilt of failure haunting your nights. Well, I do." He turned back to the fireplace, his voice now filled with sorrow. "I do. When Morag offered me that damned bargain, I almost took it, almost offered my life in exchange. But I had a duty to the Fae." He laughed grimly. "Look what my duty has brought me."

Aiden stood up, a sick feeling rolling through him. "What are you talking about?"

"Ari." Lucian put his hands on the mantel, letting his arms take his weight as he sagged in defeat. "I'm talking about Ari."

Aiden took a step forward, unsure what to do. Lyrra held his heart, and if something happened to her because of something he hadn't done, the grief would crush him. He knew that. But . . . "I know you cared for Ari," he said carefully, "but I never suspected it was more than you've felt for any other lover."

"Why should you have suspected anything?" Lucian's voice broke. "She sent me away. Did you know that? I was no longer welcome at her cottage because she had decided to marry that . . . human. So I wasn't close enough when the Black Coats came. I wasn't fast enough to save her."

Aiden raked a hand through his hair. Something wasn't right. *Couldn't* be right. "If you cared for her, why have you fought against helping other witches?"

"Because I couldn't stand knowing that Ari died because I had failed. And there you were with your eloquent pleas and demands to protect the witches, constantly reminding me of the woman I had lost, shoving it down my throat until I was sure I would choke on it. So I dismissed their importance, denied what they are. I couldn't seem to do anything else."

"I . . . I didn't know, Lucian. I didn't know." Would a man deny so much to diminish grief? Yes. Oh, yes. And looking at it that way changed Lucian's actions into something Aiden understood. But he was too tired and couldn't quite get his brain to think past his heart even though he sensed something was off-key about the conversation. Still, he said hesitantly, "She would have left Brightwood anyway. She couldn't have a decent life there."

"She would have had us instead of those paltry humans," Lucian said fiercely, regrets giving way to anger as he faced Aiden again. "We would have dealt with the villagers, and they wouldn't have dared slight her."

"You didn't do that while you were her lover. She wouldn't have any reason to think you'd do it when you were no longer lovers."

"We *would* have been lovers. The Fae would have been her companions. She would have wanted for nothing."

Except love, Aiden thought bleakly. *Except respect and loyalty.* But was that true? Had he misunderstood the depth of Lucian's feelings for Ari? "You wouldn't have been faithful to her, Lucian. You know that."

"Faithful." Lucian spat out the word. "That's a human word. *I cared for her.* But if what I offered wasn't enough to convince her to stay, I would have let her go with that fool. Despite the problems it would have caused for my Clan, despite my own feelings, *despite everything, I would have let her go.*" His voice broke. He put his hands over his face.

Aiden couldn't stand seeing a man who had once been a friend and was still kin break under a year's guilt and grief.

"Lucian . . ." He stepped forward, rested a hand on Lucian's arm. "Do you mean that? You really would have let her go?"

Lucian lowered his hands away from his face, and said wearily, "If it had been Lyrra, wouldn't you rather know she was living somewhere without you than to have died under the Black Coats' hands?"

"She survived." Aiden tried to stop the words, tried to think it through, but he couldn't think anymore, could only feel. "She got away from the Black Coats."

He watched all emotion drain from Lucian's face.

"Morag lied to me?" Lucian said in a queer voice.

"No," Aiden said quickly. "No. She told you Ari was gone, and that was true."

"She knew what I'd think. What Dianna and I both thought."

Lucian stared at Aiden. "You knew, didn't you? You knew Ari wasn't dead."

Aiden shook his head. "I suspected. I hoped. But I didn't know for sure."

Lucian took a step to the side. "You knew. All this time, you knew."

"I *didn't* know."

"Then how can you be certain now?" Lucian demanded. "Just because she got away from the Black Coats doesn't mean she survived."

"We saw her when—" Uneasy now as he watched anger fill Lucian's eyes, Aiden finished clumsily, "We saw her when we were traveling in the west."

"You saw her, and yet you said nothing until now, sent no messages to me or Dianna."

"There was no reason to say anything, no reason to send any messages. Ari is happy where she is. She'll never come back to Brightwood."

"My sister was challenged and lost to that cold-blooded bitch because her power was being drained by having to be the anchor for our Clan's territory—something Ari should have been doing."

"No," Aiden said. "You said you would have let her go."

"Where would she have gone?" Lucian said furiously. "If Morag had gathered that human when Dianna asked her to, Ari would have stayed."

"And she would have died! Neall got her away from the Inquisitors. *That's* the reason she survived." This wasn't right. Where was the grief, the guilt, the regrets that had filled the room a few moments ago? Where was the relief that the woman Lucian cared about had survived?

"So he survived as well. That's something that can be changed, and once Ari is back at Brightwood—"

"Lucian, *no*." Aiden grabbed Lucian's arms. "They're in love, and they're happy, and she's growing fat with their first child. You can't take her away from her husband and home. You said you cared for her. Be glad she's well, Lucian, and let her go."

"Be glad of what?" Lucian snapped, jerking his arms to break Aiden's hold. "That she let a *human* fill her belly?"

Was that what the anger was about? That Ari had chosen a human over the Lightbringer? "Not a human, Lucian. Neall is

Fae. A Lord of the Woods. He has a human face, true enough, but he's Fae."

"No!"

"Yes!"

"Where is she?"

Aiden shook his head.

Lucian stared at Aiden. "You went west to find the Hunter, didn't you? You brought that bitch down on us."

"She would have come regardless. After the Black Coats attacked her Clan, she would have come east to fight them whether I found her or not."

"You wouldn't have stayed long in one place while you were looking for the Hunter. And you would have wanted to stay, at least a day or two, if you'd found Ari first."

Aiden didn't dare say anything. Here was the anger he'd seen over the past year—the sneering anger that had cost them all so much.

"The Bretonwood Clan. Isn't that where the Hunter comes from? Yes, I'm sure that's the Clan that was mentioned. Does Bretonwood have a witch to anchor the shining road in the Old Place? *A witch who should be living at Brightwood?*"

Aiden said nothing.

"Just as well you don't answer. You lied to me, Bard."

"No more than you've lied to me this evening. You used my heart against me, Lucian. You used our kinship as a weapon. I won't forget that, nor will I forgive it."

"And I won't forgive your betrayal, Aiden. You should have supported Dianna and me. But that doesn't matter now. Once Ari is back at Brightwood, Dianna will regain her full power, and we'll take care of that usurper who stole her place as the Lady of the Moon." Lucian took a step toward the door.

"No!" Aiden grabbed Lucian's arms.

Heat filled his hands. Searing, staggering heat. He screamed as they burst into flames.

Lucian shoved him. He fell against the bed, scrambled wildly to pull the covers around his burning hands and smother the flames. He heard Lucian fling the door open and run down the corridor.

He howled out his anguish, but he couldn't have said if the cry was for the pain in his hands or his heart.

*   *   *

Half-listening to the story Lyrra was telling Morphia, Sheridan, and Morag, Ashk moved closer to the door. Her keen hearing was picking up the sound of male voices—arguing. Who was arguing?

She opened the door a crack. Morphia and Sheridan had the room next to this one, which she was sharing with Morag. Aiden and Lyrra were across the hall from Morphia and Sheridan.

When Lyrra knocked on the door a little while ago, she said Aiden wanted a little privacy. But the voices were coming from their room. Who was Aiden talking to? Why not tell Lyrra he wanted to talk to someone instead of implying he wanted some time alone?

Unless he didn't want anyone to know he'd arranged to talk to someone. And there was only one person she could think of whom Aiden would prefer to meet in secret.

Her stomach tightened. She turned away from the door. She didn't want to lose her trust in Aiden, not only because she liked him but because the Bard was a strong ally.

Then she heard a scream of pain, heard a door flung open.

Whipping her own door open, she saw Lucian running down the corridor to the staircase.

Hearing an anguished cry, she rushed into the other room, then froze for a moment when she saw Aiden half sprawled on the bed, a thin curl of smoke rising from the covers bunched over his hands.

She was across the room, grabbing the pitcher of water, before Lyrra reached the doorway and screamed, "Aiden!"

Lyrra stumbled in her haste to reach Aiden, catching herself before she fell against him. She rested her hands on his shoulders, her eyes full of panic as she stared at the covers hiding his hands.

Ashk tugged at the covers just enough to get past the top layer, then poured the water over the rest. The sheet was charred, but she couldn't see Aiden's hands yet.

Sheridan burst into the room. "Ashk?"

"More water. *Now!*"

Gasping, Aiden said, "I'm sorry," over and over.

"Who did this?" Ashk snapped. "Was it Lucian?"

Aiden nodded.

Sheridan returned, carrying two water pitchers from other

rooms. As Ashk grabbed one from him, she saw Morag standing in the doorway.

"Where *is* Lucian?" Morag asked.

Ashk bared her teeth. "Who cares where—" She stopped. Stared at Morag. Then she looked at Aiden. "Does he know about Ari? Does he know where to find her?"

"I didn't tell him," Aiden gasped. "Only that she was alive. But he guessed . . . because I'm traveling with you."

Ashk looked up.

Morag was already gone.

One thing at a time. "Get the basin and fill it with water," she told Sheridan. When the basin was on the bed and filled, she reached for the sodden cloth over Aiden's hands.

Shuddering, Aiden closed his eyes. Lyrra turned her head.

Carefully, Ashk lifted the cloth—and sighed with relief. Lightly gripping his wrists, she raised his hands high enough for Sheridan to push the basin under them. Then she gently lowered Aiden's hands into the water.

Not what she'd feared. Nothing like she'd feared. A few blisters were rising, and his hands were a bright red. She'd seen skin that red when young farmers foolishly stripped to the waist and worked in the fields all day early in planting season. She doubted Aiden would be comfortable for a few days, but he would be all right.

"Stay with him." She ran out of the room and down the corridor, passing Morphia and the Clan healer the Sleep Sister must have fetched.

Down the stairs and through the communal rooms. Out of the Clan house, running through the gardens until she reached the stable.

"Have you seen the Lightbringer?" she panted. Her anger grew fangs when no one answered until one of her own men stepped forward.

"He came out of the Clan house a little while ago," the huntsman said. "He changed to his other form and galloped toward the bridge that connects to the Clan just west of here." He shrugged. "We thought he'd decided to guest elsewhere tonight."

"What about the Gatherer?"

Now he looked uncomfortable. "She saddled her horse in a hurry and headed out in the same direction.

Ashk stared at him, a cold lump growing in her belly.

He shifted his feet, uneasy now. "She didn't have her saddle-bags. Said there wasn't time to fetch them when we offered to get them for her, so we made sure she had a canteen for water and a small bag of grain for the horse. She wouldn't wait for anything else."

Ashk nodded. "You did what you could."

She walked back to the Clan house, fighting the urge to ride out after Morag. Lucian had the advantage—at least until he reached the western Clans. After that . . .

She couldn't catch up to them. Foolish to even try. Besides, the waxing moon was growing larger every night—and her task was still ahead of her, in the east.

As she reached the terrace, she stopped and looked toward the west. "Find him, Morag," she said softly. "Find him . . . and do what needs to be done."

Chapter 26

waxing moon

Mihail gritted his teeth against the pain from the burns on his shoulder and back. His first mate was a good sailor, but right now they needed *him* at the wheel, needed his connection to the sea to draw every breath of speed he could coax from *Sweet Selkie*. When he was at the wheel, he felt like a bridge between wind and water, knew exactly how to turn his ship to keep the sails full and fast.

The Black Coats' ships were still gaining on them. Bigger ships. More sails. They would catch up to them. Sooner or later. He couldn't think about that. He had to keep his mind on his ship, on the sea, on the wind.

His first mate stepped close to him, and said quietly, "We don't have enough fresh water to see us through the journey. Not enough food, either. The smaller boats that fled with us couldn't have taken on enough supplies for the people they're carrying."

"I know," Mihail replied. "But if we stop anywhere, the Black Coats will have us."

"And if we don't, the lack of water will finish us off for them."

"I know." Mihail swallowed, wishing violently that his first mate hadn't mentioned water. "We can't lead the Black Coats to Sealand. We can't lead them to safe harbor." *Can't lead them to Jenny and the boys.* "That big island we pass on our way north, the one across from the western bay. What have you heard about it?"

The first mate rubbed his chin and gave Mihail an uneasy look. "Awhile back, when it was still safe enough to visit a tavern in Seahaven, I had a drink with a man who usually sails out of Wellingsford. He said the folks north of there call it Selkie Island. Said it's not a place to go unless you've no choice. Strange folk there."

"Fae?"

"Maybe. He wasn't sure—or wouldn't say. Just said the captains he'd shipped with preferred to stay closer to the mainland shore, but if a captain spotted a lot of seals that seemed a bit too interested in his ship, he'd lower some sails and call out to any fishing boat nearby, asking if they could deliver a small gift to the Lord of the island. Said the captains always kept a little cargo in easy reach for just that reason."

"Did the fishing boats take the gifts?"

"Aye, they did—and most headed straight back for that island. Safe waters. That's what the man said. Sea pirates are afraid to sail within sight of that island. Those that do usually don't sail away again."

Safe waters. They needed safe waters. Could they find food and fresh water on the island? Could they find any help against the Black Coats?

He looked up at the sky sliding toward twilight. There were still birds riding the air currents. Were they real birds, or were the Fae already watching them? If there were Fae on Selkie Island, did they know the Fae on Ronat Isle?

Safe waters. They needed safe waters.

"We'll adjust our course," Mihail said. "We'll head for that island. If the Fae do live there, maybe they'll help us." Maybe.

Right now, it gave him a grain of hope—and a grain was more than he'd had an hour ago.

Chapter 27

waxing moon

Despair. Fear. Anger. Determination.

As Liam stood in front of his family's home and watched Varden gallop away, those emotions churned inside him, a messy stew of feelings. He turned and hurried back to where Donovan waited near the stables with the horses and guards. If Varden had shown up a few minutes later, they would have already left to check the tenant farms. Of course, one of the huntsmen would have found them, but the delay would have cost them all.

Maybe it wouldn't make any difference in the end, considering what Varden had just told him.

As he closed the distance to where Donovan waited, anger rose to the surface, coating the fear.

"Mother's tits, Donovan," Liam said, his voice sharp. "Why are you still here?"

Donovan gave him a mild look. "I was waiting for you. Didn't seem right to visit your tenants without you."

"That's right," Liam panted. Muscle and bone clamped around his lungs and wouldn't let him draw a full breath. "They're my tenants. This is my land. You should have gone home days ago. Why didn't you go home?" Despair churned up through the anger.

"Gwenn insists there's something she needs to do here and won't leave. And I won't go without Gwenn." Donovan stiffened. "What's wrong, Liam? What did Varden tell you?"

Liam rubbed his hands over his face. "Armed men, marching this way. Three hundred men. Maybe more. Not a whole army . . ." But enough. More than enough. "Varden has sent one of his men back to Tir Alainn to warn the Fae . . . and to get any other Fae at the Clan house who have any skill with weapons. He sent another man to Squire Thurston's. Thurston's closer to the village. He'll have time to get the villagers assembled in case . . ."

"In case?" Donovan narrowed his eyes. "Where are those men heading, Liam?"

"Here. They're heading right for us." Liam closed his eyes. Despair would gain nothing. Anger was the better weapon, but the despair kept drowning anger's fire before it had a chance to kindle. At least his mother and Brooke were at the Old Place. He didn't have to worry about them being trapped here. And maybe there was a way to keep them safe. "Twenty Fae, your guards, and the two Willowsbrook guards assigned to protect me. Less than thirty men against three hundred."

"There are the men at the Old Place," Donovan countered. "The villagers. The farmers."

"And leave those places vulnerable? It's me they want." *If they take me, if they kill me, maybe it will be enough. Maybe they'll leave my people, my family, alone.*

"That's right. Eliminate the baron, eliminate the leader, and the county splinters into each village trying to defend itself instead of joining together into a large-enough force to repel an attack. They won't stop with you, Liam. Oh, I've come to know you well enough during the time I've been here to know you're considering it. A sacrifice offered to appease. But it won't appease. They'll keep on killing until they're stopped—or until there's nothing and no one left here to destroy."

"If you go now, you and Gwenn could stay ahead of them, could reach the Mother's Hills before . . ." Liam swallowed hard. Too easy to picture Old Willowsbrook looking like the places he'd thought were fever dreams when Padrick had helped him get home. Too easy to see faces, familiar and loved, on bodies that had been— No. He couldn't think about it.

"I don't want to die here," Donovan said quietly. "But we're not fighting just to save Willowsbrook. We're fighting to save Sylvalan. In the end, it doesn't matter where I pick up the sword . . . as long as I pick up the sword."

Hoofbeats. Heading toward them.

The guards whirled, short swords in their hands.

Breanna and Gwenn reined in—and Liam felt the heat of power under his skin, burning away despair and clearing his mind. He had a weapon at his fingertips that the enemy didn't know about. A weapon that would help even the odds.

Calm settled over him, although his heart still beat too fast as he walked over to the sister who had become dear to him.

"You shouldn't be here now," he said, looking at Breanna. Hoping he'd be able to look at her again.

"You're not going to stand alone," Breanna said quietly. "I will not let my brother stand alone."

They'd been in this place before, when the nighthunters had first attacked and he'd refused to leave her, refused to let her sacrifice herself to give him a chance to escape. He should have known she would stand with him.

"You two," he said, flicking a finger at the two women. "Get the servants out of the house. Have them take whatever food they can put together quickly, and get them out. They aren't fighters. There's nothing they can do here." When Breanna turned, he grabbed her arm. "Fetch my bow while you're in there."

Breanna gave him a cool stare. "Do I look like your valet?"

He grinned. He couldn't help it. "My valet never fetches my bow. That's a loving sister's duty."

Her only response was a grunt as she stepped away from him and ran to catch up to Gwenn, who was dashing up the steps to the front door of the manor.

"That's what I like most about Breanna," Donovan said dryly. "She's so articulate."

"She can say a lot while saying little," Liam agreed.

The small banter and Breanna's presence settled him, grounded him. He would do what he could, protect what he could—and hope they were still together when the sun set on this day.

Brisk orders now to saddle horses, hitch others to wagons. If they had to retreat and abandon the manor house, which Liam expected they would have to do, it would be easier to escape on horseback and regroup at another spot. The rest of the horses and other livestock—the few cows and chickens—were set free. It would be a headache to round them up again, but he wasn't going to leave them as easy supplies to feed the enemy.

It didn't surprise him that most of the men who worked in his stables left with the younger servants when he gave them the choice. They were, after all, his father's men and felt no loyalty to him. It didn't surprise him that Arthur stayed, looking pale and grim as he took up a position near the horses he loved, a pitchfork in his hands.

What did surprise him was how many of the servants stayed, armed with fireplace pokers and the longest of the kitchen knives.

Not surprising, Breanna told him. The house servants were Elinore's people, and he was Elinore's son.

To her, it was as simple as that.

He had a bad moment when he caught movement among the trees close to the manor until he spotted Varden and realized the Fae huntsmen were moving quietly to take up their positions.

Maybe that would be better. Move up to the low stone wall at the top of the drive and meet the enemy on the road.

Then it was too late to move. Crows exploded from the trees. A hawk screamed.

And Liam saw the dust kicked up by hundreds of feet as the gentry leaders on horseback turned into the long drive that led up to the manor. The flood of men behind them ran up the drive, arrows already nocked in their bows.

He took up a position just inside the manor's half-open door, hoping the wood was thick enough to give him some protection—especially since Breanna was with him.

He felt the power of fire flow into him, making his skin hot and his fingers tingle. He felt a light wind and knew Breanna was gathering the branch of air.

Closer. Closer.

He nocked an arrow. Drew back the bowstring, taking aim at the first man on horseback. Waited.

"There's a Black Coat among them," Breanna whispered fiercely.

"You take him," Liam whispered back.

She sighted, then shook her head. "Can't. He moved. I'd have to step out into the open to try for him."

The horsemen reined in. The men flowed in a double line to either side of them.

"Baron Liam!" one of the horsemen yelled. "Surrender now, and your people will not be harmed. You have my word on that."

"None of the men, you mean," Liam muttered. "You don't consider women to be people. You bastard."

"Liam! If you don't surrender, your people will suffer for it! What is your answer?"

"This." Liam let the arrow fly. It hit the horseman high in the chest.

Horses screamed. Reared as arrows flew from the trees and the barn's hayloft, answered by the enemy archers. He caught a glimpse of the black-coated Inquisitor. Heard someone shouting to fire the catapult.

"I can't see from here," Breanna said. "I just can't see."

She was out the door, running for the stables before Liam could grab her.

"Breanna!"

The wind staggered him. Saved him as he stumbled forward and the arrow that would have pierced his heart suddenly shot upward to hit the top of the door.

Bent over, he ran as fast as he could. Arrows swirled around him, tumbled like sticks in a storm. He saw Breanna behind the watering trough. Heard her yell of anger and surprise. Saw her pop up, a target begging to be killed. He knocked her down. Felt an arrow slice through the left sleeve of his coat.

"You fool!" he yelled.

"No! Let me up. Liam!" She struggled to get out from under him. As her head smacked his chin, he looked up—and saw the ball of fire arching toward the barn.

Wind roared around him, but it was too late. The flaming ball smashed through the barn roof. The hay would go up instantly, and the men inside—

He looked up and saw one of the Fae in the hayloft. Saw him change into an owl and take flight. Saw him fall, impaled by three arrows.

He shifted enough to let Breanna get to her hands and knees. "We've got to get away from here. The barn's going to go up."

Spitting out dirt, she twisted around enough to look at him. "I know—" Her face paled. Her eyes widened. *"Mother's mercy!"* She grabbed his shirt and pulled him back down.

He looked over his shoulder—and felt his heart clog his throat as the spinning funnel of dirt that towered over his home raced past the manor house and drove right into the center of the enemy's men.

They had no chance, Liam thought as that funnel captured the living, the wounded, and the dead, captured earth and stone, spinning it up, up, up.

Arrows flew at it. Became more debris to impale those who had been alive when it caught them.

It raced down the drive, a straight path of destruction. Men who scrambled out of its path met the Fae's arrows. They couldn't turn fast enough, couldn't run fast enough. And when it reached the catapult with another ball of flame ready to be released, he heard the savage snap of wood, heard the roar of fire—and covered Breanna's eyes and closed his own when he heard the screams of those who were still alive in that spinning fury.

"We surrender!" several voices yelled. "Please! We surrender!"

Breanna jerked. "The ground's hot."

Liam scrambled to his knees. The ground around them smoked gently. The grass near the barn was withered, as if it had been burned by an unrelenting sun. When he glanced up, he saw smoke rising from the barn roof but no flames.

He pulled Breanna to her feet and led her back toward the manor house, keeping himself between her and the drive.

"We surrender!"

Men, holding their empty hands above their heads, looked toward the trees. Slowly, cautiously, the Fae appeared and herded the prisoners toward the manor house.

And at the end of the drive, now moving slowly back toward them, was that funnel. Flames still flared at the top of it like captured lightning. Charred wood and bodies began falling from it.

"Mother's mercy, Liam. What *is* that?"

Liam looked over, relief flooding through him as he saw Donovan—dirty and with a bloody scrape along his jaw—guiding Gwenn toward the manor house. She was limping a little, and her face had no color.

As they got closer to each other, he heard Gwenn muttering, "I can do this. I can. This is what I stayed to do. Mother's mercy. Calm calm calm. I can do this."

Donovan's eyes held worry and fear. Breanna was a quivering mass of tension beside him. The prisoners hurried toward them, terrified. And Varden and the rest of the Fae who gathered on the edges of the drive looked equally pale and frightened.

And still that funnel moved slowly toward them, losing height now, losing its prey.

He swallowed hard as he watched the bodies fall. More and more of them until there was nothing left but a thin veil of dirt.

Three hundred men—and they'd had no chance.

"I can do this. Let go of me, Donovan." Gwenn pulled away

from her husband, shook out her skirt, and brushed at the dirt on her shirt. "I can do this."

"Do what, Gwenn?" Breanna asked, her eyes narrowing as she watched the funnel.

Liam stared. Was he seeing what he thought he was seeing?

The last of the dirt fell away as the funnel faded into a gentle swirl of air around the black-haired, cold-eyed woman riding a gray stallion. A beautiful woman. The kind of woman who could take a man's breath away.

The realization that his heart wasn't just pounding in fear scared him to the bone.

The horse stopped. The woman just stared at them.

Gwenn took one step forward. Her smile was as wobbling as the curtsy she tried to perform. "Blessings of the day, Selena."

After a painful moment of silence, the woman said, "Blessings of the day, Gwenn."

Breanna stared at the tea and thin sandwiches on the table in front of her. She wasn't sure if she was queasy because she was hungry or because it didn't seem right to be hungry after what she'd seen. At least her hands had stopped shaking. Sneaking a healthy nip of whiskey before Sloane brought in the tea things had coated her nerves with the illusion of calm.

There was no reason *not* to be calm. It was over. They'd won this battle. Liam and Donovan were questioning the prisoners. And the guest she was waiting to offer tea and sandwiches to was just a witch, just another Daughter of the House of Gaian.

She lowered her face into her hands. Felt her breathing hitch as she struggled to remain calm. It would be ill-mannered to show fear, but . . .

Selena wasn't just another witch, wasn't just another Daughter of the House of Gaian. Mother's mercy. How was she supposed to act around a woman who could create a funnel of wind so powerful it could have ripped grown trees out of the ground and flung them aside like a child throwing a toy with gleeful abandon. And the speed of it, racing down the drive at a fast gallop. A few seconds, a few ticks of the clock. That's all it had taken for that twisting fury to destroy three hundred men.

Feeling her hands tremble, Breanna sat up and pushed her hair back. Offering Selena a guest room and a chance to wash off the dust had been the polite thing to do. And it gave them all a chance to let their nerves settle a bit before facing her again. Gwenn's doing. If she hadn't played lady of the manor, they might all still be standing out there, uncertain of what to say or do.

Mother's tits. Where *was* Gwenn? She promised to be down as soon as she washed up a bit and changed into something borrowed from Elinore's wardrobe.

Breanna brushed her fingers over the skirt and tunic she'd borrowed, certain Elinore would have been more offended if she'd sat in the parlor looking dusty and bedraggled while offering tea to an important guest than helping herself to the other woman's clothes.

Sloane opened the door. As Selena walked into the room, Breanna decided a false, sick smile would be more insulting than a serious expression. Besides, she didn't think her parlor skills were sufficient under these circumstances to produce even a sick smile.

Where was Gwenn?

"There's tea and sandwiches," Breanna said.

Selena barely glanced at the tray on the table. "It looks lovely." She walked over to the windows half-covered by the heavy draperies that were usually pulled closed over the sheers at night. She stared out the window but didn't push aside the sheers to get a clear view.

"Do no harm," Selena said quietly. "That's the creed. That's the scale on which we balance all we do when we channel the power from the Great Mother. The Lady of the Moon is a wonderful dance, a celebration of the Mother's sister. But I'm also the Huntress, the protector of witches. I am justice . . . and I am vengeance. Because of that, I can no longer balance what I do on the scale of our creed."

And it hurts you, Breanna thought, studying the lovely woman who now wore a simple green gown. *It hurts you that you can't live by the creed.* The quiet pain under Selena's words tugged at her and she said the first thing that popped into her head. "You made a mess of Liam's drive. It will take his men days to rake it smooth again." She didn't mention the men who were out there now, searching for any wounded, gathering up the dead.

Selena turned away from the window, her expression slightly puzzled.

Good. That was good.

"I thought Gwenn said Baron Liam was your brother. Isn't it your drive, too?"

Breanna shook her head and poured tea into two cups. "Oh, no. This is Liam's house. I don't live here."

"I see."

It was like feeling the sharp blade of a winter wind cutting through a summer day.

"No," Breanna said firmly, "I don't think you do." Since her hands were trembling again, she didn't try to pick up her tea. "I live in the Old Place with my family. Liam and I only got to know each other a few weeks ago. His mother, Elinore, is kin to us, and his gift from the Mother comes down through her. He didn't know it was in him until the need to save me from the nighthunters broke the barriers inside him. And now . . ." She trailed off, remembering the mortified expression on Liam's face.

"It's a natural function," Selena said.

"So is farting, and he'd probably have preferred to embarrass himself that way in mixed company than setting a pile of arrows on fire," Breanna replied tartly. She picked up her cup and saucer. Selena's sudden, rich laughter surprised her enough to bobble the cup, slopping tea into the saucer.

"You're younger than he is, aren't you?" Selena's gray-green eyes danced with humor.

"What makes you think that?" Breanna asked warily.

"Younger sisters have no mercy."

Breanna tipped her head. "You have a younger sister?"

Selena walked over to the table, took her tea and a thin sandwich. "I do."

"Would she like a dog?"

It was the caution in Selena's expression, overlaid with humor, that confirmed for Breanna that, however powerful Selena might be, she was still one of the Mother's Daughters at heart.

"I don't think so," Selena said just as Gwenn limped into the room.

"Is the tea still hot?" Gwenn asked, sounding grumpy.

"Hot enough," Breanna replied, setting her own down to pour some for Gwenn. "What took you so long?"

"Donovan." Gwenn flopped on the couch with no grace whatsoever. "First he tries to convince me to stay upstairs, in bed, to rest my ankle, which wouldn't have gotten twisted in the first place if he hadn't shoved me to the ground and thrown himself on top of me. Then, when I tell him I'm going to come down and have tea with the two of you, he wants me to have a bowl of chicken soup. I don't want chicken soup. I don't *like* chicken soup."

Breanna glanced at Selena, relieved to see the same puzzled expression she was sure was on her own face. "Chicken soup for a twisted ankle?"

"I swear gentry fathers take their sons aside on the night before the wedding and tell them that chicken soup is the secret to a happy marriage, that it is the cure for anything that ails a wife," Gwenn grumbled.

"I never would have guessed chicken soup as the subject to discuss on the night before a wedding," Breanna said blandly.

Selena leaned forward, her expression innocent. "Do you eat a lot of chicken soup, Gwenn?"

Gwenn just grunted. "Then, when I tell him to go on since Liam's waiting for him, he waits for me and carries me down the stairs."

"It would have been difficult to get down the stairs otherwise," Selena said.

"No, it wouldn't. I could have slid down the banister most of the way."

Selena made a strangled, gurgly sound. "Oh . . . Gwenn. You're not still doing that, are you? You're a baron's wife. When the Grandmothers caught you at it, you used to tell them you were checking for dust."

"Which is exactly what I tell the servants if *they* catch me at it," Gwenn said. She sniffed primly. "Besides, how am I going to teach my daughters how to do it if I don't practice once in a while?"

Breanna choked on her tea.

Selena's face was turning red with the effort not to laugh.

Gwenn gave Breanna a helping swat on the back that almost shoved her nose into the teacup, then said, "Breathe, Selena. You're starting to look like a holly bush."

Maybe it wasn't right to fill the room with laughter when there was so much death just beyond the door.

And maybe, Breanna thought as she wiped her streaming eyes with the napkin Gwenn handed her, laughter was exactly what she needed to see Selena as a woman who could be a friend instead of a power to be feared.

Liam noticed the tremor in Donovan's hand as his friend raised the glass of whiskey and downed its contents in one swallow.

"Do not wake the Mother's Hills," Donovan said softly, staring into his glass. "Well, they're awake now, aren't they? Mother's mercy, Liam. Gwenny said Selena was powerful, and I hadn't doubted her word, especially after seeing the storm that passed over Willowsbrook, but I'd never imagined a witch could do . . . *that.* And I've *met* some of the women who come from the Mother's Hills."

"Nobody imagined they could do that," Liam said wearily. But he looked toward the closed study door and shivered, remembering the whirl of wind Breanna had created when he met her. She'd captured the earth Keely was flinging at him in a misguided effort to protect Breanna from the baron. If she could create a small whirling of wind and earth, could Breanna create something larger, something more destructive? If she needed to protect her family, *would* she create a funnel of earth and air that could be used as a weapon?

Would *he* have used the fire at his command to burn men as he'd burned the nighthunters? Yes, he would have. He didn't like knowing that about himself, especially after seeing the bodies that had been caught in that rage of wind and fire, and understood now why the creed to do no harm was constantly reinforced every time Breanna or Nuala gave him another lesson in using and controlling the power that lived inside him.

"Liam? Where have you gone?"

Liam looked at Donovan and shook his head. A knock on the study door saved him from a discussion he didn't want to have.

Varden walked in, and said bluntly, "We need to talk."

Before he could say anything more, two Fae led a prisoner into the room.

Liam studied the man dressed in the homespun tunic and trousers that were commonly worn by farmers. A pleasant-looking man in his mid-twenties, who appeared more relieved than fearful.

"Sit down," Liam said, indicating the chair in front of the desk.

"Yes, sir," the man said. "Thank you, sir."

He'd never dealt with prisoners before, but it baffled him that the man was acting more like a tenant farmer talking to his landlord than a man who'd just been captured in battle.

"You do understand that you're a prisoner," Liam said.

"Yes, sir, and grateful to be so."

"Why?"

The man shifted in the chair. "You stand against the eastern barons." Not quite a statement; more a request for confirmation.

Liam nodded. "I stand against everything the Inquisitors brought to our land—and I stand against any baron who supports them."

The man nodded. "That's why the lads and I were grateful for the chance to surrender. We didn't want to fight you. The Black Coat kept stirring up the men by saying you were a servant of the Evil One and had to be destroyed to keep our homes and families safe." Bitterness filled his face. "We've seen what the baron and the Black Coats did to our families, and if *that's* keeping them safe—" He swallowed hard.

"If that's how you feel, why did you come to fight at all?" Donovan asked.

"No choice. Any man who refused was condemned on the spot and hung for being ensnared by the Evil One. A man isn't much good to his family once he's dead. And it wouldn't have done any good to try to slip away at night because the rest of the army is just a few days behind us, and the Black Coat said the Witch's Hammer himself is leading them."

"If that's true, why did your troops attack us now?" Liam asked.

The man shrugged. "Don't know. They weren't for telling us much. But the lads and I talked it over last night and decided that if you were against the Black Coats you had to be a good man, and it wasn't right to be fighting against you. So we decided we wouldn't raise a hand against your people and we'd surrender as quick as we could." He shuddered. "Nobody expected that lady witch to . . ." His voice trailed off.

Liam rubbed his forehead, trying to soothe the headache building behind his eyes. "I've never had prisoners before. I'm not sure what to do with you."

The man leaned forward. "There's work to be done, isn't there? Your people can't do all the work and get ready for the fight?"

Liam frowned. "You want to work for me?"

"We're farmers, most of us. We can chop wood, take care of livestock. Baron . . . Baron, you have to win. You have to. You can't give us back what our baron and the Black Coats took from us, but we want Sylvalan to be what it used to be. We don't want to be afraid of what might happen to our wives or our sisters or our mothers anytime a guard rides by. We don't want to be afraid anymore. If you win, you can force the barons to change things back to the way they were before the Black Coats came."

"I'll think about it," Liam said. "That's all for now."

The man nodded and walked to the door, the Fae guards behind him. When he reached the door, he looked back. "Baron? We didn't raise a hand against your people. But if you give us back our weapons, we'll fight alongside them when the Witch's Hammer comes."

The door closed behind the prisoner and guards. Liam leaned back in his chair and closed his eyes.

"I'll send out messengers to warn the Clans east of here," Varden said. "Won't be enough Fae to stand against an army, not alone, but if they can get down the shining road in time, they may be able to save the witches in the Old Places and make sure a few less men arrive at Willowsbrook."

"What makes you think they'll listen now when they never did before?" Liam asked.

"Your sister is entertaining the Huntress and you ask me that?" Varden smiled grimly. "I doubt there's a Clan in Sylvalan that wants Lady Selena looking in their direction—even more so when they find out what happened here today." The smile faded. He shifted uneasily. "Besides . . . we're to blame for the Black Coats."

Liam straightened up and stared at Varden.

"What are you talking about?" Donovan snapped.

"The Black Coat almost escaped. He was wounded but he got away and got caught by Squire Thurston and the men the squire had gathered to come here to help you."

"How could a wounded man get away from a group of armed men?" Liam asked, wondering why Varden looked so sick.

"He'd almost persuaded them to let him go when some of my men rode up. The Inquisitor's Gift of persuasion works well on humans, but it doesn't work on the Fae. We've the same gift, you see."

Donovan sank into the chair in front of the desk. "Inquisitor's Gift of persuasion? They can *persuade* someone to believe what they want them to believe?"

"They can. But since the gift comes from the Fae, we're better at it—and we persuaded the Black Coat to tell us a few things."

"Varden, you make no sense." A sick feeling churned in Liam's belly.

"He makes a great deal of sense," Donovan said slowly, his eyes fixed on Varden. "He's talking about magic, Liam. The Fae's kind of magic. Which means the Inquisitors . . ."

"Are part Fae," Varden said bitterly. He shook his head. "I never left a child in the human world, but I know plenty of men who enjoyed a girl until he'd filled her belly and then left her and never looked back. Among the Fae, a man sires a child, but it's the woman's Clan who raises it. But that's not the way in the human world, and we understood that once—at least, understood it enough to provide gifts and bestow favors on the woman's family so that having a child by a Fae Lord wasn't something to be ashamed of. But things changed, and the Fae started abandoning the woman and child, making both outcasts among their own people. Outcast children, unwanted by either race, until someone recognized they had a power that could be shaped into a weapon."

"Mother be merciful," Donovan said. "And some of those children would have been born of witches."

Varden nodded. "Fae Lords always found the women who lived in the Old Places appealing, even if we never understood who those women were."

"You provided the vessels for the Master Inquisitor to fill with his own fever of destruction," Liam said. "Your people can shoulder the blame for abandoning the children and the women who bore them, Varden, but you didn't shape them into what they've become."

"Which begs the question," Donovan said. "If the Master Inquisitor was able to recognize a power he could shape to his will, what, exactly, is *he*?"

Silence.

Liam stared at Donovan.

Do no harm.

Varden swore under his breath and turned away.

"Witch's Hammer," Liam said quietly. "Does he hate what he once loved?"

"Or what he once wanted to love him?" Donovan countered. "The son of a witch whose bloodline also carried the magic of the Fae?"

"Whatever he is, he's not just a human," Varden said, turning back to look at them.

"No," Donovan agreed, "he's not just a human."

Do no harm.

Liam suddenly stood up, unable to stay in that room anymore. He wanted, *needed,* to see Breanna, to feel grounded again in that blend of practicality and power, that promise that being something more than just a human wouldn't turn him into something monstrous.

"I'd better see to my guest," he said as he restrained himself from bolting for the door.

As he opened the door, he heard Donovan ask, "What happened to the Black Coat?"

And Varden's heavy reply, "Baron, your people and mine are just getting to know each other and neither side feels easy yet. It's better not to ask about some things."

Out of the study and down the hall to stand at the parlor's closed door. Liam took a couple of deep breaths to steady himself.

"You won't find out anything until you open the door," Donovan said, coming up beside him.

Bracing himself for another encounter, Liam opened the door, took two steps inside the room, and stopped. The table was strewn with tea things and a large bowl of water.

"Look," Breanna said, giving him a sloppy smile. "It's Liam. And he's wearing his baron's face."

Selena looked blearily at the men. "How can you tell?"

"I'm his sister. I can tell. And if you don't believe me, I will phoof you." Breanna struggled into an upright position. *"Phoof."*

A gust of wind lifted Selena's hair.

"Well," Selena said. "I'll phoof you back. *Phoof."*

A gust of wind blew Breanna's hair around her face.

They both collapsed in their seats, giggling.

Gwenn stared sadly at the bowl of water. "I can't phoof. I just burble."

The water in the bowl rose in the center, creating a small fountain that . . . burbled.

Donovan just shook his head as he walked around the couch to get a good look at his wife. "What have you been drinking?"

"Tea," Gwenn said, spoiling the prim tone with a hiccup.

Donovan picked up the cup and sniffed. "This isn't tea."

"It's in a teacup. Therefore, it is tea."

Donovan put the cup down, kissed his wife's forehead, and picked her up. "Come on, Gwenny, you need to take a little nap now."

"Don't want any chicken soup," Gwenn said, pouting.

"Just a little nap." Donovan carried her out of the room.

Liam looked at the two women who were staring rather owlishly back at him and raked his fingers through his hair. If anyone had asked him what he'd expected to find when he walked into the room, three tipsy witches wasn't it. What was he supposed to do with these two?

"Well," Breanna said, slowly getting to her feet. "I'd better get home and give Gran a hand with things." She took a step forward and teetered.

Liam caught her, wrapping one arm around her waist.

Selena stood up. "And I'd better . . . do something, too." She took a couple of tottering steps and fell against him, almost sending the three of them to the floor.

"The only thing either of you is going to do is take a nap," Liam said sternly, trying to turn them around to head them toward the door.

"Oh, phoof," Breanna said.

"No more phoofing," Liam said.

"Do you have children?" Selena asked.

When he turned to look at her, he realized all it would take was bending his head just a little to indulge in a kiss. Heat washed through him. "No, I don't have children."

"Funny. You sound just like my father."

Liam sighed. "Come along, you two."

He'd finally gotten them into the hall when someone pounded on the front door. Suddenly, Varden was there, an arrow nocked in his bow before Sloane could reach for the door.

As soon as Sloane opened the door, a Fae woman rushed inside. The man with her, seeing Varden, grabbed her and pulled her behind him, shielding her from the arrow.

"It's Gwynith," Selena said. "You missed tea," she added—and hiccuped.

"Lady Selena?" Gwynith stepped away from her escort. "Are you all right? I waited for you at the Old Place, but when you didn't return . . ." She frowned. "Selena?"

"She needs a nap," Liam said.

"Yes, I can see that." Gwynith hurried over to slip Selena's arm across her shoulders. "I'll help you—" She looked at Liam.

"She's using my mother's room. Upstairs."

Gwynith sighed. "Stairs. All right then. Up we go."

Selena balked at the foot of the stairs. "I won't take a nap unless you promise to do something."

"Whatever I can," Gwynith replied.

"Tell the Sleep Sister I don't want to dream tonight."

"I'll tell her, Selena."

"Do you know where she is?"

"No, but I'll tell her anyway."

Hoping that wasn't supposed to make sense, Liam half carried Breanna up the stairs, paused long enough to point out his mother's room to Gwynith, then led his tipsy witch to Brooke's room.

He dumped her on the bed and knelt down to remove her boots.

"It hurts, Liam," Breanna said quietly.

He looked up, wondering how undoing her boot laces could hurt. Then he looked into her eyes and realized she wasn't quite as tipsy as he'd thought.

"It hurts," she said again. She pressed a fist over her heart. "In here. What Selena did, she did knowingly, but that doesn't mean it didn't hurt her to break our creed. We're all going to dance on a knife's edge until this war is over, and some of us will be cut to the bone. We needed to forget that for a little while. Selena most of all."

"I understand." He got her settled, tucked a quilt around her, and kissed her the same way he would have kissed Brooke—comfort and love. "Get some sleep."

When he stepped back into the hallway, he saw Donovan leaning against the wall, waiting for him.

"At least they're cheerful when they're tipsy," Donovan said.

Liam rubbed his hands over his face. "I wish we'd joined them."

"Are you going to tell them what Varden said?"

Tell the Huntress. That's what Donovan really meant.

"Tomorrow," Liam said. "We've all dealt with enough today." He walked to the stairs, feeling much older than he'd felt that morning.

Chapter 28

waxing moon

"S top, Minstrel."

The horse has more brains than I do today, Aiden thought as Minstrel moved out of the line of horses to avoid bringing all the huntsmen behind him to a stop.

"Aiden?"

It was worry that made Lyrra's voice sound sharp as she maneuvered her horse out of the line to join him. Or, perhaps, it was his own fretfulness and embarrassment that made him hear sharpness where there was none. It wasn't easy for a man to be dependent on someone else to feed him and help him take care of natural functions.

He couldn't use his hands. The Clan healer had lightly wrapped them in gauze that morning to protect them, but now the bandages felt too tight.

"Aiden?" Lyrra said as she brought her mare alongside Minstrel. "What's wrong?"

"The bandages are too tight. I have to get them off. Please, Lyrra."

Sheridan and Morphia rode back to join them.

"What's wrong?" Sheridan demanded.

"Aiden says the bandages are too tight," Lyrra replied. "I think he needs to rest."

I'm not a child. I can speak for myself. But he felt like a child for whom the adults had to slow their pace. Wasn't that why Ashk had left with some of the huntsmen early that morning? She planned to pass through two Clan territories before going down a shining road and riding on to deliver Padrick's letter to one of the midland barons whose county bordered the southern part of Sylvalan. The rest of them, led by Sheridan, were to travel at an easier pace, go down the same shining road, and find a place to camp in the Old Place that anchored that road.

He knew she was riding extra miles so that he wouldn't have to, doubling back to join them after delivering Padrick's letter instead of going on to reach the next Old Place. She hadn't suggested that he remain at a Clan house until he healed, and he was grateful for that. But if he slowed her down too much, she would never reach Willowsbrook by the full moon.

Sheridan studied Aiden's hands and frowned. "The bandages do look tighter than they did this morning. Can you ride on a bit further, Aiden? Some of the men have scouted up ahead. There's a good stream and pasture for the horses. We can set up camp there."

"I can ride awhile longer," Aiden said.

Sheridan and Morphia rode back to the head of the line. Huntsmen reined in to let Lyrra and Aiden slip into the line.

Aiden slumped in the saddle, his hands crossed over his chest. He couldn't even rest them lightly on the saddle for balance as he'd done that morning.

He wasn't sure how long they continued to ride. He'd begun worrying about his harp, carefully secured to one of the packhorses. He craved the feel of it as a thirsty man craved water. Would his fingers ever dance over the strings again? That morning, his hands hadn't looked that bad. The skin was red and more blisters had formed, but they hadn't looked bad. Lyrra had been so relieved by the healer's brisk assurance that he would be fine in a few days that he hadn't told her the look of his hands was a lie. He *knew* Lucian's fire had damaged him under the skin. He could *feel* it. And now his hands seemed to be straining against the confinement of the gauze bandages.

Finally they reached the place where Sheridan had decided to set up camp. After praising Minstrel for keeping him safe in the saddle, Aiden stood out of the way, pushing aside impatience while the others took care of the necessary chores.

He was ready to use his teeth on the bandages' knots when Ashk and her escorts rode into camp. Seeing her so grim and exhausted shamed him into patience. Her brusque "Later" when Sheridan asked if there was news warned everyone that whatever Ashk had to tell them wasn't good.

"Now, then," Lyrra said with a brisk cheerfulness that struck

Aiden as being off-key, "let's unwrap the bandages and let your hands breathe for a bit."

He tried not to flinch as she tugged at the knots. He tried not to see the worry in her eyes as she realized how large his hands looked. And he tried to deny the stab of fear when she got the bandages off his left hand—and she screamed.

"What is it? What's wrong?" Ashk demanded, rushing up to them. She stared at Aiden's left hand before quickly unwrapping the bandages on his right. "Mother's mercy."

They were so swollen, they didn't look like hands anymore. The skin was stretched so tight, he thought it would split open if he tried to move a finger.

I'm going to lose my hands. What kind of Bard can I be without my hands?

"Sit down, Aiden," Ashk said, leading him to hollowed log. "Sit down."

Blind to everything but his hands, he paid no attention to the crows cawing a warning until Ashk's snarl startled him.

"Riders coming," Sheridan said, reaching for his bow and arrows.

"Our men," Ashk replied, moving forward. "And someone with them."

The huntsmen rode up casually, reining in a few feet from Ashk. The dark-haired woman with them placed a soothing hand on the neck of her dark horse, who pawed the ground and laid his ears back. The gold pentagram around the woman's neck flashed in the sun.

"Blessings of the day to you," Ashk said.

"Blessings of the day," the woman replied.

"The lady has been traveling," one of the huntsmen said. "Alone." He packed all of his disapproval into that word.

The dark horse snorted.

The woman's lips twitched. "Not quite alone."

"We suggested that she camp with us tonight," the huntsmen said.

Ashk studied the woman. "You're most welcome to share our camp. You really shouldn't be traveling alone. Not anymore. And not any farther south."

The woman closed her eyes. "I know. Blood stains the land. The Mother drinks it and weeps bitter tears." She shook her head and opened her eyes. "I would be pleased to share your camp tonight."

"Come and be welcome," Ashk said.

When the woman dismounted and took a step toward Ashk, the dark horse nipped her sleeve and tried to tug her back.

"Fox, behave. We're guests." She untied her saddlebags, slung them over one shoulder, then grabbed the horse's ear when he tugged at the saddlebags. "Let the Fae Lords take off your saddle and bridle so you can have a nice roll and play with the other horses. I'm staying right here."

Snorting with every step to let them all know he wasn't happy, Fox allowed the men to lead him away.

"I'm Ashk, from Bretonwood."

"I am Rhyann."

Before Ashk could continue the introductions, Rhyann dropped her saddlebags, walked over to Aiden, and knelt in front of him, studying his hands.

"Do you have any healing skills?" Ashk asked.

Rhyann's fingers hovered over his hands. "Fire trapped in earth. Water seeks to quench it, but is trapped between its banks and presses on the earth it seeks to protect." She paused a moment. "How did this happen?"

"The Lord of Fire did this to him."

The cold anger in Ashk's voice didn't chill Aiden as much as what he saw in Rhyann's woodland eyes before she turned to look at Ashk.

"One of the wiccanfae did this?" Rhyann asked softly.

"I doubt Lucian wants to think of himself as wiccanfae," Ashk said.

"It doesn't matter what he wants to think. What matters is what he *is*," Rhyann replied sharply. She looked toward the stream. "Sweet, flowing water. Come with me." She rose, gripped Aiden's arm, and pulled him to his feet.

With Ashk, Sheridan, Morphia, and a silently weeping Lyrra trailing behind them, she led Aiden to the stream. She took off her boots and stockings, waded into the stream, and knelt down facing the bank.

"Kneel there." She pointed to the bank in front of her.

Ashk and Sheridan held his arms to support him as he sank to his knees.

Rhyann grabbed his wrists and pulled his hands into the

water. She closed her eyes, and said, "Fire, release your hold on
the earth of flesh and bone. Give your heat to the water that flows
free. Water, seep up from the banks of skin and join with the
water that flows from the Mother. Earth, give your strength to
flesh and bone to mend what has been harmed. As I will, so mote
it be."

Aiden felt power gather around him. Heat poured out of his
palms, constantly washed away by the stream's current until
there was no more heat. He felt sweat bead on his skin, rising up
and flowing away. He felt a different kind of warmth flow into
his hands, traveling slowly from his wrists, where Rhyann held
him, all the way to his fingertips. When that warmth faded, the
power faded with it.

Rhyann lifted his hands out of the stream. "Can you move
your fingers?"

Aiden stared at his hands. Normal hands. Even the blisters
were gone, healed. He cautiously curled his fingers until he made
loose fists. His hands felt tight, tender. He would have to work
them slowly to regain the dexterity he needed to play the harp.
But he *would* play again. He was certain of that.

Tears filled his eyes as he uncurled his hands. "Thank you."

Rhyann smiled at him, then accepted Sheridan's help out of
the stream. After picking up her boots and stockings, she followed Sheridan and Morphia back to the camp.

Aiden felt a hand on his shoulder. He looked at Ashk, surprised as much by the tears in her eyes as by the delighted smile.

"I'll play again," he said, his voice rough.

"That you will, Bard. That you will." Ashk kissed his cheek
and helped him stand.

When he turned toward the camp, he saw Lyrra standing
there. He took a step toward her. She ran into his arms.

"There was nothing I could do," she said, still weeping. "If I
could have traded my hands for yours, I would have done it, but
there was nothing I could do."

"Lyrra, my love, even if you could have offered, I wouldn't
have let you." He ran one hand over her hair, thrilled by the feel
of it. "Come on, now. No more tears."

Lyrra eased back and rubbed her cheeks dry. "No more tears."

With their arms around each other, they walked back to camp.

*   *   *

Ashk waited until the evening meal was done. Seeing Aiden's hands had shaken her. Seeing Rhyann restore his hands had shaken her in a different way. She knew the pentagram Rhyann wore gave her a comfort that might well be illusion. The witch sitting beside her was a stranger—and a powerful one. Since they were most likely traveling in the same direction for a while, she needed to know just how powerful Rhyann was—and she needed to find a way of asking without giving offense.

"It's time, Ashk," Aiden said.

Yes, it was time. Ashk sighed, allowing herself that one indulgence before she sat up straight. She had to believe they could win. Despite what she'd heard from both the baron and the Fae, she had to believe.

"An army is marching toward the southern end of the Mother's Hills. They've already crushed two counties when the barons there tried to stand against them. Our forces are still too scattered. The barons are gathering and leading their men at best possible speed, but they may not have time to come together as an army of their own."

"What about the Fae?" Aiden asked.

Ashk smiled grimly. "I don't know if it's fear of me or the Huntress, or if they've finally seen the enemy in a way that makes the danger to Sylvalan clear even to the most stubborn among them, but they're all on the move as well. I just don't know if they'll be in time to hold the Inquisitors' army." *Or defeat it.*

"The storms will slow down the Black Coats' army," Rhyann said quietly.

Ashk looked up at the clear night sky. "What storms?"

"Rain will turn roads into rivers of mud," Rhyann said, her voice sounding dreamy in a way that made Ashk shiver. "Creeks and rivers will rise, becoming impassable, and stone that had held a bridge strong for a hundred years will tumble into water. Wind will sing so fiercely no other voice will be heard. And lightning will be fire's steed. Yes, the storms will slow them down, and your people will have time to gather."

"What makes you certain there will be storms?" Aiden asked.

Rhyann smiled at him. "I can taste them on the air. I felt them in the water. The Grandmothers will not let the Inquisitors harm Sylvalan."

"They didn't do anything to stop the Inquisitors before now,"

Ashk said, suddenly feeling like she was standing on a cliff that could crumble beneath her at any moment.

"Did the Fae do anything before now?" Rhyann countered.

"No," Aiden replied. "To our shame, we did not."

Rhyann brushed her hair back. "The wiccanfae did not ask for help, and the House of Gaian doesn't usually interfere in the lives of others."

Aiden shifted uneasily. "The witches who died by the Black Coats' hands didn't ask for help because they didn't know there was anyone they *could* ask."

Rhyann nodded. "They have forgotten much of who and what they are. Just as the Fae have forgotten who and what they are."

Ashk stiffened. "Meaning?"

Rhyann gave her a considering look. "Do you not know the story of how the Fae came to be? It is an old story. Have your Grandmothers never told you?"

Chills raced through Ashk. "No, I've never heard the story. Have you?" She looked at Lyrra, who shook her head.

"Do you know the story?" Aiden asked, leaning forward. "Could you tell us?"

"Do you really want to know?" Rhyann replied.

"Why wouldn't we?" Ashk wanted to throw another log on the fire, but she doubted it would ease the chill inside her.

"Because you're the Hunter," Rhyann said gently.

Ashk twisted around to stare at the witch. "Why would that make a difference? And how did you know?"

Rhyann smiled. "You said the Fae feared you and the Huntress. Since the Huntress is justice and will not harm those who do no harm, you must be the Hunter, the one who rules the Fae."

"I don't rule the Fae. Not in the way you mean."

"Yes, you do. Because the Hunter was the oldest, the strongest, the first. And it was the Hunter's love of a witch that created the Fae.

Long ago, there was the Great Mother. She was earth and water. She was air and fire. Everything that lived depended on her for food and shelter, and while she was not always benevolent, she was generous with her bounty and the world thrived.

But the animals and birds and creatures of the sea and stream were not the only ones who were nurtured by the Great Mother.

There were people who lived in the long ridge of hills, and they had a gift of sensing the Mother in a way other creatures could not. They became Her vessels, drawing in the power of Her branches and breathing it out again. They became the Sons and Daughters of the House of Gaian.

In that long ago time, there were also spirits in the woods. Small spirits . . . and powerful spirits. They had no shape of their own, so sometimes they slipped into a living thing to enjoy the feel of wind on leaves or water through gills or the warmth of the sun on a furred body. Many of the spirits remained in a small piece of the woods or in the meadows around it, needing the familiar. Others wandered the land, residing in a part of the woods for a season or two before moving on.

One of those wanderers was a very powerful spirit, the oldest and strongest of them all. He did not need a host body in order to have form because he had the power to draw on the branches of the Great Mother to create a cloak of flesh. He needed to slip into a host body once in order to learn its shape, but after that, he could change at will. His favorite form was a stag, but he also walked the woods as a wolf or rode the air as a hawk. The other spirits quickly learned that when he walked as a stag, he was simply there to live among them. But when he appeared as hawk or wolf, he hunted—and when he hunted, he was feared.

One day, he had wandered close to the long ridge of hills and caught unfamiliar scents on the wind. So he followed them, curious to see what kind of creature smelled that way.

They walked on two legs and lived in strange stone burrows above the ground. Smoke rose from the burrows, a warning of fire, but he saw no fire that would be a danger to the woods. The ground was turned in a way he'd never seen before, and plants grew in even rows.

For many days, safely hidden at the edge of the woods, he watched the creatures. Then one morning, just after dawn, he approached the turned earth and nibbled one of the plants. Pleased by the taste, he ate more, forgetting to be cautious—until he heard something running toward him and harsh sounds filled the air.

The scent of female filled his nostrils and delighted him in a way he didn't understand. What he did understand was the sounds she was making were like snarls and growls. The female was not pleased. When she picked up a stone and threw it at him, he bounded back into the woods.

But he kept coming back, day after day, to watch the female and her mate and the two small ones. And because he remained there, other spirits became curious and wandered to that part of the world to watch the strange creatures.

She danced with the earth. She sang to the wind. She was not of the woods, but she understood the woods. Her joy filled the air with a rich sweetness. Her anger was the sharp edge of a storm.

He watched her through the turn of the seasons, followed her when she walked through the woods gathering nuts and berries and plants, followed her mate when he hunted or gathered wood.

Most of the spirits were content to watch the female and her mate, but there were some who resented the two-legged creatures coming into the woods, some who were filled with a darker nature and preferred to inhabit host animals that could express that nature.

One day, that old spirit felt the presence of one of those angry spirits moments before he heard a startled cry, smelled blood. He ran toward the sounds and smells—and saw the female's mate on the ground, being gored by the angry spirit in the form of a wild pig. As the pig ripped open the male's flesh with its tusks, he felt a fury toward his own kind that he'd never felt before. He lashed out with his power and ripped spirit from flesh, destroying both.

As the other spirits who were nearby fled from his rage, he stared at the male on the ground. Releasing his stag form, he flowed as spirit into the body of the male.

Death surrounded him, and another spirit, another will strove with all its remaining strength to reach him, touch him. Afraid of Death, he still reached out for that other spirit. Knowledge and feelings flooded into him, then pushed him away.

He drew on the branches of the Mother to create a cloak of flesh that matched the new shape he'd learned from the dying male. As he knelt beside the man, the whispered sounds became words.

"Please look after her. Help her. Please."

When the flesh no longer lived, he walked to the stone burrow—cottage—and stood at the edge of the garden until the woman noticed him. Fear filled her face as she stared at him. He didn't know enough words yet to tell her about her mate, so he *pointed toward the woods and started walking back the way he'd come. She followed him, and her young followed her.*

Her grief shuddered through the woods when she saw the body of her mate. Her tears turned the streams bitter. Wind keened her heartache.

For a while, she clung to her young, grieving with them. Finally, she wiped her face and called the Great Mother to take the body of her mate.

Earth shifted, moving under her mate's body until the flesh sank deep into the ground. Earth shifted again, covering flesh.

When it was done, the woman took her young and walked out of the woods.

For days, he watched her but kept his distance. She feared him now that he had taken a form like her own. How could he tell her she would be safe in the woods when he couldn't get close enough to use the man words?

Perhaps . . . Perhaps he had done something wrong with the form and that was why she feared him?

He found a pool of water on a still day and stared for a long time at the face looking back at him.

The woods looked back at him. The wild places of the world. A human face, but not completely human. Never completely human. The small pointed ears still looked like a stag's ears—and small antlers rose from his brow.

Discouraged, he stayed away from her cottage for several days.

Then, one day at dawn, he saw rabbits feeding in her garden and chased them away, understanding now that these were the kinds of plants she and her young needed to eat, and if the rabbits ate them, she would not have enough to eat over the winter.

When he chased the last rabbit away, he turned and saw her watching him. He struggled to say the man words, hoping she would hear him before she ran away.

"I did not harm him."

She smiled at him, and he felt the warmth of the sun again.

"I know," she said. Then she went back into her cottage.

Slowly she got used to him. Slowly she began talking to him while she worked in her garden.

One day, when he brought her a rabbit he'd hunted for her, she invited him into her cottage, gave him clothes that had belonged to her mate, and let him eat with her young.

She called him Fae, which meant Other.

The other spirits called him Hunter, because now he walked through the woods with a different purpose.

Eventually the cottage became home to him.

Eventually her feelings for him ripened, and one night she took him to her bed and taught him the human way of mating.

Eventually, when he watched her suckle the child that had come from his seed, he knew he would never go back to being what he had been.

And when the other spirits saw his joy, they, too, wanted to know this form. And slowly they learned. And slowly they changed, becoming spirit always cloaked in flesh, but flesh that retained the gift of changing into a form that belonged to the woods. Some of the smaller spirits became the Small Folk. Other spirits became the Fae. And as other Sons and Daughters of the House of Gaian came down from the hills to cherish other parts of the Great Mother, the Fae lived with them, learned from them, mated with them. Some of those children were witches, vessels of the Mother. Some were Fae, with their gift of changing form and their ties to the woods. And some were called wiccanfae because they had gifts from the Mother as well as the woods.

The Hunter still rules the woods. That old, powerful spirit lives on in flesh of his flesh, blood of his blood, bone of his bone. It is still the guardian and predator, the Green Lord and Hunter, the one who commands the other spirits of the woods.

That is the way it was, a long time ago. And that is the way it still is.

Ashk felt a tear trickle down her cheek. She wiped it away, unsure if Rhyann had just given her a gift or a burden.

"It's just an old story," Rhyann said quietly.

Ashk sniffed. "Do you believe that?"

"No," Rhyann admitted. "I think it's truth handed down as story so that it would be remembered."

"And as much as I'd like to believe it's just a story, I can't dismiss the truth of it, not when I feel the power inside me, not when I know—I *do* command all the gifts of the woods. I *can* destroy the Fae, stripping them of any gift that comes from the woods."

"And you can command the woods to fight back and defend itself against those who want to destroy it."

Ashk turned her head and studied Rhyann. "What do you

command, Rhyann? What branch of the Mother is your primary gift?"

"All of them."

Stunned silence.

Rhyann shrugged. "It is not common among us, but it's not that rare, either."

"Among us," Aiden said. "Where are you from?" He shook his head. "There's only one place you *can* be from. The Mother's Hills."

Rhyann nodded. "I am a Daughter of the House of Gaian. I come from the Mother's Hills."

Ashk licked her dry lips. "Do you know a witch named Selena?"

Rhyann laughed. "I know her well. She's my sister."

Another silence.

Ashk felt as if the ground had suddenly dropped out from under her.

"I had a dream that fire had silenced music," Rhyann said. "That's why I've been traveling. I knew I couldn't stop the fire, but I could help the music." She smiled at Aiden. "Now my journey is done, so I'll head north to join Selena."

Ashk stared at the fire. "I'm to meet her before the full moon."

Aiden shook his head. "We'll never make it to Willowsbrook. Since they're already fighting in the south, we can't chance using the bridges and the shining roads. We could ride down in the middle of a battle or become trapped if the shining road closes."

"I know." Ashk rubbed her hands over her face. "I know. But what choice do we have? There's no telling how many Clans are left on the eastern side of the Mother's Hills. If we can't get huntsmen from the midland Clans to Willowsbrook to fight the third arm of the Inquisitors' army, they'll drive right through the center and crush our fighters from behind."

"In order to drive through the center, they would have to go through the Mother's Hills," Rhyann said. "They'll never get through the hills. But you can use those roads to get to Willowsbrook."

"I can't bring an army of Fae through the Mother's Hills."

"Why not, since they're traveling to defend the land?"

"Because your kind have the power to destroy the world!"

Ashk bit her lip. Too tired to be cautious, to walk carefully.

"That's right," Rhyann said softly. "We can. That's why we hold so strongly to our creed to do no harm. But the Mother isn't always benevolent—and neither are Her Sons and Daughters. If you fear us so much that you'll stand aside instead of taking a road offered—" She jumped up and turned as if to walk away.

Ashk grabbed Rhyann's arm and stood up to face her. "I'm tired, and I spoke in haste. And, frankly, having to meet Selena frightens me."

Rhyann tipped her head. "What is your other form?"

"I'm a shadow hound."

"So is Selena. So it's simple, isn't it? You snarl at her, she snarls at you, and then the two of you go off and bite someone else."

A laugh burst out of Ashk. "Fair enough. Are you offering to be our escort through the Mother's Hills?"

"Since it appears I'm going the same way, I could do that."

They settled back around the fire. This time there was no tension in the silence.

Ashk was about to suggest they turn in when Lyrra said, "If the Hunter is the oldest spirit of the woods, I wonder who the next oldest is?"

"Can't you guess?" Rhyann replied.

Ashk suddenly felt the darkest shadows of the woods brush against her. She shivered. "The Gatherer. Death's Mistress."

Rhyann nodded. "Or Death's Sister, as she's called in some stories. Like the Hunter, hers is an old and powerful spirit. And like the Hunter, hers is a dual nature."

"Why?"

"Because Death's Sister is both mercy and destruction."

Ashk said nothing. She simply unrolled her sleeping bag, pulled off her boots, and settled herself for sleep. With her eyes closed, she listened to the quiet sounds of the people around her, knew when her companions around the fire finally fell asleep.

She opened her eyes and stared at the night sky.

Death's Sister. Mercy and destruction.

She thought of Ari and Neall—and what could happen if the Lightbringer reached Bretonwood.

Find him, Morag. Find him . . . and do what needs to be done.

Chapter 29

waxing moon

She chased him relentlessly, and still he remained ahead of her. He had the advantage. When he tired of running in his other form, he changed back and demanded a horse, which that Clan provided. The Fae ran to fetch him food and water, rushed to make up a comfortable bed for him to sleep in for a few hours. Anything for the Lightbringer.

But for the Gatherer . . .

The Clans had no horses to spare. No, none at all. And no one could be spared from his duties to look after her dark horse or bring her food. No one at all. So she fed and watered the dark horse, unsaddled and groomed him. She stumbled to the Clan house's kitchen, reeking of sweat and reeling from exhaustion, to devour whatever food was easily available. Sometimes she collapsed in the dark horse's stall and slept for a couple of hours, but the dreams chased her as relentlessly as she pursued the Lightbringer, driving her away from any possible rest until she saddled the dark horse and headed out again.

She did what she could to spare the dark horse. He had courage and stamina, but he'd already made a hard journey across Sylvalan. So she changed to her raven form and flew until she thought muscles would tear. She walked beside him to spare him carrying the extra weight. And she rode when fear of what she might find at Bretonwood overwhelmed her concern that she was ruining a good horse.

So she chased the Lightbringer relentlessly—and the dreams relentlessly chased her.

Chapter 30

waxing moon

Dianna cantered over the bridge to the next Clan territory.

The new Huntress had turned the Fae into panicked children scrambling for a crumb of approval. Oh, they acted pleased to see her when she arrived at a Clan house, but they didn't have time to talk with her, barely had time to show her to a guest room and have the Clan healer look at her arm. So much to do. Hurry hurry. Scramble scramble.

The Black Coats had sent whole armies against the humans in Sylvalan. Why should the Fae care about the humans? The fewer of them, the better. They'd caused nothing but trouble lately. Just like the witches.

It was the Black Coats' fault. All of it. *They* were the ones who started all the trouble in Sylvalan. At the core of it, *they* were the reason she was now shunned by her own Clan and cautiously welcomed by others. If *they* hadn't come, she wouldn't have been trapped at Brightwood, wouldn't have lost the challenge to that usurping bitch.

If you'd listened to Morag, Aiden, and Lyrra a year ago, you could have gathered the huntsmen from the Clans and driven the Black Coats out of Sylvalan. You could have been the one who protected the witches and the Old Places . . . and Tir Alainn. You would still be the Lady of the Moon, and the Fae would still love you . . . as they used to love you.

Maybe she *had* been mistaken about a few things, but she'd done her best for the Fae. *For the Fae.* They didn't seem to remember that. They certainly hadn't wanted to live in the Old Places or deal with humans or do any of the things they were now scurrying to do.

Her pale mare stumbled over something, almost fell. Mist

suddenly enclosed them. Dianna slowed the animal to a trot while fear produced jagged spikes to scrape her nerves.

She should have reached the other side of the bridge by now. At the very least, she should be seeing the glow from the arch that indicated the end of the bridge. And . . . why was she riding through mist? There was no mist *on* the bridges.

But there had been. Thin wisps of it that swirled around her mare's knees. She remembered that now.

She dug her heels into the mare's sides, desperate to get clear of the mist.

A few strides later, the mist thinned. A few strides after that, she was galloping over flat green land—and the Clan house was no more than a few minutes away.

Reining in the mare, she looked back.

Mist. Swirling, spreading, devouring.

When the mare stumbled . . . She must have stumbled at the end of the bridge, where it connects to this Clan's territory. Which means I've been riding through mist in Tir Alainn.

She wheeled the mare and galloped toward the Clan house, then changed direction to intercept the stream of people hurrying toward the markers that indicated the shining road.

As she reached the markers, she reined in and shouted, "What's happening?"

A woman holding a baby stared at her with terror-blank eyes. "The road is closing! We have to get away *now*!"

Two boys shoved the woman, causing her to stagger against Dianna's mare. They continued pushing and shoving through the crowd in front of the markers until they'd gotten clear and were running down the shining road.

A moment later, a male voice shouted hoarsely, "Go back! Go back! Mother's mercy, you can't go down there!"

The pain in that voice silenced the Fae crowded in front of the markers. And in that silence, Dianna thought she heard faint screams.

A few moments later, a man lurched into sight, sweating and struggling to get up the last few steps of the shining road. He had an arrow in one shoulder, another arrow in his thigh. Two men near the front of the crowd dropped their bundles and rushed to help their wounded Clansman.

Dianna's heart pounded as the wounded Clansman was helped past the markers.

"Stand back now!" an older female voice ordered. *"Stand back."*

There were mutters and low curses as people trod on the toes of those behind them in an effort to obey.

Seeing the woman who stepped into the cleared space around the wounded man, Dianna muttered a curse of her own. She'd forgotten this was Sorcha's Clan. The woman had always disapproved of the way the Fae interacted with the human world and never hesitated to say so. And Dianna had the feeling Sorcha hadn't really approved of her and Lucian becoming the leaders of the Fae, which is why she'd never felt comfortable around the old woman. But when Sorcha demanded obedience, she was obeyed, and that strength of will would help all of them now.

"What's happening down there?" Sorcha demanded.

"They're killing us," the wounded man gasped. "They're killing us. The Black Coats are down there *with an army of men.*"

Gasps and murmurs ran through the crowd.

"What about the huntsmen who were down there keeping watch on the Old Place?" Sorcha asked.

One tear spilled down the man's cheek before he closed his eyes. "Dead. Slaughtered. And the witches . . . I saw what the Black Coats did to the witches. *I saw.*"

A man's voice rose from the crowd. "The Black Coats couldn't have killed *all* the Fae. My *sister* went down the shining road with her children."

"Mine too!" another man's voice said. "I sent her down as soon as we saw the warning signs that the road was going to close. She *must* have gotten away."

The wounded man shook his head. "Dead. All dead. Women, children, babes, old men. The Black Coats didn't care. They were waiting at the end of the shining road. Just waiting for us with swords and bows. They killed all of them."

A woman cried out, "The shining road is fading!" Another cried, "The mist!"

Dianna twisted in the saddle. The mist was creeping across the land, a wall more formidible than any wall of stone could be. She twisted back around and stood in the stirrups to look at the road. It was flickering now, fading. When it vanished, the mist would consume everything. Everyone.

"No!" She threw herself out of the saddle, heedless of the

pain the movement caused in her arm, equally unaware that she'd shoved the woman with the babe to the ground in her haste. They would never find the bridges in all that mist, even if the bridges still existed. The shining road had to stay open long enough for them to escape.

Escape where? To a fast death rather than a slow one?

She didn't know, didn't care. She flung herself at the shining road, closing her left hand over that flickering shimmer.

Power flooded out of her, making her gasp. Down her arm, through her hand, flowing into the flickering golden air enclosed by her hand. Down, down, racing down until it touched something old, something that was still strong. The golden air stopped flickering as power flowed back up to her hand, her arm. Not filling her, not giving back as much as it took, but completing a circle.

More power flowed out of her, draining her strength before the circle of power sent it back. Different somehow when it came back. She could almost smell earth, almost hear the ominous rolls of thunder, almost feel the lash of rain that gave the land more nourishment than just water. Power, soaking back into the land, flowing back up to that bit of shining road to anchor Tir Alainn.

Gasping, weeping, she felt someone's arm around her shoulders, felt a hand close around her left wrist.

"That's enough now, Dianna. That's enough. You did well, darling girl. You did well."

With effort, she opened her hand. Watched it shake as she held it above a shining rope no more than three fingers wide. A Fae whose other form was a tiny whoo-it owl might be able to walk down that rope to the human world, but nothing else would be able to escape.

"You did well, Dianna," Sorcha said again. "You've given us a chance to survive."

Dianna just stared at the shining rope.

"Sorcha!" a man yelled. "The mist has stopped moving forward!"

She felt Sorcha's forehead rest on her shoulder for a moment.

"What do we do now?" a woman asked.

Sorcha slowly got to her feet. "We survive. That's what we do."

"How?" someone wailed.

Sorcha huffed. "We turn over some of the flower gardens and plant more vegetables. We turn the earth on some of the open land and plant grain, which will hopefully be able to feed the horses we keep. The cock and hens that were recently acquired in the human world for the cookpot will be kept for eggs, and if the cock does his duty, we'll get chicks from some of those eggs, and when they grow, we'll have more food. It will be hard for all of us, and it's going to be some time before any of us goes to bed with a full belly. But thanks to Dianna's gift, we still have an anchor to the human world—enough to keep our piece of Tir Alainn. If there are witches with the power to close a road, then they must also have the power to open one."

"How long will that take?" someone asked fearfully. "When will the Huntress come and free us?"

Sorcha shook her head. "The Huntress and the Hunter and all the Fae who are joining them to fight must defeat the armies the Black Coats have set against Sylvalan. They must drive the Black Coats and their followers out of the land. Until that is done, they cannot spare thought or strength for anything else. So we will wait until the shining road is opened again—and we will survive."

"The new Huntress is very powerful. She'll defeat the Black Coats." "With the Hunter joining the fight, it won't take long to rid Sylvalan of these creatures." "The shining road will be open again before the season changes."

Voices swirled around her. Hopeful. Fearful. It made no difference. Dianna stared at the shining rope. She heard Sorcha giving orders to take the wounded man to the Clan house, heard someone else say it was fortunate the Clan's healer hadn't gone down to the human world.

Voices swirled around her as the Fae slowly returned to the Clan house, still not realizing how much their lives had changed. It made no difference. She just stared at the shining rope.

"Come now, Dianna," Sorcha said with brisk kindness. She pulled and tugged until Dianna got stiffly to her feet. "You need to rest now. I'll have someone keep watch on the anchor to the human world. Never fear about that." She rested a hand on Dianna's cheek and smiled. "I don't know how you managed to cross that bridge or what brought you here today, but I'm thankful for it."

Dianna stared at the older woman. Tears filled her eyes.

"There now, girl, no need for tears. We'll survive. You'll see."

Blinded by tears, Dianna didn't resist when Sorcha led her to the Clan house.

No need for tears? Did the old fool actually thinking she was weeping out of relief—or even joy?

Survive. She'd fought against returning to Brightwood, fought against having to *survive* there. She'd thought of it as a cage, confining her to a place. A bright, rich place, despite the crowded rooms in the cottage. There was meat from the woods there, wood for the fire. She could have ridden with her shadow hounds to hunt for meat. With so much land within Brightwood's borders, she could have avoided riding through the crops her Clan had worked hard to plant and grow.

Petty anger had made her strike back at her own Clan. Petty anger had made her take and take and take because she felt her people wouldn't *give* enough to make up for her having to live in the human world. She'd wanted to live in Tir Alainn. She'd wanted to do what *she* wanted to do—as she'd always done.

Well, she was in the Fair Land now, being exactly what she'd sulked over being for her own Clan. Except there was no hope of escaping *this* cage until someone else decided to turn the key. Knowing that, unshakeably certain of that, she realized she hated Tir Alainn.

Chapter 31

waxing moon

Selena rode beside Liam, tucked in the middle of a company of human and Fae escorts. A few months ago, those same men wouldn't have considered riding together, would have met each other on the road with uneasiness and suspicion. Now there were murmurs of conversation, the occasional muffled laugh that said plainly enough that, despite the differences in how their peoples lived, there was also common ground.

As they crested the low rise that gave them a clear view of the land beyond the village, she reined in. So did Liam. A sharp whistle from one of the escorts behind them was sufficient warning to those who rode ahead that the company had halted.

"It would be better for my people if we could meet the enemy before they reach the village or the farms and estates around it," Liam said quietly as he studied the land. "But I doubt the enemy will accommodate my wishes."

"It isn't likely," Selena agreed. "But the land . . ." She closed her eyes. Connecting to the land here was as easy as breathing in and breathing out again. Did Liam realize that the people in his home village prospered so well because the magic that flowed out of Old Willowsbrook was so strong and far-reaching? Even here, miles from the Old Place, she could feel the ripples of it in the air, in the ground beneath Mistrunner's hooves. She would be able to taste it in the water. A celebration of life. The acknowledgment of harvest. The spiral dance that takes and gives back.

"Lady Selena?"

Liam's voice pulled her back to the here and now. She opened her eyes. "But the land will be our ally—and our weapon."

As soon as she said the words, she heard the low rumble of thunder, felt the sliver of cold air on the wind as the dark clouds raced overhead, coming out of the west from the Mother's Hills, shutting out the sun.

"We're in for a storm," Liam said.

Selena watched the clouds for a moment, then shook her head. "A soft rain. A farmer's rain, soaking in deep to nourish the crops. It will wet down the roads, making it easier to travel without all the dust. But when the storm reaches a place where there is no Mother's Daughter to greet it and ask it to be gentle, that's where it will break. Roads will turn to mud and creeks will run too high to cross. The Black Coats will struggle through the storm's wrath, and that will give us time."

"Time for what?" Liam asked with a trace of bitterness. "The barons from the neighboring counties have sent messages, promising men to help fight the Inquisitors, but there's no sign of those men. Other barons have declared themselves neutral, hoping to be spared if either army marches through their land—and hoping their estates will remain intact because, even if they didn't fight for the winning side, they didn't support the losing side, either. The Fae from the nearby Clans have sent men, but they're also guarding the Old Places to keep their Clan territories protected."

"Do you blame the Fae for that?" Selena asked, curious about this bitterness.

Liam shook his head. "No, I don't blame them. We've gotten more help from them than I ever expected, and they're more skilled with weapons than the farmers and merchants I can bring to the fight from the villages under my rule." He sighed. "But we've heard nothing from the midland barons, and without their support, we can't win. And even if they *are* gathering men and marching toward Willowsbrook, they'll have to fight their way here from either the north or the south, and that delay, and the loss of men, will work in favor of the Black Coats' army that's marching toward us."

"There is an alternate route," Selena said dryly. "There *are* roads through the Mother's Hills."

Liam looked at her. "Forgive me for saying this, but the Fae are afraid to enter the Mother's Hills, and anyone who has seen the power a witch can wield understands that fear. As for the humans . . . If I didn't have a sister who was a witch, I'd think long and hard about taking my men into those hills. I'd think long and hard about it anyway."

Selena dismissed the sharp pang beneath her breast. There were men at home who were just as handsome, just as intelligent. She knew as much about the gentry as she knew about the Fae, which wasn't much. The courtesy and interest he'd shown her could be nothing more than gentry manners. But the turn of conversation reminded her of the other reason she'd agreed to ride out with him.

She turned Mistrunner to head back the way they'd come. She waited until the escorts had turned and started back down the rise before signaling Mistrunner to follow them.

"I've offended you," Liam said, matching his gelding's pace to Mistrunner's.

Selena shook her head. "You merely said what the rest have been thinking. There *is* power among those of us who live in the Mother's Hills. But if you enter the land of the House of Gaian and do no harm, you will come to no harm." She smiled mischievously. "At least, not from the House of Gaian. We can make no promises for the wolves that live in the northern part of the hills or the wild pigs that live in the woodlands."

Liam stared at her for a moment, then smiled. "I suppose you make no promises about rabbits in the kitchen garden, squirrels in the attics, or foxes in the hen house."

"Of course not. If you want help with *those* things, you must deal with the Fae. The woods and what lives in it is *their* duty in the world."

"If the witches deal with the land and the Fae deal with the wild creatures of the woods, what's left for humans? Where do we fit in?"

Selena looked away, studying the land as they rode back to the Old Place. "We have an old story that says the witches and the Fae were in this land long before the first humans traveled over the mountains and the first ships touched the shore. The story doesn't say why they made such perilous journeys, only that they were looking for a new place, a home where they could put down roots and live in peace. They promised to honor the Great Mother as the witches and the Fae honored Her, promised to give something back for the bounty they received. And while there were few of them, they did live in peace with the Fae and the Small Folk and the House of Gaian. But as more of them came to settle on what they saw as open land, free for the taking, they built fences to keep their animals in and opened the land with plows.

The Daughters saw the world changing. They did not mind change, for the world is always changing and ever constant. But that was when they walked the boundaries, establishing the Old Places, the places that would belong to the wild things, so that all the Mother's children would have a home." She looked at Liam. "Where do your people fit in? Perhaps you were supposed to be the stewards of the tame places, just as the Fae are the stewards of the wild places. Perhaps you aren't sure of your place because you haven't yet learned the first lesson—to live kindly with the rest of the Mother's children."

"If that's the case, maybe the Inquisitors did us a favor," Liam said. "Their obsession to eliminate anything and anyone who would prevent men from ruling with impunity forced the rest of us to work together again. The Fae are remembering their place in the world and humans are remembering that there are others with whom we have to share the world." He paused. "What has the House of Gaian learned?"

"That we, too, need to be more present in the world," Selena replied. Getting to the subject she wanted to discuss with him wasn't as easy as she'd thought. Well, she wasn't that good at being subtle, so why try? "I wanted to talk to you about your sister."

Alarm flashed over Liam's face before he regarded her warily. "What has Brooke done?"

Anger sizzled under her skin, coated with disappointment. Maybe he was more cold-hearted than he seemed. "Brooke isn't your only sister."

"That's true," Liam agreed, "but she's the only one who would wheedle to have a third party intervene for her. If Breanna has a problem with me, she just marches up to wherever I am and yells at me."

Selena tried to muffle a laugh and ended up snorting, which made Mistrunner stop and turn his head to look back at her.

"Oh, go on," Selena said. After giving a snort of his own to let her know what he thought about these odd sounds she was making, he moved on.

"So what does Breanna want to discuss with me that requires a third party?" Liam asked.

"Well . . . she didn't actually *ask* me to intervene—"

"Ah."

"—but there are things a sister can't really discuss with a brother."

"There's a subject Breanna won't discuss with me? The Mother truly is merciful."

The urge to stick her tongue out at him was almost overwhelming. She settled for turning prim. "Why don't you like Falco?"

Liam frowned, obviously confused at the turn of conversation, which wasn't a turn at all as far as she was concerned. "I do like Falco."

"But you don't approve of him as your sister's lover."

"Lover?" Liam sputtered. "He's not— They're not—" He fumed for a minute. "It's not that I object, it's just— They barely know each other. There's no need to rush into being . . . intimate."

Jackass, Selena thought, amused at the way he was blushing—and thinking it rather sweet that he *would* blush.

"Liam, a few days from now, we'll be meeting a vicious enemy on a battlefield. There is no way to tell who will walk away from that battlefield and who will travel on to the Summerland. Today may be all the time there is. Falco cares about Breanna, and she cares about him. Would you deny them the comfort and pleasure they can have from each other?"

"I'm not denying her anything. She'd be the first to tell me it was none of my business, which isn't true, but she'd tell me that. If she wanted to take him as a lover, she would have done so."

"Where? From what I've been told, there are so many of her kin living in the Old Place, there's barely room there to pee in private let alone spend time with a man."

"If a man wants a woman, he can usually find a private place," Liam said darkly.

"Oh, I'm sure he can find a dark corner someplace if he wants to use a woman for a few minutes of sex—"

"What?" Liam's yelp made half the escorts riding ahead of them twist in their saddles, their hands reaching for weapons. He shook his head and waved at them to indicate there was no danger.

"—but a man who wants to make love with a woman he cares about needs more than a corner of an empty stall in the barn," Selena continued.

"I. Do. Not. Want. To. Discuss. This."

"No, you just want to be pigheaded and uncaring."

"Uncaring? *Uncaring?* What do you want me to do? Throw out all the Fae and other guests staying in my house and tell Breanna she can have her choice of the guest rooms for a romp between the sheets?"

Selena felt a tingle in her fingertips, the sizzle of temper. Remembering that the man riding beside her also sizzled when his temper rose and still hadn't learned to completely control his gift from the Mother, she put all her desire to smack him into one word. "Jackass."

His mouth opened and closed, opened and closed. He reminded her so much of a hooked trout tossed up on the bank that she found his expression much more satisfying than calling him a jackass.

"Very well, Baron Liam. You win. Your sister should remain chaste because spending time with a man she cares about would inconvenience the people who supposedly love her. Although, I suppose if there was a woman *you* wanted in your bed for the next few days, *you'd* find a way of having the privacy to have sex with her. If you deny Breanna what you'd take for yourself, that just makes you—"

His face was such an alarming shade of red, she forgot what she was going to call him.

You gave his toes a good stomp that time, didn't you? The thought made her fiercely curious to know what woman he yearned for at night but didn't think he could approach.

"I'll think about it," Liam said through gritted teeth. "I-I'll think about it."

He dug his heels into his gelding's sides. The horse leaped forward, galloped past the startled escorts. Half the escorts galloped after him. The rest stayed with her, looking anxiously over their shoulders until Varden rode up beside her.

"Lady? Is something wrong?"

She looked at Varden. Liam was right about that. The Fae *were* afraid of her. She smiled at him, wanting to put him more at ease. "No, Lord Varden, there's nothing wrong. Baron Liam is just . . . acting like a man."

Varden frowned. "Is that a bad thing?"

Her smile warmed with real humor. "It depends on one's point of view. Come along. I rode through the Old Place so fast the other day, I didn't get a good look at it." *And it will give Liam*

*time to find his balance again before he has to deal with having
me in his house as one of his guests.*

Liam paced his study, ignoring the blend of humor and alarm on
Donovan's face as the other man stretched his legs out and
slouched in a chair.

Finally, Liam whirled around to face his friend. "Did you
have sex with Gwenn before you married her?"

Donovan stiffened, all humor gone. "That's none of your
business, Baron Liam."

"Don't turn into a gentry prude, just answer the question like
a man."

Donovan rose slowly. "What's this about?"

Just thinking about it made his skin hot. "Selena said Breanna
wants— That Falco wants— That I'm—" He rammed his fingers
through his hair and curled them into fists. "She called me a jackass."

Donovan settled back in his chair and stretched out his legs
again. "It's no more Lady Selena's business than it is mine, but if
I've translated that sputtering correctly, I have to agree with her."

"What?"

"To answer your first question, yes, Gwenn and I were lovers
before we married. And her brothers made my life a misery while
I was trying to get to that point."

The pain of pulling his own hair slowly cleared Liam's mind.
He lowered his arms. "How did you get around it?"

"I finally invited her to go for a long ride one afternoon, took
her to my house, and scandalized my servants by taking her up to
my room, locking the door, and spending the day in bed with her.
We had quite a few long rides between the sheets after that—
until the night we had a storm and I insisted that she stay
overnight since I didn't want her riding out in that weather, even
if I was escorting her home. Her brothers showed up bright and
early the next morning. A little too early. The House of Gaian
may have more leniency when it comes to legal contracts, but
they're far stricter than any blustering gentry father when it
comes to heart loyalty. Gentry men have indulged themselves
often enough that the Sons of Gaian don't always respond with
enthusiasm when a man who isn't one of their own looks toward
one of the Daughters."

Fascinated now, Liam eased a hip onto the corner of his desk. "What did you do?"

Donovan grinned. "Told them if they gave me a few more days, I'd convince Gwenn to marry me. Took me a little longer than I'd expected to win her family over to the idea, me being a baron and fine husband material, but in the end, I got the woman who owned my heart."

Liam looked away. "This isn't the same thing."

"For you? Or for Breanna?"

He felt the heat rising in his face and cursed softly.

"Liam . . ." Donovan shook his head. "Breanna is a grown woman. She's not someone whose head will be turned by flattery or florid phrases whispered in the moonlight. We're prejudiced about the Fae. You know we are. We expect them to seduce women, enjoy them, and then leave. But I don't think Falco is going to leave. You see a man who wants to have sex with your sister. I see a man whose eyes light up whenever he sees her. I'm not saying you should actively do anything, I'm just saying you shouldn't stand in the way."

"I wasn't aware that I was," Liam muttered.

"Of course you weren't. But until you stop being a barrier between Breanna and Falco, Lady Selena will continue thinking you're a jackass and you won't win any ground with her."

Liam shifted. "I don't know what you mean."

"Don't you?" Donovan smiled. "I've seen the way your eyes light up, too, my friend."

Selena studied the small black dog yapping at the trees that bordered the large back lawn. "So. That's the dog you want to give me for my sister? He doesn't notice twenty strangers riding in with horses, but vigorously defends you against unwanted squirrels."

Breanna scowled. "Squirrels can be pests. Besides, he'll notice you. Eventually."

"When?"

Before Breanna could reply, Fiona walked out of the manor house and came toward them smiling. Introductions were made.

"Here," Fiona said. "I've packed an overnight bag for you."

"I didn't say I was doing this," Breanna muttered, staring at the bag on the ground in front of her.

"You're doing it."

"Doing what?" Selena asked.

"She's going to spend the night in Tir Alainn," Fiona replied. "With Falco."

"I see."

Breanna shifted her weight from one foot to the other. "I should wait until Liam gets back."

"No!" Fiona and Selena said. They looked at each other and smiled in understanding.

"You don't have to be afraid of falling off the shining road," Fiona said. "You're riding double with Falco."

"I'm not afraid." Breanna narrowed her eyes. "I never said I was afraid."

"And if the Fae get all snotty about a witch being in their Fair Land, you can just threaten to call up a wind that will spin their little piece of their world like a child's top. That'll impress them."

A snort of laughter escaped before Selena could prevent it.

"See? Selena agrees with me."

Breanna turned her narrowed eyes on Selena. "I could phoof you."

"Do something better with your time," Selena replied. "Go up to Tir Alainn, find a room with a bed and a stout lock, and let the man seduce you until you're breathless."

"Blessings of the day, ladies," Falco said, leading his horse up to where they stood.

Selena looked back and noticed how the grins on all the escorts' faces disappeared when Breanna turned to stare at them. Falco looked adorably nervous, although she hoped his nerves settled before he got Breanna into bed.

"Are you ready, Breanna?" Falco asked.

"I—"

"Yes, she is." Fiona snatched up the bag and handed it to Falco. He tied it to the saddle, mounted, then held out a hand for Breanna. When she didn't move, Fiona grabbed her arm and tugged her toward the horse.

"Stop that," Breanna hissed. "Since everyone knows why we're going to Tir Alainn, why don't we just strip naked and have sex in the middle of the lawn?"

"While that would be handsomely entertaining for the rest of us," Selena said, grabbing Breanna's other arm, "you really should have a bit more privacy the first time."

"You'll look after Gran?" Breanna said when she was mounted behind Falco.

"I'll look after everything," Fiona promised. "Just forget the world for one night."

Falco urged his horse into a canter and headed for the woodland trail that would take them to the shining road. They disappeared into the trees just as a blond-haired girl walked out of the kitchen.

The strength of the need to change into a shadow hound and attack was the only thing that kept Selena from making the shift. One look at this girl, a complete stranger, and she wanted to rip flesh, taste blood.

"What do you want, Jean?" Fiona said.

"Where's Breanna?" Jean demanded in a sulky voice.

"She's gone for a few hours."

"Where?"

"What do you want?"

The flash of hostility in the girl's eyes made Selena snarl. She took a step toward the kitchen door, watched Jean's eyes widen with apprehension. She took another step.

Jean dashed inside the kitchen and slammed the door.

Selena turned on Fiona, who paled. "Who is she?"

"She's"—Fiona nervously cleared her throat—"she's kin. She isn't being pampered the way she thinks she's entitled to be. And she's jealous of Breanna."

With effort, Selena leashed the shadow hound side of her nature.

Fiona shrugged. "It's Jean's nature to be petty and spiteful. She wants to be married to a wealthy gentry man or, barring that, have a Fae Lord who will shower her with lavish gifts. Since none of the men have shown interest in providing for her and some are now openly hostile after being entangled in one of her love charms, she's even more resentful of Falco's affection for Breanna."

"There's more than pettiness and spite in that one's nature," Selena said. She had to get away from here, had to get away from that girl before she did something that couldn't be undone. "I'd better—" She looked over to where her escorts waited with the horses and saw Liam ride through the arch.

Fiona sighed. "Who's going to tell him?"

"I'll tell him." There was something else she had to tell him now. Varden, too. They both needed to be watchful. She trusted her instincts, and those instincts were insisting that something inside that girl was *wrong*.

"Better you than me," Fiona said. From the open kitchen window, they heard a crash followed by raised voices. "I'll just go sort out the latest squabble."

Selena nodded and walked toward Liam, giving Varden a signal on the way to tell him to accompany her. After she got done talking to him about Jean, she didn't think Liam was going to put up much of a fuss about Breanna.

Chapter 32

waxing moon

"Morag! Lady Morag!"

"What's happened to her?"

"She's exhausted. Lady, let go of the horse."

Unable to straighten up, Morag bared her teeth. "Get away from me." Voices swirled around her. Faces drifted in and out of her blurred vision. "Get away."

The dark horse rose up in a half-hearted rear, barely able to lift his front legs above the knees of the men around him.

"Steady, lad," a strong voice said. "Steady now."

"Get away," Morag rasped, her dry throat scraped raw from the effort to speak. "I killed the last man who got in my way. I'll kill you, too."

"There now, Lady Morag," the strong voice said. "There now. You're so tired you're not thinking clearly. Come on now, darling. Let us help you off the horse so we can tend to both of you."

Darling? Tend to her? Morag struggled to see the face that went with that voice. It finally came into focus. She didn't remember his name, but she remembered his face. A Lord of the Horse. A Clan's stable master.

"I have to keep going," Morag said. "I have to reach Bretonwood before he does. I have to."

"And you will, darling. You will. But now you have to get down off the horse. You're too tired to ride, and he's too tired to carry you." A huff of exasperation. "And what is it we should tell Lady Ashk when she returns if we let you ride off without looking after you?"

Ashk. She'd seen him when she'd ridden east with Ashk.

"If I could have some water . . . and a little food."

"That's the way of it," the stable master said. "Here now. Let us give you a hand down."

She dismounted and would have crumpled to the stable floor if the stable master hadn't been ready to support her.

"Bring a stool for Lady Morag and a dipper of water. Put extra straw in that stall. Give the lad a good bed. Let him have some water and feed him by hand once you have the tack stripped off of him. There now, Lady. Just sit down here. Easy now. Here's some water. Sip it, now. Just sip. Boy, run up to the Clan house. Tell our Lady of the Hearth that the Gatherer is down here and needs something warm and easy to eat. Hurry up now."

Hands brushed her tangled hair away from her face, tucked a blanket around her.

She sipped the water and watched in a daze as men gathered around her dark horse, stripping off the saddle and bridle, bringing him water, feeding him handfuls of grain, wiping him down with a soft cloth. The soothing murmur of voices talking, reassuring, leading the horse to the stall.

"Don't shut him in," she said. "They tried to lock him in to stop me. He almost hurt himself trying to get out. That's when—" That's when she'd done to one of her own kind what she'd done to no one except Black Coats: gathered a man who was healthy and whole, ripped his spirit out of his body and left it there for another of Death's Servants to take up the road to the Shadowed Veil. She remembered loud voices, angry voices, hands grabbing at her. Dead flesh. She'd done that to a Black Coat, too—unfurled enough of her power to kill a piece of a man without taking his spirit, without killing all of him. She should have killed the Witch's Hammer that day. That moment of mercy, that moment of pity that she'd felt when she'd seen him on the wharf at Rivercross had cost so many so much. It hadn't been pity that had stopped her at the Clan house where they'd tried to keep her from pursuing the Lightbringer. Perhaps it had been nothing more than a hesitation to harm her own kind despite their clear intention to harm her. There was no pity in her anymore, no hesitation. The dreams that haunted the little sleep she'd gotten had burned those feelings out of her.

"Here, Morag." The stable master was back, holding a bowl with a thick cloth under it. "Here's soup, and some bread and cheese there. Eat now, and we'll fix you a place to sleep."

"Can't stay." Her hands shook with the effort to hold the bowl. He took it from her, knelt down, and held it for her. "Can't. He's too far ahead of me."

"He won't be far ahead of you for long. Eat up now. It won't do you any good inside the bowl."

She picked up the spoon and began to eat. The first taste made her want to gulp it down. When had she last eaten? She couldn't remember. The days had blurred. So she ate slowly, chewing the small chunks of bread and cheese when he offered them to her.

She almost wept when she put the spoon down, unable to eat any more with the bowl still two-thirds full.

"That's good," the stable master said, setting the bowl on a bale of hay. "We can warm it up again if you get hungry later. Now." He took her hands. She couldn't tell him how painful simple kindness was right now. "I know you've no time to waste, so we can put a cot in one of the stalls here. We keep a couple handy in case we need to keep a close eye on a sick horse. We can put it in the same stall with your lad if that will make you both rest easier."

"I can't."

"You can and you will." He shook her hands. With effort, she focused on him—and realized there was no longer any kindness in his face. "He'll not be as far ahead as you think."

"He can run until he tires, then use another horse—"

"And where would the Lightbringer be getting another horse? There's not a spare horse to be had, what with the huntsmen needing riding horses and pack horses to join the other Fae heading for the coast. And the rest of the horses are needed to protect the Old Place. No, Morag. Whether on four legs or two, they'll be his own. If he wants food, no one will stand in his way of going to the kitchen and getting some for himself, but there's no one who will fetch and carry for him. He'll have to travel harder and won't get as far. As for you, you'll get a few hours sleep. Tomorrow, we'll give you a horse you can ride through the next Clan territory or two. You can leave him there, and the Clan will send him back to us."

The dark horse snorted, stamped a foot.

The stable master grinned as he looked over his shoulder. "Never fear, lad. She'll not be leaving you. But you'll run easier if you're only carrying yourself, and I'm thinking she'll need you strong at the end of the journey."

Morag frowned. "You said there weren't any horses to spare."

He turned back to her, no longer amused. "We've none to spare for the likes of *him*. You're in the west now, Morag. Things are different here. The Lightbringer will get no help from us, and you'll get all the help we can give."

The west. She'd reached the west.

She let him lead her to the cot in the stall. Before she could collapse on it, female voices suddenly filled the stable. Women came into the stall carrying a basin of steaming water and bundles of cloth. They shooed the stable master out and closed both halves of the stall doors before she could warn them not to. The next thing she knew, she was stripped out of her clothes, given a hurried sponge bath, bundled into a clean nightgown, and tucked into bed like a weary child. The women promised they'd have her clothes washed and dried by first light. Then they were gone.

She heard the quiet creak of a door opening and struggled away from the sleep that pulled at her.

"There now, lad," murmured the strong voice. "Don't fret now. We're not shutting you in. Just keeping the bottom half closed to give your lady a bit of privacy. Rest now. Rest. You've work to do soon enough."

Morag gave up the struggle, let sleep pull her down. And for the first time in too many days, the dream didn't chase her.

Chapter 33

waxing moon

In the deepening twilight, Ashk watched cookfires bloom in the fields like exotic flowers. She was in the Mother's Hills. The House of Gaian lived here. The House of Gaian ruled here. Power breathed here, in the land, in the water, in the very air. She drew in air slowly, savoring its richness—and caught the slight stink of fear from the army of humans and Fae that were spread out over the land.

Yesterday evening, she and her companions and huntsmen had ridden into that army camped near the hills. Thousands of men, human and Fae, waiting for the midland barons and the Fae leaders to decide how to reach Willowsbrook. The quickest way lay right in front of them, but none of them had dared send as much as a small party of men into the Mother's Hills to request passage to the other side.

Then she rode up to the tents that were the barons' quarters and both sides dumped the decision on her shoulders with a swiftness she'd found a bit staggering. The Fae would follow her because she was the Hunter. The barons would abide by her decision because, they were relieved to discover, she was Baron Padrick's wife and, therefore, would not dismiss the safety of humans simply because they were humans. She had no idea how or why they came to that conclusion, even though it was true, but it had allowed all of them to get a few hours' sleep instead of arguing half the night about choices that weren't choices at all since they couldn't go around the hills without tangling with another piece of the Inquisitors' army. So, early the next morning, with Rhyann as their guide to show them the closest road, she led her companions into the Mother's Hills—and an army marched behind her.

She took another deep breath. Power seeped into her, brushing away cobwebs of fatigue. She would sleep well tonight—and hopefully not dream too intensely about Padrick. It was a bit embarrassing to wake up aching and wet and wonder if she'd made any sounds that had disturbed the other sleepers around her.

"Does it feel strange to you?"

Relieved to have her thoughts pulled away from that particular path, she smiled at Rhyann. "No. It feels like home. It's the first place since I left the west that feels like home."

Rhyann studied her, looking slightly puzzled. "How does it feel like home?"

Ashk shrugged. "It just does. More potent than the magic that flows through Bretonwood, but not so different. It soothes—and also makes me aware of how much I miss my home woods, my husband and children, my Clan. And it makes me realize again how much we can lose if we don't drive the Inquisitors out of Sylvalan. The people in the east have been wounded. Lives have been torn in ways we cannot fix. But we can lance the wound and drain the pus from it so that it has a chance to heal."

"There will be scars from those wounds," Rhyann said quietly. "Scars that may not fade for generations."

"Yes. And those scars will require careful attention to make sure nothing that may be festering beneath them has a chance to take hold."

"We'll all have to make some changes if we want to keep Sylvalan safe."

"Then we'll make some changes." Ashk looked over the fields. "We'll learn from one another, come to know one another better. We can learn to see the whole of the land that anchors all of us instead of our individual pieces of it." She smiled. "And I know just how to begin—with music and stories."

"You can't expect Aiden and Lyrra to spend the night going from camp to camp singing and telling stories," Rhyann protested. "They've put in a hard day's travel, too."

"There are bound to be a few bards and minstrels among the Fae here. A few storytellers, too. What Aiden and Lyrra begin will ripple through the rest of the camps. Others will pick up the tunes, tell the tales."

"And humans and Fae will take comfort in the songs and stories they discover they have in common and pleasure in the ones one side or the other hasn't heard?"

"Exactly."

Rhyann crossed her arms over her chest. "And what about the House of Gaian?"

"I imagine you have a few stories to tell, too," Ashk replied blandly. Was it just the way the firelight had flickered over Rhyann's face at that moment, or had she really seen a flash of mischief in the witch's face?

"I know some stories," Rhyann said, her voice equally bland. "But I think the storytellers among us would have more suitable fare."

Oh, how I'd love to give you one glass of wine too many and hear the stories you might tell about your sister. She'd been very careful not to ask Rhyann anything about Selena. She wanted to know about the Huntress. Oh, how she wanted to know. But it didn't seem right to lure Rhyann into revealing family matters, and Rhyann hadn't offered any information after the night they'd met her.

"I'd better tell the Bard and the Muse their gifts are needed," Ashk said. She walked away from Rhyann—and temptation. By her estimation, they were a day and a half away from Willowsbrook, so she'd find out soon enough what she needed to know about the Huntress.

Chapter 34

waxing moon

Adolfo opened the door that led out onto a terrace, letting the rain lash his face, soak the fine carpet beneath his muddy boots. The mud and the wet carpet were a small way to punish the baron's wife. The woman was not docile, despite the fact that the baron had followed all the procedures to make her so. Oh, she did what was required, said what was required . . . but hatred burned in the back of her eyes. Should he warn the baron to watch his back? No. If the fool ended up with a knife plunged into his heart one night after using her, it was no more than he deserved.

There was hatred in the baron's wife that discipline would never exorcise. There was fury in the storm that chained him to this house.

A bitch of a storm.

Adolfo stared out at it, as if his stare alone could crush it. Instead, it was crushing him. His army was mired in roads turned to mud. The wheels of supply wagons were sunk to the axles, and even with men straining until muscles tore in their effort to help the horses pull the wagons out, they advanced a handspan at a time. Their only choice had been to empty the wagons and have men carry supplies along with their own packs, exhausting the men to the point where they weren't fit to meet the enemy. Lightning struck old trees that fell across the road, forcing more men to expend time and effort to chop and haul enough aside to let men and wagons pass. Fields were drowning under lakes of water. Creeks had risen and washed away bridges.

A bitch of a storm, reeking with magic and fury, aimed right at him.

He knew who to blame for that.

Leaving the door open so that the storm would frame him, he turned to look at the pale, trembling baron.

"Were my orders so difficult that you found them impossible to follow?" Adolfo asked gently.

"No, Master Adolfo," the baron replied, looking at his hands clasped white-knuckle tight in his lap.

"All you had to do was gather the complement of men from your county and wait for the rest of the army to arrive. Why couldn't you do that?"

When the baron just hunched his shoulders, Adolfo said nothing more, letting silence take on the weight of a weapon. *You're a weak man,* he thought as he watched the baron, *used to being guided. You resented knowing it was your wife's strength and intelligence that kept your estate and your county from being mired in debt, that it was her will that kept you from gobbling up the prosperity of the villages under your hand like a greedy child. What glee you must have felt when my Inquisitors helped you tame her, what pleasure you must have had every time you disciplined her for defying her new place in the world, what joy you must have experienced when you raped her after a beating. But like a greedy child who now has the means of punishing the once-restraining hand, you thought there were no restraints, no one to whom you had to answer. You will learn differently—and you will learn the lesson so well you will never dare disobey again.*

"I thought—" The baron stammered, struggled to collect his thoughts. "I only wanted to help our side win the battle. I thought if Baron Liam was eliminated, it would make it easier for the army to march through his county and meet the real enemy, the bitch servants of the Evil One."

"But you didn't eliminate him," Adolfo said, his voice viciously gentle.

"We should have!" The baron finally looked up, confusion and defiance in his face. "He wasn't expecting an attack. He didn't have that many men gathered at his estate. Certainly not enough to defeat my men."

"But he did have enough men."

"He didn't! Even with those Fae helping him, he didn't. He wasn't prepared for an attack. We would have captured him or killed him if . . ." The baron swallowed hard. "If it hadn't been for that wind."

"A wind that was able to defeat three hundred men." Adolfo put just enough skepticism in his voice to sting, even though the storm raging outside was sufficient testimony that the witches in this cursed land were far stronger than any he'd encountered in Wolfram or Arktos. "A wind *killed* three hundred men."

He had questioned the one man who had escaped the slaughter and managed to make his way back to his home county. Had questioned him carefully. A huge funnel of wind that consumed everything in its path. A *controlled* funnel of wind. The spot in his lower back that always turned cold when he was afraid felt icy now.

The baron looked away. "I lost my son, my *heir.* That wind killed him."

And that would be the punishment. The baron hadn't yet considered what the loss of those other men would mean to the farms and villages in his county, wouldn't think of the cost of those lives until his steward made the trip to collect the tithes that filled the baron's pockets. Those pockets would be less full this year. He would insist that the tithe be lowered for every family that had lost a father or a son because of this ill-conceived attack as a compensation for the loss of a worker in his prime. That loss of income would be a punishment, too. But the son, the heir . . .

Adolfo drew on his Inquisitor's Gift of persuasion, let it roll through his voice, turning the mildly spoken words into whiplashes on the heart. "That wind didn't kill your son. You did."

The baron's head snapped up, his eyes full of shock . . . and a kernel of anger.

"*You* decided to attack the Baron of Willowsbrook on your own instead of waiting for the rest of the army. *You* sent your heir to lead the men who died without considering *all* the enemies that might be waiting for you there. *You* ignored the dangers in order to indulge in some childish rivalry with the other barons. *You* wanted to be the first to encounter the enemy, to defeat the enemy, to be praised for your courage, to be envied for your vigor. Because of your willfulness, *you* sent those men to their deaths. And *you* killed your heir."

The baron wept silently, his kernel of anger crushed under the weight of persuasion.

Watching him, Adolfo felt nothing but contempt. "And because of your recklessness," he continued, "they're aware of the army now." The storm raging outside was confirmation of that. "We no longer have the advantage of swiftness or surprise. Men will die, fighting for ground we should have conquered with ease. Because of you."

"I'm sorry," the baron whispered. "I—"

Adolfo turned and walked out the terrace door, walked into the storm. Fury grew inside him, and his desire to punish was more excessive than prudent.

It wasn't just that men were going to die. *Wolfram* men were going to die. The army led by the Arktos barons was expendable. So was the army led by the Sylvalan barons from the east and south. Distractions to split the enemy's strength. A bonus if either army actually made it around the north or south ends of the Mother's Hills and threatened the midlands. But *this* army came from Wolfram, came from *his* people. There would be losses. He knew that. Now there would be more. They knew he was coming, knew his army was aimed at Willowsbrook and the hills beyond Willowsbrook.

He didn't know how Liam had managed to persuade the Fae to join the fight, and he didn't like the fact that those creatures were suddenly paying attention to the human world. Bad enough that Ubel had encountered them the first time he'd gone to Breton, but if they were actually joining forces with the Sylvalan barons who dared to defy him . . .

He shuddered. There had been no mention of a black-haired woman riding a dark horse. There had been no sign of *her* around Willowsbrook. With so much death in one place, *someone* would have seen the Gatherer if she had returned to this part of Sylvalan.

Perhaps he should change the place of attack anyway. Swing around the county Baron Liam ruled and strike somewhere a little farther north or south. It would force the human enemy to march fast to meet him before he reached the Mother's Hills and began cleansing them of the foul magic that lived there. If the Fae had some alliance with Liam, they would lose interest if Willowsbrook wasn't threatened.

He could turn the army away from Willowsbrook . . . but the Sylvalan barons would see it as fear. They would think he was afraid of whatever unnatural allies that young bastard Liam was gathering, would gain strength and courage from misinterpreting his decision, and would pursue him more relentlessly because of it.

Soaked to the skin, Adolfo closed his eyes and lifted his face to the storm. The rain stung his skin, reeked of magic.

Magic.

He smiled.

He wouldn't need to find an Old Place. The bitches were providing him with pools and pockets of magic he could drain for his own use, twist to his own will. He would still need a witch to create his finest gift, but he could use these pockets of magic to create the smaller gifts.

So he wouldn't turn away. He would drive his army to Willowsbrook, would fight against the elements that had become the enemy's weapon. He would capture a witch, soften her enough to remove any threat to himself or his men—and he would give Baron Liam and his allies a gift from out of a nightmare.

Chapter 35

waxing moon

Filled with fierce triumph, Ubel gripped the railing and watched the Wolfram warships gain on the enemy. That witch-loving bastard was heading for the big island, probably hoping he could circle it and find a place to hide. There was no place to hide. There would *never* be a place to hide from an Inquisitor's righteous judgment. He had the bastard now. *He had him.*

Turning his head, he shouted at his ship's captain, "We're in range of that last ship. Signal the other Wolfram captains. Put fire down on those witch-lovers!"

The ship's captain shouted orders. Sailors scrambled to obey as the first mate changed course to give them the best shot and the flagman waved the signal flags to alert the other warships. The guard captain shouted orders, too, and guards scrambled along the deck to prepare the catapult while others carried up one of the boxes of round clay pots that contained shards of metal floating in liquid fire.

Ubel turned back to watch the fleeing ships. The Wolfram captains knew what to do and needed no further orders from him.

The guard captain shouted the order. Ubel watched the round clay pot sail over the water and hit the side of the closest enemy ship, setting the wood on fire. The metal shards flew from the pot, ripping into the flesh of people on deck.

Another pot was prepared and fired. It hit the sails and was cradled in the cloth for a moment before it fell to the deck, spraying its liquid fire and metal shards.

As the other warships engaged their catapults and shot clay pots toward the other ships, Ubel heard the screams of the burned and wounded aboard the now-floundering ships. He bared his teeth in a vicious smile.

Try to run, you bastards. You won't escape me. What fire doesn't cleanse from the world, the sea will.

Jenny stepped out of the cottage and saw men running toward the stone stairs that led down to the harbor. Saw Murtagh striding toward her, his face grim and determined. She ran to meet him.

"What's happening?" she asked, chilled by the comforting hand he laid on her arm.

"We've sighted some ships heading for the island," Murtagh replied.

For a moment, her heart leaped into her throat, making it impossible to breathe. "Mihail?"

"Can't tell yet. But they're being pursued by warships. Since sea thieves know better than to come into these waters, I suspect it's Black Coats in pursuit. One of those ships running ahead of them could be your brother's." Murtagh squeezed her arm lightly. "Not to worry, sweet Jenny. My selkies are getting our own ships ready to sail to meet them, and the coastal barons whose land touches the bay all have ships out to keep watch. We'll get the people on those ships to safe harbor."

Turning away, he hurried after his men.

Jenny took one step to follow, then spun and ran for the cliffs. She would be in the way down at the harbor, but she would be able to see the ships from the cliffs. Even from a distance, she would be able to identify *Sweet Selkie*.

She ran until the village was almost out of sight, then stopped, reluctant to go too much farther. From her vantage point, she saw the Fae ships leaving the harbor, heading for the neck of water between the coast and a spur of the island. That spur kept her from seeing the ships running toward the island. So she waited, her hands clenched, her heart pounding. Waited for that first sighting of a sail. When she was younger, how often she'd waited on the home docks in the same way, watching the Una River until she saw the sails and knew her father or brothers were coming home. Now the only brother left to wait for was Mihail.

Birds screamed. Looking up from the sea, she noticed the flocks of gulls circling and swirling. Sea hawks flew above them, around them. Were they really birds or were there Fae among them, guiding the birds that answered to their particular gifts?

She saw the sails now—and her blood turned to ice.

A handful of ships. *Sweet Selkie* ran ahead of the smaller ships, but the warships had closed the distance. As she watched, flames appeared on one side of the smallest ship. Moments later, fire bloomed on the deck, spreading to the mast and sails.

The sails of the warship closest to *Sweet Selkie* burst into flames. *Yes!* Someone on that ship had the gift of fire and was fighting back.

Fighting back.

Jenny stared at the warships. "No," she whispered. "No. You accuse us of being evil and take our land. You take away our way of life, and then you take our lives." Her voice rose as she watched the burning ship flounder and roll. "You've taken our homes, our families, everything we held dear. Now take our grief, take our rage, *take our pain.*"

She drew on the branch of water, filled herself with the power. Then, charging that power with all the feelings raging in her heart, she gave it to the sea.

The sea went insane.

One moment, Ubel was watching the burning ship roll to its death and the people on board leap into the sea in an effort to escape. One moment, the guards not manning the catapult were shooting the gulls that flew around the ship, Fae spies for the witches. One moment, the enemy was almost in his grasp.

And the next moment, the sea went insane. Walls of dark water rose out of nowhere, curled into foaming white fists, and smashed down on his warships. Waves rose as high as cliffs, with a ship teetering on the crest before it rolled and smashed to the base of the wave, only to have the wave arch and dive back into the sea, taking the ship with it.

Ubel clung to the rail with all his strength, listening to his men screaming as the box of clay pots broke and liquid fire spilled out over the deck and the men trying to cling to anything they could hold onto. They screamed as the fire washed over them. They screamed as they were pitched into the merciless sea.

The sky suddenly turned dark. Looking up, Ubel realized his ship was caught in a tunnel made by two waves coming together at the crests.

Then the tunnel collapsed, and there was nothing but the sea. Nothing at all.

                    *   *   *

"Jenny! *Jenny!* Mother's mercy, *what have you done?*"

Rough hands gripped her arms and spun her away from the sea. She stared into Murtagh's face, seeing fury and fear—seeing him, but feeling only the sea.

"Jenny! Ground the power now! Ground it, Jenny!"

She bared her teeth. "They kill us and kill us and kill us. But they will kill no more of us. *No more!*"

He was breathing deeply, roughly, as if he struggled to complete a ferocious task. "That's right," he said, his voice straining for calm. "They'll kill no more."

His eyes were dark and intense as he stared into hers. His voice smoothed out, a balm to raw emotions.

"You defended your people, and you defended them well. Now help me, Jenny. Help me get them to safe harbor. My ships can't reach them until you calm the sea. Help me, Jenny. Help me get your brother to safe harbor."

"Safe harbor," she whispered, unable to look away from his eyes.

"Yes. Safe harbor. Calm your heart, Jenny. Calm the sea."

Safe harbor. Help the selkies get Mihail and the others to safe harbor.

She closed her eyes, but Murtagh's voice still washed over her. She breathed in the power she'd given to the sea, and breathed it out again, flowing on the path of that soothing voice. Calm the heart. Calm the sea.

"That's good, Jenny. That's good."

She opened her eyes. She saw relief in his eyes now—and still a hint of fear behind it. When she tried to turn to look at the sea, Murtagh shifted to place himself on the seaward side of the cliff. With his arm firmly around her shoulders, he led her back toward the village.

"We'll go down to the harbor and welcome your brother," Murtagh said. "When he sees you, he'll know he's among friends."

Mihail. Yes. When he saw her waiting for him, he would know he'd reached safe harbor.

It didn't occur to her until much later that Murtagh had deliberately kept her from seeing what her fury and the sea had done.

Ubel clung to the broken mast, surrounded by debris that had once been a Wolfram warship. Surrounded by bodies. There were a few other men clinging to anything that would float, but not many.

A pained, garbled sound came from the guard captain, who was also clinging to the mast with his good arm. Ubel kept his face averted. The captain had been splashed in the face with liquid fire. The area around his right eye had been spared, but that normal eye, dulled with shock and exhaustion, made the rest of the ruined face look more obscene.

He didn't know how long he'd been in the water when he saw the line of ships slowly sailing through the debris, looking for survivors. He didn't know how long he watched them before he noticed all the seals swimming ahead of the ships, before he heard their odd barks that guided the ships' crews toward the living.

He waited. When a sleek brown head rose from the water and the creature stared at him, he shuddered. Not seals. Not here. Selkies. An animal body with a man's brain.

Seconds passed, stretched, turned into agonizing years before the selkie made that odd barking sound. Then it sank beneath the water.

Finally a ship approached. Beyond throwing out two loops of canvas attached to ropes, the crew offered no help. Since the ship continued moving past him, his choices were to abandon the mast and swim as best as he could to reach the canvas loop or to remain in the sea until his strength gave out.

He splashed and floundered, came close to sinking when his foot almost tangled in one of the lines from the sails, but he managed to reach the canvas loop and slip his arms through it. They pulled him toward the ship, used the rope to steady him as he climbed the rope netting attached to the side of the ship. He glanced back once. There was no one clinging to the mast now, and the other canvas loop being hauled up was empty.

He barely had time to collapse on the deck when he was lifted to his feet and dragged to the stern. In the bow, people were wrapped in blankets. Some were sipping from mugs. Others were having wounds tended. He caught no more than a glimpse of them before he was shoved to his knees, and his hands were tightly bound to the stern railing. The first mate was there, but not his ship's captain. A few guards, a few sailors. Almost all of them were wounded in one way or another.

"Water," Ubel croaked. "We need water."

The man with a face that wasn't human just stared at him.

Curse these Fae, Ubel thought. "We need water. The wounded need tending."

"When we reach the harbor, we'll turn you over to the barons who rule that part of the coast. If they want to give you water and tend the wounded, that's their choice." The Fae Lord turned away.

"Have you no mercy?" Ubel cried.

The Fae turned back and smiled at him. "No more than you, Black Coat. If you want mercy, ask one of the Mother's Daughters. They're the ones who believe in doing no harm."

Ask one of those evil bitches for mercy? Ubel shuddered. No. Never. He would conserve his strength, let these creatures bring him to the shore. Once he was dealing with the barons, his Inquisitor's Gift of persuasion would convince them to give him food and water—and a horse. He would need only a few hours head start to stay far enough ahead of the enemy to reach the arm of the Inquisitors' army that was crushing the southern end of the Mother's Hills.

Jenny wept silently as she stood on the dock and watched the battered *Sweet Selkie* limp into the harbor. Murtagh had taken a ship and gone out to meet her brother, and it was Murtagh she saw standing in the bow. But there was no sign of Mihail.

She saw Fae piloting the ship to the dock instead of Mihail's crew. She saw Fae securing the lines and lowering the gangplank.

Her heart broke. She wrapped her arms around herself. Had she done this?

Then she saw Murtagh motion her to come aboard. She ran up the gangplank and would have fallen when she reached the deck if he hadn't reached out to steady her.

"He's in the bow," Murtagh said, guiding her. "He collapsed shortly after I got on board and convinced him we weren't the enemy."

"He's wounded?" Jenny asked, feeling breathless.

"He's been hurt, but it's exhaustion and lack of food and water that finally pulled his feet out from under him. They ran out and couldn't stop to take on supplies."

When she saw Mihail, she rushed forward and sank to her knees. "Mihail. *Mihail.*" She brushed a shaking hand over his hair. He looked so pale, so worn. "Mihail."

He opened his eyes and stared at her. Finally he said in a hoarse voice, "Jenny?"

She choked back a sob. "Yes, Mihail. It's Jenny."

"Safe harbor, Jenny?"

Tears spilled down her cheeks as she gently pressed her lips to his dry, cracked ones. "Yes, Mihail. Safe harbor."

Mihail closed his eyes. His body relaxed.

Panicked, Jenny pressed a hand against his chest, trying to feel his heart.

Murtagh placed a hand just above Mihail's nose. "It's all right, Jenny. He needs to rest."

Sobs ripped out of her. Tears of grief. Tears of joy.

"It will be all right, sweet Jenny," Murtagh said, putting his arms around her to offer warmth and comfort. "It will be all right."

Chapter 36

waxing moon

Ashk and Aiden slowly rode out of the trees, heading toward the manor house at the other end of the big sweep of lawn. Two of the midland barons rode behind them, having insisted on coming. The rest of her companions, her men, and the combined Fae and human army were waiting in the woods. She still wasn't sure if it was because it was reasonable or because Aiden's gift as the Bard had influenced her decision, but she couldn't deny his genuine concern that Breanna's hostility toward the Fae might cause her to shoot first and ask questions later, and it would be easier to persuade her to see them as allies if the Old Place wasn't suddenly flooded with humans and Fae.

Of course, that was before they'd met up with several pairs of Fae from different Clans patrolling the woods, all of whom informed her quickly, and with wary relief, that men from their Clans had set up camps in meadows and pastures in the Old Place. They told her Varden, the Willowsbrook Clan's Lord of the Woods, was working with Barons Liam and Donovan as well as Lord Falco and Lady Breanna on a way to meet the enemy while protecting the Old Place and the human village. And they told her, with a hint of fear in their eyes, that the Huntress rode among them.

So she'd held to her decision and rode ahead with the Bard and two barons—not because the witches who lived at Willowsbrook might still feel hostile toward the Fae but because she wanted to take the measure of the Huntress before exposing her men.

As she rode toward the manor house, she noticed the small black dog sound asleep under a tree. She noticed the large hawk who watched them from its perch on a pole that supported lines of pegged clothes. She noticed the men around the stables, who put down grooming brushes and picked up pitchforks and cross-bows. And she noticed the dark-haired woman who strode out of the house and headed right toward them, followed by a man and woman.

She reined in. Aiden stopped alongside her, and the barons swung their horses to either side to flank them.

Aiden raised his hand. "Blessings of the day, Breanna."

Breanna's eyes flicked from Aiden to Ashk, and Ashk saw a question in those woodland eyes that a man would never notice and any woman would understand.

"I am Ashk, the Hunter," she said. "My husband guested with your family a few weeks ago and asked me to send you his regards."

"Husband?" Breanna studied Ashk. "You mean Padrick?"

Ashk nodded.

"He was a sensible man," Breanna said, her voice turning sour. "Even if he is gentry . . . and Fae."

Oh, dear. It didn't sound like the barons were going to be warmly welcomed, either. And there was still doubt in Breanna's eyes.

"Lyrra will be pleased to see you," Aiden said with a smile, proving that he had understood the question in Breanna's eyes as well. "She's waiting with some of our companions. We didn't want to impose on you until . . ." He trailed off, now looking uncertain.

"Until you were sure I wouldn't shoot you?" She threw up her hands, a gesture of sheer exasperation. "Didn't I promise Falco and Varden I wouldn't threaten to shoot any Fae just for riding into the Old Place? They said it made the Fae nervous."

"That's because they've seen you shoot," the man who had followed her said.

Breanna twisted around to look at him. "I'm a good shot!"

"Exactly." He looked at the two barons. "Good day, gentlemen."

"Good day, Baron Donovan," one of the barons replied. "I'm surprised, but pleased, to see you here."

"The fight is here," Donovan said grimly. "And the Master Inquisitor is heading for Willowsbrook, so we win or lose here."

"We must talk with Baron Liam as soon as possible," the other baron said.

Donovan rubbed the back of his neck. "Liam is involved in a rather . . . delicate . . . discussion at the moment."

Breanna snorted. "What Donovan is trying to say is my feath-erheaded jackass of a brother is having a bang-up argument with the Huntress over something that is none of his business." She paused, then added, "It isn't any of Selena's business, either, but since she's on my side, she can say what she pleases."

The other woman snickered.

"Gwenn," Donovan warned.

The muscles in Ashk's back tightened painfully. "The Baron of Willowsbrook is having an argument with the Huntress?"

"You'd think he'd have better things to do, wouldn't you?" Breanna said sourly.

She would have hoped a baron would have more sense. Perhaps he didn't realize the kind of power the Huntress wielded— in which case, someone should tell him. Fast.

Before she could phrase a request that someone inform the Huntress that the Hunter had arrived, a soft wind blew out of the woods, riffling the grass and dancing past the leaves on the big tree.

Breanna snapped to attention. "Gwenn?"

"Yes," Gwenn replied softly. "I think so."

Her patience worn thin, Ashk dismounted, prepared to insist that they discuss where the army waiting for orders could make camp.

Then she saw the black-haired woman race around the side of the manor house and come to an abrupt stop, her attention focused on the woods. Joy lit her face, and her resemblance to Rhyann was strong enough for Ashk to guess her identity. When her attention shifted to the newcomers and the joy faded, there was no doubt in Ashk's mind that this was the woman who had shaken the Fae enough to come down from Tir Alainn. There was no doubt that the woman now walking toward them was Selena, *the* Lady of the Moon . . . and the Huntress.

Ashk walked forward to meet her, aware of the tension starting to fill the people behind her. They stopped at the same time, close enough that one leap in their other forms would have them at each other's throats.

"I am Ashk, the Hunter," Ashk said.

Selena studied Ashk, her eyes searching for something. "Shadow hound."

"Yes."

They studied each other, searching, measuring—and finally smiling in approval of what each saw in the other.

"Are you being bossy again?" a voice asked.

Ashk clenched her teeth. It had been too much to hope that Rhyann would follow orders—and seeing the temper flash in Selena's eyes made her wish she could change into her other form and give Rhyann a sharp nip.

"Some people wouldn't have to be bossy if other people did what they were told," Selena snapped.

Here, here, Ashk thought, turning enough to see Rhyann walking toward them, followed by Breanna and the others.

"And some people just like being bossy," Rhyann replied with a sweetness designed to spike another woman's temper. "I kept my promise to Father. I came to this side of the hills with an entire army as an escort. Who came with you?"

Selena made an indescribable sound.

"There's an army?" Breanna asked.

"Yes," Rhyann replied. "Fae, human, and Sons and Daughters of the House of Gaian." She gave Selena an annoyingly sweet smile. "Why don't you and the Hunter go discuss whatever you need to discuss, and I'll help—" She looked inquiringly at Breanna.

"Breanna," Breanna said.

"I'll help Breanna sort things out here."

Mother's mercy, Ashk thought, wondering how much longer it would be before Selena simply exploded.

But the Huntress gave Ashk a look that could sear flesh and snarled, "I'll saddle my horse and meet you at the arch near the stables."

Watching Selena stride toward the stables and the arch, Ashk grabbed Aiden's arm, pulled him aside, and said in a low voice, "Use your gift, Bard, and smooth things over as best you can here."

Aiden gave her a weak smile. "I'll ask Lyrra to join us. She and Breanna deal well together."

"Do what you think best." She saw a dark-haired man come round the corner of the house, check his stride when he noticed the new arrivals, and continue toward them slowly.

"Do you have any advice about dealing with featherheaded older brothers?" Ashk heard Breanna ask.

"Of course," Rhyann replied cheerfully. "I'm very good at being a younger sister. I've been practicing all my life."

Aiden grabbed Ashk's arm, his blue eyes filled with alarm. Ashk just patted his hand and pulled away. "Do what you can, Bard."

As she hurried back to her horse, she knew with absolute certainty that, no matter what mood the Huntress was in, by leaving Aiden to deal with annoyed barons and younger sisters, she was getting the better side of the bargain.

Aiden wondered how he was supposed to smooth things over and get a message to Lyrra that he needed her. Then he remembered the letter in his saddlebags—and the hawk.

Hurrying back to Minstrel, he made a "come here" gesture to the hawk. His stride faltered when he saw the hawk flutter to the ground and change into a man.

What had Falco been up to here that he felt comfortable enough to change form where outsiders could see him?

"Merry meet, Aiden," Falco said, smiling but a bit wary, as if he anticipated criticism from someone he considered a friend.

"Merry meet, Falco," Aiden replied. "I see you've become acquainted with the ladies here."

Falco stiffened. "You're not the only one who has a heart, Aiden. Breanna's brother has no reason—yet—to believe in a Fae Lord's ability to be loyal to a lover, but I thought you would understand since you and Lyrra—" He stopped. Looked away. "But it is different because you're both Fae."

Falco and Breanna? Aiden wisely hid the grin of delight that might be mistaken for mockery. "I take it her brother disapproves?"

"I can't blame him," Falco said quietly. "Not after—" He closed his eyes for a moment before looking at Aiden. "Do you know where the Black Coats got their Inquisitor's Gift of persuasion? Do you know where they got the power to draw magic from the land and twist it to create those nighthunter creatures?"

A chill went through Aiden as he shook his head.

"From us. They're children we abandoned in the human world because they weren't pure Fae. We enjoyed the women, both human and witches, and ignored the children we sired."

"You don't know that," Aiden protested.

"Yes, I do. Varden's men caught a Black Coat when Baron

Liam's home was attacked a few days ago. We've kept it among ourselves—so far—but we *know*, Aiden."

Staggered, Aiden rubbed his hands over his face. "The Inquisitors came from Wolfram."

"Which only means it wasn't the Sylvalan Clans who had ignored *those* men when they were young. What about the children here? There are some. You know there are. Mother's mercy, Aiden, the *Huntress* is one of them. So I don't blame Liam for being reluctant to accept that I'm staying."

Aiden stumbled as he reached Minstrel. Leaning against the horse, he noticed how his hands shook while he tried to open the saddlebag. "We'll talk more about it later, Falco. Right now, I need you to go into the woods and fetch Lyrra."

He waited until Falco changed form again and flew off toward the trees before he pulled the letter out of the saddlebag. After he closed the saddlebag's flap, he leaned over and rested his forehead against the leather.

As soon as she got back from her ride with Selena, he would have to tell Ashk what he'd learned about the Inquisitors. She needed to know about every weapon the enemy could bring to the fight—including their ability to control people through persuasion. But, right now, he had to do his best to smooth things over between men and women, brothers and sisters, gentries' sensibilities and witches' feelings. And he was gambling that the piece of wax-sealed paper would help him do that.

As he walked back to the others, he noticed they'd split into two groups. Breanna and Gwenn were talking with Rhyann while the barons stood a few feet away, probably making plans for the army. He also noticed that the dark-haired man he assumed was the Baron of Willowsbrook—and Breanna's brother—kept glancing her way, as if to keep an eye on her.

"Breanna?" Aiden held out the folded paper. "This is for you."

Looking puzzled, Breanna studied the blob of sealing wax, then looked at him. "What is it? A song?"

"I don't think so. We met up with a messenger heading east. Since I was coming to Willowsbrook anyway, he entrusted me to deliver this to you in exchange for taking messages back to the west."

Still puzzled, she turned the paper over—and stared at the writing.

"Mother's mercy." She broke the wax seal, opened the paper,

and started to read. Her eyes filled with tears. Then she laughed. "Jenny. It's from my cousin Jenny. She and Mihail have found safe harbor somewhere in the west. And Tremaine's sons are with them. They got out. They escaped."

As Gwenn slid a comforting arm around Breanna, Aiden saw her brother break away from the other men.

"Breanna?" he enquired, his voice sharp with concern, his eyes fixed on Aiden with suspicion.

Laughing and crying, Breanna shook her head. "They found safe harbor. I have to tell Fiona and Gran. And Mihail's wife. Oh, she's been desperate for any news of him." She threw her arms around Aiden's neck and choked him with the hug. "Oh, thank you, Aiden. Thank you." Spinning around, she almost knocked Liam over as she ran to the house.

Gwenn and Rhyann hurried after her.

Aiden looked at the man who continued to stare back at him. "You're the Baron of Willowsbrook?"

"I'm Liam."

Aiden extended his hand in the human way of greeting. "Aiden. The Bard."

Some of the tension in Liam eased as he slipped his hand into Aiden's. "Breanna has mentioned you."

"No matter what she's said, I'm not taking the dog."

Liam grinned as they turned and looked at the small black dog, who was still sound asleep under the tree. They watched Lyrra ride up, slow her horse as she, too, looked at the dog and shook her head, and finally rein in when she reached them.

"I saw Breanna run into the house," Lyrra said. "What's wrong?"

Aiden shook his head. "The letter I had for her was good news. The kind women like to cry over."

"And men never shed tears? Ha!" Lyrra shoved the reins into the closest pair of hands—which happened to be Liam's—and ran to the house.

"I'll take those," Aiden said, holding out a hand for the reins. "You've other business to attend to."

Nodding, Liam returned to the other barons.

Well, Aiden thought as he led Lyrra's horse toward the watering trough in the stableyard, with Minstrel and the barons' horses following, *it isn't exactly what Ashk intended when she'd asked*

*me to smooth things over, but it will keep everyone occupied for
a while.*

They ran. There was no need for human speech. A yip, a soft
growl, a wag of a tail was all either needed as commentary about
the sounds and smells their heightened senses picked up.

It felt strange to roam the land with another shadow hound,
especially another strong bitch. Selena fought against the instinct
to surrender more to the animal nature and push a confrontation
that would decide dominance. Perhaps because she knew, deep
down, that Ashk had lived in this form in ways that she had not,
and that experience would win in a fight.

So she trotted beside the Hunter, pleased with how easily they
moved together.

Then she picked up a strange scent and moved off on her own
to investigate. A bad smell. Bitter. Foul. The trail seemed to lead
to the dead tree among the stand of trees up ahead.

She started forward, then yipped in pain and surprise when
Ashk nipped her flank. She rounded on Ashk, her teeth bared, her
hackles raised. But Ashk's attention was focused on the trees, and
the snarl rising from her throat spoke of deadly anger.

Ashk backed away, her attention never leaving the stand of
trees.

Selena paused a moment to sniff the scent again. When she
was in human form, the smell would be much weaker, but she
would recognize it again.

Ashk trotted away, stopping every few yards to look back and
study the trees. Selena followed, puzzled by the Hunter's behav-
ior. When the trees were a field away, Ashk settled into a ground-
eating trot that a shadow hound could sustain for hours.

Finally they reached the top of a rise beyond the village of
Willowsbrook. Flat land stretched before them—grass and wildflowers. Beyond the field, more woodland took over. The road
cut through the woodland and the field, curving leisurely around
the rise they stood on as it continued on its way to the village and
the surrounding farms and estates.

Almost in the center of the field was a tumbled pile of huge
stones, as if a giant child had taken blocks of stone to play with,
built them up, then knocked them down. There would be a war-
ren of hiding places among those stones. An enemy entrenched
there wouldn't be attacked or driven out easily.

She didn't like those stones. She didn't know why, but they made her hackles rise.

Ashk shifted back to human form. Reluctantly, Selena did the same.

"This is the place," Ashk said quietly as she studied the land. "This is where we'll stand and fight. The Black Coats will take cover among the trees to hide the strength of their army, but they won't hide as well as they hope to. The woods will watch them. Birds will give warning. We'll know when they arrive. We can hold this high ground, use it to cover our own movements. The village is behind us, and if we defend the road here, we can keep it protected. The wounded will be sent to the Old Place. It's closer to the Mother's Hills, and that will give our people a better chance of getting the wounded to safety if we're forced back and have to choose another battleground."

Selena looked out at the grass and wildflowers. Looked away from the tumble of stones. "That's what you see here? A battleground?"

Ashk nodded. "It's a good place to fight. As good as any I've seen today."

A shiver went through Selena. Not because there would be a fight, but because Ashk sounded so calm about it. Feeling unsettled, she asked, "What was that smell back there? The foul one?"

"Nighthunters. I'll have to talk to the witches, maybe even the baron, to find out how many we have to cleanse from the woods here." Ashk continued to study the land. She paused for a long moment as her eyes focused on the stones, then went on. "We have to hunt them down. And I'll have to find out if any of the Clans brought Fae who are Death's Servants. We can bury the bodies of the dead, but their spirits will still be a feast that will draw the nighthunters, no matter what we do to stop them."

Selena swallowed the sick feeling rising from the pit of her stomach. "Feast?"

Ashk looked at her. "Some of us will die here, Huntress. Many of us will die here. It's not just flesh and blood that nighthunters devour. They feast on the ghosts, the spirits of the dead. So the spirits of our dead need to be taken to the Shadowed Veil as quickly as possible. To keep them safe. To let them go on to the Summerland."

"Mother's mercy," Selena whispered.

"We'd better get back," Ashk said, turning away from the field. "We need to put the time we have left to good use."

Selena followed Ashk down the rise. Changing back into shadow hounds, they loped to the field where they had left the horses.

Many of us will die here.

She'd known that. Of course she had. But it had remained unspoken when she and Breanna, Fiona, Nuala, and Elinore had discussed the best places to house the wounded and how to divide the people with healing skills among those places. None of them had mentioned Death's Servants or the Shadowed Veil.

And that is the difference between us, she thought as she and Ashk rode back to the Old Place. As the Huntress, she would be justice . . . and vengeance . . . when it was needed. But the Hunter always saw the things that lived within Life's shadows and wouldn't ignore or deny them. As the Hunter, Ashk would be Death's ally . . . and Death's weapon.

Aiden resisted the urge to shift position again, but after his hands had curled hard enough to hurt on the top stones of the pasture wall, he tucked them under his arms. His fingertips were sore from the few minutes he'd taken to work with his harp before Ashk and Selena returned, and he was still very aware of how much he might have lost if it hadn't been for the power of Rhyann's gifts.

But it wasn't Ashk's silence that made him edgy as they leaned against one of Baron Liam's pasture walls. It was learning that there were nighthunters out there, somewhere, that made him yearn for solid walls and thick doors and shutters. He was grateful Liam had found room for them at his house. Several of the gentry had offered accommodations to the midland barons and the Fae leaders, but knowing there were some of those creatures out there wasn't going to let anyone rest easy—not when there were so many men living out on the land. At least a warning had been sent to the farms nearest the place where Ashk had caught the nighthunters' scent, and all the camps would post guards to keep watch.

Aiden found no comfort in the fact that he and Ashk were in the open, or that despite the distance the Fae and humans were giving them for privacy, they were hardly alone. Or unarmed.

Ashk had her bow and a full quiver, and even in the waning light, he doubted she would miss anything within range of her arrows.

Still, he shifted again, unable to remain calm when every rustle of leaves or snap of a twig made his heart jump.

As if telling the Hunter what he'd learned about the Inquisitors wasn't enough to make his heart bounce inside his chest.

"Well," Ashk finally said, "that explains, in some part, why the Black Coats hate witches and the Fae as much as they do."

"In some part? I think it explains it well enough," Aiden replied.

Ashk looked at the land. "No. Only in part, Aiden. When the Fae who had lived in the pieces of Tir Alainn anchored to the Old Places in Wolfram ignored the children they had sired in the human world, it would have created some hardship for those human families—and ill feelings in others. The Fae didn't understand, or chose to ignore, the consequences of indulging their whims. It changed them, distanced them from the world. But some of the humans must have changed, too, and some of the witches as well. Maybe they were too far away from their roots to remember who they were. Maybe they saw what others had and envied it to the point where they could no longer see what *they* had. Maybe they tried to grasp too hard to gain the thing they desired, and by doing so, pushed it further away. The world is always changing, Bard, and we change with it—even those of us who are firmly rooted in who and what we are. So maybe everything changed in Wolfram, or nothing changed, or the wrong things changed, and a hole full of wanting was created in people's hearts—and that wanting opened the way for a man like the Master Inquisitor to come into power. We'll never know what happened in Wolfram. All we can do is take care of what is here."

"We have enough reason to regret what we haven't done here," Aiden said with a trace of bitterness.

Ashk turned her head and looked into his eyes. "Do you?"

Aiden hesitated, then shook his head. "My friends used to tease me, saying that I was too in love with music to taste the other pleasures to be had in the human world." He smiled self-consciously. "That wasn't quite true. There were some moonlit walks with pretty maids and sweet kisses. But that was all. When I left a village, the only thing I left with a maid was a song and a memory." His smile faded. "I'm grateful for that now, grateful I'm not one of the men who has to wonder if he'll meet a son on that battlefield. Even more grateful I don't have to wonder if a daughter I sired has died under the Black Coats' hands. When this is over, I imagine there will be some Fae men who will travel to a village or an Old Place they haven't thought of in years. Just to see. Just to know."

"And, perhaps, to begin to change things for the better," Ashk said gently. She sighed and pushed away from the wall. "Come along, Bard. It's been a long day. Tonight we'll eat and rest."

"And tomorrow?" Aiden asked reluctantly.

The gentleness drained out of Ashk's face, reminding him of the mask she'd worn during the Summer Solstice dance. Reminding him of the dance itself—and what it meant.

"We will do what needs to be done," the Hunter replied.

Chapter 37

waxing moon

Morag came down the shining road into a world of smoke and flame. The dark horse squealed, then sat back on his haunches, preparing to wheel and take them back to the shining road—and safety.

She wanted to let him turn back, wanted to escape the heat that made her feel like a dried husk and the air that fouled her lungs and made her choke as she struggled to breathe. But the path of fire was also the Lightbringer's path, so she dug her heels into the dark horse's sides, bent low in the saddle, and gasped, "Run."

He gave her his heart and his courage—and he ran. Trees exploded from the heat, showering them with bits of flaming wood. She screamed in fury, in fear, and guided him as best she could through the tunnel of fire, her eyes slitted against the smoke and heat.

Death roared in that fire, and when the dark horse almost stumbled on something soft, she hoped it was a rabbit and not one of the Small Folk who lived in Bretonwood.

Curse you, Lucian. May you never have a moment's peace for the rest of your life.

The trail split. The fire hadn't reached the right-hand fork, leading to the Clan house. For a heartbeat, she thought of taking that trail, circling round. But images from the dream flashed in her mind—Neall, dying on the trail; Ari, fleeing from an enemy. She didn't have time. Whatever it cost her, she didn't have time. So she turned the dark horse onto the left-hand fork that burned, burned, burned all the way to Neall and Ari's cottage.

The dark horse's breathing was harsh and labored, but he ran. He ran until they burst out of the trees into the meadow where she saw a nightmare—and hope.

She let him turn toward the kitchen garden, toward the grass untouched by the battle taking place in the meadow. Choking, gasping for air, she watched, not daring to do more at that moment when her vision was blurred and her control too shaky to summon her power.

The black horse and the stag circled each other, looking for an opening to strike a blow. Merle circled with them, also looking for an opening. The stag had a hoofprint branded onto his left flank, but Morag didn't think Neall even realized he'd been struck. Flames rose wherever Lucian's hooves touched the ground, but they were quickly extinguished, as if someone was grounding the power as fast as Lucian could summon it.

Morag looked at Ari, who stood a few feet from the cottage. Tears ran down the young witch's face, mixing with the sweat that soaked her hair and the bodice of her dress. Her teeth were gritted, and her hands pressed against a belly that looked ripe enough to burst.

"No, Lucian! *No!*" Ari screamed. "I won't go back with you. I made my choice. *Lucian!*"

Horse, stag, and shadow hound kept circling, paying no heed to the woman they fought over.

Ari screamed again—and Morag shivered at the rage she heard growing under the fear. "You think if you burn out my life, I'll crawl back and accept whatever crumbs you give me because you've left me with nothing else? I won't crawl. I won't go back. *I'm not some trinket for you to play with!*"

Smoke rose from the cottage roof, but Morag saw no flames. She looked at Ari and saw determination etched in a face that would never again look as young and fresh as it had even just a few hours before. *She's grounding the fire. She's matching his power and holding it back. But how long can she do it without harming herself or the babe?*

Morag straightened in the saddle, still fighting to take a full breath. If Neall slipped . . . If Lucian got in a lucky blow . . . She couldn't wait for Death to tell her whom to gather.

Then Merle dashed in, snapping at Lucian's belly. Lucian whirled to strike back at the shadow hound—and gave Neall the opening he'd been waiting for. His antlers raked across Lucian's side, cutting through the skin. Fire roared up in front of Neall, forcing him to leap away. But the flames died fast, and he was back, circling, circling. He moved forward, putting himself in reach of Lucian's front hooves.

Screaming in fury and triumph, Lucian reared—and Merle struck from behind, his jaws closing on a hind leg, his teeth ripping muscle and tendons.

Lucian fought for balance while Neall leaped away. As his front hooves slammed into the ground and blood poured from his side and his crippled hind leg, Ari yelled, "Neall! Merle!" The power of earth rolled in her voice.

They backed away from Lucian, moving toward her.

Ari and Lucian stared at each other. Morag watched them, waiting. Then something else caught her attention and she turned her head to stare at the trees—at the fire disappearing from their blackened skeletons.

She looked back at Ari, alarmed. And she felt a moment's pity for the man who was the Lord of Fire. *Lucian, you fool. There is good reason why witches are called the Mother's Daughters.*

"You want fire, Lightbringer?" Ari said. *"Then I will give you fire!"*

A column of flames roared up in the meadow, rising toward the sky. Trapped in the center of it, Lucian screamed—and Morag heard Death howl. She watched the dark shape of a horse rear, too panicked now to remember the crippled leg until it buckled under him. As he fell, as the smell of burning flesh reached her, she gathered him. Tore his spirit out of that burning body and pulled him to her.

Ari's legs slowly buckled. Neall changed form and ran toward her, his limp becoming more pronounced with each step as his body finally recognized the burn on his hip. He caught her as her knees hit the ground.

"Ari? Ari!" He looked around, as if desperate to find someone to help.

Morag saw him pale when he noticed her. She didn't have time to tell him that Death had turned away from their cottage and was summoning her to many other places around Bretonwood because Padrick rode up at that moment.

"Mother's mercy, Neall! What happened?" Padrick demanded. "Did the Black Coats slip past us and attack you?"

Neall shook his head, then looked at the column of fire that had died to a flicker around the burned corpse.

Padrick stared at the charred lump in the meadow. As he

turned his head toward Neall, he saw Morag. His eyes flicked from Ari and Neall back to her. She shook her head, brushed her heels gently against the dark horse's sides, and rode away.

She circled around to a place that would be an easy distance from the Clan house before she opened the road that led to the Shadowed Veil. The dark horse faltered halfway up the road, dropping back from a canter to a trot. His breathing still sounded too labored. She pressed a hand against his neck, noticing the bloody pock marks where he'd been burned. Death was close by, calling her, but not for her loyal dark horse—and not for her. Whatever harm the fire had done to them would heal.

When she finally reached the Shadowed Veil, she released Lucian's spirit. His ghost appeared before her in human form, and he stared at her with gray eyes full of hate.

"At least now you'll have to keep your bargain, Gatherer," Lucian said.

"I made no bargain with you, Lucian," Morag replied.

"Of course you didn't," he sneered. "But we all know you're a liar, Morag, so there's no reason to think you won't lie about this, too."

"I didn't lie. I told you Ari was gone. And she *was* gone. Neall got her away from the Inquisitors, got her away from Brightwood . . . and got her away from you."

"And now that you've gathered me, you'll return Ari to her proper place at Brightwood."

Morag shook her head. "That wasn't the bargain. You didn't offer your life in exchange for hers."

"What man *would* make an offer like that?"

"Neall did."

Lucian stared at her.

Morag smiled sadly. "That is the difference between you, Lucian. You wanted her. Neall loves her."

"I cared about her!" Lucian clenched his fists. "And she cared about me. I know she did. She was *mine* until that mongrel enticed her away from me. She turned me away without giving me a chance to show her what I could give her. And even if she didn't choose to be my lover, she still belongs at Brightwood. She would be there now if you hadn't lied to us, made us believe she was dead. Dianna wouldn't have been trapped there and—"

"You," Morag snapped. "Dianna. It's always about you and Dianna, isn't it? What you want, what you didn't get, what someone else should do or give up so that nothing inconveniences *you*." She bent in the saddle and leaned toward him. "Are you going to stamp your feet and throw a tantrum now, *child*?"

He took a step back from her, stunned.

"I am the Gatherer of Souls," Morag continued. "I answer to no one, and I do not care what you want."

"You have to care!" Lucian shouted. *"I am the Lightbringer."*

"You were the Lightbringer." Morag brushed the reins against the dark horse's neck to signal him to turn and go down the road. "Now you're a spirit who has to finish the journey to the Summerland."

She rode back into the human world, then reined in and sat for a moment, listening. No whispers from the direction of Neall and Ari's cottage. But in the direction of the Bretonwood Clan house, Death was a chorus, and the woods still burned.

As she turned the dark horse toward the Clan house, she heard the first rolls of thunder and felt the first drops of rain.

Morag rode toward the cottage, swaying in the saddle from exhaustion and grief. The fire hadn't reached the Clan house itself, but it had swept through the woods around the shining road so fast, the Small Folk who lived in that part of Bretonwood had had no chance to escape. Some of the Fae were missing, but the Clan tried to remain hopeful that their kin had been able to outrun the fire and were taking shelter elsewhere until morning. Since Death no longer tugged at her, she hoped they were right.

The cottage was dark except for the kitchen. When she saw light flicker in the barn, her heart bumped against her chest. No. Too steady to be uncontained fire. A lamp most likely.

Then Glenn stepped out of the cottage, a pitcher in his hand. "Lady Morag?"

"How are you, Glenn? Is everything all right here?" Morag grabbed at the saddle as she felt herself slip sideways.

"I'm fine. We're all fine. Baron Padrick had a carriage brought over and took Ari, Neall, and Merle back to his house. Said he wanted his physician and the midwife—"

"Physician? Midwife?"

Glenn raised his hand in a placating gesture. "Neall's got that burn on his hip which I think is paining him more than he'll admit, and he and Padrick both wanted Ari looked over to make sure she and the babe came to no harm because of— Well, because. And the baron said they'd get no rest with the smell of smoke and—" He shifted uneasily as he glanced at the meadow. "Ari doesn't need to see that. The baron will send men over in the morning to take care of things."

Morag lifted her chin toward the barn. "Something wrong with the animals?"

"No," Glenn said quickly. "It's just . . . well . . . some of the Small Folk showed up. Didn't have anywhere to go for shelter. Too dangerous to try traveling any distance in the woods tonight. Wouldn't stay in the cottage for anything, but they were glad of the offer of a couple of stalls in the barn. Forrester came back with some blankets and a small keg of ale. Brought some bread and cheese, too, to have with the day soup Ari had simmering on the stove. So they're snug enough for the night."

She wanted bread and soup, too—and enough ale to dull the memories of the bodies she'd seen.

"Will you be staying, Morag? There's plenty of soup left."

With regret, Morag shook her head. "I'll go on to Padrick's house."

Glenn nodded. "You tell Ari not to worry. Plenty of neighbors have stopped by to say they'd be back in the morning to air out the cottage and put things to right."

Morag lifted a hand in farewell, then signaled the dark horse to move on. Halfway to Padrick's house, she wondered why she hadn't stayed at the cottage. She was almost blind with exhaustion and the dark horse wasn't in any better condition.

She needed to see Ari. That's why. She needed the assurance that Neall would recover. She needed to tell Merle he was a wonderful shadow hound. She needed her family.

So she rode on until her dark horse snorted in surprise and a hand closed over her arm. Startled, she tried to pull away—and found herself staring into Padrick's grim face.

"I thought you wouldn't have sense to stay at the cottage once you got done gathering," he said, exasperation making his voice rough. He released her arm and signaled his horse to walk on. "The two of you staggering down the road, asleep on your feet—"

"I'm not on my feet," Morag protested.

"And your horse is barely staying on his. Damn fool of a woman."

"Who's a fool?"

"You. Ari. All of you. You're all too stubborn to know when you need to stop, when you've done all you can—more than you can. No, you'll just keep pushing until your brain shuts down or your body quits."

Stung, Morag made an effort to sit up straighter in the saddle. "You can't speak to me that way."

"I can and I will, just as I'd speak that way to Ari or Caitlin if they were being too stubborn to show some sense. Ashk, too, for that matter—although she'd change into her other form long enough to nip me for it."

Wish I could do that, Morag thought sourly.

"Damn fool of a woman," Padrick muttered. "She was trying to ground the whole fire. Did you realize that? Not just the meadow. Not just keeping that stunted excuse of a man from burning her home down around her or killing the man she loves. No, she was trying to hold the whole thing back."

Alarmed that Ari would even think of trying to do that much, Padrick's tone nevertheless compelled her to defend the decision. "Did it occur to you that Ari was trying to protect the Clan?"

"Of course it occurred to me," Padrick roared. "The Clan house would have been lost before the witches who had come up from Wiccandale could do anything about it."

"Witches from Wiccandale?"

Padrick waved that away. "They had business with me. Two of them had the gift of water, and when they saw the fire, they summoned the rain."

"Did you yell at them, too?"

"No, I did not."

"Then why are you yelling at me?" Morag blinked, furious with Padrick because tears were filling her eyes.

Since they were riding Fae horses, there wasn't even the *clip-clop* of hooves to interrupt the sudden silence.

Finally, Padrick said quietly, "Because I was scared to the bone today. Because I know what could have happened here. Because I know what *did* happen here. Because I was helpless to stop it. Because I'm just a foolish man who was so relieved at finding you're both all right that I yelled at you."

"Did you yell at Neall?" Morag asked, wiping the tears off her cheeks.

Padrick chuckled. "Couldn't. My physician took one look at

Neall's hip and dosed him with something that put him to sleep before he could finish arguing that he didn't want it."

"But he'll be all right?"

"Yes, he'll be all right. So will Ari. The physician and midwife agree that she needs bed rest. The babe's not due for another week or so, but they were concerned that the strain of channeling so much magic might have brought her to childbed early. However, the babe is content to stay where it is a while longer, and Ari will be recovered before she brings her son or daughter into the world."

Morag tried to stay alert, but after Padrick's assurance that Ari and Neall were all right, her attention drifted. The next thing she knew, he was helping her out of the saddle, assuring her that the dark horse would be well taken care of, and leading her into the house. From there, the housekeeper and the lady's maid to Ashk took over, helping her take a quick bath and wash the stink of smoke out of her hair, bundling her into a borrowed nightgown, and feeding her a bowl of stew and bread. She resisted their attempts to put her to bed, insisting that she had to see Ari first.

Ari gave her a tired smile when she entered the guest room and settled on the edge of the bed.

"I'm glad I'm not gentry," Ari said. "Lady's maids are very intimidating. Seems every time I twitch, the bed covers get straightened, the pillows get fluffed, and I spend five minutes arguing that the physician and midwife don't need to come back."

Morag nodded. "I kept trying to picture how Ashk and her maid deal with each other—and decided I didn't want to know."

Ari plucked the bedcovers. "He's gone? Really gone?"

"Yes, Lucian is really gone."

"I keep thinking I should be sorry for what happened. But I'm not. That hurts almost as much as knowing he would have killed Neall without a second thought. And for what?"

"Because he was the Lightbringer, and the Fae have catered to the Lord of Fire and Lady of the Moon for so long, he believed he should have what he wanted whenever he wanted for as long as he wanted."

"People's lives as trinkets?" Ari's eyes filled with tears until one slipped down her face. "Did that make him any different from the Inquisitors, Morag? They think of people as trinkets, too—things they can reshape to suit themselves . . . or destroy if it suits them better."

"I think he did care about you," Morag said. "I think he wanted you for himself as much as for Brightwood."

"I cared about him, too, but not enough to stay, even if the Black Coats hadn't come to Brightwood." Ari hesitated. "I wanted to remember him kindly, as a lover I'd had for a little while. A small romance that was outside the world in many ways. Now I'll remember him as the man who tried to destroy the people I love. As the man I killed."

There it was, the festering pain Morag had been waiting to lance. "You didn't kill him, Ari," she said, resting her hand over Ari's to stop the nervous plucking. "I did."

Ari shook her head. "I'm the one who used my gift from the Mother to send the fire back to him, knowing he would burn."

"And I'm the one who gathered him while he lived."

"The fire would have killed him anyway."

"He was the Lord of Fire. He might have controlled it enough to escape it. I didn't give him the chance."

Ari looked at her for a long time, then said softly, "As you will, so mote it be."

Morag leaned over and kissed Ari's forehead. "Get some rest."

As she reached the bedroom door and opened it, Ari said, "Morag?"

"Yes?"

"Thank you."

Morag stepped into the hallway and found Padrick leaning against the wall, waiting for her.

"Is she all right?" Padrick asked quietly.

"I'm the one who killed Lucian. I took a spirit from a body that still lived."

"From what Glenn told me, the fire would have killed him anyway. You're standing on one side of a line that's no more than a hair's width of difference."

"Perhaps," Morag agreed. "But that hair's width of difference is one Ari can live with."

She stood beside the cradle, smiling at the babe who stared at her. As she leaned over, pudgy hands waved in the air, trying to catch strands of her black hair. The babe made gleeful sounds, kicking its feet against the blanket that covered it.

She raised her hand to brush her finger down one round little cheek . . .

. . . and saw another hand reaching to do the same thing. A dark hand with leathery skin and talons at the ends of its fingers.

The enemy's hand. Right beside her.

No. No!

She threw herself to one side, intending to shove the enemy away from the cradle, to put herself between this destroyer and the babe. The hand lashed out and disappeared.

There was nobody to shove against, no enemy to fight.

However, the movement turned her toward the doorway. Ari sprawled there, her eyes Death-blind, her torn body empty of life and spirit.

Spinning around, she looked into the cradle and saw what those cruel talons could do to a small body. Empty of life. Empty of spirit.

It had taken everything. Everything!

But where was the enemy? Where?

A last exhalation, a death rattle from someone already gone as Ari said, "As you will—"

I don't want this! I don't will this!

"—so mote it be."

NO!

Morag's hands shook violently as she pulled on her clothes and boots. She had nothing else to take with her. Her tack was in the stable, along with the canteen for water.

She'd had one brief hope that the dreams would end now that Lucian was dead, that the dreams had been a nightmarish warning about his coming here. But he wasn't the only enemy after Ari and Neall. There was another one. A far more deadly one.

And she understood now that it would find its way here because of her, that it was following *her,* and through her would destroy what she held dear. So she had to leave, had to get away, tonight, right now. She had to lead it away from here until she found a way to fight it, destroy it.

She ran through the corridors and clattered down the stairs, too driven by the need to escape to care about the noise she made. The lock on the front door thwarted her until she almost screamed with frustration. Finally, she forced herself to slow down enough to look, to think. After that, it took mere seconds to deal with what was, after all, a simple lock.

She ran to the stables, pulled open one side of the double door. A chimney lamp with a candle burning low hung on the wall above a cot where a stablelad snored softly.

As she hurried down the aisle, the dark horse put his head over the stall's half-door and snorted an inquiry. Ointment glistened on his neck and face where cinders had burned him. Not too many. Not too bad, considering what they'd run through. When she opened the bottom half of the door, he stepped forward, and she watched his legs, his feet. No lameness. No injuries. She was almost sorry she didn't have a reason to leave him behind.

He snorted again, a bit more forcefully.

"I'm sorry, boy," she whispered, resting a hand on his muzzle. "I am sorry I can't let you rest, but we have to go now. We have to get away from here."

"Huh? Wha'?" The stablelad sat up, rubbed sleep from his eyes, and blinked at her. "What are you doing with the horse?"

Morag spun around, desperation changing to fury. "Get out of here. Get out. Now."

The lad stumbled away from the cot, his fear-widened eyes watching her as he backed toward the outer door. He tripped when his shoulder hit the edge of the door. He was up and running almost before he fell.

Morag barely had time to throw the saddle over the dark horse's back before Padrick burst into the stable.

"Morag?" he said, striding toward her. "What's happened? What's wrong?"

She turned on him, her teeth bared, her hands curled like claws. "Stay away from me. Leave me be. I have to get away from here. Now."

Padrick raised his hands and stopped moving toward her, but he didn't back away. "Why?"

"I have to leave!"

"Why?"

The whip-crack demand in his voice doused her with cold reason. She couldn't kill *him* because he was in her way, and he wouldn't get out of her way without an explanation.

Raking her hands through her sleep-tangled hair, she tried to explain. "I've had dreams. On the journey east and all the way back here. Not always the same dream, but the same kind of dream."

"About what?"

"Something is hunting here. Something evil. I can sense it, almost feel what it feels, know what it thinks. But I can't find it, can't stop it. It . . . kills Neall. And then hunts Ari and the babe. But this time, it was right in the cottage with them. I was standing right there, and it . . . still . . . killed them. I think it can find them through me. Somehow, it will find them through me. So I can't stay here. If it's following me, I have to lead it away. Once I'm gone, they'll be safe."

"Ashk?"

For a moment, she didn't understand him. Then she let his voice, stripped of all emotion, all heart, sink in. She shook her head. "I've only dreamed of Ari, Neall, and the babe. Ashk . . ." She stopped, felt a swell of hope. "It wouldn't go near the Hunter because Ashk could defeat it. She's strong enough to win."

Padrick slowly lowered his hands. "Then you have to head back east and join Ashk as quickly as you can."

"Yes." Morag sighed with relief before she turned to finish saddling the dark horse.

"You're not leaving tonight, Morag."

She gripped the saddle to keep from striking him as he stepped up behind her.

"Morag. You're exhausted. The horse is exhausted. How far do you think you'll get before one or both of you ends up injured or crippled? Listen to me. There's another way. It's only a few hours until sunrise. Do you know Sealand?"

She nodded warily. "I went there with Ashk."

"A day's ride from here, even by carriage. The horse can follow behind."

"A day's ride in the wrong direction."

"In the right direction," Padrick countered. "To the sea. We'll get a ship there that can take us all the way down to the bay near Selkie Island. Once we land, if you go up the closest shining road and ride through the Clan territories and cross between them on the bridges, you're a day's ride, a day and a half at most, from the Mother's Hills. If you ask them, the House of Gaian will allow you to ride through their land. You'll get to Willowsbrook just as fast, if not faster, and you'll have the sea journey in which to rest."

He had a point, especially when she wasn't sure she could finish saddling her horse by herself. "If I agree to this, will you promise not to call me a damn fool of a woman for trying to leave?"

After a pause, he asked, "Can I think it?"

Morag rested her forehead against the saddle. "I can't stop you from thinking, Padrick."

"That's settled, then. Take the saddle off the horse. We'll all get a few hours sleep and be on our way at first light."

Morag debated for a moment, then decided the horse was worth more than her pride. "I don't think I'm strong enough to lift it off him."

Padrick shouldered her out of the way. She chose not to hear what he muttered under his breath while he put the saddle on the nearest rack, made sure the dark horse had feed and water, and led her back to the house. He was still muttering when he pushed her into her room and closed the door with a firmness that was just short of unfriendly.

Morag stared at the door for a long time before she changed her clothes and climbed into bed.

Since Ashk often wore a pleased, lazy smile after spending time alone with Padrick, Morag suspected there were compensations for putting up with the man. But she also decided that every nip Ashk gave him was a nip well deserved.

Chapter 38

waxing moon

Jenny stood on the cliffs, staring out at the gentle sea. Fishing boats rode easy swells. She shuddered at the thought of what they might bring up in their nets.

"I thought I would find you here."

She turned and watched Mihail walk toward her. "You shouldn't be up yet. You need to rest."

He smiled and shook his head. "My shoulder and back were burned, not my legs. I needed to move, needed the fresh air."

Jenny turned back to the sea, felt the warmth of his hand when he rested it on her shoulder.

"If you're going to brood and feel guilty, I can remind you of all the people who wouldn't have survived if you hadn't used the sea to defend us against the Inquisitors' warships."

"Will you also remind me of all the people who didn't survive?" Jenny asked softly. "There are empty chairs around the tables in this village, Mihail. There are empty chairs around the tables in the other Clan houses."

"That wasn't your doing, Jenny." Mihail squeezed her shoulder. "Murtagh made a point of telling me the Fae who were flying around those ships weren't killed by the sea. Arrows killed them. Or fire if they were splashed when one of those pots of liquid fire struck a ship. They fought for themselves and their land and their way of life just as much as they fought to help us. Just as we would have fought to help them."

The words washed against a different kind of pain, a different kind of grief, trying to break through and smooth the rough edges of emotion, like the sea's relentless dance with stone.

"Murtagh said he tried to tell you this, but you weren't ready to hear it, weren't ready to accept it. Will you listen now, Jenny?"

Tears filled her eyes, blurring her vision. "The anger and the grief that swelled the sea and created that storm . . . They were mine. They came from me."

"So did the love."

She obeyed the pressure of his hand and shifted to face him. "I know what I gave to the sea. What I chose to give to the sea. I didn't choose love."

"You didn't have to choose. It's part of who you are." He released her shoulder to rub the back of his neck, and his voice ripened with frustration. "I know the sea, and I know you—and I know how the sea feels when you channel your gift through it. Mother's mercy, we've sailed together enough times. How could I not recognize the feel of you in the water?" When she just stared at him, he swore. "Sometimes you can be as stubborn as stone. So tell me this, Jenny. If there wasn't love in that storm, how do you explain the two children? A sister and brother. They were on the ship the Inquisitors burned. The children's parents threw them off the ship while it burned and broke up around them. Threw them into the sea, doing the only thing they could to spare their children from burning.

"Those children were too young to survive in the sea. They were too far from land and any help, and they were in that storm with nothing but the sea around them. They should have drowned, Jenny. And yet, when the selkies swam out to look for survivors, they found those two children riding the swells. They said there were currents in that water like they'd never felt before—currents that constantly pushed upward, under those children, keeping them in that place where water meets air. The selkies used those currents, pushing the children to one of the boats that had come out to help. When the children were safely on board, the currents disappeared. The selkies didn't know what to call it. I do. That was love.

"And what about the rest of us? We rode through that storm, too, and we came to no harm. Because the part of you that you never have to think about kept guiding the sea around our ships. Swells that would have destroyed a ship if they'd crested, never crested. We sailed through mountains of water that didn't tumble in on themselves until the ships were past them. That wasn't luck, Jenny. That was love. You *have* to know that. This fight isn't over, and the day may come when you need to shape the sea into a weapon again to save those you hold dear. I'd take that burden from you if I could, and do it with a glad heart, but I don't have your strength and I can't command the sea the way you do."

Mihail put one arm around Jenny, drawing her against him. "So you have to know, sister dear, that if you give the sea your fury to fight against the enemy, love will always flow under it to protect your friends."

Jenny broke, weeping bitterly as she clung to her brother. It felt as if the sea crashed inside her, fierce waves breaking the foundation upon which she'd built her life, the security she'd always had that her creed was her protection against using her gift to harm instead of help.

"You've lost your innocence, Jenny," Mihail said when her sobs had finally eased back to sniffles. "And I'm sorry for it. It's no comfort, but you're not alone. There will be other witches who will weep bitter tears when they make the same choice and break the creed. But they'll break it because they must, and they'll weep to ease the grief in their hearts—and they'll go on with their lives."

"It will never be the same," Jenny whispered.

"No, it will never be the same."

Jenny said nothing for a while, finding comfort in the steady beat of Mihail's heart beneath her cheek. Finally, she eased back, fumbled in her pocket for a handkerchief, and wiped her face. She looked away, feeling a fresh stab of grief, which had been hidden under the storm but had been raging inside her. "The selkies are afraid of me. Murtagh is afraid of me."

Mihail laughed.

Jenny stared at him, insulted. "How can you laugh about it?"

"I'm sorry, Jenny. I am. But—" He winced when he moved without thinking. "Mother's tits. My shoulder is going to be tender for a while." He smiled at her and shook his head. "I am sorry, but you're thinking like a woman."

"And that's bad?"

"No, it's just"—he let out a gusty sigh, and winced again—"the selkies sometimes fear the sea, too, with good reason. But that doesn't keep them away from it. As for Murtagh . . . well, his visits to my sick bed weren't just to keep me company."

"Then why was he there?"

"He hedged a bit—and I got the impression Murtagh rarely hedges about anything—but the gist of the talk was to find out if I'd have any objections to his visiting us to become better acquainted. And before you say anything that makes you sound dim-witted, I'll tell you now he really isn't interested in becoming better acquainted with *me*."

Jenny turned away and frowned at the sea. "He hasn't come to his grandmother's cottage in the past two days. Not even to visit you."

"That's because he's gone to the mainland across the bay to talk to the young baron who rules there, and also to purchase a mainsail for *Sweet Selkie*. They've canvas enough to replace the smaller sails that were damaged, but he'll bring the mainsail back with him."

"You gave him the coins to pay for it?"

Chuckling, Mihail slipped his arm through hers and started walking back to the village. "Craig gave him the coins for it— and the commission for acting as the family's agent in the purchase."

Jenny blinked. "The Lord of the Selkies had to barter with *Craig* to pay for the mainsail and get a commission?" She pitied anyone who had to barter with her cousin.

"Murtagh was ready to pull his own hair out by the time it was done, then insisted that he'd given in only because Craig was still recovering from his injuries."

Jenny frowned. "Craig didn't barter well?"

"He bartered as he always does."

"Oh, dear. Poor Murtagh." She laughed, but the laughter faded quickly. "Craig will heal, won't he?"

Mihail looked sad and grim. "He was badly burned, Jenny. His face will always be scarred. But the healers are hopeful that he'll regain the use of his hand, and there's nothing wrong with his wits. Time will heal the body, and work will heal the rest. In a few days, we'll be able to go on to Sealand, and he can set up the stock we have and start to rebuild the family business."

He didn't call it home, she noticed. Sealand wasn't home for him. Not yet. But it was safe harbor. She knew he would wait anxiously for the day when his wife and daughter would be able to leave Willowsbrook and join him there. Then Sealand would be home.

She hoped that day would come. She hoped Mihail's family and Fiona and Rory and the others had made the journey to Willowsbrook safely. And she hoped they would remain safe despite whatever battles were raging in the eastern part of Sylvalan.

Chapter 39

waxing moon

Ubel nursed his hatred until it was a living thing crawling inside him.

They had chained him—*him! The Master Inquisitor's Assistant!*—as if he were an animal. The shackles around his ankles and wrists jangled with every movement, dragged the straw that had been put down on the warehouse floor as rough bedding under the thin blankets they'd been given. A handful of chamberpots, emptied twice a day, kept the men who had survived the destruction of Wolfram's great warships from living in their own filth, but there was no privacy. Every time a man unbuttoned his pants to squat over one of those pots, those bastards—those cold-eyed, silent Fae—watched him.

Their prison inside the warehouse had no walls, just crates no more than waist high to mark the perimeter. Even in chains, it wouldn't take much effort to get over the crates, but any man who tried to escape was dead before he'd taken two steps, arrows bristling out of his chest and back. The Fae didn't warn or wound. They simply killed. Baron's son, minor gentry, soldier, sailor, Inquisitor. It didn't matter to them.

There was no way past these cold-eyed Fae. They didn't speak, not even among themselves, while they stood guard. His men couldn't get close enough to fight them, and his Inquisitor's Gift of persuasion had no effect on them. Humans didn't come into the warehouse—at least, they didn't come in far enough to be useful to him. And the one time he'd managed to snare a human youth's will by raising his voice as if to offer encouragement to his fellow prisoners, the young man was pulled out of the warehouse as soon as the Fae realized the human had been ensnared—and a Fae Lord with eyes colder and more dangerous than the sea came in a little while later and told him that if he raised his voice again, they would cut out his tongue and feed it to him.

He believed the bastard.

So he nursed his hatred and waited, waited, waited for the enemy to come to him. Because there were barons' sons and minor gentry among the prisoners, because the baron who ruled this piece of Sylvalan was so young and inexperienced in doling out harsh punishment, a message had been sent to Padrick, the Baron of Breton, to assess the prisoners, to pass judgment.

The enemy he had failed to punish the last time was coming within his reach. He wasn't a fool. Killing Padrick would guarantee his own death, but destroying Padrick would be a deep wound to western Sylvalan. And when the Master Inquisitor conquered this part of Sylvalan, Adolfo would hear of it and know his Assistant had served him well to the last breath.

Chapter 40

full moon

B reanna walked into the kitchen and almost walked out again. Too many people. Too much heat. Too much confusion. Too much noise. Keely and Brooke were sitting at one end of the long work table, shelling peas and chattering as if they could actually hear each other. Fiona and Glynis were dealing with some crisis around the stove, which meant they'd give her snappish replies if she asked them what, if anything, was supposed to be done with the big kettles simmering on the stove in the summer kitchen. Elinore was at Liam's house that afternoon, responding to pleas from her son's housekeeper and butler that someone needed to provide the servants with some instructions for dealing with so many important guests—and Liam's response to household questions, Elinore had told her dryly, was a distracted look and a promise to look into matters soon . . . which meant never.

She needed to tell some other passably sane adult that Idjit, living up to his name, had gobbled something he shouldn't have eaten, thrown up on the flagstones in front of the summer kitchen, and one of the boys helping Clay with the horses, too intent on sneaking into the kitchen to grab a snack, had slipped in the mess, hit his head on the edge of a work table, and was now on his way to the village physician with Clay and Falco to have his head stitched up.

And why was Jean standing in the corner of the kitchen with that smug, I-know-something-you-don't-know smile?

"Where's Gran?" Breanna asked, raising her voice enough to be heard.

Her face flushed with heat, Fiona turned away from the stove. "She went upstairs about an hour ago. She was sitting here, having a cup of tea while we talked about what to serve for the evening meal. She said the tea tasted odd, poured out the rest of it, and went up to her room to lie down for a bit."

Breanna headed for the door that led into the rest of the house. Pausing, she looked back. Jean watched her, eyes bright with something Breanna would have called malicious glee.

Shaking her head, she left the kitchen and walked to the stairs that led up to the bedrooms. She didn't like Jean—liked the girl even less with each passing day. But they were stuck with each other, so she'd have to grit her teeth and try to be more tolerant of adolescent snits.

Breanna tapped on her grandmother's door. When she didn't get an answer, she slipped into the room. Nuala was lying on her side, asleep, a summer quilt pulled up to her waist.

As she moved closer to the bed, Breanna's nose twitched at the smell. Was Nuala more ill than they'd realized? Had she soiled herself in her sleep, unable to rouse enough to reach the chamberpot?

"Gran?" Breanna said softly. The hand reaching for her grandmother's shoulder froze as she stared at Nuala's face, then at the chest that did not rise nor fall. "Gran?"

No sound. No flutter of breath. No flicker of movement, not even a twitch of an eyelid. And cold skin. Cold, cold skin.

Breanna backed out of the room, shaking her head. She clung to the banister as she walked down the stairs because her legs suddenly had too many joints and moved in strange, unpredictable ways.

She would send someone for the village physician. She would send one of the Fae to find the closest healer staying in the camps with them. They would know what to do. Gran was ill. Very ill. But they would know what to do because Gran was . . . Gran was . . .

She was standing in the kitchen, with no memory of walking from the staircase to the kitchen door. Too many people. Too much heat. Too much confusion. Too much noise.

Then Selena, Ashk, and Liam walked through the back door, and no longer were there too many people. Strength had walked into the room. But there still wasn't quite enough air to breathe, everyone but those three people were blurs of color and movement, and voices were nothing more than sounds until Liam said sharply, "Breanna?"

Things began to slip back into focus. She saw the chair that was pushed away from the smaller work table in front of her, as if someone had been sitting there recently and hadn't bothered to push the chair back again. Saw Fiona turn in response to the sharpness in Liam's voice—turn and look at him before looking closely at her. Saw Keely rest a hand on Brooke's arm, signaling the girl to be quiet.

"Breanna?" Fiona said. "Is Nuala awake? Would she like a bowl of soup or another cup of tea?"

Tea.

Breanna looked at Jean, who still stood in the corner, wearing that smug smile and watching her.

Clarity became knife-edged.

"What did you put in the tea?" Breanna asked calmly, staring at Jean.

Jean shifted her feet, the smile changing into a pout. "I didn't make any tea."

"What did you put in the tea?"

"Breanna?" Liam said, taking a step toward her.

She took a step closer to the table. "Nuala said the tea tasted odd. She didn't drink all of it, but she drank enough." Another step. Close enough now to jump from chair to table to—"I'm going to rip your heart out with my bare hands, just to see if you really have one."

"I didn't do anything!" Jean wailed.

"Breanna." Now Fiona's voice had turned sharp. "Is something wrong with Nuala? Is she ill?"

"Nuala is dead." Breanna's voice broke. Her control shattered. "You little bitch, *you killed my grandmother!*"

Chair to table, and she was flying through the air straight at Jean. Strong arms caught her around the hips, hauling her back.

Kicking and flailing, she screamed her grief and rage. "You killed my grandmother! *You killed her!*"

Her legs buckled. The strong arms that had held her back now eased her to the floor, wrapped around her to hold her close as she howled her pain.

"I'm sorry, Breanna," Liam murmured, his voice more a rumble in the chest she was held against than words she understood.

Keely, yelling, "Mama! Mama!"

Fiona, shouting, "Keely! No!"

Someone brushing past her, someone with strength as formidable as earth.

Ashk, implacable, saying, "Get out of here. Stay out of the house until we get her calmed down."

Aiden's voice, and Lyrra's. Part of a swell of voices lost in the waves of pain.

Another voice saying, "Are you sure? She needs to grieve."

Ashk. "Yes, she does. But not like this."

A woman's hand on her hair. Gentle. "Sleep now. Sleep."

She tried to fight against it. "I'll die."

"I'll keep watch over you until Falco returns," Liam said. "We won't let you die. I swear it."

The woman's voice again. "Sleep now. Sleep."

Nothing she could do but follow that voice. Nothing.

Selena moved away to the window, leaving Ashk standing at the foot of Nuala's bed.

"Is Breanna right?" Ashk asked. "Did the girl put something in the tea, intending mischief but resulting in this?"

"I don't know," Selena replied, moving the curtain enough to watch the people milling around on the back lawn. "I stayed away from the girl as much as possible."

"Why?"

She let the curtain fall and turned to face Ashk. "Because every time I saw her, I wanted to change into a shadow hound and tear her throat out."

Ashk stared at her. No revulsion, no criticism in that look. Just assessment.

Finally, Ashk stepped away from the bed and blew out a breath. "If your instincts were that strong, the girl's lucky to be alive."

"And I'm wondering if I have reason to regret not following that instinct."

Now Ashk's look sharpened. "Don't think that way. If we find proof that Nuala's death was not natural, then we'll deal with it. But you and I can't afford to be swayed by Breanna's grief. We hold too much power, Huntress. When *we* pass judgment, there is no turning back."

"I know." Selena looked away.

Ashk raked a hand through her short hair. "Besides, we have a more immediate problem. At this time of year, it's too warm to let the body remain above ground while people call to pay their respects. We have to give Nuala back to the Great Mother."

Selena nodded. "Breanna will choose the place."

"And we'll have to have watchfires around it at night. And guards. Fae who have good night vision in their other forms, archers who can shoot clean in the dark. And someone there with the gift of fire."

She shook her head, puzzled.

"There are nighthunters still out there, Selena," Ashk said with biting patience. "They don't just devour flesh and blood. They feast on the spirits of the dead. There aren't any Fae here who are Death's Servants. They've all headed north or south since that's where the fighting is. I've sent a call to have some of them return here, or have some from the midlands join us here, but until there's one of them among us who can take Nuala's spirit up the road to the Shadowed Veil, she is still prey for those creatures. So we have guards. We keep watch. We protect our dead until they are safely out of reach."

A chill went through Selena. "The men who made the first attack on Baron Liam's estate. Their . . . ghosts . . . might still be there?"

"Where the bodies are buried, yes."

"But there's no way to tell?"

"Not until one of Death's Servants—or the Gatherer—joins us." Ashk paused. "Would it ease your mind if we put guards around those graves as well?"

Selena hesitated, then shook her head. "We can't risk too many of the living when the battle is still ahead. There will be more dead before this is done."

"Yes," Ashk said quietly, "there will be."

Jean ran across the bridge that spanned Willow's Brook, then stopped, no longer sure where to go. Her first thought had been to run to Baron Liam's house and tell Lady Elinore how mean Breanna had been to her. But Elinore would want to know why Breanna had gotten angry. If she lied, Elinore would know, and if she told the truth, Elinore would forget all about her and hurry to the Old Place to comfort Breanna.

She headed for the field, refusing to even look in the direction of the *baron's* house.

For a moment, there in the kitchen, she'd thought Liam was protecting her from Breanna's vicious attack. But, no, *he* just wanted to comfort that . . . *bitch*.

It was *always* Breanna. Mean, nasty, spiteful Breanna. Always wanting her to do *chores*. As if she were some *servant*. And here she was, walking through these fields wearing her best dress—which she'd spent *hours* pressing because Nuala had refused to order one of the other women to do it. So she was *ruining* her best dress and hadn't even gotten the chance to let the Bard see how pretty she was and *so* much more interesting than that homely red-haired woman he was sleeping with. How *could* he want to sleep with a woman who looked like that?

He hadn't noticed her because Breanna had to grab every-one's attention. Poor, poor Breanna. Nobody was saying poor Jean, were they?

And it *wasn't* her fault. She hadn't meant to hurt Nuala, but the old woman had been so *mean* about the dress that she'd wanted to get even. Just a little. It had been so easy to slip into the tea a pinch of the crushed plants she'd had in a handkerchief in her dress pocket. And Nuala was supposed to have spent the day sitting on her chamberpot. She wasn't supposed to *die*. But . . .

Jean stopped walking, put both hands in her dress pockets, and carefully pulled out two rounded handkerchiefs.

Could she have gotten the handkerchiefs mixed up and put the foxglove mixture in Nuala's tea?

She stuffed the handkerchiefs back in her pockets and walked faster.

That mixture had been for Breanna. Or Falco. Or both.

Breanna was so stupid. She'd had sex with Falco. He'd even taken her up to Tir Alainn to do it to her, and all she'd gotten out of it was his cock making her wet and messy. No gold necklace. No rope of pearls. Not even a *bracelet*. Stupid Breanna.

Well, *she* wasn't stupid. And she was *not* going to go back and have Breanna and Fiona be mean to her. No, *she* was going to have *everything*. She'd find a baron's son, a baron's heir—a *wealthy* baron's heir. And he'd see how pretty she was and know she was too special to do *chores* like some *common* woman. He'd hug her and kiss her, and whenever he wanted sex, he'd give her presents. *Lots* of *wonderful* presents. She'd have car-riages and beautiful gowns and jewels. And *then* she'd go back to the Old Place, and Breanna would be so envious of all the things she had that mean, stupid Breanna would choke. She'd just choke.

Jean stopped again and looked around. She'd already walked a long way, hadn't she?

Maybe they were already sorry they'd been mean to her. Back home, they'd felt sorry for her because she was the Abandoned Child, and after they'd scolded her for something, the old women would give her an extra sweet at dinner and sometimes one of the men would give her a scarf or a shawl that was supposed to be sold with the rest of the ship's cargo.

But the younger ones, like Fiona . . . and Jenny . . . had never been nice after they'd been mean. And Nuala had been the only elder at this Old Place, so there had been no one else to take her side and tell her she was a darling girl but it was naughty to cause such mischief.

Just mischief. It wasn't her fault if she'd gotten the mixtures confused. Breanna and Fiona were always watching her, just waiting for her to make a little mistake. And there wasn't any privacy to work out the proper mixture that she half-remembered learning from her mother before her mother went away. It was *their* fault that she'd been in a hurry and hadn't paid enough attention to which mixture she'd put in which pocket.

Maybe she wouldn't go to any of the camps just yet. She was tired and hot and getting all sweaty. Maybe she'd go to the village instead. Someone there would give her something to eat and a place to wash up and rest.

And when her *family* realized they were sorry for being mean to her, she wouldn't be that hard to find.

So she walked until the dress she'd spent so much time pressing became limp and her legs quivered and burned and her shoes pinched her feet. She was close to tears when she reached the top of a rise and saw the field stretching out before her. A field with a jumbled pile of huge stones—and the road winding out of the trees beyond the field, curving around the rise she stood on.

Dress, legs, and feet momentarily forgotten, she hurried down the other side of the rise and headed for the road. Someone would be coming from the village or heading to the village. Or one of the estates. Or a farm. Surely whoever was traveling would give her a ride.

As I will, so mote it be, Jean thought smugly as a one-horse cart came out from behind that pile of stones. The young man driving the cart seemed startled when he saw her, but he turned the horse in her direction.

"Blessings of the day to you," Jean said when he finally got close enough, giving him her best smile—and wishing she could have smoothed her hair and dress before he'd seen her. No matter. He obviously wasn't gentry, so she didn't have to impress him much. Just enough to get a ride.

"Blessings of the day, mistress," the young man said after a brief hesitation. "Are you alone?"

A little wary, she watched him loop the reins around the brake and get out of the cart. "My family is nearby."

"These are dangerous times, mistress. A young lady shouldn't wander about on her own." When he got a man's length away from her, he stopped suddenly. His eyes widened. "Are you one of them?"

"Them?"

"A— One of the Mother's Daughters."

She was more hedge witch than witch, and wouldn't have been called one of the Mother's Daughters around *them*, but her grandmother had been a witch and that counted for something, didn't it? "It is best not to mention such things," she said coyly, looking up at him through her lashes. "As you pointed out, these are dangerous times."

"Of course." He smiled. "If being seen in such a humble cart would not offend you, may I offer you a ride?"

"You are very kind."

He extended a hand to indicate the cart. "The daylight is waning, mistress. We should be on our way."

"Yes. You're right," Jean replied, walking toward the cart. She lowered her head and smiled. He seemed nervous. And the way he kept looking around, as if to reassure himself that there was no one who could see them, he was probably hoping to coax her into giving him a kiss or two. And maybe she'd let him since he *was* nice looking.

As he placed one hand on her arm to help her into the cart, she noticed him reaching inside the leather vest he wore over an unpressed shirt. Was he going to offer her a present in the hopes of getting more than a kiss?

Then the hand on her arm yanked her off balance. As she teetered on the edge of falling backward, his other hand whipped out of the vest, and something soft yet heavy struck her on the head.

As he lowered her to the ground and her vision dimmed, the look on his face made her very afraid.

He looked back at the bundles in his cart, then grinned as he slapped the reins over the horse's back.

He'd done it! Succeeded beyond expectation. He'd no longer have to work at the charity house where he'd grown up, receiving nothing more than lodgings and a few copper coins each month. When he returned to Master Adolfo's camp, he'd receive the promised reward of an apprenticeship. He'd be trained to be an Inquisitor, a man of power, a man who was *somebody*.

Never again would the squire who was his grandfather look past him if they saw each other in the village. Never again would he have to pretend he didn't recognize his mother when he saw her shopping with her proper children. Never again would he lie awake at night remembering the arguments between his mother and grandfather before he'd been taken to the charity house.

My son's father is a Fae Lord!

Convenient to say that, daughter, when no man is here to say yay or nae.

He went back to Tir Alainn!

And hasn't made even a token effort to provide for his child? No, daughter. No. I never asked who fathered the boy, and I won't ask now. But you have a chance to marry, and no gentry man is going to want to raise his own sons with a groom's or footman's leavings.

A Fae Lord!

Enough! You can cut yourself off from a good life for yourself, and condemn the boy into the bargain, or you can let him go now while he's still young enough to forget and let him make a life for himself. Make your choice, daughter—and live with it.

She made her choice. And the squire made his choice. But the boy had been old enough to remember, and grieve, the life that had ended when the squire's servants left him at the charity house. And the boy had felt the weight of being a nobody for years—until Master Adolfo had stopped and visited the charity house. Had stopped even though he had an army to command and important work to do in the world.

Master Adolfo had known the boy was special. He'd given the boy a chance to prove he was worthy of the training that would make him a powerful man one day—a man so powerful that even the old squire wouldn't dare ignore him.

And he'd succeeded. Almost within sight of the enemy, he'd succeeded. The Inquisitors had given him the horse and a cart filled with small sacks of flour, sugar, and tea. They'd told him to take the supplies to the more isolated farms and offer them to the females as thanks for the other provisions the army was taking from the surrounding farms.

The females had accepted the supplies with delight, had offered him small glasses of ale and fresh-baked bread. They had given him time to be eyes and ears for the Witch's Hammer. And they had given him time to obtain the special creatures Master Adolfo needed for the coming fight.

The Master had been specific. Find one or two of the special creatures, then get back to the army that was marching toward Willowsbrook. Take no chances, because discovery could destroy everything.

He'd been careful, but he'd had a rough minute or two when he spotted the female. Luckily she'd suspected nothing, had seen nothing. So now he was heading back toward the army that was no more than two or three days' march away from this place. He was returning in triumph.

Not only had he gotten the special creatures the Master Inquisitor wanted, he'd gotten something Master Adolfo wanted even more.

A witch.

Aiden tied the sash around his waist, then tugged at the hem of his dress tunic to make sure it still hung straight. He looked at his harp, rubbed his thumbs over the pads of his still-tender fingers, and shook his head. It would have to be one of his pipes tonight.

"Maybe it's for the best."

Turning, he studied Lyrra's reflection in the mirror. She, too, had worn her best outfit, and she'd left her hair loose so that it flowed down her back. Her eyes were puffy from the tears she'd shed, but it only made her look more beautiful—the Muse who not only touched the world but was touched by it. "What's for the best?"

"That Nuala died now."

Aiden frowned. "How can you say that?"

Lyrra turned to face him. "She went to sleep and never woke

up. Isn't that better than dying slowly from a mortal wound, or feeling an arrow bury itself in flesh? She won't know the fear and pain, she won't watch anyone she loves suffer. She won't know what happens here if . . . we fail."

He walked over to her, drew her into his arms. "We won't fail. What has gathered here is more than I'd dared hope for. The Fae have come down from Tir Alainn, the House of Gaian has come out of their hills, and the humans are standing with us. Even the Small Folk are preparing to fight. This battle won't be shining and glorious. It will be desperate and brutal . . . and people will die. Neither of us can be of any use on that battlefield when the time comes, but we have the power of words, Lyrra. We can sing the songs that feed the heart, tell the stories that offer comfort. And later, we can sing of the glory of courage and tell stories about how all the peoples of Sylvalan stood together to face a common enemy. We need to remember that we stood together— and we'll need to honor the dead." He drew back enough to kiss her forehead. "And that's what we need to do now."

He released her long enough to fetch his pipe, then slipped an arm around her waist to lead her out of the room.

Liam waited for them in the front hall, along with Baron Donovan; his wife, Gwenn; and Gwynith, a western Lady of the Moon. They went out to the open carriage that was big enough for all of them since Liam was driving and invited Aiden to join him on the driver's seat.

"Selena, Rhyann, and Ashk have already gone to the place Breanna and Keely chose," Liam said quietly after flicking the reins over his team's back to signal them to move on. "My mother has gone to the Old Place to drop off some dishes for the supper afterward. We've still got a few hours left before full dark, but I doubt anyone will want to linger after paying their respects."

"Where is the place where Nuala will be laid to rest?" Aiden asked.

"Near the brook. There's a place that has a 'sitting stone' and a curve of rose bushes close by that Nuala had planted years ago. She liked to sit there and listen to the water." Liam sighed. "We would have given Nuala back to the Great Mother wherever Breanna chose, but I know Ashk is relieved that it's open ground, and, frankly, so am I."

Aiden nodded. "No chance of nighthunters attacking before they can be seen."

"Yes."

They made the rest of the trip in silence until they crossed the bridge over Willow's Brook and saw all the conveyances lined up beside the road.

"I didn't expect so many humans to come here," Aiden said.

"My father made certain I remained ignorant of the witches who lived here," Liam replied with a trace of bitterness. "But I've learned since that my ignorance wasn't common. Nuala was a fine woman. She was respected by her neighbors, which is more than I can say about my father." He secured the reins and got down, then nodded to the boy who came forward to lead the carriage away as soon as the others had stepped down.

Taking Lyrra's hand, Aiden followed Liam to the spot where the mourners gathered. People stepped aside to let them through, and Aiden wondered if there had ever been a time before this when barons had stood side by side with farmers and Fae Lords, oblivious of the differences that separated them in the day-to-day world.

Nuala lay on the grass, dressed in a blue gown. No coffin, no shroud. Nothing between her and the earth.

For a long moment, Aiden stared at the gold pentagram around her neck, then glanced around. Now that he thought about it, he couldn't remember seeing Breanna or Nuala or any of the other witches wearing the pentagram openly. Even Selena hadn't worn hers openly. But the witches were wearing them now, and as he looked around, he felt a jolt when he saw men—strangers to him—wearing that symbol over shirts or tunics.

"I didn't know there were men who were witches," Lyrra whispered to Rhyann, who had come over to stand beside them.

Rhyann smiled. "They are the Sons of the House of Gaian. They have the same power that comes from the branches of the Great Mother that the Daughters do. Why wouldn't they wear the symbol that acknowledges the bond to the Mother?"

"You don't usually wear it openly," Aiden said.

Rhyann looked puzzled. "Why would we? We don't wear it to remind anyone but ourselves of who and what we are and what we honor. Earth, air, water, fire"—she looked at Nuala—"and spirit."

Seeing two Fae with instruments at the edge of the crowd,

Aiden excused himself and made his way over to the minstrels. One carried a small harp; the other had a pipe.

"We've never seen a burial for one of the Mother's Daughters," one of the minstrels said. "What should we do?"

Aiden smiled dryly. "We'll play it by ear."

The quiet conversations around him faded.

Selena, all in white, wore the split gown over trousers. She moved away from the others until she stood alone, facing Nuala, and turned to look at Gwynith. "Will you dance with me this time?"

"I don't know the steps," Gwynith said.

Selena smiled. "Just follow me—and follow your heart."

"Is this dance only for the Ladies of the Moon?" Ashk asked.

Selena shook her head. "Anyone who wishes to honor the one who has left us can join this spiral dance." She turned away from the people watching, her arms extended, her palms up.

Power flowed, as soft as moonlight. Balls of white light filled Selena's palms. Tendrils of light twined down her arms and over the rest of her body until she glowed with the light of the moon.

Then she began to dance. Solemn and simple, just a few steps and a turn, over and over again. But as she moved, moonlight followed her, forming a path.

Rhyann stepped onto the beginning of the path, her steps matching her sister's.

He could feel the song of those steps, those solemn turns. "Follow me when you have the tune," he told the minstrels quietly. Raising his pipe to his lips, he let his music follow moonlight down the spiral path Selena created as she danced. A simple tune, repeated like the steps. When he glanced at the minstrels, they nodded, and harp and pipe joined him, taking up the melody while he let his own pipe's notes twine around it.

Ashk stepped onto the shining spiral, followed by Breanna . . . and Liam. Gwynith followed them, then Falco. Fiona and Rory. Gwenn and Donovan. Elinore took Keely's hand, and the two of them stepped into the dance. Sheridan and Morphia. Clay, Edgar, and Glynis. Varden. Squire Thurston and his wife. Kin and neighbors, humans and Fae, Sons and Daughters of the House of Gaian joined the dance. And last . . . Lyrra, her eyes wet with tears.

Finally Selena stood at Nuala's feet. She extended her arms

again, palms up. Raising her face to the sky, her voice soared as Aiden let the last notes of the song fade.

"Great Mother, we give back one of your Daughters. Let earth take her body. Let air remember her voice. Let water remember her laughter. Let fire remember her heart. Let her spirit fly to the Shadowed Veil and pass through to the Summerland. She is no longer with us, but she will be remembered until she is back among us. Merry meet, and merry part, and merry meet again."

The ground in front of Selena swelled with moonlight, dazzling the eye. When it faded, there was a gentle mound of bare earth—and Nuala was gone.

As if hearing an unspoken command, people turned and walked out of the spiral until only Selena remained. Then she too turned and walked out—and moonlight filled in the path of the spiral dance, leaving a circle of light around the new grave.

After thanking the minstrels, Aiden tucked his pipe through his sash and joined Lyrra. He held her close and felt her shuddering effort not to cry.

"It was beautiful," she whispered.

He felt his throat close, felt the sting of tears. "Yes, it was. Come along, my heart, we have to help Breanna and her kin get through the rest of it." Slipping an arm around her waist, he led her back to the carriage.

Most of the mourners came back to the house to say a few words to Breanna and Keely and have a bite to eat. But even as they talked and ate, they kept glancing at the ever-darkening sky, and soon those with any distance to travel were saying their good-byes. Until all the nighthunters were destroyed, people wouldn't feel easy about being far from home at night.

Aiden wandered among the people still gathered on the back lawn, making a point to talk to the villagers and farmers who hadn't had any contact with the Fae yet. As he was making his way back to the house, a voice asked, "Bard?"

"Yes?" Aiden answered, turning toward an exhausted Fae male.

"Lord Aiden?"

"Yes."

The Fae pulled two pieces of wax-sealed paper out of his inner vest pocket. "I've a message for you from one of the northern bards. And a message for Baron Liam, but I don't know where to find him."

"I'll take it to him." Aiden held out his hand for the letters.

"Why don't you get something to eat? I'll talk to Lord Varden. He'll make sure you have a place to stay tonight."

Impatience mingled with dread as Aiden hurried over to the group of barons talking to Liam and Donovan.

"A message for you," Aiden said abruptly, handing over the paper addressed to Liam.

He hesitated before breaking the seal on his message. Noticed Liam did the same.

Then he read the message. "Mother's mercy."

"What is it?" Donovan asked sharply, looking from Aiden to Liam.

"Wait," Aiden said, looking around. "Hunter! Huntress!" When Ashk and Selena turned in response to his call, he signaled them to come over. Lyrra, catching the signal, said something to Fiona before hurrying to join them.

Liam looked at him. Aiden nodded.

"It's a message from one of the northern barons," Liam said. He cleared his throat quietly. "The Arktos and Sylvalan barons we were fighting in the north have surrendered. Or more to the point, the men they were leading put down their weapons and surrendered, leaving them no choice. The elders of the House of Gaian who were from the northern end of the Mother's Hills drafted the terms of surrender, which our barons seconded. The men are being allowed to return home. The Arktos barons and the Sylvalan barons who sided with the Inquisitors will be held until the army has disbursed. Then they'll be permitted to go home." Liam closed his eyes. His hand fell limply to his side. "That part of the fight is over. We've won that much."

"Did the baron say anything about captured Inquisitors?" Donovan asked.

"There were no captured Inquisitors," Ashk said softly. "Were there, Bard?"

Reluctantly, Aiden looked up from his own letter. "No, Hunter, there were not."

The barons around Liam muttered, but it was Donovan who expressed the outrage. "They escaped?"

Aiden shook his head. He glanced at Ashk—and remembered the chill that had gone through him after the dance the Breton-wood Fae had performed at the Summer Solstice, when those masked faces had stared at him. When *her* masked face stared at him. And Morag's words: *They're the Fae.*

"The Wild Hunt?" Ashk said, her voice still soft.

Aiden swallowed hard. "The Inquisitors who were caught were released in a woods, where the Lords of the Woods and the Ladies of the Moon were waiting for them . . . with packs of shadow hounds."

"Justice," Ashk said. "And vengeance. There is nothing quite so terrifying as trying to flee a shadow hound—or the Wild Hunt. The Fae were absent for too long, even when they were present. Now they have returned."

The barons shifted uncomfortably.

"Was there anything else in your message?" Liam asked after an awkward silence.

"Just something a minstrel reported overhearing," Aiden said, hoping Liam would understand the dismissive tone and let it go.

"Well?" Liam demanded.

"When the Arktos men were told their barons would be released once their army had gone back through the mountain pass between Sylvalan and Arktos, one of the men said 'we'll be waiting for them.' The barons assumed it was a sign of loyalty. The minstrel heard something different in the words."

"They hate their own rulers," Selena said. "Hate them enough to kill them."

Aiden nodded. "The minstrel's opinion was that the barons might reach the mountain pass, but he doubted any of them would reach home."

"I wonder how long the Inquisitors still in Arktos will survive once the army returns home," Ashk said.

"Not long." Aiden carefully folded the letter. He might as well say the rest. "The bard who wrote the message to me witnessed the terms of surrender and said they were fair. But the elders from the House of Gaian told the Arktos men that if another witch in Arktos was harmed simply because she was a witch, they would bring down the mountains and bring in the sea."

Another awkward silence as everyone except Ashk avoided looking at Selena.

"It's not a bluff," Selena finally said. "If the Grandmothers gather and bend their will to it, they can do exactly what they said. And Arktos would be no more than a memory of a place." She looked around. "Would you have me lie to you? We are the House of Gaian. We are the Great Mother's Sons and Daughters. We are the Pillars of the World. It is not just Tir Alainn that answers to our will. This world answers as well. It has always been so. It will always be so. You cannot defeat air or water or earth or fire. As long as they exist, we will exist. And as long as we exist, as we will, so mote it be."

Quiet and troubled, the barons said good night. Aiden wondered how easily the barons staying with Liam would sleep, knowing the Huntress was also a guest in his house. He wasn't surprised that Ashk slipped her arm through Selena's as the two of them walked away.

"I'll say our good-byes to Breanna and find Gwenn," Lyrra said.

Donovan's smile looked a little brittle. Aiden almost asked him what was wrong—then remembered that Donovan was married to a witch.

"She's the same woman she was yesterday," Aiden said.

"I know," Donovan replied. "My darling Gwenn."

"We don't own the land," Liam said quietly. "We're just its stewards. It's humbling to be reminded of that."

"And it's troubling to be reminded that they're different from us," Donovan said.

Pricked by anger, Aiden tucked the letter into his sash, next to his pipe. "Are they really so different, Baron Donovan? You've never sat beside the bed of a witch whose body was so broken by torture there was no hope of healing. You've never listened to her plead with you to let her die. You've never buried the rest of her family and then listened to the screams of the ghosts when the nighthunters attacked. They have the power to shatter the world yet they still live by a creed to do no harm." He paused. "And maybe that does make them different from the rest of us."

"Are you saying that message didn't frighten you?" Donovan asked.

"Which part? Mother's tits, man. Do you understand what the Wild Hunt means? Do you understand what happened in that woods? *My people* did that. And it's only because I met Ashk and saw the Fae in the west that I've come to realize my people are *meant* to do that. But it still frightens me. And it comforts me, that that can be awakened inside the Fae. Your people have suffered, too, and I'll not deny that. But your kind wasn't slaughtered first, and none of your counties—and all the people who lived in them—disappeared when the witches died. You still have the land, and your people have a chance to rebuild their lives. We may never regain the pieces of Tir Alainn that were lost, and no one can bring back the dead. So if it comes to a choice, I would rather face the House of Gaian than the Black Coats."

He started to walk away when Liam placed a hand on his arm.

"You're forgetting something, Bard," Liam said. "I'm not just a baron. I'm also a Son of the House of Gaian. I'm still a stranger to myself, still learning to accept this part of me that awakened a few weeks ago. Yes, we're frightened. Things that have been hidden, or barely glimpsed, are suddenly being revealed, and we can no longer pretend those things don't exist. In some ways, we've all been children. We can't be children anymore."

Donovan scrubbed his hands over his face. "Well, if the two of you are done with these delightful bedtime stories, I'd like to take my wife back to our room and get some sleep."

"Would you mind seeing Lyrra back to the house as well?" Aiden asked.

Liam gave him a curious look. "You're not going back?"

Aiden shook his head. "My night vision is good, so I've agreed to take a watch tonight." He smiled ruefully. "My other form is an owl."

"You can't go fluttering around in the dark," Liam said. "You'll get stepped on." He shrugged. "You can perch on my shoulder."

Donovan looked at his friend. "You're staying, too?"

"I have the gift of fire."

Donovan shook his head. "You two get to stand out in the dark while I escort two beautiful ladies home. I guess there are compensations to being just human."

Gwenn and Lyrra joined them, both women sensing something and searching faces to try to discover the answer.

"I'll see you later," Aiden said after kissing Lyrra. He handed her the pipe and message. "Take these for me."

When Donovan, Gwenn, and Lyrra were gone, Liam said, "Come on, then."

Aiden hesitated a moment before changing to his other form and fluttering up to the arm Liam held out.

Liam studied him for a moment. "The feathers look good on you, Bard."

Aiden climbed up Liam's arm to his shoulder, then nipped his ear.

"Do that again and you'll have to find another perch," Liam growled.

"Whoooo?"

Since Liam didn't say anything, Aiden fluffed his feathers, pleased to have gotten in the last word.

"I wonder if I can persuade Morphia to send the barons quiet dreams," Ashk said as she walked around Breanna's house, her arm still tucked through Selena's.

"Why would they need them?" Selena asked.

"Because, Huntress, between the two of us, we've given them the stuff of nightmares. How many of them will dream of being pursued by the Wild Hunt while the ground drops out from under their feet and stones suddenly grow mouths filled with fangs?"

"Stones don't have mouths. Or fangs."

Ashk smiled. "But dreams don't always show you the true form of what you fear, do they?" Her smile faded as she thought of Morag and wondered if the Gatherer was still plagued by dreams.

"I hope not," Selena said, her voice quivering with some strong feeling.

Ashk let it go, suddenly too tired to explore strong emotions. They'd already been through enough for one day. "Let's check on Breanna and the men standing watch and call it a day. We could both use some sleep."

Selena nodded. "I need to saddle Mistrunner."

"Why?"

"Because it's a bit too far to walk back to Liam's." Selena's eyes widened. "Oh. *Oh.* No, we couldn't. Not after telling them about shadow hound packs."

"But the barons who heard that are already back at whatever houses they're guesting at," Ashk said, then added, "Besides, wouldn't you like to know if Liam's any good at petting?"

Selena choked on a gasped laugh. "Ashk! That would be . . . Well, it would be—"

"Pleasant?" Ashk suggested.

"You really expect him to pet a shadow hound? What if he realized who he was petting and got—"

"Excited?"

"Intimidated," Selena said with a different kind of quiver in her voice. "I was going to say intimidated."

"Of course you were. Because there he would be, running his hands through all that lovely fur, and when he realized who it was, he'd think, 'Oh, my. I'm touching Selena. I'm intimidated.' Phah. On the other hand, if you change back while he's got his hands all over you, it might be more of a thrill than he's ready for, depending on where his hands are at that moment."

Selena just gaped at her.

There, Ashk thought, satisfied, *that's got your mind off thoughts of troubling dreams.* "Trust a woman married to a baron. They like fur."

Selena shoved her hands through her hair. "It wouldn't be fair, just trotting up to him and wagging my tail. Besides, he gets so gentry prim whenever he thinks about Breanna and Falco being lovers—"

"He's not his sister. And you're not his sister. And if you'd ever noticed the way he looks at you, you'd know he'd jump through a couple of hoops for the chance to pet you."

Selena sputtered. Muttered. "It's out of the question. I'm sharing a room with my sister."

"He's not sharing a room with anyone."

"This is none of your business."

"I know. It wouldn't be half as entertaining if it was any of my business."

Selena lowered her hands. "Bitch."

Ashk just smiled.

"All right. Let's check on Breanna and Keely first. Then I'll decide what to do about Baron Liam."

As soon as they walked through the kitchen door and saw Fiona, their humor fled.

"Breanna?" Ashk asked.

Fiona shook her head. "She's asleep, thanks to Morphia. So is Keely. It's Jean."

Selena's sigh sounded more like a growl. "Now what?"

"I can't find her anywhere."

Two shadow hounds ran through the moonlight. They didn't pause when the men standing guard over Nuala's grave turned to watch them race past.

Selena wanted to howl with frustration. Fiona was certain the girl wasn't sulking in the house somewhere, but they still spent time searching the more unlikely places—pantry, cold cellar, wine cellar. They would have searched the attic, but that was pointless. The boys were sleeping up there on beds made of straw and blankets. She wasn't in the stables or any of the other out-buildings. It was possible that she'd run off into the woods and couldn't find her way back to the house after dark, but there were Fae keeping watch around the shining road and at least half of them were in their other form so that their sharpened senses would warn them of any kind of enemy approaching. If she was out there, they'd have seen her and brought her back to the house.

If the girl had gone in any other direction in the Old Place, she would have ended up at one of the camps—and they would have brought her back to the house. So that left the bridge that crossed over to the lane on Liam's estate.

Once they were over the bridge, Selena went right, toward Liam's house, while Ashk moved off to the left.

Too many people. Too many scents. For a moment, Selena thought she'd found Jean's scent at the edge of the bridge, but there were too many fresher scents over it for her to be certain.

Then Ashk growled, and Selena turned back to follow the other shadow hound.

They had followed the scent over one field when another scent drifted on the air. With no warning, Ashk spun around and trotted back the way they'd come. Recognizing that scent, Selena ran to catch up with the Hunter.

When they got close to the bridge, Ashk paused long enough to change form.

"Why are we walking the rest of the way on two legs?" Selena asked.

"Because I want to warn the men on watch. I'm almost certain the nighthunters are nesting in that stand of trees on Liam's land. It makes sense. The Fae patrolling haven't seen them. Probably too many people around. Too much fire at night. We'll hunt in the morning, and bring Morphia with us."

"Morphia? She's not a hunter."

"No, but her gift is the best defense against nighthunters," Ashk replied as they crossed the bridge. "She can put everything in that stand of trees to sleep. We can search for the nest and destroy those creatures without being attacked."

"You still won't be certain you'll have found all of them."

"No, but we'll burn the ones we find and the carcasses of their prey. Then if we catch the scent again, we'll know it's fresh."

"What about Jean?"

Ashk stopped at the end of the bridge. "There are a dozen farms and estates in that general direction, not to mention camps. Or she could have easily circled around and reached the village." She sighed. "She's not my kin. I can't make the choice." She looked toward the men standing near the grave still glowing with moonlight, then shook her head. "I'll talk to them on the way back." After changing back into her shadow hound form, she trotted off toward the house.

Selena watched Liam, who had been walking toward them, check his stride when he saw Ashk change. Would any man really be comfortable around a woman who could change into a shadow hound?

Memories of her father sitting in his rocking chair by the fire, cuddling her as a puppy. Memories of him walking through the woods with her trotting ahead of him, growling happily when she caught a scent.

Not the same. Not the same at all.

With a pang of regret, she shook her head, changed, and raced after Ashk.

Ashk found Fiona sitting at the small work table in the kitchen. A cup of cold tea was pushed to one side. Her hands cupped a glass of whiskey.

"I made myself a cup of tea," Fiona said, "but I was afraid to drink it."

Ashk sat across from her. "That's understandable." She reached for Fiona's hand. "I'm sorry to force something else on you, but it's a decision I can't make. We found a scent in one of the fields on Liam's estate. I also picked up the scent of nighthunters. I won't send men into those fields in the dark, Fiona. That I won't do. But I'll send pairs of riders out on the roads to the neighboring farms and estates and to the village to find out if anyone has seen her."

"You'd send men out on dark roads for Jean?"

"No. I'd do it for you. For Breanna."

The kitchen door opened. Selena walked in, closed the door, and came to stand near the table.

Fiona took a long swallow of whiskey. Then she pulled a bundled handkerchief out of her pocket. "After you left, I searched the drawers Jean was given for her clothes. I found this, tucked in the back of one drawer under the camisoles. I can't identify everything she collected during her forays in the woods and through the gardens, but I do recognize foxglove. So, no, Ashk, I don't want you to send your men out on dark roads to search for Jean. Because Breanna was right. If this is what was in the tea, then Jean did kill Nuala."

Chapter 41

full moon

*A*shk doesn't avoid being around the gentry because they're *human*, Morag thought sourly as Padrick escorted her off the ship. *She avoids them so she doesn't have to dress like a . . . lady.* "I feel—"

"Lovely?" Padrick asked innocently.

"Foolish."

"But you look lovely. And that split skirt with matching jacket and linen shirt is both practical and stylish."

Morag slanted a look at him. "You've had this argument with Ashk, haven't you?"

"Me? Never. But her lady's maid has had this . . . discussion . . . with Ashk on several occasions and then vented her frustration over my wife's stubbornness to my valet, who, of course, tells me everything. So I'm kept informed without ever becoming involved. An ideal solution for a husband when it comes to such matters."

No doubt that explained the woman's delight—and the trunk of clothes borrowed from Ashk's wardrobe—when Padrick asked Ashk's lady's maid to accompany them on the voyage. The fiend now had a captive female to play with—a female who didn't know enough about gentry ways to argue when told "this is what's done in a gentry household." Remembering the twinkle in Padrick's eyes every time she stepped out of the ship's cabin after submitting to another change of clothes and restyling of her hair, she suspected gentry ladies didn't usually change outfits four or five times a day—especially when they weren't going anywhere.

As if he could hear her thoughts, Padrick patted the arm linked through his. "You do look lovely, Morag. You could pass for a gentle gentry lady."

Morag snorted. "How many gentle gentry ladies do you know who ride a dark horse?"

"That's beside the point. With your hair coiled up like that and wearing those clothes, and with the glamour, no one would look at you and realize you were Fae, let alone the Gatherer of Souls."

"What I am is not something that should be hidden," Morag said quietly.

Padrick's teasing smile faded. "No," he replied solemnly. "Ashk can put aside the Hunter because she is also the Green Lady. But you are always the Gatherer."

"Yes." And during the voyage to this harbor town, having the borrowed attention of an attractive, intelligent man, she'd found herself regretting that being Death's Mistress was all she would be. All she could be. Padrick had been right, though. Sailing to this place had cost her nothing in time and given her the rest she'd badly needed. The greatest blessing had been the dreams. No nightmares of blood and death. No glimpses of an enemy who could destroy those she loved and disappear before she could fight back and protect them. She and the dark horse had simply cantered through green—green woods, green meadows and fields. Not going anywhere, just enjoying the green, the heady sense of life. Those dreams had been as restorative as the sleep at night and the delight during the day of watching the ship dance with the sea.

But the quiet time was over. Her dark horse and the horses of the two Fae escorts Padrick had insisted go with her were already being led to a nearby inn where they would be saddled and waiting. She'd have a light meal with Padrick because he'd also insisted on seeing her fed before she began her journey, and then she'd be heading up the nearest shining road to race through the Clan territories to reach the Mother's Hills and travel through them to Willowsbrook, where the Hunter waited.

Padrick gestured to his right. "The inn is this—"

"Baron Padrick! Baron!"

Padrick stopped, turned toward the Fae Lord striding toward him.

Morag glanced at Padrick. It was clear by the expression on his face that he didn't know the man and wasn't pleased to be interrupted before he'd completed what he considered his duty toward her. But *she'd* seen this Fae Lord before, so she gave Padrick's arm a quick squeeze of warning.

The Fae Lord gave her a quick, dismissive look before turning his attention fully on Padrick. "My apologies if I'm intruding at an inconvenient time, Baron, but the magistrate pointed you out to me. I don't know how the message got to you so fast, even going through Tir Alainn, but I'm glad you made it here in such good time."

"Message?" Padrick raised one hand to forestall further explanation. "If you'll tell me where to find you, I'll join you as soon as—"

The Fae Lord wasn't listening to him. He was staring at her in an almost comic doubletake. "Lady Morag?"

She smiled. "Blessings of the day to you, Lord Murtagh. Padrick, this is Murtagh, Lord of the Selkies. Murtagh, this is Padrick, the Baron of Breton."

"I didn't recognize you," Murtagh blurted out. "You look like— I thought— Mother's tits." He raked a hand through his hair. "The last time I saw you, you looked Fae and you were with the Hunter."

"I had to return to the west. Now I'm on my way back east to join the Hunter."

"A long way to travel," Murtagh said.

There was something calculating in the way he looked at her now, but she couldn't figure out what he wanted. "The Lightbringer is dead."

"You came all the way back to take *his* spirit to the Shadowed Veil?"

"I came back to gather him."

It only took Murtagh a moment to understand the difference. The smile he gave her was sharp and feral. "Then you might want to postpone your journey for a short while and take a look at the prisoners I want Baron Padrick to see."

"Prisoners?" Padrick said.

Murtagh nodded. "Survivors of the warships the Inquisitors had sent to deal with the west. They were attacking a convoy of ships that had fled out of Seahaven. The baron here does well by his people, but he's young and didn't feel easy about passing judgment when the attack hadn't occurred in waters that are under his rule and the people harmed weren't his people. So a message was sent to you, asking that you come here and offer your advice."

"There are other experienced barons that could have offered advice," Padrick said.

"But they aren't Fae as well as gentry. And they aren't married to the Hunter. You're respected for your own strengths, Baron Padrick, but there's not a baron in this part of Sylvalan—or a Fae Lord or Lady, for that matter—who doesn't realize you have more influence than any other man in the west."

Morag wasn't listening to the men. A cold fist settled in her belly. Seahaven. Ships fleeing from Seahaven. "Mihail," she whispered.

Murtagh studied her a moment before nodding. "If you're meaning the captain of *Sweet Selkie*, he doesn't need your gift. He was wounded, but he's healing well. His ship needs to be fitted with new sails, which I promised to bring back to Selkie Island once my business here is done."

"You said the prisoners are survivors," Padrick said. "What happened to the rest?"

"Mihail's sister is a witch who commands the sea," Murtagh replied. "She was staying with us to watch for her brother's ship. When she saw the attack . . . Let's just say she let the sea speak for her." He waited until Padrick nodded. "Among the prisoners are barons' sons, minor gentry, sailors, warriors—and two Inquisitors."

"I want to see them," Morag said tightly.

Murtagh gave her another quick, assessing look. "They're in the warehouse right over there. The Fae are guarding them. We aren't influenced by the Inquisitor's Gift of persuasion, as they call it, but humans can be manipulated by it in the same way they can be influenced by the Fae's gift of persuasion. So we've kept the humans away from them. To put it bluntly, you look like a gentry lady the Black Coats could twist around their little fingers."

Morag smiled. "That's perfect."

Ubel watched that bastard Fae Lord walk into the warehouse . . . with two humans. His heart sped up when he recognized the man, so he turned away, pretending disinterest.

"You there!" the Fae Lord snapped. "Baron Padrick wants to speak to you."

Moving with feigned reluctance until he stood close to the barrier of crates, Ubel studied the man these fools thought worthy of judging *him*. An active man, not gone soft and fat like some of the other barons he'd seen when he'd observed the barons' council in Durham. This baron's grim expression made him look hard and ruthless, but that might have been nothing more than the contrast between him and the woman he stood beside, her arm linked through his. She was too tall and thin to be appealing for sex, but the coiled black hair looked soft and enticing, and her dark eyes held nothing but vulnerability and dependence.

As she stared at him, he felt himself sinking into her eyes. When she stepped away from Padrick and came to stand on the other side of the crates, so close he could have lunged over the barrier and snapped her neck before the Fae could have reacted, he stopped thinking about Padrick and the bastard Fae Lord and the other Fae around them. There was only her, only the need to have her submissive. Drawing up every drop of his Inquisitor's Gift, he aimed his will directly at her.

"You're the one, aren't you?" she asked quietly, her voice roughened by a thrilling touch of fear. "You're the leader."

"Lady, I appeal to your sense of what is right and just," Ubel said. He knew better than to answer a question like that, but he *wanted* to answer. Why was it so hard to avoid giving her an answer? "We are being held unfairly. We've done nothing to harm the people here."

"Perhaps not here, but elsewhere. You harmed so many."

Her eyes looked so soft, so sad. "The ones who stand in the way of men claiming what is rightfully theirs must be punished."

"You torture them, burn them, rape them, kill them."

"I . . ." He fought against the need to answer her.

"You've been in the west before, haven't you? You came to Bretonwood."

"I . . ." He shook his head, as much to try to break the hold her dark eyes had on him as to indicate a refusal to answer. But he couldn't look away, couldn't break her hold. Why couldn't he break the hold of this soft, useless female? He struggled to impose his Inquisitor's Gift on her. "You have to let me go. I shouldn't be held in this place. I should be released."

"Yes," she whispered. "You should be released. All of you should be released."

Triumph surged through Ubel. Triumph so keen it felt like a sharp, momentary pain in his chest.

He smiled at her. When he raised his hands, he realized the shackles were gone—and also realized he could see the crates through the flesh of his hands. He heard cries of fear from the men imprisoned with him. He noticed the startled, yet satisfied, look the Fae Lord exchanged with Padrick. But his attention was still on the woman.

He watched as she pulled the pins from her coiled black hair, letting it tumble down her back and over one shoulder. He watched while her face changed from human to Fae, as the softness in her dark eyes changed to something exquisitely merciless.

"I have released you, Inquisitor," she said. "But one of Death's Servants will have to take you to the Shadowed Veil. I have to return to the east. I have a gift for the Witch's Hammer."

Ubel tried to move forward, but couldn't get past the barrier of crates. Why couldn't he get past them? He was free now.

"What have you done?" he shouted at her.

She flicked a glance at the floor, then smiled at him.

He looked down—and stared at his body, the shackles still around his wrists and ankles. He looked at the other bodies on the floor inside the barrier . . . and the ghosts standing beside them.

"What have you done?" he screamed. She just watched him. The face, the hair, the eyes. He knew who stood before him now. "You can't do this!"

"It is done. My choice. My judgment. I have given you the release you have given others." She turned and started walking away.

"You think you're strong?" Ubel screamed. "You think you can defeat the Witch's Hammer? He'll crush you, bitch! You're not strong enough to defeat the Master Inquisitor!"

She stopped walking and looked at him over her shoulder. "I'm strong enough to defeat anyone. Haven't you realized it yet, Inquisitor? The only thing stronger than Death's Mistress is Death itself." She looked at the Fae Lord. "Don't move the bodies until one of Death's Servants gathers the spirits. That will keep the ghosts leashed to the flesh and contain them in this place."

"As you command, Gatherer," the Fae Lord replied.

Ubel screamed at her as she walked away. Kept screaming at her even after she left the warehouse. Kept screaming as the Fae who had guarded him and the others silently moved away from the barrier and took positions in front of the warehouse doors.

He screamed and screamed as he stared at his dead body, but no one heard him, no one saw him. Except the other ghosts.

Morag walked over to where the dark horse waited. "I should change out of these clothes. I imagine it's one of the few outfits Ashk actually likes."

"Keep it," Padrick said quietly. "The skirt is designed for riding. Besides, your own clothes are already packed in the saddlebags. You'll need them when you reach Willowsbrook." He made an effort to smile. "If Ashk misses having that outfit, she can order another one—which will please the village seamstress *and* her lady's maid."

She rested one hand on the dark horse's neck. "I don't need escorts."

"You'll have them anyway."

She didn't bother to sigh. Padrick had given in when she'd insisted she didn't have the appetite for a meal, but he wasn't going to yield about the escorts.

"It wasn't enough," she said abruptly.

"What wasn't enough, Morag?"

She turned away from him and placed her hands on the saddle as if to mount. But she stayed there, staring at leather instead of the man.

"They tortured. They maimed. The witches and other women they'd taken had suffered. But the Black Coat and the others . . . They didn't even hear Death's whisper before they died. Was that justice, Padrick? Did that balance the scales for all the harm they've done?"

"Would knowing they suffered balance the scales?"

"I don't know. Maybe."

Padrick placed his hand over hers. "If you wanted them to suffer, then you succeeded, Morag. Until they pass through the Shadowed Veil, they will know something men like that would consider worse than death."

Slowly, reluctantly, she turned her head to look at him. "What could be worse than death?"

"Defeat."

Chapter 42

waning moon

Adolfo slowly crumpled the letter, working it until it was a ball enclosed in his fist.

The Arktos barons had failed him. *Failed him.* Instead of continuing the fight until there wasn't a man standing, instead of destroying as many of the enemy in Sylvalan as they could, instead of fighting on to keep Sylvalan's forces divided, *they had surrendered.* Put down their weapons and crawled to the witches with their tails between their legs. And they *were* given their lives while his Inquisitors, his *men,* were taken away and hunted down like animals, slaughtered by the Fae.

He wouldn't even know that much if the messenger he'd sent north hadn't been delayed by a few critical hours because his horse had thrown a shoe. The man had arrived in time to learn of the surrender and the Inquisitors' deaths, had thought quickly enough to lie by claiming to have been sent by the southern barons to request news about the fighting in the north.

So he had the report that had been written for the enemy, had the enemy's taunts and boasts burning behind his eyes, had confirmation, based on the questions his messenger had been asked, that the midland barons and some of the Clans among the Fae were gathered around Willowsbrook, waiting for him.

They could wait. And they could die. He wasn't going to Willowsbrook with sniveling barons from Sylvalan or craven barons from Arktos. Wolfram was behind him, and Wolfram would not fail him. They would annihilate the army Liam had gathered. They would break the Mother's Hills and crush them into dust—and everything that lived in that foul place. They would extinguish magic once and for all.

But before he brought his whole army up, he would take a small company of men and ride up to the very edge of Willowsbrook, and he would give that witch-lover Liam, and all the fools who followed him, a gift that would break their hearts.

Chapter 43

waning moon

What's wrong with him? Ashk wondered as Liam offered her a sickly smile and gestured for her to take the chair in front of his desk. He took his seat and placed his clasped, white-knuckled hands on the desk.

"I'm sorry to trouble you with this, but I have to ask. I have to be certain. And since this concerns the Fae . . ." He pressed his lips together.

Ashk suppressed the urge to rub her forehead to ease the headache building there. "Liam, if you're trying to tell me some of the Fae have taken . . . liberties . . . with some of the girls who live around here—"

"No," Liam said quickly. "No, it's nothing like that." He offered another sickly smile. "Truth be told, I think the girls are a little disappointed that there haven't been any offers to take moonlit walks. Of course, the girls don't realize that the thought of having to deal with you, Selena, or Breanna afterward has pretty much stifled the urge for romance—among the human army as well as the Fae."

"I understand why they'd be nervous about me or Selena, but why Breanna?"

Liam winced. "Stories travel. You know how it is. And the Fae . . . Well, from what Varden and Falco told me, they all figure that any witch who would threaten to shoot the Lightbringer when he appeared interested in a girl wouldn't hesitate to shoot any of *them*."

Ashk shook her head and smiled. "I'm sorry I missed seeing that." Then she sighed. "Whatever the problem is, Liam, just tell me."

"There are Fae who are predators in their other form," Liam said carefully.

"Yes, there are."

"And those predators might do some hunting while they're here."

"They might."

"They might hunt people."

Ashk tensed. Her voice chilled. "Say what you have to say, Baron."

Liam took a deep breath. Let it out slowly. "Two young children are missing from outlying farms. At first, their families thought they'd wandered off, saw something intriguing among the trees and followed it. They reported it to the guards who make a daily round to all the farms and estates, and there was a search. But when the children weren't found . . ."

"People started wondering if the Fae might have indulged in a quick hunt—or had taken the children for some other reason," Ashk finished for him.

"Yes."

"Well," Ashk said after a long silence, "I understand why they would ask the question."

Liam looked slightly alarmed. "You do?"

Ashk gave in and rubbed her forehead. "I'm a mother, Liam. I have two children. If one of them was missing, I'd wonder about the Fae, too, but for a different reason. Or, perhaps, for the same reason." When she saw no comprehension in his eyes, she sighed. "If one of the Fae in the form of a predator killed those children, it is only the bodies that are gone. The loved one will go to the Summerland and return to the world one day. There's a comfort in that. But if it was a different kind of predator that took those children . . ."

"Nighthunters," Liam said, turning pale.

Ashk nodded. "If I were the mother of either of those children, I'd rather wonder about the Fae than consider the other possibility. There is no hope in the other possibility. When the nighthunters feast, there is no spirit left to gather, no one to take to the Shadowed Veil."

"Mother's mercy," Liam whispered. "I know that. I've talked to Fae who have encountered nighthunters. Breanna and I were attacked by them. But I hadn't thought of it that way."

Ashk pushed herself out of the chair. "We found the nest of nighthunters we scented, and the creatures have been killed and burned. I'd just gotten back when I got your message. I can't say with certainty, but hopefully that was all of them that remained around Willowsbrook. If any more appear . . . Well, there are plenty of Fae around here now who can detect the scent. We'll hope we can detect them before they do any harm. As for the children, I'll send some of the winged Fae out to search. A hawk can see a great deal more than any of us can see on foot."

Liam stood. "Thank you, Hunter."

She shook her head. "Thank me when we've found the children. You didn't say how old they were."

"Young. Two or three years."

Children, Ashk thought as she went upstairs to wash up and indulge in an hour's rest. Toddlers, really. Old enough to scamper off in pursuit of a butterfly in a meadow or a fawn glimpsed in the woods. Caitlin had done it to her once. Had wandered off during a moment when her attention had been required elsewhere. She and the Clan had searched for a frantic day before she'd found her girl in a fox's den, sound asleep with the kits snuggled around her, all of them being guarded by a very confused vixen.

She could wish for something that simple. Hope for something so screamingly normal. But she knew in her gut it wasn't simple or normal. So she was left with the question of what had happened to two small children—just as she was left with the question of what had happened to Jean.

Chapter 44

waning moon

Hearing the guard captain call a halt, Adolfo pushed aside the cloth covering the carriage window and waited. No further orders were given. He'd heard no urgency to indicate a company from the enemy's army was approaching. So he waited until the guard captain rode back to the carriage and bent low in the saddle to look at the Master Inquisitor.

"What is the delay?" Adolfo asked.

"One of the Sylvalan brats who were sent out with carts has returned. Says he's found what you're looking for," the guard captain replied.

The Wolfram captain knew better than to let anything in his voice imply criticism of a decision made by the Master Inquisitor, but Adolfo knew the man hadn't been pleased to have a choice assignment given to unknown, untried, unwanted bastards who came from the enemy's land. After all, what man wouldn't want to be the one to supply the tools the Witch's Hammer needed to hamstring the enemy?

Adolfo leaned forward, but the guard captain dismounted quickly enough to open the door for him.

A good man, Adolfo thought approvingly. He had the proper balance of subservience and authority, and his ambitions didn't outstrip his common sense. "Where is the Sylvalan boy?"

"Just up ahead. He was stopped by our outriders. I can have him brought to you, Master Adolfo. There's no need for you to walk."

Adolfo raised his right hand in a gesture that was dismissive but not slighting. "I welcome the opportunity to stretch my legs," he said mildly as he walked toward the head of the column of men. The column split, men stepping to the sides of the road to leave the center clear for him and the guard captain, who handed his horse's reins to one of the men.

The boy stood to one side of the road, flanked by two guards. Two others flanked the cart, while the fifth held the horse.

Catching sight of him, the boy brightened and took a daring step away from the guards. "I succeeded, Master Adolfo. I found what you were looking for."

Adolfo moved a few steps closer, then stopped to give the boy that mild stare that had shattered the nerves of Wolfram barons when the Master Inquisitor showed up at their estates unexpectedly.

"I am the only one who decides if you succeed, boy," Adolfo said softly.

The boy paled and looked at the ground. "Yes, Master. I— My apologies for speaking out of turn."

Adolfo smiled. "We'll see if your success is reason enough for a loss of manners." He walked over to the cart and frowned. Then a scent wafted up from the cart, and his heart began to race. He pointed to the smaller sacks. "Show me."

The guards flanking the cart moved to one side, reached in, and untied the tops of the sacks.

Perfect, Adolfo thought. Of the eight carts he'd sent out, only three others had returned with anything he could use. When added to these . . . Five tools weren't as many as he'd hoped for, but they would be enough to distract the enemy leaders. Now all he needed . . .

Tipping his head to indicate the large sack, he looked at the guard captain. "Show me." Sweat beaded on his forehead. His heart hammered in his chest as the captain opened the sack and pulled it down enough to show him what was inside.

The girl's terrified eyes stared at him as she made distressed sounds, muffled by the gag. She stank of fear and sweat. She also stank of magic.

Adolfo turned away from the cart. He studied the boy, now watching him anxiously. "You were right, boy. You did succeed. Well done."

The boy sagged in relief, then recovered swiftly enough to ask, "Then I'll become an apprentice? I'll become an Inquisitor?"

That combination of brashness and hopeful fear. Ubel had been like that when he'd found him years ago. Yes, perhaps he would keep his promise to this boy and mold him into a useful tool. Take him back to Wolfram to shape him and train him, then send him back here to be a hammer against his own people.

"You have much to learn before you can become a warrior against the Evil One and its servants," Adolfo said. "As for your apprenticeship . . . You can begin by looking after the creatures you brought me. Take good care of them."

He hurried back to his carriage, the guard captain beside him. "We must act swiftly now. Send messengers back to the main army. Have them come up with all possible speed. Question the boy. See if he noticed any land near Willowsbrook that would serve us well in a fight. And assign some of your best archers to join the outriders. As we get closer to the enemy, they may use the Fae to try to spy on us. Kill any bird that flies near, any beast that stops to watch men pass instead of fleeing, any hawk soaring overhead."

The guard captain nodded. "I have some archers who can shoot the eye out of a soaring hawk."

Adolfo paused at the carriage door. "That's exactly what needs to be done." He swung into the carriage. "You have your orders."

"As you will, Master Adolfo." The guard captain saluted, then moved off to give his orders.

As I will, Adolfo thought as he settled himself in the carriage and closed his eyes. He smiled. *Yes. As I will.*

Chapter 45

waning moon

Morag knelt in front of the open window, her chin resting on her crossed arms. Quiet conversations drifted up to her from the inn's garden courtyard where men and women were enjoying a still summer night. The voices were nothing more than sounds, as soothing as air flirting with leaves or water murmuring over stone. Just another part of the Mother, those voices. Not surprising, since she was in the part of Sylvalan ruled by the House of Gaian. She was in the Mother's Hills.

Odd how she'd never thought to describe Tir Alainn to Ari and Neall but found herself trying to remember everything she could about these hills. When she returned home, she wanted to tell them about the horses, the people, the land . . . and the shadow hounds.

As she followed the innkeeper across the courtyard, she spotted the children playing with a litter of puppies under the shadow hound bitch's watchful eyes. She walked over to them, unable to resist getting a better look at the little bundles of fur.

"Hadn't intended to breed her," the innkeeper said, grinning. "But females of all kinds are tempted to take a walk on the night of the Summer Moon."

She knelt and picked up the little bitch of the litter, who was more black than gray and had tan markings on her legs and face. An adorable bundle of fur.

Cuddling the puppy, she looked up at the innkeeper. "What are you going to do with them?"

"Oh, most of them are already spoken for," the innkeeper replied. "Pure shadow hounds are hunters, but a shadow hound mix tends to be happiest with a family where it can be both com-

panion and protector. So there's no worry about any of them find-
ing a place around here."

Reluctantly, she put the puppy down and got to her feet. She
wanted that little bitch. Merle had never been hers, not really.
She wanted something of her own to care for and cuddle. And Ari
and Neall wouldn't mind having another shadow hound around
the Old Place.

The innkeeper studied her. "The little bitch isn't spoken for
yet."

She hesitated, then shook her head. "I'm headed for Willows-
brook. I couldn't take her with me."

The innkeeper nodded. "Lots of folks traveling to Willows-
brook lately. Tell you what. The pups aren't ready to leave their
mother quite yet. I'll hold her for a while longer, and you think
on it. If you decide you don't want her, just send a message back
and I'll let her go to someone else."

Morag rested her forehead on her arms. She'd reach Willowsbrook in four days. Maybe three if the dark horse and her escorts'
horses could maintain the pace. She'd get there in time to help
Ashk and the Huntress stop the Witch's Hammer from devouring
any more of Sylvalan. And when it was over, they would all go
home.

Aching and stiff from long days in the saddle, Morag rose and
got ready for bed. As she blew out the bedside candle and settled
down to sleep, she thought about the feel of the puppy's fur and
its eagerness to belong to someone.

She would give the innkeeper her answer in the morning. The
puppy would stay here a while longer, waiting for her in a land
that flowed with the power of life while she rode to a place that
would be a banquet for Death.

Chapter 46

waning moon

Adolfo walked into the small clearing. He'd spent the entire morning searching for the right place—a place within the cover of the trees just beyond the field with the tumbled stones, a place shielded from the eyes of curious men.

Now, as afternoon waned toward evening, he studied everything carefully to be sure his Inquisitors had followed his orders. Finally, he nodded once to show approval—and was amused to see the relief in their faces . . . and the curiosity they allowed to show now that they knew they wouldn't be reprimanded for some oversight.

"Leave now," Adolfo said. "This is delicate work, and I must focus all my power as the Master Inquisitor to take the foul magic of our enemy and transform it into a weapon that will be used against them. I must not be disturbed. I will summon you when the task is done and we are ready for the next step."

One by one, the Inquisitors left the clearing, their eyes flicking from the cage covered with blankets to the witch tied to a stool. But they asked no questions, and when this was all over, none of them would ever dare question him, even in their own minds. When they finally saw what he could do, they would know having a dead arm had not diminished the power the Witch's Hammer could wield. They would do anything for him, be anything for him. They would know that the foulness in Sylvalan that had crippled his body had not really crippled him at all. And when they'd cleansed this land of the witches and the barons and the Fae who stood in the way of men ruling what was rightfully theirs, his Inquisitors and the barons in Sylvalan, Arktos, and Wolfram would know once and for all that *he* was the true power in the world. And everything would be as it was meant to be.

Adolfo walked to the cage and adjusted the blankets covering it to create a small opening. The creatures stirred, drawn to the sliver of light. One of them started whimpering. They must have consumed the food his Inquisitors had put in the cage—or had lost interest in it.

He moved away from the cage and bent his will into creating a circle of power that would contain what he was going to do. What he sent into the circle would remain within the circle until it was absorbed by flesh that would be twisted and transformed into something glorious and deadly.

Once the circle of power was completed, he turned his attention to the witch. Not much of a witch. Barely a witch, despite the initial stink of magic he'd sensed when she was revealed to him. If she'd been merely a hedge witch, she would have been no use to him. He would have handed her over to the guards to enjoy. But she had enough connection with the branch of earth that he could use her as a channel for power. Her own strength might not have been enough to transform all five of the creatures, but the land here was saturated with magic, more than he'd felt anywhere else. So she would be his tool for draining that power to feed his spell.

More whimpers from inside the cage. The witch, bridled and blindfolded, whimpered too.

Placing his right hand on her shoulder, Adolfo began draining the magic out of her, drawing it into himself. Tapping into the power in the land once he'd drained her own pittance of magic. More. And more, until he was so swollen with power he thought his skin would burst.

Then he raised his hand and released the power in a fierce wave, twisting it as he sent it flying into the cage, as he said the words, "Twist and change. Change and twist. Become what I would make of thee. As I will, so mote it be."

Power crashed into the cage, snapping a few of the wooden bars as it sought living flesh. It crackled in a way that grated on the ears, dazzled the eyes with tiny bolts of lightning.

Finally, the power he'd gathered was spent. He waited, listening. When he heard faint stirrings from inside the cage, he released his breath in a deep sigh of satisfaction. He hadn't been sure these creatures would survive the transformation. They were much larger than the squirrels or birds that were usually changed when Inquisitors twisted magic and sent it back into the world. It would take longer for the transformation to be complete.

Adolfo looked up at the patch of sky visible between the trees. He would wait an hour or two before checking on the progress of his new creations. The guards who had been selected for the next step would need the cover of darkness to ride through enemy territory to deliver his gifts to Baron Liam and the witches in the Old Place, so there was no hurry. There was time for a meal and a glass or two of wine.

After one dismissive glance at the witch, still bound and blindfolded, he walked away from the clearing.

Wanting a few minutes of solitude, Liam almost retreated back to the house when he saw Aiden sitting on a stone bench in the garden, the Bard's fingers gently plucking the strings of a small harp. Then Aiden looked up, and Liam, cursing gentry manners, walked over and sat on the other end of the bench.

After listening for a minute, Liam asked, "Is that a new tune?"

Aiden smiled. "No, it's just a way of letting my mind wander while my fingers regain some of their skill."

Since Aiden didn't seem to expect conversation, Liam slowly relaxed, letting the drift of notes melt into the softening light and the scents of the flowers his mother fussed over.

There was nothing to do but wait now. The enemy had been sighted, but Falco, Sheridan, and the other winged Fae hadn't been able to get close enough to get an idea of how vast the army moving toward Willowsbrook might be because archers were shooting any birds that came within range. Falco had a couple of wing feathers tattered by an arrow, and Sheridan had barely avoided being hit. If there were Fae who hadn't made it back to the camps, neither Ashk nor Selena had mentioned it. Maybe because there had been no losses—or maybe because the weight of grieving for Nuala still hung over all of them, and the Hunter and Huntress had made the decision not to add to the grief, knowing there would be more to come in the days ahead.

Think of something else, Liam scolded himself. "Do you think I'm being an ass about Breanna and Falco?"

"I don't think it's my place to have an opinion, one way or the other," Aiden said mildly.

Liam turned on the bench to look at Aiden directly. "You're

the Bard. I had the impression you have opinions about most things."

Aiden chuckled. "Is that your impression? Well, you might be right."

"So?" Liam prodded when Aiden didn't say anything more.

"So, yes, I think you're being an ass." Aiden glanced over and smiled before turning his attention back to his harp.

Liam waited. "That's it?"

Aiden stilled the harp strings, then cradled the instrument in his arms. "Love is precious, no matter how long it lasts. We sing the songs, we tell the stories, we glory in those moments when love begins. We sing the songs and tell the stories of love lost, of love offered and refused, of love betrayed. I suspect you're a man who feels deeply for the people he cares about, a man who wouldn't make a commitment he didn't intend to keep. You look at Breanna and see a woman who also has deep feelings, a woman who would honor her commitments in the same way you do. You look at Falco and remember stories about the Fae—and of love betrayed. You doubt his feelings because he's Fae and because you're afraid for Breanna's sake. But Falco isn't the brash Fae Lord he was a year ago, and Breanna is a strong woman, not a girl who would be swayed by a bit of romance. I see two people working toward a partnership rather than temporary lovers whose only interest in each other is what they find in bed."

"I've only known her a few months," Liam said softly. "It feels like I've known her all my life, that she's always been a part of my life, but, in truth, I met Breanna at the beginning of this summer. Maybe I'm . . . jealous?"

"Maybe."

He sighed. "Selena thinks I'm an ass."

Aiden laughed. "Then maybe you should spend less time thinking about Breanna and Falco and more time giving Selena a chance to change her opinion of you."

"Maybe." Liam smiled reluctantly and rose. "I have a few things to do. I'm taking the early watch at Nuala's grave so that I can get some sleep tonight." He hesitated. "It's rather extraordinary, the way the grave still glows with moonlight. It's a beacon in the dark, but it also feels like a barrier against the dark things in the world."

Aiden just looked at him for a long moment. "I suspect Selena is also someone capable of deep feelings for people, whether she's known them for a long time or not."

Adolfo walked back into the clearing, followed by eager Inquisitors and wary guards. Hearing footsteps, the witch made muffled, distressed noises, but he ignored her, his attention on the cage.

Alarm danced up his spine when he saw the broken cage bars—until he remembered the wood had snapped when he released the power. It wouldn't do to have *these* creatures loose among his own men. It wouldn't do at all.

Then he heard wood cracking, saw the blankets shift as limbs pushed through broken pieces of the cage.

"Quickly," he snapped. "Put the meat in the cage. Push it through that broken section."

The guards moved forward cautiously, jumping back when the creatures screamed, having caught the scent of meat and blood.

"Quickly!"

The first guard approached, the body of a dead falcon tied to one end of a long tree branch. He thrust the branch through the bars.

The cage rocked with the impact of the creatures lunging for the offered prey. Something snapped the branch. Sounds of fighting. Of bones snapping.

"More!" Adolfo ordered. Two other birds that the longbowmen had brought down were thrust into the cage. Then a rabbit, recently snared and still barely alive, was shoved into the cage. Then a chunk of meat from the hind leg of a deer that had been fleeing from one group of men and had run into the middle of another pack of guards hunting to supply meat for the cookpots.

Five meals, all smeared with a paste he'd made to put the creatures to sleep for a few hours. Long enough for the guards to get them close to the Old Place—and Baron Liam's estate.

When the sounds inside the cage diminished to snarls and crunching bones, Adolfo took one of the branches, caught the edge of one blanket, flipped it aside, then did the same with the other blanket. He stepped back to admire what his power had wrought. One of the creatures was still transforming, and its leg revealed clearly what it had been.

He turned and looked at the faces of the Inquisitors and guards. Shock. Revulsion. Fear.

Smiling gently, he walked over to the witch. He fumbled with the blindfold before managing to pull it off. Leaning down, he whispered, "Look what your magic created."

She just stared at him as he moved to one side, as frightened as the rabbit that had been caught in the snare.

"Look," he said again, turning her head to focus her attention on the cage.

She stared and stared. Then she screamed, the piercing, terrified sounds muffled by the bridle.

Suddenly the screaming stopped.

Leaning over her again, Adolfo studied the blank eyes, pressed a hand to her chest. Her heart still beat. She still breathed. But her wits had fled, and he wasn't sure they would return. Not a strong witch in any way. No matter. She could be used for one more spell before she became too worn out to be useful.

One by one, the creatures inside the cage fell into a drugged sleep.

"Swiftly, now," Adolfo said. "There's enough time to ride to the Old Place before they rouse from this sleep, but not much more time than that."

The guards hesitated.

"Move!"

One guard pulled a knife from his boot sheath and sliced at one of the blankets until it could be ripped in half. Gingerly opening the cage, he took one of the creatures, wrapped it in half the blanket, and hurried out of the clearing to the spot where other guards held the horses.

Three guards, following the example of the first, ripped the other blanket and bundled creatures into the pieces. The last creature in the cage was the one not fully transformed. The guard hesitated. There was nothing left to wrap the creature in. His hands shook as he finally grabbed the creature and ran for his horse.

Adolfo waited until the guards rode off. Then he turned to his Inquisitors and gestured toward the witch. "Take it back to a tent. Give it water. Feed it if it still has enough wits left to eat. Take care of it. I need it physically strong and healthy for an-

other day or two. After that . . ." He shrugged. "The men will
have another use for it."

Aiden was already dozing off in the saddle as Minstrel crossed
the bridge that would take them back to Liam's house. If he'd
been riding another horse, he might have stayed at the Old Place
after finishing his watch at Nuala's grave. But Minstrel knew the
way to Liam's as well as he did, and he trusted the horse to get
them there safely. Besides, if he didn't come back, Lyrra would
worry about him and never get any sleep. And he didn't sleep as
well if he didn't fall asleep holding her. Too bad they were usually so worn out that they didn't do much else when they fell
into bed.

Minstrel stopped so suddenly, Aiden wobbled in the saddle
before regaining his balance. The horse's attention was focused
on the fields.

Reaching down to give the horse a reassuring pat, he felt the
muscles quivering beneath his hand. Alarmed, he strained to see
if there was anything out there in the dark. Nothing. But *something* was spooking Minstrel.

Then he thought he heard a muffled cry of pain. Was someone in the field?

He looked back toward the grave and saw two of the huntsmen moving toward the brook, their attention focused on the
field as well.

Horses galloping away. Not Fae then. He wouldn't have
heard Fae horses. Humans who had lost their way in the dark
and realized where they were when they saw the glow of moonlight around Nuala's grave? Possible. But Minstrel still trembled
under his hand, and his own skin was starting to crawl.

"Come on, boy," he whispered. "Let's get away from here."

Wide awake now, he let the horse run. He didn't want to be
out in the dark. He didn't want to be near that field.

When he reached Liam's house and led Minstrel into the stable, Arthur sleepily offered to bed down the dark horse. Accept-
ing the offer, Aiden gave Minstrel a farewell pat and hurried to
the house. It was locked at night now, but guards kept watch at
the front windows, so the door was open for him as soon as he
reached it.

He rushed up the stairs, then hesitated in front of Liam's bedroom door. Had he spooked himself over something that had a

simple explanation because he wasn't easy about being out at night anymore? But that didn't explain Minstrel or the huntsmen who had also heard or sensed something. So he knocked on the door, grateful he didn't have to rouse the whole house in order to wake Liam.

Liam opened the door partway and raked a hand through his hair. "What is it?" he asked, his voice sleep-roughened.

"We have to talk," Aiden said, keeping his voice low. "Ashk and Selena, too."

Liam stared at him, then seemed to really wake up. "I'll join you in a minute."

Nodding, Aiden hurried to the other rooms. Selena was harder to rouse, but Ashk was still dressed, which meant she hadn't even tried to get any sleep yet.

They gathered in the hallway outside Ashk's door. As soon as Liam joined them, Aiden told them what he could. When he'd finished, the others said nothing.

Finally, Ashk shook her head. "Are you certain the huntsmen were aware of something out in the field?"

"I saw two of them moving toward the brook. Since we were all looking at the same field, I'm assuming they sensed something," Aiden replied.

"Then they'll warn the others when the watch changes. I'll go out and take a look around."

"You can't go out there in the dark," Selena protested.

"Shadow hounds hunt in the dark," Ashk replied quietly.

"Then I'll go with you."

Before he or Liam could argue, another voice said, "No," sharply enough to silence all of them.

They turned to find Morphia, pale and shaking, walking toward them.

"You can't go out tonight," she said.

"Morphia—" Ashk began.

"You can't." Morphia closed her eyes. "Dreams. Blood in the water . . . and blood-soaked fur. And . . . more." When she opened her eyes, they were glazed with fear. "We can't lose either of you. Something's coming. Something terrible. And something is already here. If you go out tonight, we'll lose you . . . and then we'll lose so much more. Please. Don't go."

Silence.

Finally, Ashk said, "All right. We'll go out at first light." She brushed a hand lightly down Morphia's arm. "Go back to bed. Try to get some rest."

They watched Morphia go back to her room. Waited until the door softly closed.

"I don't want you to go out either," Liam said slowly, "but it is just a dream."

Ashk looked at him. "Liam, do *you* want to tell the Sleep Sister it's just a dream?"

After a brief hesitation, Liam shook his head.

"Then let's get what rest we can. It looks like we'll be hunting in the morning."

Adolfo took a long sip of wine. The guard captain's uneasiness didn't please him, but he would hear the man out before deciding what discipline was required. "Well?"

"The guards managed to get deep into Baron Liam's estate, almost to the water that divides his land and the Old Place."

"But they didn't get to the Old Place?"

The guard captain shook his head. "They didn't dare move closer. They said there was a strange light. Not torches or a campfire. They said it looked like a circle of moonlight rising up from the ground. And there were men guarding the place. Then . . ." He hesitated. "One of the creatures roused sooner than expected, bit the guard on the forearm, and escaped. The sounds alerted the guards on the other side of the water."

"What happened to the other four creatures?" Adolfo asked quietly.

"They were released in the field. The guards rode away. They're certain the creatures weren't seen."

Adolfo thought this over and finally nodded. "They are close enough, and when they wake, the fresh prey within sight will keep them close to the water. That is adequate. Tomorrow we will attack. We'll set our catapults on the low rise beyond the field with the tumbled stones and fire on them as the enemy moves to meet us."

"As you will." The guard captain turned to leave the tent. He stopped and turned back. "Master Adolfo, the guard who was bitten . . . In the time it took to return to camp, the flesh around the wound turned putrid and the rot is spreading. The physicians don't know how to stop it. I wondered . . ."

"Tell the physicians to take the arm."

The guard captain tensed. "But the bite itself wasn't that serious!"

"There is nothing that can be done. He can lose an arm or lose his life." Adolfo smiled horribly. "And what is an arm compared to crushing this enemy once and for all?"

Chapter 47

waning moon

Ashk stepped out of Liam's house, annoyed with herself because she'd slept past first light. As Aiden had pointed out, the sun was barely up, but she couldn't shake the dream she'd had last night that she'd tried to catch something fragile and it had slipped through her fingers and shattered all around her, couldn't shake the feeling that this small delay would make a difference . . . somehow.

"Ashk?"

She turned to look at Selena and almost smiled. The Huntress was dressed in soft gray trousers and a short-sleeved tunic. The tunic had been done up hastily, revealing the white camisole she wore beneath it. Not practical garb for a hunt, since the light color would make her too visible in the woods. But . . .

Shadow hound colors, Ashk thought suddenly, studying the gray clothing and the black hair carelessly tied back with a ribbon. *And the dark and light of the moon. Perhaps the Huntress was right after all in her choice of garb, since she would usually partake in a very different kind of hunt.*

Then something shivered through her. She turned away from the house and walked toward the grass and trees that formed a park on one side of the house.

"Ashk?" Selena said again.

She raised her hand to acknowledge that she'd heard and kept walking until she reached a big shade tree. She paused there and rested her palm against the tree. Now that she was away from human things and human noises, her senses sharpened, her gift flooded her with messages.

Something wrong nearby. Something unnatural. Something that doesn't belong in the woods.

She swore silently. She'd hoped they'd cleared out all the

nighthunters when they'd found that nest, but there were more of them out there. But this shiver beneath the land's skin hadn't been there since they'd cleaned out the nest. Had the Black Coats marching toward them created more of the creatures and managed to capture and transport them somewhere close by? Was that what Aiden had heard in the field last night? From the information she'd gotten from the Inquisitors who had been captured at Bretonwood, the magic they drew from an Old Place and twisted struck randomly when it was released, and its manifestation could range from a good well suddenly going dry to small creatures in the woods being changed into nighthunters. They simply unleashed that magic with no way to control it. But what if one of them had learned to contain that power while twisting it so that it flooded a particular place?

A hint of sound made her look up just as something small and black floated down from the branches above her head. She caught the feather, then studied the crow that was preening itself while watching her. Just a crow. And yet . . .

She watched the crows drift across the small clearing. One took flight, flying so low she could have reached up and touched it. Then another followed. Then a handful. Finally the rest of the rook flew over the clearing to the trees on the other side.

"Seeing them reminds me of something I've wondered about," she said.

Morag's attention remained focused on the crows. Eventually she relaxed and looked at Ashk. "What have you wondered about?"

"All the Fae who are Death's Servants are crows or ravens in their other form. They aren't the only Fae who have that form, but I don't recall one of Death's Servants who wasn't one or the other. Why is that?"

Morag looked at her a long time before saying softly, "Perhaps it's because crows and ravens are Death's servants, too."

Ashk dropped the feather, turned on her heel, and hurried over to where the others waited with the saddled horses. Too many others. This wasn't some gentry hunt where they chased a fox over the fields for exercise and amusement. What she was hunting this morning could kill them. Of course, what was coming toward them could kill them all just as swiftly.

As she reached them, Varden was speaking: "—mentioned hearing something moving near the brook, but nothing came near the grave. One man thought he saw something. From the size of it and how it moved, he figured it was one of the Small Folk. They haven't approached any of the men guarding the grave, but we've seen them a couple of times at dusk or right before dawn. I guess they're keeping their own watch."

When Liam noticed her, he stiffened, obviously braced for an argument. "I'm coming with you. My land, my people. If something is out there, I'm not sitting back and letting someone else protect what's mine."

"You have another task," Ashk said brusquely. "We need to move up companies of men to guard the road into the village. The villagers and the barons will listen to you. Sheridan, Varden. Do you know the low rise that borders the field with that tumble of stones?"

"We've both seen it," Sheridan said, looking at Varden, who nodded.

"Sheridan, you take the western huntsmen. Varden, you take the huntsmen from your Clan. I want that rise guarded. Now. The Black Coats' army has to move across that field or down the road in order to strike at the village or the Old Place."

"They're moving?" Liam said. "Are you sure?"

Ashk hesitated, then shook her head. "It's not something I know, it's something I feel."

"Messages from the spirits of the woods?" Selena asked.

Ashk jolted, too startled for a moment to reply. *How—? Of course.* Selena must have heard the story about how the Fae came to be, just as Rhyann had.

"It is my gift that hears the warning, not my head," she said slowly.

Selena nodded. "Then it's a warning we should heed."

Liam shook his head. "We aren't sure the Black Coats are moving, but we *are* sure there was something close to the Old Place last night."

"It's easy enough," Donovan said. "I'll ride to the village and on to Squire Thurston's place to coordinate the defense of the village and the guarding of the main road."

"I'll go with Donovan," Aiden said. "I can take care of sending and receiving messages. Lyrra can do the same here."

"I—" Lyrra began to protest. She pressed her lips together, then took a deep breath and nodded. "All right. Yes, you're right. If the Bard and the Muse can't relay messages, no one can.

Gwenn, Gwynith, and Rhyann can help me with that—and with keeping a record of any wounded who may be brought here."

Ashk walked over to her horse. As she swung into the saddle, she found comfort in the feel of a full quiver of arrows resting against her back. "Let's ride."

"The men are ready, Master Adolfo," the guard captain said.

"You understand your orders?" Adolfo asked as he sipped his wine. No sign of disapproval that he took wine so early in the morning. Not today. Never again.

"Yes, Master. One arm of the army will seize the village. The other arm will take possession of that low rise, set up the catapults, and crush the Fae and the other witch-lovers when they move against it."

"Let it rain fire."

"Yes, Master."

"But I must have some prisoners," Adolfo said firmly. "Males." He waited until the captain nodded. "You may tell the men one other thing. Today I will give fifty gold coins to every man who kills a witch."

"Fifty!" With effort, the guard captain regained his professional stance. "They'll kill every female they encounter in an effort to claim the reward."

Adolfo smiled. "Yes, they probably will. But the foul creatures I want are easy enough to identify. Most of them wear an ornament hidden beneath their clothing. A five-pointed star within a circle. Any man who brings me one of those ornaments—and the tongue of the bitch who wore it—will receive the gold."

He saw a glint of greed in the captain's eyes and did not disapprove of it.

"I'll tell the men," the captain said.

Tell the other captains, Adolfo amended silently. "Go on, then."

"We'll have the Old Place cleansed by nightfall," the captain promised.

"A pretty thought," Adolfo murmured as he watched the man leave with more haste than dignity. He drained his wine glass and set it aside. "A very pretty thought."

Breanna walked toward Nuala's grave, Keely a few steps ahead of her. Keely, still grieving and displaying an unshakable stubbornness, had insisted on walking to the grave that morning. The men who stood the last watch until dawn had already left since it was safe to leave the grave unattended in daylight. Clay, Rory, and Falco had agreed to ride into the village for supplies they'd run short of with so many people to feed. Fiona and some of the other women threw themselves into household chores with grim single-mindedness, but work hadn't provided solace for Nuala's daughter or granddaughter. So the two of them walked to the grave in order to touch the earth, feel the air.

A healthy walk, Nuala used to call it with a smile. It was that. For the first time since she'd found Nuala, Breanna felt a tightness in her chest and shoulders ease. Even in daylight, the grave glowed in its circle of moonlight. She wasn't sure if that light simply offered some comfort to the living or was protection for the dead, but she was grateful for this gift from the Lady of the Moon.

As they reached the grave, Keely stopped and cocked her head. "Do you hear something?"

No, she didn't, but her nose picked up an unpleasant smell in the air that made her uneasy. A . . . decaying smell. Not wanting to think about why she might be smelling something like that, she summoned a light wind and guided it over the crescent of rose bushes Nuala had planted years ago. Even though the bushes were trimmed every year, they were chest-high now, and, despite being so late in the season, there were still enough roses blooming to scent the air.

"I *do* hear something," Keely said. "There's someone behind the rose bushes, crying. It sounds like a child." She moved toward the bushes, altering her course to come around the nearest end.

Breanna wasn't listening. The wind had stirred the long grass on the bank of the brook, revealing a patch of red cloth for a moment. Puzzled, she walked toward the spot where she'd glimpsed the cloth.

"Hello?" Keely said, moving closer to the bushes. "Are you lost?"

A small sound. A click of pebble on stone. Breanna looked toward the bridge and saw the three riders, still distant, heading toward her. Liam, she thought affectionately. Coming for his daily brotherly inspection.

"Don't cry. You don't have to be afraid. Are you lost?"

Another click of pebble on stone. Another small sound, muted but still filled with agony. Dismissing Liam and his companions, she turned her attention back to the brook and moved closer.

Keely rounded the end of the crescent, stopped when she was close to the middle of it, and asked, "Who are you?"

Ashk reined in so hard and fast her horse almost tumbled over in its effort to obey. She patted its neck as both comfort and praise, but her attention was on the light wind blowing in her face.

Selena and Liam pulled up and looked back at her.

"Ashk?" Selena said.

"Can't you smell it?" A tremor went through Ashk's body. "That smell. That *scent*."

Selena turned her face into the wind. "I don't—" She gasped, then twisted in the saddle to look at the Hunter. "It's coming from the direction of Nuala's grave. And there's someone near there."

"Breanna," Liam whispered. He whipped his horse into a frenzied gallop, leaving Selena and Ashk racing to keep up with him.

Get away from there, Breanna, Ashk thought as she rode recklessly toward the bridge. *Get away from there!*

Breanna felt her gorge rise as she reached the bank and looked down. Fear hammered in her chest, in her head.

Not a piece of red cloth. Part of a bloody arm. The small man had been ripped apart before the remains had been flung up on the bank, abandoned.

She saw other things now. Mangled bodies of water sprites caught among the stones. Blood still dripping over the stones into the water.

"Who are you?" Keely asked again, her voice now holding a touch of fear.

Blood still dripping over the stones. Breanna shivered.

Pebble on stone.

She whipped her head toward the sound so fast, she felt a muscle pull in her neck.

The water sprite clung to the rocks, her side nothing more than ripped flesh and broken bones. "Run, Breanna," she whispered. "Moonlight. Circle. Can't . . . touch . . . circle. Run."

The sprite stared at her with dying eyes as Breanna backed away from the water. Fresh blood. Fresh death. "Keely?" She turned to look for her mother, the woman who had remained a child. She saw Keely's head and shoulders above the rose bushes. "Keely?"

"W-what are you?" Keely took a step back.

"Keely! Get away from there!" Breanna ran toward the rose bushes. The circle would protect them. She could warn Liam that there was danger here before he got too close. But first . . .

She heard Liam shouting at her, but she didn't stop, just ran.

Keely spun around, stumbled, and grabbed the rose bushes to keep from falling, screaming in pain and terror.

Breanna rounded the end of the crescent and stopped, too frozen to do more than stare.

They were big. Much bigger than the ones that had attacked her and Liam a few weeks ago. And . . . different. Not wings, but flaps of skin that stretched from hips to front limbs, like the squirrels that could glide from tree to tree.

As she watched, unable to move, one of the creatures sank its sharp, jagged teeth into Keely's leg, ripping off a chunk of her calf and gulping it down while another slashed at the other thigh with teeth and talons. When a third scrambled up Keely's back and sank its teeth into the flesh that joined shoulder and neck, her scream raked through Breanna.

"Keely!" She took a step forward, unable to think past the fear and yet certain she needed to do *something*.

Until the fourth creature turned and stared at her—and her courage shattered.

It had a long, deep gash down one limb, as if it had been slashed with a sharp stone. Tears still glistened on its dark, leathery face. Snot still bubbled from its nostrils. It let out one whimpering cry as it held up its arms to her—and then snarled and leaped.

And Keely's screams of terror turned into a shriek of rage as she let go of the rose bushes and grabbed one of the creature's legs. "Not my girl. *You can't have my girl!* EARTH!"

The ground around Keely moved, shifted, churned. She sank into the earth so fast there was no time for the creatures attached to her to escape.

Breanna watched Keely disappear. Watched her mother's hand convulse around the leg it held, pulling the last creature down with her until it was buried up to its waist. It screamed, clawing at the ground as it fought to free itself. She watched, too numb to move, until an arrow whistled past her and buried itself in the creature's chest.

Silence.

Keely.

She wanted to scream to break the silence, to beg Keely to come back. But she couldn't move, couldn't speak.

"Liam, get Breanna away from here. Get her away *now.*" She recognized Selena's voice, but it was just a sound.

She knew Liam picked her up. She knew he got her on his horse somehow and they were galloping to her house. But she was too far away to feel him, too far away to feel anything. Even the wind.

"Mother's mercy," Ashk said, her voice rough with pain and pity. "That bastard turned children into nighthunters." She closed her eyes and shuddered. "He turned them into nighthunters."

"Could they still be alive down there?"

There was something cutting about Selena's voice—and there was something odd about that cutting tone.

"They're buried in the earth," Ashk said. "Buried alive."

"But they might be able to survive longer than her?"

What difference does it make? "I don't know."

Selena raised her hands and pointed at the nighthunter that stared at them with dead eyes. "I call fire to cleanse and air to give it breath."

The nighthunter burst into flames, burning so hot Ashk took a step back. Moments later, spears of fire shot out of the ground, and she thought—she imagined—she heard something shriek.

The fire was gone as quickly as it had been summoned. It was only her refusal to give in to the urge to back away—and keep backing away—that made Ashk stand where she was.

Mother's Daughters. House of Gaian. They aren't the same as the witches who live among us. And this one . . . Mother's mercy. This one.

Selena watched the tendrils of smoke rising from the ground. "You said nighthunters feasted on spirits as well as flesh and blood. If, by some chance, they were able to live even a minute longer than she did, they could have destroyed more than her body. I couldn't save the flesh, but I could save the spirit."

"She wouldn't have survived long in any case, but she might have been alive when you sent your fire into the earth."

"I know," Selena said softly. "That's why I had Liam take Breanna away from here."

No, Ashk thought, *we do not know your kind at all. We do not understand the power that walks in the Mother's Hills.*

"Do you fear me, Hunter?"

"At this moment, I am feeling cautious, Huntress," Ashk said carefully.

"It is wise of you to feel that way when you deal with the House of Gaian. That is something our enemy has yet to learn." Selena raised her hands. "Earth."

The ground shivered. Softened. The nighthunter, with Ashk's arrow buried in its chest, sank into the earth.

Selena raised her hands higher. "Sister moon." She glowed as moonlight washed over her skin, pooled at her feet, then spread out until it became a shining circle bordered on one side by a crescent of rose bushes.

The glow faded from Selena's skin. She turned and walked back to where Mistrunner waited.

Ashk studied the glowing circle for a long moment before going to her own horse and mounting.

"Selena?" She waited until the Huntress looked at her. "I am cautious, but I do not fear you."

"Why not?"

"Because I think your heart matches your power."

A film of tears covered Selena's eyes before she blinked them away. "We'd better see if Liam needs help with Bre—"

"Hunter!"

Ashk dropped the reins, freeing both hands for arrow and bow. She relaxed a little when she saw the Fae male cantering toward her—until she got a good look at his face.

"The Muse sent me to find you," he said. "The fight's started."

"Where?"

"At the field with those tumbled stones. We got to that low rise ahead of them, but not by much. That's where the fight is—and along the road leading to the village."

"Warn the witches in the Old Place, then ride to the Fae camps and tell the leaders to get their huntsmen to that rise as fast as they can."

As she and Selena rode over the bridge and galloped over the fields that provided the fastest route to the battleground, she wished there was some way to convince Liam to stay out of the fight for Breanna's sake—and knew the wish was a futile one.

Liam slowed his horse as he rode through the arch. When one of the boys came forward to take the horse, he shook his head and turned the animal toward the kitchen door. Since Breanna was in no shape to walk, it was easier to let the horse carry them both.

The barking caught his attention for a moment before he shook his head. Idjit was dancing under the big tree, defending the world from another squirrel.

The kitchen door opened. He heard Fiona's voice, sharp with annoyance. "Either shut him up or lock him up. I don't need his yapping today."

"I'll get him." Brooke came out of the house, waved at him, and trotted toward the tree. "Idjit! You stop that now, you hear? You're giving Fiona the headache."

Suddenly Breanna went rigid in his arms. "Keely, no," she whispered.

Liam tried to shove aside the worry that flooded through him. They didn't look anything alike, but Brooke and Keely had been about the same age mentally. That's why she was confusing the two. She was still stunned by what she'd witnessed. That was all.

"Keely, no!"

Breanna rammed her elbow into him, breaking his hold so that she half fell, half slid off the horse. The momentum took her forward a couple of steps before she fell to her hands and knees.

He flung himself off the horse, giving it a slap to send it to the stables. He tried to lift Breanna, but she clung to the ground, making horrible, mindless noises while she stared at the tree. He glanced at the tree. Idjit's barking had become frenzied, and Brooke had slowed down, her attention also caught by something in the tree.

Wind riffled the leaves, just enough for him to catch a glimpse of a dark shape hiding in the branches. Something too big to be a squirrel.

"Mother's tits!" Fiona burst out of the kitchen, a poker in her hand. "Can't I have a minute to tend the fire without having to deal with some kind of ruckus?"

He closed the distance between them without realizing he'd started to move, grabbed the poker out of Fiona's hand, and ran just as the nighthunter jumped out of the tree, its flaps of skin turning the jump into a gliding fall. Heading straight at Brooke.

Heat pulsed under his skin, but he couldn't unleash the fire because Brooke was standing between him and the creature. He couldn't burn one without burning the other.

He ran as if his world depended on it—and knew he wouldn't reach her in time.

The nighthunter landed, but before it could leap on the girl, Idjit attacked, sinking his teeth in the flap of skin and bracing his legs to play a deadly game of tug.

Shrieking, the creature turned on the dog, ripping and tearing.

Liam reached Brooke. Grabbing the back of her dress, he flung her behind him, then braced for the attack.

The nighthunter, crouched over the still dog, lifted its face. Blood spilled over its chin. As it gathered itself to leap at him, Liam stepped forward and swung the poker at its head with all his strength. He heard the sharp crack of bone. Felt the poker sink into something softer. Watched the poker slide out of the smashed skull as the body slumped over the dog's haunches.

And saw the perfectly shaped human foot. The birthmark on the back of a pink-skinned calf. A birthmark a distraught mother had described to the guards who had searched for her missing child.

He dropped the poker and backed away. He'd seen, briefly, when Ashk shot the creature that Keely had prevented from attacking Breanna. He'd seen, but his mind had refused to understand.

His gorge rose as he remembered the feel of the poker connecting with that small head. He turned, caught a glimpse of Elinore running out of the house while Fiona tried to comfort Brooke, who was crying hysterically. Then he stumbled away from them as far as he could manage before he fell to his hands and knees and was violently sick.

Breanna slowly got to her feet. On legs that felt as fragile as cracked glass, she walked toward the tree, wobbling as if she'd been ill for a very long time. Her legs buckled before she reached the tree, so she crawled the rest of the way on her hands and knees. She saw a foreleg twitch, heard the bubbly, labored breathing as she crawled to the dog.

Nothing to be done for him. His belly was ripped open, and

blood bubbled from the wound in his neck, soaking his fur and the ground under him.

He whined when he saw her. Tried to lift his head.

She bent over him, petted him, whispered to him. "Idjit. You foolish dog. You foolish, brave, idjit of a dog. Thank you for loving her. Thank you for saving her. We'll give you back to the Mother at your favorite spot under the tree, where you liked to nap. That way you'll always be with us. And Aiden will write a song about you so you'll always be remembered."

The dog sighed out a breath—and didn't breathe again.

"Merry meet, Idjit . . . until we meet again." She gave the dog a final caress, and whispered, "Keely."

Then she laid down beside the dog, too broken inside to do anything else.

Liam staggered to his feet and moved away from the smell of sickness before it brought him to his knees again. Fiona must have taken Brooke into the house, but Elinore waited for him. Edgar stood beside her, glancing uneasily at the figures under the tree.

His heart lurched when he saw Breanna on the ground beside the dog. Before he could decide if Breanna or Elinore needed him more at that moment, a rider came through the arch, paused long enough to have one of the boys point at Liam, then trotted to the kitchen door. The rider glanced at the figures under the tree, then averted his eyes.

"You have news?" Liam called, moving quickly to join Elinore and Edgar.

"Yes, sir. The Hunter said to warn the ladies of the house that the fighting has started along the road to the village and the low rise where she sent some of the men this morning. I'm to ride to the camps around here and give the word they're to come and be quick."

"Go on then, and be quick yourself," Liam said. "Ashk didn't send enough men to hold that rise if the Inquisitors start throwing companies of men at them."

The Fae rider wheeled his horse and galloped toward the pasture gate. Before any of the boys around the stable could run to open the gate, his horse cleared it and kept running.

Liam stripped off his coat. Pulling Edgar aside, he thrust the coat into the man's arms. "I want you to stay here."

"Aye, that's what I was told when the rest of the men headed out with Varden's huntsmen this morning." Edgar smiled grimly. "Everyone agreed we needed one man to stay to keep the boys on their chores, and I drew the short straw."

In more ways than you know, Liam thought grimly. Keeping his voice low, he said, "Cover the nighthunter with the coat, and make sure it's completely covered. Then get Breanna into the house."

Edgar nodded. "I'll get a hand cart and take the creature away from the house before I bury it."

"You'll take kindling and lamp oil with you. After you dig the hole, you put that thing in and burn it before you finish burying it."

"Burn it!"

Liam gripped Edgar's arm hard enough to make the other man wince. "Listen to me. That creature, no matter what it once had been, was a nighthunter, and we burn nighthunters. That's all the ladies need to know. That's all they ever need to know."

"All right, Baron. If it's that important to you, I'll do just as you say."

Stepping away from Edgar, he approached Elinore.

"Where's Keely?" Elinore asked quietly.

Liam swallowed hard. "Keely's dead."

Elinore looked at Breanna. "You have to go. I know that. But be careful, Liam. Please be careful. Not just for my sake, but for hers."

He kissed her cheek. "I'll be back."

"See that you are. We'll look after Breanna."

Since he could think of nothing more to say, he strode to the stables, mounted his horse, and rode away toward the battle.

Chapter 48

waning moon

When they were in sight of the low rise, Ashk and Selena reined in.

Ashk scanned the land in front of her, troubled by the smell of burned meat that hung in the air. There were too many men moving toward the rise for her to see much, but the skittish way they swung around objects caught her attention.

"What's burning?" Selena asked.

At that moment, a ball sailed over the low rise and smashed into a company of men. Blood fountained from the neck of one man as he fell. Others screamed as clothes and skin burst into flames.

"Mother's tits! What is *that*?" Ashk saw one of the western Fae riding toward her and raised her hand in a commanding summons. When he reined in, she looked at the barely conscious man he carried in front of him and felt her gorge rise. She hoped he was a stranger and that was the reason she couldn't recognize his face. "Report."

"We're outnumbered," the huntsman said. "And spread out too thin. Our longbowmen have managed to keep them from coming up the rise, but there's hundreds of them marching across that field and we—" He glanced at the burned and wounded men.

"What is that?" Ashk said.

"Fire," Selena replied in a queer voice. "But not natural fire. Not the Mother's fire."

The huntsman nodded. "One of the humans said the Black Coats have catapults. They're firing clay pots that shatter when they hit the ground or a man. Some are filled with scraps of metal that are flung in all directions when the pot breaks. Some have a liquid that burns when it meets air. Some have both.

We're losing a third of the men before they make it up to the rise to fight."

"Where are you going with him?" Ashk asked.

"Message from Lyrra and Gwenn. They're sending carriages, wagons, anything they can to bring the wounded back to the gentry houses. They should be— There!" The huntsman pointed.

Ashk looked over her shoulder. Lyrra might have thought to send the conveyances, but Gwenn, married to a baron, would have known which ones to send. A pony cart, an open carriage, a farm wagon. They could travel over rougher land, but how would they get through the stone walls?

As the thought took shape, she watched a section of the stone wall in the path of the conveyances break apart, watched the stones roll out of the way. And noticed the man on horseback.

"That Son must have the gift of earth," Selena said. "He's clearing the way for the wagons."

Another ball sailed over the rise, hit the ground, and set the grass on fire. Ashk tensed. If the field on this side of the rise began to burn . . .

The flames diminished. The ground smoked.

She breathed out a sigh of relief. They might not be able to stop men from getting burned, but as long as the House of Gaian was fighting with them, they wouldn't have to worry about being trapped between the enemy's army and a wall of fire.

"See those trees?" Ashk pointed and waited for the huntsman's nod. "Tell the men driving those conveyances they are not to go beyond those trees."

"The catapults are positioned midfield," the huntsman said. "I don't think they have the range to reach that far. But if they push us back enough to move them—"

"They won't," Selena said. "Go now. We have work to do."

When the huntsman rode away, Selena pointed to the stretch of rise right in front of them. "You have to get up there and pull our men off that piece of the rise."

"If we open up a hole, the enemy will pour through it," Ashk protested.

"No, they won't. Because I'll be there to meet them."

Selena's hair fluttered, as if caught by a light breeze. Dust stirred around Mistrunner's hooves. The Huntress looked at her with cold, cold eyes, and the face was a perfect mask that held no hint of the woman Ashk was coming to know.

Saying nothing, Ashk urged her horse into a canter and headed up the rise. She stopped a few lengths from the top and went the rest of the way on foot, pulling an arrow from her quiver and nocking her bow as she got her first look at the field and the enemy.

The huntsman was right. There were hundreds of men marching toward the rise. Longbowmen marched at the back of each company, pausing long enough to aim and fire, then marching on again while they nocked another arrow. Men worked the catapults in midfield, sending their deadly balls over the rise. The road, barely visible from where she stood, had become a cloud of dust, stirred by the feet of men who clashed and maimed and killed.

It would take hours for all the Clans and human companies to reach this place, Ashk thought with despair. The camps were spread out all around Willowsbrook while the enemy must have come up in one mass hidden by the trees at the other end of the field.

She shook her head. Time to get on with the task at hand.

"Huntsmen," she said, pausing a moment to draw her bow, aim, and fire. "Move the line to either side of this position. Stagger the archers in a double line."

"But . . . Hunter," one of them protested, "we can't—"

Ashk looked over her shoulder and saw what was coming up the rise at the speed of a cantering horse. "Move!" she shouted, shoving the man on her left. "Move, move, *move!*"

The men looked back, cried out in fear, and scrambled away from that part of the rise.

Ashk ran a few steps to the left, then flung herself to the ground, pressing herself into it while it quivered beneath her.

Shouts of triumph from the enemy as they surged forward. Screams of fear as that funnel of earth and wind topped the rise and went down the other side, straight into the men who had been rushing up to break through the opening.

She crawled back up to the top of the rise and watched that fury suck men into itself. Watched others, caught by the edge of it, flung aside as if they were nothing more than dry leaves. Archers fired into it, but nothing touched the center of that storm, and men who hesitated before turning to run couldn't match the speed of a galloping horse.

How long could Selena channel that much power? How long

before that funnel of earth and wind diminished, leaving her vulnerable to attack? How long before someone managed a lucky shot that wounded Selena or the horse, leaving the Huntress trapped?

Ashk leaped to her feet. "Archers! Now!" She fired. The men around her rose as well, firing at the companies of men who had changed direction now that the wind funnel was past them and were rushing up the rise to break through the open space and attack her people from behind.

She fired until her quiver was empty. She dropped her bow and unbuckled the quiver. They were useless to her now. But when she reached for the hunting knife in her boot, she remembered she had a better weapon.

The first man to reach the top of the rise had his throat torn open by a shadow hound.

She used her fangs to slash, her speed to dodge. She went for the throat if she could, but hamstringing a leg or tearing an arm down to the bone worked just as well to end that attacker's ability to fight.

She saw the sword slashing down, but she slipped in the grass slick with blood and gore and knew she couldn't dodge it. The stroke never fell, but the man did when a wild pig ripped open the back of one thigh with its tusks.

Their human weapons exhausted, the Fae used the weapons they had. Stags used antlers and sharp, cloven hooves. Wild pigs charged through clusters of men, ripping at legs with their tusks. The wolves among them gathered in packs and tore into flesh with fangs and fury. Hawks and falcons dove, raking heads and faces with their talons. And humans, who would have run from a wolf or a wild pig a few weeks ago, fought beside them now.

They slashed. They maimed. They killed.

And many of them died.

Then ribbons of fire swept down from the rise, racing through the grass, fanning out as they reached the middle of the field and swept over the catapults. The balls filled with metal and liquid fire burst, spraying the enemy with their own weapon. Wind funnels twice as tall as a man danced over the field, breaking up the enemy's efforts to attack. Parts of the field turned soft as water was called to the surface, and men stumbled as they sank into mud between one step and the next.

She saw it all in glimpses, in heartbeats. But the sight of Mistrunner galloping over the rise, alone, pierced her heart—until the other shadow hound leaped on the man who had closed in on her during that moment of inattention, ripping his throat open.

They fought for hours, for what felt like days, until she was exhausted and desperate for water.

She'd tried to keep them close to the top of the rise, but the fighting had brought them down into the field. A handful of men armed with knives rushed toward the two of them. There was no one else around them now. She braced for the attack. Two hounds, five men. Even if they got them all, they would also feel the knives.

Then fire streamed over their heads and hit the men chest-high. The five men rolled in the grass, screaming, burning.

She nudged Selena and scrambled back to the top of the rise. Liam stood there, his face bruised and dirty, his left sleeve soaked with blood, the fingers of his right hand still sending out little drops of fire that seared the grass around his feet as he fought to ground the power he'd summoned.

Selena reached the top of the rise, clamped her teeth around Liam's right wrist, and dragged him down the other side far enough to be out of sight of the enemy longbowmen.

Ashk stopped as soon as she was safe, changed back into human form, and collapsed. Her muscles screamed in protest, but she crawled the arm's length needed to peer over the rise.

The enemy was retreating, heading back toward the cover of the trees on the other side of the field. She looked toward the road. Yes, men were retreating there, too. They'd held them off, but they hadn't won. Would never win until they'd dealt with the Master Inquisitor once and for all. But there was time now for the rest of the Clans and companies of men scattered around Willowsbrook to reach this place.

Her throat tightened as she looked at the bodies in the field, some moving but more laying still. She saw a stag struggle to its feet and begin its painful way toward the rise, hobbling on three legs. And she saw the arrows pierce it—arrows from the enemy longbowmen who had taken up position in the tumble of huge stones. She bared her teeth as other wounded, trying to make their way to safety, were shot down.

She rose to her hands and knees, snarling when a strong hand pushed her back down.

"You've done all you can today," the man said, dropping down beside her.

"I'll do what needs to be done," she snapped.

"You already have."

Impotent rage filled her as she watched more wounded fall. "Mother curse them! May their land and their women be barren for a hundred years."

"Do you really mean that?" he asked quietly.

She turned her head to say something cutting—and saw the pentagram hanging from a chain around his neck. And was suddenly afraid of what might happen if she said yes to this Son of the House of Gaian.

She looked away. "No. The Black Coats and the barons who followed them in the name of greed and ambition deserve whatever comes to them. But not the men and women who just want to live free of fear. Not the children. Not the land." She hesitated, then added, "Do no harm."

He nodded. "But even within the words of our creed there is room for justice, and justice can sometimes be harsh."

Not knowing how to respond to that, she focused on the low-voiced argument going on behind her and shook her head. "Don't waste your breath, Selena. He's gentry and he's a baron. The only way you'll get your point across is to nip him so that he's reminded of it for a week every time he tries to sit down."

"Is that what you do with your man?" the Son asked.

"On occasion. When he needs it."

He grinned, then sobered as he looked out over the field again. "Fog."

"What?"

He nodded toward the field. "A heavy fog. If we blanket the field, their longbowmen will be blind. We can go out and help the wounded to safety."

"If they're blind, so are we. Anyone going out too far could end up walking right into the enemy."

"Would you rather leave them out there?"

Ashk shook her head.

"Problem is, fog is even harder to hold than a storm. We can create it, but it will drift. It's well into the afternoon now. By dusk, there will be banks of fog as far back as the Old Place. But I think it's our best chance."

"What's our best chance?" Selena asked, coming up behind them.

"Fog," Ashk replied.

Selena considered this and nodded. "It will drift, but that's not a bad thing. The Black Coats haven't been here long enough to know the lay of the land. I don't think they'll be anxious to move men when they can't see if they're about to tumble down a creekbed or walk into a tree."

"We'll take care of it," the Son said.

Selena studied him. "My thanks. In that case, I'm going to take Liam back to his house to get his arm sewn up. He stands there bleeding like a stuck pig and insists he's fine. The jack-ass."

"Thank you very much, Lady Selena," Liam said stiffly. "It's always a pleasure to discuss things with you."

"Just nip him," Ashk muttered.

"I heard that."

"You were meant to."

"You'll go with them," the Son said.

Ashk gave the man a cool stare. "I'll decide when to go back to the house."

"Which is now because you're a sensible woman who needs food and rest in order to prepare for what will come tomorrow. You're only annoyed because you know I'm right."

Ashk looked at Selena, who shrugged. Studying the Son, she said, "Have you spent much time among the human gentry?"

He shook his head. "Do you think I need lessons in persuasive speaking?"

"No, I think you could give them."

Ashk stepped out of the house. The Son had been right about the fog drifting. It was eerier somehow when it parted suddenly, providing a clear view for a few seconds before drawing a veil back over the land. But it had hidden the men who had gone into the field to search for the wounded, and they had brought back more than she dared hope for. Many of the Fae were too hurt or dazed or frightened to change back to their human form, but as one human told her when he walked up to the house with a Fae in his arms, it was easier to carry a fox than a man.

So many wounded. So many dead. She was grateful to Gwenn and Lyrra for making a record of the men arriving, writing down names and Clans or a human's home village. It had helped to see the names of those who had come back to them, even if they were wounded. And it helped to receive copies that had been sent from the other gentry houses who were taking in wounded.

But it squeezed her heart to see how many names were missing. Clay had lost an eye but had managed to get back to the village on his own. But Rory was missing. Squire Thurston had lost his right leg below the knee and was being nursed in his own home. But no one remembered the last time they'd seen Donovan. Varden had come through the battle unharmed, but Sheridan was missing.

And no one had seen Falco. Or Aiden.

She tensed when she heard the door open, then forced herself to relax. There were no enemies here. She didn't have to guard her back.

Morphia stepped up beside her. "I wish they hadn't made the fog."

"It was needed," Ashk said quietly.

"I know, but . . ." Morphia wrapped her arms around herself and shivered. "I didn't tell you everything about the dream I had last night. I couldn't. I still can't."

"Why not?"

"I told you something terrible was coming, and it is. I know it. I can feel the echo of it from the dream. But I can't tell you what it is because my mind won't let me see it."

A fist of dread settled in Ashk's stomach. "Is there anything you can tell me?"

"Only that it will come among us shrouded by fog. And it hunts."

"It was a damned fool thing to do," Donovan said in a low voice roughened by exhaustion and pain.

"You've mentioned that already," Aiden replied, keeping his own voice low in the hopes the sound wouldn't carry.

"But I'm grateful. Have I mentioned that, too?"

"Several times."

"Will you write a song about it? The Bard's Rescue of the Baron?"

Aiden snorted softly. "That'll be good for two verses and a chorus, if that."

Donovan was quiet for a moment. "They were close. I could hear them moving around in the fog, searching for survivors. For prisoners, they said. If you hadn't found me, I'd be in the hands of the Black Coats now."

"I didn't find you, I tripped over you. If I hadn't, I would have walked right into them. So we both have reason to be grateful." He would never forget those tense minutes when he lay sprawled in the road next to Donovan, who was desperately trying to stifle moans of pain, realizing they both might have the misfortune of meeting the Master Inquisitor. And he would always be grateful for Minstrel's uncanny sense of direction. Twice the horse had balked when he'd tried to turn him, so he'd finally given Minstrel his head and let the horse choose where they were going. What Minstrel couldn't see, he could smell and hear, and he seemed to know if the sounds or smells belonged to friend or foe.

He *had* been a damned fool to go out once the fog started rolling in. He'd gone anyway to help lead the wounded back to Squire Thurston's estate or the village proper. And he'd been a twice-damned fool for going out again when he couldn't see the road or the land around him beyond his stretched hand. He'd gone out anyway because there were two people he knew who had been fighting on that part of the battlefield. He'd found one. He hadn't found the other.

"Aiden—"

"Hush," Aiden said at the same time Minstrel snorted. "I think I see lights up ahead."

He felt a lightness in Minstrel's stride, an eagerness that gave him hope. As they got closer, the horse bugled.

Dark shapes moved in the fog, and a hard voice said, "Who's there?"

Aiden drew back on the reins enough to slow Minstrel to a walk. "Aiden, the Bard, and Baron Donovan."

Excited voices now. Relieved voices.

"Donovan's hurt," Aiden said.

"Here, sir." A man moved toward him, holding up an oil lamp. "You just follow me to the house. It'll relieve the Squire's mind that Baron Donovan's been found."

Aiden followed the man up to the front door of the house. When he dismounted, he got a good look at Donovan's side—and wished he hadn't.

Donovan gave Aiden a pained smile. "I couldn't leave Gwenny. That's reason enough to fight to live—and keep on fighting. You'll send her a message in the morning, won't you, Aiden?"

"I will."

Donovan closed his eyes and slumped in the saddle. Men caught him and carried him into the house while Aiden, leading Minstrel, followed the man with the oil lamp back to the stables.

"We'll take good care of him, Bard," one of the men said. "That we will. You'd best go back to the house before your legs give out on you."

Pausing long enough to promise Minstrel an extra song in the morning, Aiden left the stables. But he didn't go back to the house. Instead he walked toward the pasture fence—or where it should have been if he could see it. He wasn't ready to enter a house full of wounded. There would be pain there and loss there, and some of those men wouldn't see the sun rise. He hoped with all his heart Donovan wasn't one of them.

The fog parted suddenly, giving him a clear view of the pasture fence—and the hawk perched on the top rail.

Aiden moved quickly, before the fog obscured his vision again. His hand touched the fence. He stopped, worried now because the bird hadn't even turned its head to look at him when he approached. "Falco?"

The fog veiled the world. Keeping one hand on the rail to guide him, Aiden moved closer. "Falco? It's Aiden."

The hawk didn't move when he touched it gingerly, fearing a mortal wound was the explanation for its lack of response. It didn't move when he lifted it off the pasture rail and set it on the ground.

"Falco. Please."

The hawk shuddered. Aiden took one step back. A few moments later, Falco stood before him in human form, still shuddering.

"Falco?" Aiden stepped forward and cautiously put one hand on Falco's shoulder. "Are you hurt?"

"Lost a couple of tail feathers," Falco murmured.

"They'll grow back." Aiden kept his voice soothing as worry lanced through him. Something *was* wrong with Falco, but he didn't know what to say or do to help him.

"I've—" Falco swallowed hard. "I've never seen men fight like that. I've never seen men die like that."

"None of us have."

"It was bad, Aiden. It was bad."

And Falco, who had been a brash young Lord last summer, put his head on Aiden's shoulder and wept.

Chapter 49

waning moon

Morag rode through swirls of fog, her heart pounding, her body clenched. Had she come too late? Had the Black Coats won? Were all the witches gone? Would the human world be swallowed by mist just as the pieces of Tir Alainn had been swallowed when the magic that had anchored them died?

"Odd time of the year for fog," one of her escorts murmured.

And that is why I fear it, Morag thought.

Then she rode out of the trees and saw slivers of light coming from shuttered windows not too far ahead of her, heard the sleepy stirring of animals.

And heard Death's summons.

But not quite here. Death passed over that house with the slivers of light, pausing for a moment before moving on. There was no one here who needed her, but up ahead . . .

"Go up to the house," she said quietly. "See if the people there know where the Hunter can be found. This is the end of the journey. She has to be nearby."

"Are you going up to the house?"

"No. I'm required elsewhere."

"Then we should come with you."

"You can't. You're still among the living."

She rode away before they could argue, letting the dark horse pick his way over unfamiliar ground.

A man's voice to her left. "I thought I heard voices. I think someone is out there."

She said nothing to the men who stepped away from the stables. She just rode through a stone arch and kept going. If they saw anything at all, it was a black-gowned woman appearing and disappearing in the fog, riding a dark horse with silent hooves like something out of a dream.

She rode on toward a steady glow that defied the fog. When she neared the place, she stopped. It looked as if moonlight had gilded the grass to form a circle. Death waited for her there, but she also felt the summons behind some bushes she glimpsed in a moment when the waning moon freed itself from its veil of clouds. Dismounting, she followed the dark shape of the bushes until she reached the end and could see what was on the other side.

Another circle of moonlight. The ghost of a short-haired woman sat in the center of that light, her arms wrapped around her drawn-up knees. One of her thighs and both her arms were tattered, as if something had slashed her spirit. And there were four strange wisps of spirit moving around in that circle of light. There wasn't enough left of any of them to take on a ghostly shape. There was barely enough for her to sense them as spirits that should be gathered. She didn't know if they would ever be able to return to the world, but perhaps they would find some peace in the Summerland.

She held out her hand to the ghost. "I am the Gatherer of Souls. Come."

The ghost floated over to her. "Are you going to take Mama, too?"

"Is she in the other circle of light?"

The ghost nodded.

Morag smiled gently. "Yes. I'll guide you both to the Shadowed Veil so that you can go on to the Summerland."

The ghost stared at the four wisps of spirit now clinging to Morag's dress. "I heard a child crying. But they weren't children anymore. They were the bad things." She sighed. "They didn't get my girl, my Breanna. I didn't let them get my girl."

As she led the ghost to the other circle of light, Morag fought against revulsion, fought against the desire to fling those four wisps of spirit as far away from her as she could. Children. Bad things. Something that could tatter a spirit after the body died. Something that had consumed almost all of the spirit within itself.

She'd known since her first encounter with them that there was nothing inside a nighthunter for her to gather, which was why her gift did nothing more than stun them. But she hadn't realized there *had* been a spirit residing in that flesh once—a spirit the creature had consumed as it changed.

Children. The Inquisitors had done this to children. Mother's mercy.

"Mama!"

The ghost of an older woman stepped out of the other circle of light and opened her arms. The short-haired ghost ran to her, held on to her.

Morag mounted the dark horse, who had followed behind her, then held out her hand. "Come."

The ghosts floated over to her, floated up behind her. The fog cleared for a moment, showing her a stone bridge that spanned the brook she could hear but not see. As she turned the dark horse toward it, the older ghost said, "Can you take them, too?"

She looked at the spot the ghost pointed to and saw the Small Folk standing on the bank, watching her. "Come. I'll take you up to the Shadowed Veil."

After she crossed the bridge, she paused a moment before turning the dark horse toward the field, riding slowly as she followed Death's summons. When she reached the field that climbed to a low rise, she guided the dark horse around it, keeping behind the trees that bordered it. Then she opened the road that led to the Shadowed Veil and took the ghosts as far as she could on their journey to the Summerland.

With eyes filled with pity, the older ghost gathered up the four wisps of spirit and cradled them in one arm. Taking her daughter's hand, she walked through the Veil. The Small Folk raised their hands in farewell, then followed the witches.

Morag rode back down the road and through the trees until she reached the big field on the other side of the rise. In whispers, in pleas, in cries, Death called her.

She rode into the field and began gathering the spirits of the dead—and the spirits of the men who, wounded and suffering, wanted to leave the world of the living.

"Master Adolfo!"

Adolfo finished pouring wine into a glass and settled himself on the blanket-padded bench inside his tent before he said, "You may enter."

A young Inquisitor almost leaped through the tent's opening, his face shining with excitement. Two guards came in behind him, dragging a bound, bridled man.

"Master," the Inquisitor said. "We caught this witch-lover."

"Any man who fights against us is a witch-lover," Adolfo replied in the tone he used as a mild scold—and warning. "What makes this one special?"

"Remember the nest of witches we cleaned out from that estate along the Una River?"

Of course he remembered. He'd drained some of those old women while learning to create nighthunters at will. "What of it?"

The Inquisitor fairly danced with excitement. "We didn't know what had happened to the young ones in the nest."

"I'm aware of that." The Inquisitor's excitement stirred his interest, but Adolfo took care not to let it show.

"This is one of them. His name is Rory. One of the men who came from a village near there recognized him. We think they ran to *this* Old Place to escape us."

Which meant the man was known to the bitches who lived in this Old Place. Was, perhaps, even kin to them. Which made him perfect.

Draining the wine glass, Adolfo set it aside and stood. "Bring him."

The Inquisitor looked crestfallen. "Don't you want to question him about the witches, Master?"

Adolfo smiled. "I have a better use for him."

There were so many. Morag lost count of the number of spirits she had taken up the road to the Shadowed Veil, and there were still so many. She couldn't keep going. She was tired. The dark horse was tired. She'd ridden all day to reach the Old Place and had been gathering spirits for hours now. Time to stop. Time to rest. She needed to make her way back to the Old Place and find Ashk.

This would be her last trip up the road to the Shadowed Veil. She would open the road right here and let the spirits nearby follow her to the Veil.

Just as she opened the road, she saw a ghost moving toward her. He smiled and raised a hand in greeting.

"Merry meet, Gatherer."

Tears pricked her eyes. "Sheridan," she whispered, then held out her hand. "Come."

As he floated up to her, he said, "Tell Ashk I've gone to the

Summerland, and"—regret filled his face for a moment—"tell Morphia I hope to meet her again one day."

"I'll tell them."

She couldn't talk anymore. She'd recognized some of the men she'd gathered, but Sheridan had been a friend, as well as her sister's lover. She wondered if he'd moved away from his body as a kindness to her, so she wouldn't have to see how he'd died.

"Don't grieve, Morag," Sheridan said. "The Summerland has sweet skies for a falcon to soar in."

Hearing what he didn't say, she was even more grateful that he'd spared her the sight of his body. So she didn't grieve for him or any of the others she'd taken up the road to the Shadowed Veil. She grieved for the loved ones left behind.

Adolfo wasn't pleased to have torches around the small clearing, but the fog and the cover of trees swallowed up too much of the moonlight for him to see without the extra light.

"Put the tether stake in the center and tie the prisoner to it," he said, pointing. "Keep him bound and bridled. There's no telling what abilities a man born of a witch might have."

He smiled grimly as he watched the guards obey his orders— as he thought of the witch who had been his mother, who had betrayed her son's love and trust in order to keep her own power a secret. He thought of the monster his father became when, spurred by his wife's accusations, he tried to beat the magic out of the boy to regain his wife's affection. Most likely, the man had been grateful when the boy, by then a youth, had run away to try to survive in the world on his own.

He hoped his mother's spirit spent a hundred years drowning in one of the Summerland's cesspools—if the Summerland had such places. He hoped his father's spirit was also in a cesspool—a place made from the foul thoughts and feelings the man had harbored for his own flesh and blood. But not the same one. No, he didn't want them to have the comfort of being together for any reason, even torment.

When the prisoner was in position, guards brought the witch into the clearing and bound her to the stool. Her wits hadn't returned at all, and her body, despite being so young, was starting to fail. She would be no use to him after he channeled the magic through her this time, but she might live long enough for some of the men to use her. After all, being passed around from man to man was a fitting end for a witch.

"Leave now," he ordered. "Stay away from the clearing. I am shaping a weapon to set against the enemy, and this clearing will be a dangerous place."

He waited until the guards were gone, waited until he couldn't hear even a muffled footstep. Then, using the witch as his channel, he began to draw the magic out of the land.

Morag signaled the dark horse to stop, no longer certain she was moving in the right direction. But Death was out there, ahead of her, whispering. Not the kind of whisper she was used to. This was almost wary, almost a warning. What would Death be warning her about?

She dismounted and moved forward, letting the dark horse follow on his own. Guided by Death's whisper, she walked until she saw flickers of light among the trees. As she moved closer, feelings scraped along her skin. A prickle of warning. A prickle of fear.

Still moving closer, she saw the small clearing lit by torches, saw the shape of a man at the other end of the space, heard the struggling efforts of someone on the ground between her and the man.

She moved through the trees, circling toward the man. Power swirled in the clearing, but it didn't feel right somehow.

Then the fog tore, and she saw the man clearly. She heard the voice she'd heard once before at the dock at Rivercross. In a moment of pity, and in the hope that mercy shown might produce a seed of mercy inside him, she had let the Master Inquisitor live, leaving him with a dead arm to remind him that there were powers in the world that were stronger than his.

He lifted his right hand, aiming it at the person on the ground.

"Twist and change. Change and twist."

She saw the faint glow of a circle of power. What was he—? Children. Bad things. No. *No!*

"Become what I would make of thee."

Rage blinded her as she charged out of the trees, straight toward him.

"As I will—"

Little flashes of fire in the clearing. The sound of leather snapping as a man hurled himself out of the circle.

"so mote it—"

She was almost on the Master Inquisitor. His head whipped around.

"—beeee."

He screamed the word as she slammed into him, knocking them both into the circle. His right hand closed on her arm. She screamed as the power he unleashed ripped through her body. He screamed as the power ripped through him as well. The circle crackled with it while they rolled over and over. She tried to gather him, but she couldn't find his spirit in the storm of power.

Then the power was gone. She rolled away from the Witch's Hammer, clawed and scrabbled until she regained her feet and stumbled toward the trees. She almost fell on the man who had hurled himself out of the circle. Grabbing his arm, she helped him to his feet.

"Come on," she gasped, her voice scraped raw from screaming. "We have to get away from here."

The dark horse waited for her at the edge of the clearing. The rope that had bound the man's feet had burned through, so he was able to mount by himself and was aware enough to kick one foot out of the stirrups to make it easier for her to swing up behind him.

She brushed her heels against the dark horse's sides. "Get us away from here. Go anywhere, as long as it's away from here."

He turned back into the trees and cantered away from the clearing.

She clung to the saddle as the horse wove through the trees, adding speed whenever he came to some open ground. Pain seared her. The power continued to slash through her, ripping her apart inside.

She had to find Ashk.

It was the last clear thought she had before she felt herself leaning sideways, felt the horse slow, felt the man try to grab her as she slid to the ground.

Adolfo rolled over onto his side, gasping as pain lanced through him.

Bitch. Thrice-cursed bitch. Not only had her interference deprived him of a valuable weapon, she'd hurt him. Hurt him worse than when she'd turned his arm into dead meat.

A mewling sound at one end of the clearing caught his attention. Made his mouth water.

Moving slowly, he managed to push himself up to his knees.

Bitch. She'd tried to gather him. He had felt her try. But his power had been stronger than hers, and he'd won.

More mewling noises. And an unpleasant smell. The useless witch must have soiled herself.

He got to his feet, swaying with the effort to stand.

He'd fought against the Gatherer . . . and he'd won.

More pain lanced through him, but he embraced it now, celebrated it. *He'd won.*

He shuffled toward the mewling sounds coming from the female tied to the stool.

Now he needed rest. Needed something to drink.

Feast!

Something warm. No. Something hot. And something to eat. He was hungry. So very, very hungry.

Morag jerked awake. Her body felt battered, and little shivers of pain still lanced through her, making her limbs jerk. And there was a thick, unpleasant taste in her mouth.

She heard the dark horse snorting nearby, little fearful sounds.

Groaning with the effort, she pushed herself up to her hands and knees.

Mother's mercy. Her dress pinched the skin along her arms and sides, and her body didn't feel right. The power in the circle had made her sick. She'd seen some people who had swelled from a kind of sickness. She had to get out of this fog. If she couldn't make it back to the Old Place, she had to find a farmer's cottage, a barn, anyplace they could find shelter for a few hours. She had to find a place for herself, the dark horse, and—

Where was the man who had escaped from the Witch's Hammer? He'd come with her. She was certain he had. Where—?

He lay near her, the wounds on his neck and chest making her stomach churn. Something vicious and terrible had killed him. A fast kill. A recent kill.

Fear got her to her feet, got her stumbling toward the dark

horse. He snorted. Took a step back as she approached, then, trembling, held his ground.

"Easy, boy. Easy." Why was he afraid of her?

She raised her hand to give him a caress and pat.

The hand that lifted out of the fog was dark, leathery, had sharp, blood-smeared talons at the ends of its fingers.

She wept silently as she stared at the hand of the enemy from her dreams.

Quiet conversations died in his wake as Adolfo walked through the camp and entered his tent, followed by fearful whispers.

He was still thirsty, but the wine held no appeal. And his sides itched, irritated by the cloth rubbing against it. He raised his hand to pull open the tunic's lacings . . . and stared, fascinated, at the skin that was turning darker, rougher, even as he watched. Stared at the nails folding in on themselves until they began to look like talons.

A hesitant scratching on the tent flap.

"What is it?" His voice sounded rough, raspy—not the smooth deep voice that had persuaded hundreds of men to help him reshape the world as he wanted it to be.

An Inquisitor stepped into the tent. "Master Adolfo? Is there something we can do for you? Is there something you need?"

Fresh meat. Hot blood. Everything he needed was standing within reach.

No. Not his own men. Not when there was prey close by. "Do we have other prisoners?"

"Yes, Master."

"Bring two of them to me. It doesn't matter which two." He turned around to face the Inquisitor. He smiled as he watched the man's face turn deathly pale. *Deathly pale.* The thought amused him. The fool had no idea how close to deathly pale he had been.

"Y-yes, Master," the Inquisitor stammered.

As the man fled from the tent, Adolfo looked at the glorious talons at the end of his right hand and laughed.

Two ghosts standing next to bodies still locked in the embrace of the fight that had killed them.

Morag slid off the dark horse, moved toward the ghosts, then stopped. No. She couldn't gather them, couldn't take them up the road to the Shadowed Veil. She was sick, hurt, exhausted. She had to find Ashk. Mother's mercy, she had to find Ashk, had to . . .

The meat was already spoiled from the heat of the day, the blood already too clotted and thick. But the best part of the feast remained.

Where were the ghosts? Where were the spirits she'd seen a moment ago?

She backed away from the bodies, shaking her head.

And realized she didn't feel quite so hungry, realized . . .

The wolf with the burned hind legs tried to drag itself away from the predator, tried to run, tried to hide. Screamed as fangs and talons ripped its flesh, as a tongue lapped at the fresh blood while it died slowly, slowly.

It didn't like the taste of animal flesh, but It was too hungry to care. And the feast that rose from the animal flesh was a rich spirit, a strong spirit in the shape of the flesh It liked best.

It devoured—and still hungered.

. . . Morag dropped the reins, wrapped her arms around herself, and doubled over, gasping and weeping. She remembered the wolf, remembered the ghost that had risen from it. One of the western Fae who had ridden east with her and Ashk. She remembered him screaming her name. Remembered him screaming as she . . . as the thing inside her feasted on his spirit until nothing was left but wisps of memories.

She'd known him and still hadn't been able to stop It.

"Mother have mercy," she whispered. "Please, have mercy."

The dark horse trembled beneath her. Loyalty and courage. How many times could he have run away during the past few hours? He had more trust in her ability to protect him from the predator inside her than she did. Would the hour come when that loyalty would be repaid with talons slashing his throat open? Would courage be rewarded by dying in terror?

She slowly placed one hand on his neck, careful not to let the talons prick him. "I won't hurt you. I will fight with everything in me not to hurt you. That much I can promise."

She straightened up and looked around. The fog was lifting. The first, soft light of the day was pushing back the night. The dark horse had brought them close to a large stone house. The baron's house? She could . . .

Hunt!

. . . find food there . . .
Flesh!
. . . and grain for the horse.
Feast!
The Old Place was too far away. She had to find food *now*—
before It got too hungry.

Chapter 50

waning moon

Breanna closed her eyes as the ponycart approached the circle of moonlight guarding Nuala's grave. She couldn't bear looking at the rose bushes—and wondered if she ever would be able to again. Best to close her eyes before the grief numbed her again. Best not to wonder if the light in the circle was really waning or if it was this soft light before dawn that made the circle look dimmer. Best not to think about what would happen to Nuala's spirit once the light waned since they could no longer spare men to guard the grave. Best not to think at all.

"I'm glad to have your company," Elinore said as she guided the pony over the stone bridge and headed for the baron's house. "And a chaperone, since I'm being escorted by four handsome men."

Breanna pictured one of the Fae huntsmen riding with them offering Elinore a hesitant smile, uncertain if flirting with Baron Liam's mother would be considered acceptable in the human world. Strange how the Fae had become more wary of dealing with humans now that they'd been forced to become more aware of them.

"Are you sure you won't come with me to the village?" Elinore asked. "I'm told the Widow Kendall wraps her hair around strips of rags at night to produce those curls other women envy. The result is certainly beautiful, but I imagine the sight of her first thing in the morning is something that takes getting used to. Since I'll be knocking on her door at an indecent hour, we might find out for ourselves."

Breanna opened her eyes and focused on the pony's ears. A safe thing to look at. "Thank you, but I'll just visit with Gwenn and Lyrra for a bit. I'm sure they'll be up by now."

"Yes, I'm sure they will be."

She was grateful Elinore didn't continue trying to make conversation. She didn't want to talk to anyone. Not really. She just needed to get away from her home, from the rooms so choked with memories she couldn't seem to breathe. She just wanted to sit with two women who weren't kin and weren't bent under the same weight of grief.

But you don't know what happened yesterday. You don't know if they're breaking under their own grief.

When Elinore pulled up in front of Liam's house, Breanna got down from the ponycart. Elinore smiled at her, but the smile couldn't win over the worry in the older woman's eyes.

"If you want to go back before I return, one of the men will escort you," Elinore said.

Breanna just nodded and walked to the front door. She turned and raised a hand in farewell as Elinore and two of the Fae escorts headed for the village. Watched the two other escorts lead their horses to the stable, where they would wait for her. Tried not to scan the fences and roofs and trees for some sign of—

She hadn't thought of him. Wouldn't allow herself to think of him. He hadn't come back to the Old Place. There were many who hadn't come back to the Old Place. She hadn't been able to help Fiona, Glynis, and the other women when the wounded arrived yesterday, but she'd heard the women talking. Heard the break in Fiona's voice when she asked if anyone had seen Rory.

How long would it take before she didn't look toward the clothes lines to see if the hawk was perched on one of the posts, keeping watch? Months? Years?

She wouldn't think of him. Or she would pretend he had gone away. Back to Tir Alainn. Back to his home Clan. Had just gone away without saying good-bye. Which, in fact, was exactly what he might have done.

As she turned back toward the door, it opened. Sloane stepped aside to let her enter.

"Good morning, Lady Breanna," Sloane said.

"Blessings of the day, Sloane. Is anyone up yet?"

"The Hunter, the Huntress, and Baron Liam rode out toward the village at first light. The Ladies Rhyann and Gwynith went with them, along with Lord Varden. Ladies Gwenn and Lyrra left for Squire Thurston's house a few minutes ago. The Bard sent a messenger to let them know Lord Donovan was badly wounded but had survived the night and was healing well."

"So Aiden and Donovan survived," Breanna murmured. "That's good."

Sloane smiled. "And Lord Falco. He made it back to the squire's house before the fog made travel imprudent."

She was suddenly lightheaded, floating. A warm hand closed on her arm, grounding her.

"Lady Breanna?" Sloane said. "Are you well? Have you eaten yet?"

"I . . . don't remember."

"Why don't you go sit in Lady Elinore's morning room? I'll have some tea and toast brought in for you."

"Thank you, Sloane. That's very kind of—"

A scream sliced through the house. A maid rushed through the servant's door at the back of the hall. She tripped over her skirt and went sprawling across the floor, still scrabbling wildly to reach the front door.

Sloane hauled her up by one arm and said sternly, "What's the matter with you, girl? There's wounded in the house. Do you want to give everyone a fright?"

"There's something in the kitchen," the maid gasped. "Something terrible."

Breanna moved toward the servant's door. This was her brother's home. These servants were her brother's people. Since he wasn't here to deal with this, she would. Somehow, she would find the strength to deal with this.

When she walked into the kitchen, she saw the cook and her helpers pressed against one side of the room, staring with terrified eyes at the black-haired woman bent over one end of the work table. Her black overdress and trousers were dirty and torn, and her breathing was as rough and ragged as her clothes.

"What do you want?" Breanna asked.

The woman spun around, snarling.

Not a woman, Breanna thought as her blood chilled. *No longer a woman.* Leathery skin. Sharp teeth. Talons at the ends of its fingers. But the dark eyes that stared at her . . . The woman was still in there, still aware, still fighting against what she was becoming.

The creature raised one hand. "Hot blood. Strong spirit." She shook her head fiercely, then turned away.

"What do you want?" Breanna asked.

"Food. Drink. Grain for the horse."

Mother's mercy. "Sloane, ask one of the footmen to fetch a small sack of feed from the stables."

"At once, Lady Breanna."

The creature twisted around, stared at her again.

A chilling calm settled over Breanna. "Cook, bring out a wheel of cheese—and one of the carry baskets Elinore uses." She took a step toward the table. The creature moved around to the other side. Moved away from her. Which gave her enough courage to keep moving forward. There was bread on the table, along with a cold beef roast and some vegetables. The cook had started to make a beef broth for the wounded and a heartier soup for anyone who could take more solid nourishment.

"Bring me some butter and a jar of preserves." She sliced bread, carved the meat. The cook crept to the table, handing her things as she asked for them. By the time Sloane returned with the sack of grain, she had built two generous beef sandwiches as well as a butter and preserve sandwich, cut a thick chunk of cheese from the wheel, wrapped it all in the white napkins that were used at the servants' table, and placed it in the basket.

"Do we have any canteens?" she asked Sloane.

"There are a few that are not in use," he replied.

"Fill one with water, the other with ale." Breanna looked at the creature who had watched her in silence. "Is ale acceptable?"

The creature hesitated, then nodded.

While Sloane filled the canteens, Breanna repacked the basket to fit the bag of feed in one end. No point having those talons ripping through the cloth and having the feed spill out. If the woman inside still cared enough about her horse to ask for feed, it would hurt her to have nothing to offer because of what her body had become.

When the canteens were placed on the table, Breanna stepped back. "If there's something else you want, take what you can gather."

The creature made a hideous sound that Breanna realized was meant as laughter. Cruelty filled those dark eyes for a moment before it was battled back by a strong will. "I can gather armies." She reached for the basket, then hesitated. "Breanna."

Breanna swallowed hard and wished Sloane had never spoken her name.

"The witches in the Old Place. In the circles of light."

Her heart pounded, throbbed in her temples. "My m-mother and grandmother."

"They have gone to the Summerland."

Tears pricked her eyes. Keely's and Nuala's spirits were out of reach now. Safe.

Grabbing the basket and canteens, the creature hurried toward the open kitchen door. Then stopped. "Have you seen the Hunter?"

"I've seen the Hunter."

"Tell her . . . *Warn* her that the Gatherer has come."

Breanna saw the dark horse waiting a few steps beyond the open door, saw the creature mount and ride away . . .

The Gatherer has come.

. . . felt the floor disappear . . .

. . . and heard someone saying, "Bless the Mother, she's all right. She just fainted, is all."

Fainted? How embarrassing.

"Nothing to be embarrassed about, Lady Breanna. Never saw anyone with so much foolish courage."

She didn't remember speaking, but she must have since Liam's housekeeper was answering her.

Her eyes popped open. They'd carried her to Elinore's morning room. A smell of burnt feathers stung the air. She'd never understood why gentry households thought burning feathers was so useful for bringing someone out of a faint, but maybe she could add a few coins to the house funds by selling Falco's molted feathers to gentry ladies. Would he be offended by the suggestion or find it amusing? She must remember to ask him, must remember . . .

The Gatherer has come.

She struggled to sit up. "Where's Sloane?"

"Here, Lady Breanna."

She focused on him. The foolish courage the housekeeper had praised was deserting her, and she had to tell him before her body began shaking so badly she wouldn't be coherent. "Send the Fae who are waiting for me. They have to find Ashk and Selena and bring them back here *now*."

"Yes, Lady."

The housekeeper urged her to lie down again, tucked a blanket around her. Fear was a runaway horse inside her, and she couldn't stop shaking. Mother's mercy, what were they supposed to do? What could Ashk or Selena or any of them do?

The Gatherer has come.

Ashk, Selena, and Liam stood on the low rise overlooking the field. The sun was barely on the horizon, but most of the fog was already gone, giving her a clear view of the field.

"The bodies are gone," Ashk said. They'd had to leave the dead on the field last night. Finding the wounded and getting them to a house where they could be tended had taken all their effort.

"We gave them back to the Mother last night," Rhyann said.

Ashk closed her eyes and wished a silent farewell to the men who hadn't returned from that field. Then she pushed aside any thoughts about those who were gone. She had to do her best for the living—and for the land.

"Those stones," Selena said softly, dreamily.

Ashk looked at the tumble of huge stones that dominated the field. "A den for their longbowmen."

"A den," Selena said in that same soft, dreamy voice. "Yes, a den for the Black Coats."

"Selena?" Worry sharpened Ashk's voice. Neither of them had gotten much sleep, and she didn't like the unfocused look in Selena's eyes.

"Earth. Air. Water. Fire. Light of the sun. Light of the moon. Dreams and will. That's what it takes."

Mother's tits! What is the woman talking about? But the way Rhyann's expression sharpened told Ashk that, while the words meant nothing to her, they were important.

"Yes," Rhyann said after studying the stones. "But how to drive the Black Coats to that spot? Fighting isn't enough. We need something they'll run from without thinking, something they'll fear in their hearts and react to."

That she could answer. "The Wild Hunt."

Selena and Rhyann looked at her thoughtfully. Varden nodded.

"The Wild Hunt?" Liam asked, sounding skeptical.

"It would be better if we had packs of shadows hounds—"

"We have them," Gwynith said, hurrying back to them. "I was just talking to one of the Fae Lords. He said three Ladies of the Moon arrived at the camps just before the fog closed in last night.

They came with their huntsmen—and their packs of shadow hounds."

"If you want something humans will fear, Huntress, there's your answer," Ashk said.

Selena nodded. "Two arrows driving the Black Coats to those stones. One coming from the road, the other from this end of the rise. The human companies will take the middle of the field, coming down from the rise."

"And the House of Gaian?" Liam asked.

"We have a different task." Selena looked at Rhyann. "I'll leave it to you to gather the Sons and Daughters."

Rhyann nodded. "And I'll gather what we'll need."

"Need for what?" Ashk asked.

Selena smiled coldly as she stared at the stones. "For justice . . . and for vengeance. I have no interest in the men who were commanded to fight, but the Black Coats, the barons, and the guard captains . . . I want them driven into those stones."

Liam raked a hand through his hair. "The barons—"

Selena turned on him. "Show me a baron who did not order the death of a witch, and he is yours to deal with as you choose. But the others come to me."

Liam stared at her as if he'd never seen her before. "What will you do with them?"

Selena's smiled turn colder. "We'll give them what they want."

"Let's move," Ashk said. "The sun's coming up, and the Black Coats will be forming their companies. We have to do the same."

As she turned to go down the rise, she saw a huntsman galloping toward her.

"Hunter!" he yelled. "Hunter!"

"What is it?" Ashk demanded. "What's wrong?"

"You have to come to the baron's house. Lady Breanna says she has to speak with you right away."

Breanna was at Liam's house? She was relieved to hear Breanna was no longer lost in that horrible frozen retreat she'd sunk into yesterday, but . . . "Tell Breanna I'll be there as soon as I can. We've a battle coming in a few hours and—"

"Hunter, you have to come *now*. And the Huntress, too."

"Go on," Liam said. "I'll stay here and start bringing our people into position."

Knowing what it must have cost him to stay, Ashk nodded. "We'll be back as soon as we can." She touched his arm lightly. "She's strong, Liam. The grief will ease, and she'll heal."

"That she wants to talk to anyone is a relief." He tried to smile.

Ashk and Selena hurried down the rise to where their horses waited and galloped away, leaving the Fae Lord who had brought the message trailing behind them.

When they reached Liam's house, it was clear by the way Sloane hovered at the front door, watching for them, that something had happened.

As they reached the door, someone called out, "Hunter!"

A young Fae Lord trotted over from the stables and handed her a wax-sealed piece of paper. "I was told to hand this to the Bard, or to you, Hunter, if the Bard wasn't here."

Ashk nodded, tucked the paper under her belt, and went inside.

They found Breanna in the morning room, wrapped in blankets, both hands around a large glass of whiskey.

Ashk went down on one knee in front of her. Selena sat beside her, putting an arm around Breanna's shoulders.

"Breanna?" Ashk touched her knee and realized Breanna was trembling. The woman was strong, but how many blows could she take before she broke?

"I have to tell you . . . *warn* you . . ."

"Tell me what?"

"The Gatherer has come." Breanna began shaking so hard, Selena had to help her raise the glass of whiskey so that she could drink.

Relief flooded through Ashk. "Morag has come? She's here?"

Breanna shook her head. "We gave It food . . . and grain for the horse. It went away."

It? "Breanna—"

"She's changed!" Breanna's voice rose, spiked with fear. "She's been changed!"

Relief turned into shards of ice that sliced Ashk's heart. "What do you mean, she's been changed?"

Tears rolled down Breanna's face. "The Gatherer has been changed into a nighthunter."

Ashk walked out of the house, bolted for trees on one side of the drive. She collapsed against one, fighting the sick churning in her belly.

Morag changed into a nighthunter? The Gatherer of Souls changed into a creature that feasted on—

"Morag," she whispered. "Mother's mercy, Morag."

"What should we do, Hunter?" Selena asked softly.

She wasn't surprised that Selena had followed her out of the house—both because the Huntress cared about people and because she would want answers.

Ashk straightened up, feeling painfully old, desperately weary. "We do what must be done, Huntress. We form the Wild Hunt. We bring up the companies of humans. We fight the battle that must be fought today."

"What do we do about the Gatherer?"

"Leave it alone, Selena."

Selena studied her for a moment, then nodded. "You know her best." She took a deep breath, let it out in a sigh. "What was the message?"

She'd forgotten about the message. She pulled it out of her belt, broke the seal, and read. "The Black Coats army in the south has been defeated. And the . . . the warships that were sent to attack the west were also defeated."

"Then this is it. It comes down to us and the Witch's Hammer. It comes down to what happens on that field today. If we win, it's over."

Ashk refolded the paper and tucked it into her belt. *Not quite,* she thought grimly. *Not quite.*

Chapter 51

waning moon

Adolfo watched swollen, putrid flesh push through the rotted skin on the prisoner's chest—and smiled. A bite to the shoulder, something a healer would think of as a simple wound. But whatever was in a nighthunter's bite that tainted a wound had spread so swiftly, the black rot had already crept down the prisoner's arm, crept toward his heart, crept up his neck.

All it had taken was one bite from him. One. The nighthunters he'd made from small animals would kill a man if there were enough of them, but a man could live after being bitten in a limb—if he was willing to sacrifice the limb. But with *his* bite, the rot spread too fast. A simple bite became a mortal wound.

A scratching on the tent flap. "Master?"

Adolfo pulled up the hood on his cloak. He'd torn off his tunic hours ago, no longer able to stand having the web of skin that had grown out of his side and the underside of his arm trapped by cloth. The cloak would cover him sufficiently until he was ready to reveal himself to his enemies.

Obeying his terse reply, the young Inquisitor peered into the tent. "Is there something you need, Master?"

"Have my horse saddled," Adolfo growled. "Today I will lead our men to victory. And you can throw that next to the dung pile. Let the flies have it."

He strode out of the tent, amused at the way the young Inquisitor pulled the tent flap back and held it in front of him as if it were a shield.

There were no shields from the glory he'd become. He would fill the battlefield with pain and fear. And then he would feast.

Crouched on the top of the rise, Ashk looked over the field. How many bowmen were already tucked among that tumble of huge stones? How many Fae would die today? How many humans? She, Selena, and Liam had agreed that the companies and Clans that had fought yesterday wouldn't be asked to step onto the battlefield again unless there was no other choice. Some of the Fae still hadn't returned to their human form, and she wondered if some of them ever would.

She couldn't think about them, couldn't pity them. They couldn't win this battle without the Clans, and if they didn't win today, they would keep fighting, keep dying, keep getting pushed back until there was nowhere to go. So they would fight to the end today—and, hopefully, some of them would go home again.

"Are we ready?" Liam asked, moving up beside her.

Ashk stared at the line of trees at the other end of the field. "We'd better be. They're coming." She moved down the rise, heading toward the huntsmen waiting for her. "You know what to do?"

Liam nodded. "My men will take up a position in the trees that border this side of the rise. We stay hidden until the Wild Hunt sweeps down into the field, breaking their lines. Then we deal with the men who are driven our way." He smiled bleakly. "I know you gave me that position to keep me out of harm's way, Ashk, but this is my land, my people."

"And they're going to need you when this is over. Sylvalan will need you when this is over."

"Sylvalan needed the barons who died yesterday, too."

"Don't argue with me, Liam."

He stared past her, and whispered, "Breanna."

She turned—and wanted to snarl. But the woman walking toward her looked too emotionally battered to endure harsh words, so she choked them back.

Ignoring Liam, Breanna came up to Ashk. "My home. My family. I couldn't help you yesterday. I won't stand aside today."

"You sound like your brother," Ashk said at the same moment Liam said, "You shouldn't be here."

"Don't argue with me, Liam," Breanna snapped.

He muttered a few extremely vulgar phrases.

Ashk looked at Breanna—and at Falco, who stood just behind her, already pale and sweating. Neither of them should go down into that field, but Breanna, for whatever reason, would do just that. And Falco would go with her.

"Do you see that jumble of wood and stone at the top of the

rise?" Ashk pointed to the place where they'd used branches and stones to build a small wall. "I want you to take a position behind that wall. Stay down."

"I—"

Ashk raised her hand. "You want to help, I'll take the help. But give me the help I need."

Breanna blinked.

"Your gift is air, isn't it?" She waited for Breanna's nod. "We want the first lines to get past the middle of the field before we move, but that means all the men on our side of the rise will be stationary targets. Blind hits, true, but that won't matter if we lose too many men before the fight even begins."

"You want a hard wind their bowmen have to shoot against."

"Yes."

Breanna smiled. "I can summon a wind."

"Go on, then. Get in position."

Once Breanna and Falco were moving up the rise to their position, Ashk turned to Liam, who looked ready to explode. "Don't ask her to be less than she is, Liam."

"And what is she, besides a woman who's lost her mother and grandmother in the space of a few days?" he demanded.

"A Daughter of the House of Gaian."

He swallowed whatever he'd been about to say and left her, signaling to his men to take up their own position.

As she reached her horse, she heard Varden call her.

"You don't have to be here today," she told him.

"There aren't many of my men who felt they could face this field again, but those of us who can . . ." Varden shook his head. "We need to do this, Hunter. Now, there's not many of us, so I thought we'd join Baron Liam's men. Besides, fighting from the cover of the trees will be an advantage to our new warriors." He jerked a thumb over his shoulder.

Ashk stared at the Small Folk being helped off the Fae horses.

"They wanted to come. They've lost friends and family to the nighthunters, too. And they've assured me they're wicked accurate with a sling."

She walked over and studied the grim-faced men and women who were no taller than the length of her arm. All of them carried slings and had a bag bulging with stones hanging from their belts.

"All right," she said. "You go with Varden and Baron Liam.

Varden, tell Liam we'll alternate between arrow and sling. When the enemy reaches the striking point, let the slings fire first. Once the first line drops, the bowmen will have a clear shot at the second line."

"Yes, Hunter."

Ashk hurried to her horse. How much time had passed? How far had the enemy advanced? Her eyes scanned the field. Gwynith and one other Lady of the Moon with a pack of shadow hounds was riding with her. The other two Ladies with their packs were with the Hunt coming up the road from the village. Her huntsmen were ready, the first waves of human companies were waiting for the order to move up the rise and descend into the field. Breanna and Falco had taken up position where she'd told them to. And Selena, dressed in white overdress and trousers, sat quietly on Mistrunner with Rhyann beside her, mounted on Fox.

They'd refused to explain what they'd meant by "dreams and will," but seeing the Sons and Daughters now gathered behind the Huntress, and remembering the Son who had asked her if she really wanted Wolfram made barren, she decided it was just as well they hadn't told her what they intended to do after the Black Coats and the barons who followed them were driven into the tumble of stones.

She felt the first gust of wind hit her back, watched men take a stagger-step to keep their balance, saw the trees bend with the force of it. And saw the first enemy arrows hit that wind and dance skyward, tumbling back the way they'd come like twigs driven by a storm.

It was time.

She unhooked her hunting horn from her belt, raised it to her lips, and sounded the call for the Wild Hunt. Lords of the Woods picked up the call, the notes from their horns flying on the wind. Finally she heard the call of a distant horn. After hooking her horn back on her belt, she nocked an arrow in her bow, and, using leg and knee commands, signaled her horse to canter up the rise.

Adolfo kept his horse at a walk as he moved into the field. Excitement filled him as he watched the lines of men marching toward the rise. Hungry lust bit at him, making it hard not to grab one of the men marching past him and begin the feast. But he waited, knowing that soon he would be able to gorge on the spirits locked helplessly to their dead bodies. And once he had destroyed the witches, he would take some of the prettier women from the village and slake another kind of lust.

Then he heard the horns. And something in him too primitive to listen to reason wanted to run, to hide, to get away from whatever was coming behind those horns.

He wouldn't run. Curse whatever shivered through him, he *wouldn't* run. But . . .

Almost without thought, driven by something he could barely control, he cut between two companies of men and rode toward the tumble of stones.

They came down the rise in terrifying silence. Silent horses, silent hounds. That was the way of the Wild Hunt. Only the horn gave the warning that the Fae were out riding to hunt.

They came down the rise with their bows drawn, but the first line of men who froze when they caught sight of them fell before the first arrow was loosed, clutching their heads or throats, dropping weapons as stones shot from slings broke hands or wrists. The second line fell from arrows flying out from the trees.

Then she was down amongst the enemy, letting her bow sing Death's song, turning her horse to cut a straight path toward the tumble of stones while the shadow hounds pulled men down, ripping open a leg or tearing out a throat before racing on to the next prey.

Men scattered, ran toward the shelter of the trees and were met with arrows and stones.

Ashk glanced to her right and saw the V of the other Wild Hunt—and saw several men fall before an arrow could touch them. Good. Morphia had joined the hunt. Yesterday, the Sleep Sister had worked with the healers to ease the suffering of the wounded. Today, she would use her gift to put some of the enemy to sleep, making it easier for the huntsmen to deal with the others.

The human companies poured down from the center of the rise, keeping the Hunt from being surrounded as it continued toward the stones.

Then an arrow struck her horse in the chest. It was more luck than skill that she managed to land on her feet when she threw herself out of the saddle.

"Hunter!" One of the huntsmen slowed, reached out a hand for her.

"Go on!" she yelled.

They flowed around her, giving her a breathing space. She reached back—and touched her last arrow. Unbuckling the harness, she dropped bow and quiver beside her dead horse, then crouched, waiting for the last of the huntsmen to pass by her.

When she could see again, she cursed viciously to herself. *Mother's tits, Liam! Don't you ever listen?*

He was in the field, fighting with a short sword now, out-matched by the guard captain, who had a longer sword and the benefit of training. Liam took a wrong step, lost his footing. As he went down, the guard captain raised his sword for a killing blow—and was struck by an arrow in the throat.

Well done, Varden, Ashk thought as she looked back toward the rise. But it wasn't Varden nocking another arrow, it was Breanna taking aim at the next man who came near her brother while a hawk, a vixen, and a whoo-it owl did their best to protect her back.

She understood Falco going into the field with Breanna, but she was going to have a talk with the Bard and the Muse when this was over. What did they think a fox and a whoo-it owl could do in the middle of a battle? The two of them had more courage—or more compassion—than sense.

She half rose from her crouch, then froze at the sight of more companies of men running out of the trees at the far end of the field. She glanced back at the rise, but there were no more fresh companies of men coming over the top to join the battle, no more Fae. Mother's mercy, how many more men did the Witch's Hammer have?

Then she realized they weren't running to join the battle. They were fleeing.

She couldn't move, could barely breathe when she saw the dark horse burst out of the trees, saw those men fall in waves as the horse and rider caught up to them, cut through them.

The Gatherer had come.

"Liam!" Breanna screamed.

He turned toward Breanna, unaware of the danger riding straight at him.

"Go!" Ashk shouted. She changed into a shadow hound and charged Liam. He saw the movement and had started to turn to meet it when she slammed into him, sending his sword flying as they hit the ground.

She spun around, crouching over him, her fangs bared as the dark horse came closer, closer. Out of the corner of her eye, she saw Breanna running back toward the rise, followed by the hawk, vixen, and whoo-it owl.

And she saw Morag—and what Morag had become.

For one long, painful moment, their eyes locked. Then the Gatherer rode past her, turning the dark horse toward the center of the field at the same moment Selena, with moonlight streaming around and behind her, came over the rise, followed by the Sons and Daughters of the House of Gaian.

Not the Huntress, Morag. Not Selena. Mother's mercy, not Selena.

She barely noticed Liam shoving her off him, barely noticed the fighting still going on in the rest of the field. All she could see was Selena galloping toward the stones, the enemy fleeing ahead of her—and the Gatherer galloping toward Selena.

Selena raised her hand and the pairs of riders broke formation, shifting to become a staggered line with her in the lead. She swung to the left, taking the line with her. Dark horse and gray passed each other with barely any daylight between them.

Morag rode on, turning back toward the trees at the far end of the field. Selena continued her wide curve around the stones. As she rode, with Rhyann behind her, a circle of moonlight and fire began to form. Wind whipped around the stones, splintering arrows before they could touch the riders.

She changed back to her human form and stood up.

"Ashk?" Liam said warily. "What's happening?"

"Can you move?" she replied, evading his question. When he nodded, she retrieved his sword and handed it to him. "Let's go."

She walked back to her horse, picked up her bow and quiver, and headed for the stones, not even looking back to see if he followed, terrifyingly aware that she and Liam were the only people alive in that part of the field.

The last rider following Selena swung into place, completing the circle. They circled again. And once more. The ground trembled. The wind howled. Lightning slashed the sky, bringing with it a brief cloudburst of rain. And fire ringed the circle made around the stones.

As the last circle was completed, Selena swung left again,

turning Mistrunner sharply back to face the stones. The others swung out of the circle and went past her, turning back until they formed a crescent with Selena at its center.

Selena raised her arms. The cloudburst ended. Moments later, the sun shown down upon the field. And still moonlight glowed around the circle, forming a barrier.

"Witch's Hammer!" Selena shouted. "Show yourself, Master Inquisitor, or someone else will bargain for you!"

Nothing happened. There were plenty of men moving among the stones, but no one answered. Finally, a cloaked, hooded figure appeared.

"What are you to think you can bargain with me?" a growling voice shouted back.

"I am vengeance—and I am justice. You tried to reshape our world to your own liking—and you have failed. We stand, and we will always stand. We are the Mother's Daughters. We are the Mother's Sons. We are the Pillars of the World. We are the House of Gaian. And we are going to grant your wish. You and your followers are exiled from this world, Inquisitor, but we will give you another to shape as you will." Selena raised her arms higher. "I call earth!"

"We call earth!" the Sons and Daughters repeated.

"I call air!"

"We call air!"

"I call water!"

"We call water!"

"I call fire!"

"We call fire!"

Power flowed into the circle. Flowed and flowed.

"By the light of the sun, by the light of the moon, by the four branches of the Mother, we make a world beyond this world, anchored to it but never a part of it. We make it out of dreams and will." Selena pointed at the Witch's Hammer. "As *you* will, so mote it be."

The ground shook. Lightning flashed. The fire that formed a circle rose so high Ashk could no longer see the stones.

The power swirled inside the circle. Swirled and swirled.

Then, with a tremendous thunderclap that knocked Ashk to the ground, it was gone.

Chapter 52

waning moon

Adolfo slowly got to his feet and looked around. Stone. Nothing but stone. And a spear of gold and silver light no thicker than a fist touching the stone a man's length in front of him and rising up, up, up until it disappeared somewhere in that vaulted ceiling of stone.

He didn't like that light. Hated that light. It felt . . . clean . . . and repulsive. He moved away from it. He had no trouble seeing. Fire burned among the stones, and the air reeked with the smell of sulfur. He tore off the cloak that now felt too hot and confining and went searching for the water he could hear trickling nearby. It spilled out from a crack and pooled in a hollowed stone that formed a basin. Bending over, he lapped the water. It tasted of blood, of gore, of rotting bodies. Delicious.

He heard voices below him, saw the rocks piled together to make rough stairs leading down into the stones and the fire.

"What happened?" asked one frightened voice. "Where are we?"

"Where's Master Adolfo?" another voice said. Then, shouting, "Master! Master Adolfo?"

He walked down those rough stairs, moving toward the voices.

"Where are we?"

"It— Mother's mercy! This is the Fiery Pit! We've been thrown into the Fiery Pit!"

There is no Mother here, Adolfo thought. *Only the Master. Only . . .*

Hunger.

He followed the curve of the stairs, stopping when he saw them. Wolfram barons. Sylvalan barons. Guard captains and bowmen. His . . .

Meat.

. . . Inquisitors. His . . .

Feast.

. . . followers. He would show them the glory of the world he'd created for them. He would show them he was . . .

Hunger.

. . . . was . . .

An Inquisitor looked up, saw him, and screamed, *"It's the Evil One!"*

He laughed as he watched them flee, running deeper and deeper into the Pit.

Feast.

He followed them deeper into the Pit. And he hunted.

Frowning, Selena studied the sky above the stones. The Black Coats and their followers were gone, so the magic had worked, but where was the anchor of light?

One by one, the Sons and Daughters rode away from the stones to help the humans deal with the prisoners and find the wounded until only Rhyann stood with her. Then Ashk joined her . . . and Liam.

"I don't see the anchor," Selena said quietly. Steam rose from the ground inside the circle—ground that was now cracked and barren.

"There." Ashk pointed to a glow barely visible among the stones.

"But"—Rhyann shook her head—"it's going down. Why would it go *down*?"

A chill went through Selena. "Dreams and will. His dreams. His will. He made the world he wanted. Mother have mercy."

"Vengeance and justice," Ashk said. "You gave him both, Huntress, in a way no one else could have."

Selena turned to look at Liam, who stared at her with unreadable eyes. "I am sorry the anchor had to be placed here." She hesitated. "Your people should build a wall just beyond the circle. What was made here . . . I don't know what would happen to anyone who stepped onto that barren ground or climbed among those stones."

"When all the bodies are given back to the Mother, this will be a field of the dead. I don't think anyone will go near those stones after what happened here today, but we'll build the wall."

Aiden and Lyrra rode up on Minstrel, followed by Breanna and Falco on another horse. Aiden helped Lyrra slide down from behind him before dismounting. Hand in hand, they came forward. "It's done?"

Selena nodded. "The Witch's Hammer and his followers are gone."

Morphia rode up, followed by a few of the Fae. She gave them a brilliant smile, her face lit with happiness and relief as she dismounted to join them. "Ashk! Morag's here. Did you see her? I only caught a glimpse of her as she rode back into the trees, but she's here."

Selena felt Ashk shudder. Then Rhyann said, "Selena," in a quiet, tense voice.

She heard a muffled cry of fear, watched men scatter, leaving a clear path for the dark horse that walked toward her.

"Morag!" Morphia called. Then, puzzled and a little fearful, "Morag?"

Selena saw Aiden and Lyrra rush over to Morphia. She heard Liam whisper, "Mother's mercy." And she felt Ashk walk away as Morag dismounted and walked closer to them.

Morphia's face crumpled in disbelief and horror. *"Morag!"*

Selena grabbed Rhyann's arm, pulling her sister behind her. An illusion of protection, nothing more. But Morag stopped a man's length in front of her. She saw something savage in those dark eyes, something that would ride through villages and leave nothing but empty corpses in its wake. But the woman Morag must have been was also shining out of those dark eyes, pained and so weary.

I have the power to shape a world beyond this world, but I don't know how to change this. I know nothing that can change this.

"What do you want, Morag?" she asked gently.

One tear spilled down a dark, leathery cheek. "I want to go home."

Silence.

Then . . .

"Merry meet, and merry part, and merry meet again."

A moment caught by the eye, frozen by memory.

Morag, standing straight and tall, turning toward that voice.

Ashk, waiting, the bow drawn back, her eyes clear and yet filled with a terrible grief.

Then the arrow sang Death's song. Pierced the chest. Found the heart.

And Morag fell.

"Noooo!" Morphia screamed as Aiden struggled to hold her back.

Ashk dropped her bow, moved forward slowly.

"How could you?" Morphia screamed. "How could you?"

Ashk stared at the body. "I promised to do what needed to be done."

Mist rose from the body, took the shape of a slender, lovely woman.

Morag turned to look at her sister. Raised a hand in farewell to Aiden and Lyrra. When she looked at Ashk, she smiled.

"You'll be missed," Ashk said softly. "Don't stay away too long."

Morag raised her arms. Her ghost changed into the shape of a raven. As she flew toward the shimmering road that suddenly opened in the field, Selena watched ghosts flow up the road behind her as Morag led the spirits of the dead to the Shadowed Veil for the last time.

Before Selena could say anything, do anything, Ashk turned away from all of them and started walking toward the rise.

Ashk reached the top of the rise before Breanna caught up to her.

"Ashk! *Ashk!*"

Ashk stopped walking, but didn't turn to look at her.

Breanna reached out but didn't touch. Ashk looked like a woman about to shatter. She knew how that felt. "She shouldn't stay in that field, Ashk. She shouldn't be buried near that . . . place. Where should we take her to give her back to the Mother?"

Ashk swallowed hard. "Morphia is her sister. It should be Morphia's choice."

"No," Breanna said slowly, "I don't think so." She waited until Ashk looked at her. "You freed Morag from what she'd become, for her sake. Morphia would choose a place that gives *her* comfort, but you'll choose a place that's right for Morag."

Ashk clenched her hands, and Breanna watched strength

battling grief. Finally, Ashk said, "Somewhere in the Old Place. A spot where there are shadows and light."

"As you will, so mote it be," Breanna said.

She watched Ashk walk down the other side of the rise. Alone.

Chapter 53

waning moon

Ashk took a deep breath to steady herself before knocking on the guest room door. "Morphia? It's Ashk."

She waited a long time before she heard a muffled, "Come in if you must."

She stepped into the room, closing the door behind her—and simply watched in silence while Morphia packed her saddlebags.

"Where are you headed?" Ashk finally asked.

"I don't know yet. Maybe back to the home Clan for a while."

"If you can wait a couple more days, you can ride with—"

"I don't want to ride with you, Ashk." Morphia's hands clenched around the camisole she'd just folded. Sighing, she shook it out, refolded it, and tucked it into the saddlebag before looking at Ashk. "I don't want to ride with you, Hunter. You did what you thought was right—and maybe it was. But you didn't give it a chance. If I'd had another moment or two to collect myself, I could have put her to sleep for a while—at least until the witches had a little time to discover if they could have changed her back."

A moment or two, Ashk thought bleakly. *You might not have had that moment or two. If she lost control of what was inside her for even a heartbeat of time, you could have ended up dead. Worse than dead. Would you have wanted Morag to fight her way back to clarity to find your torn body, to find no trace of your spirit, knowing what must have happened to it?* But she couldn't say those things to the woman staring at her with dark, grief-filled eyes.

Morphia shook her head and went back to packing her saddlebags. "Maybe if Sheridan had lived . . . Maybe when enough time has passed . . . But right now, Ashk, when I look at you, all I see is the person who killed my sister. So I don't want to travel with you. I don't want to be in the part of Sylvalan where you rule. There's work to be done in the world. I'll find a place to do it."

"Safe travel, Morphia," Ashk said as she opened the door.

"Ashk." Morphia hesitated. "For Morag's sake, and in her memory, I wish you gentle dreams."

Ashk bolted out of the room, turned blindly down the hallway, and ran straight into Aiden.

He caught her arms to keep them both from a tumble. When he saw the door, still partially open, he slipped an arm around her shoulders and led her to the room she shared with Gwynith. She was grateful Gwynith wasn't there and wished desperately that Padrick was.

"Liam asked us to stay for the council meeting tomorrow," Aiden said. "He seems to think my writing is neater than his, and he wants to be sure the other barons can read the decisions that are made without stumbling over half the words. You're staying, too?"

Ashk nodded. "I'll leave after the meeting." *I want to go home.* The words echoed in her head, in her heart.

"You'll be heading back to Bretonwood?"

She nodded again.

"In that case, if you don't mind the company, Lyrra and I will travel with you for a while."

"Your company is always welcome, Bard."

After giving her shoulder a comforting squeeze, he left her.

She stared out the window for a long time, not really seeing anything. Finally she stretched out on the bed and did something she hadn't allowed herself to do. She cried.

Breanna sat on the bed, feeling awkward as she watched Fiona pack. "You're welcome to stay. You know that."

Fiona joined her on the bed and rested a hand on Breanna's cheek. "I know, darling Breanna. We all know that. But the Hunter knows where Jennyfer and Mihail found safe harbor, so his wife and daughter will travel with her as far as the western bay and take a ship from there. And the rest of us . . . We have to go back."

"You don't know what you'll find there. You don't know if there's anything left."

"Then we'll start again. Build again. And one day our ships

will sail down the Una River and out to sea again. But whatever we find there, it's still home. We need to reclaim what was ours."

"I understand."

Fiona's brows drew together in a worried frown. "You're welcome to come with us. You don't have to stay here alone."

Breanna forced herself to smile. "I won't be alone. Clay, Edgar, and Glynis will still be here." Neither of them mentioned Falco, who had made a fumbling excuse about needing to do something before riding away an hour ago.

Fiona went back to her packing. "You'll write to me on a regular basis, just to let me know how things are going."

"Yes, I will." Breanna stood up and hugged her cousin. "I'm glad you were here."

When she went outside a little while later, she found Falco sitting on the bench beside the kitchen door. He sprang up as soon as he saw her.

"Breanna? Could we talk?"

Why not? she thought, suddenly weary. She sank down on the bench. He sat on the other end—the polite distance required between strangers. Were there some standard phrases gentry women used when a lover was trying to say he was leaving? She'd have to ask Elinore so she'd be prepared next time. If her heart was ever willing to risk a next time.

"Breanna, maybe it's too soon, all things considered, but . . ." He reached down, picked up a basket, and set it between them. "I got this for you."

She lifted the cloth folded over the top of the basket—and stared at the sleeping black puppy. She wanted to run her fingers over that soft fur, but she couldn't quite bring herself to touch him.

"Squire Thurston's bitch had a litter," Falco said. "He wasn't going to keep them. And since he's pretty sure the wild oats the bitch got into came from here, I thought . . ."

"Wild oats?" Breanna asked, bewildered. "From here? What kind of . . . *Oh.*" She looked at the puppy again, and her throat tightened. But she still hesitated to pet him.

"I thought he'd be company for you, once winter sets in. And I thought you'd like him better than a salmon."

"Better than—" Remembering the condition of the salmon he'd brought her, she grabbed the puppy out of the basket and cradled him against her chest. "Falco! You didn't fly over there and snatch him, did you?"

"Fly? Snatch?" Falco's eyes widened. "*No.* I rode over with the basket. Just got back a little while ago."

"Oh." It wasn't so hard to cuddle the puppy, who was content to be petted back to sleep. "I thought . . . after everything that's happened, I thought you'd grown tired of this world and were going back to Tir Alainn." *Where it's peaceful . . . and safe.*

After a long silence, he asked quietly, "Do you want to live in Tir Alainn?"

She didn't have to think about it. "No."

"Then I'm staying. I love you, Breanna. And I think . . . I think Willowsbrook needs us."

She heard it again. The same hesitation and uncertainty she'd heard when he'd finally shown himself to her in human form. He was looking for some assurance that he had a place in the world.

Smiling, she held out her hand. "Yes, Falco. Willowsbrook needs us. Both of us."

The following morning Aiden set two fresh stacks of paper at one end of the dining room table at Liam's house, made sure the quills were sharpened and the ink bottles filled. He and Lyrra would make notes of this barons' council, then combine them into one document for Liam's review and approval.

He looked at Donovan, who sat in a cushioned chair to his left. "Are you sure you should be out of bed?"

"If I didn't get out of that cursed bed, I'd either have to strangle Gwenny or have an affair with the cook. The woman has taken a fiendish delight is serving me chicken soup for two out of three meals."

"The cook?"

"No," Donovan growled. "My wife."

Aiden coughed to disguise his laughter.

Looking sulky, Donovan turned to Liam. "You've had news from the west?"

"I'll tell you when we're all gathered," Liam replied, fingering the folded sheet of paper.

To distract Donovan—and satisfy his own curiosity—Aiden asked, "You've had news as well, haven't you, Ashk?" She looked more exhausted now than she had during the days of the battle, so he was relieved to see a little color in her face again.

"From Padrick," Ashk said, smiling. "He and the children are well. And Ari gave birth to a strong, healthy boy. Padrick says Neall is hiding his disappointment in not having a daughter by wearing a silly grin, walking into walls, and generally making so much of a nuisance of himself that the Clan's Lady of the Hearth has taken to locking him out of the cottage for a couple of hours every day so that Ari and the babe can get some rest. Of course, since he sounds too sulky to be complaining just on Neall's behalf, I suspect Uncle Padrick has also been locked out of the cottage on a regular basis."

"That's wonderful news," Lyrra said, having paused in the doorway to listen. As she walked to her place at the table, she pointed at Aiden. "You should write a song."

"You should write a poem," he countered.

"We'll collaborate," she said primly, taking her seat.

Aiden leaned close to her and whispered, "We did that quite well last evening."

Watching her color rise, he busied himself with examining his quills, fully aware of the interested, and speculative, glances the barons were giving Lyrra as they walked into the room.

Ashk took her seat at the table, followed by Selena.

The table had been pushed to one side of the room so that chairs for the surviving barons who had fought at Willowsbrook could be placed in rows facing the table. Fae Lords and Sons of the House of Gaian stood against the wall, and two chairs were set to one side for Breanna and Elinore. The barons had argued that their council should be private while they decided the fate of the eastern counties ruled by the barons who had followed the Inquisitors, but Liam had insisted that the Fae and the witches should be present if they so wished since they would be affected by any decisions made here.

When everyone was assembled, Liam opened the piece of paper. "I have a message from Padrick, Baron of Breton. You are all free to examine the contents."

One of the barons waved the offer away. "Just tell us what it says, Liam."

Liam cleared his throat. "Recognizing that the fate of Sylvalan would have to be decided swiftly once the battle was won and that it would be better not to delay such discussion by waiting for those who would require days of travel to reach us here,

Baron Padrick states that I have been granted a proxy vote—for all the western barons."

Stunned silence.

Aiden made hurried notes. If his understanding was clear on the way the council worked, Liam's vote counted for more than the rest of the men combined.

When no one made any comment, Liam folded the paper and set it aside. "Shall we begin?"

The door to the dining room opened. Aiden glanced up and dropped his quill, spattering ink all over the top sheet of paper. Pushing the paper aside, he retrieved the quill and dipped it in the ink pot.

"Oh, my," Lyrra whispered.

Her hair was pinned up in a becoming fashion instead of scraped back in a tight knot, and her gown was as finely made as any gentry lady's, but Aiden had no trouble recognizing Skelly's sweet granny. And the way Breanna and Selena leaped to their feet when she entered the room made him very nervous.

"Grandmother," Selena said.

The Crone smiled at Selena and Breanna. "Granddaughters."

"Take my seat, Grandmother," Breanna said, touching the back of her chair.

The Crone sat down and folded her hands in her lap. Her eyes touched every man in the room before they fixed on Liam. "The Crones have discussed what has happened in Sylvalan. Since I am the one who lives closest to this place, I have to come to tell you what has been decided."

"Begging your pardon, Lady," one of the barons said. "But it is up to the barons to decide what happens to the land owned by—"

"You do not own the land." Her voice cut like a knife. "You have never owned the land. The Great Mother is held by her Sons and Daughters. It has always been so. It will always be so. We granted your people stewardship over portions of the land, giving you a place to live in your own way, just as we set aside portions of the land for the Fae and the Small Folk and the wild things of the world. Stewardship, Baron. Stewardship. You do not own the Mother."

Aiden wrote frantically, part of him fearful of what she was going to say and another part hoping she wouldn't object if he shaped those words into a song.

"This is what we have decided. The barons in the west, in the midlands, and in parts of the north, south, and east will retain stewardship of the lands they now hold. But the land that was held by the barons who followed the Inquisitors is forfeit. *All* of it."

A swell of protest rose from the barons, cut off abruptly when Liam raised his hand.

"Wise of you, Grandson who is also a baron."

Aiden wrote frantically, aware that Lyrra was scribbling just as fast.

"The land is forfeit. However, we recognize that your people have already suffered much, and turning them off the land they have worked would be cruel and unjust. Therefore, they may stay if they wish—but under the rule of the House of Gaian.

"Sons and Daughters who are willing to leave their homes in the Mother's Hills will take up stewardship of those lands. The boundaries of the Old Places will be walked again. The land will be reclaimed as a home for the wild things and the Small Folk— and the Fae. Other Sons and Daughters who have the strength and skill will do what they can to reopen the shining roads and free the Fae who were trapped there. This is what we have decided."

"And if we don't agree?" one of the barons asked.

The Crone raised one hand, palm up. "Earth. Air. Water. Fire. These are what we hold in our hands. Can you live without them?"

Aiden stopped writing, suddenly aware that his pen scratching on the paper was the only sound in the room.

"It is justice," Liam finally said, bowing his head.

The Crone nodded. "As we will, so mote it be." As she walked out of the room, she paused and looked at Breanna. "We will talk, Granddaughter."

"As you will," Breanna replied.

Ashk rose from the table. "Breanna? Are you nervous about talking to her?"

Breanna smiled weakly. "A little."

"She isn't really your grandmother."

"She and Nuala were cousins. So she is the elder most closely related to me now."

Liam stood up. "It would seem this meeting is concluded." He turned toward Breanna. "We can talk to her in the morning room."

"She wants to talk to me, Liam, not us."

"Well, she gets to talk to us." Pushing past Ashk and Selena, he strode to the doorway and stood beside it.

Breanna muttered, "Featherhead," and walked out of the room with Liam right behind her.

"Selena?" Donovan asked. "If I may ask a question? What makes the Crones entitled to make such decisions about the world?"

Selena hesitated, then raised one hand, palm up. "The Crones who rule the Mother's Hills are the ones whose power comes from all four branches in equal measure."

"Could she do what she implied? Could any of those women take away the world?"

Selena lowered her hand. "That is not a question you should ask of the House of Gaian. But there is a poem that gives the answer."

"I know it."

After Selena walked out of the room, the rest of the people trickled out as well until only Donovan, Aiden, and Lyrra were in the room.

Lyrra glanced at Aiden and gathered up her papers, quills, and ink pot. "I'd better make a fairer copy while I remember what all these scribbles mean."

When he and Donovan were alone, Aiden asked, "What is the answer?"

"'If roused, their wrath can shake the world / And men will not see the light of day again,'" Donovan replied.

"Mother's mercy."

"That's what we all stake our lives on, Bard. The Mother's mercy. And the mercy of Her Sons and Daughters." Donovan struggled to stand up.

"Do you want help getting back to your room?"

Donovan gave Aiden a wan smile. "I wouldn't refuse it. Right now, I wouldn't turn down a bowl of chicken soup."

The Crone gave Liam a cool stare. He stared back, not sure why he was so primed to fight, except that Breanna had already been through enough.

"I asked to talk to Breanna," the Crone said.

"Then talk. But I'm staying."

"Oh, sit down, Liam," Breanna said.

He sat on the sofa, close enough to her that their shoulders brushed.

"Now, Granddaughter, since you have no family here—"

"She has family here," Liam snapped. "She doesn't have to live alone in the Old Place. She can live here with us."

"I'm not living alone in the Old Place," Breanna snapped back. "I'm living with Falco and a puppy."

Liam frowned. "A puppy? When did you get a puppy?"

"Yesterday. Falco brought him for me." Breanna squirmed. "Now that I've figured out what he meant about the salmon, I think the puppy was intended as a courting gift."

His frown deepened. "Courting gift? Giving a woman a pet is more a betrothal gift than a courting gift."

"Whatever. The point is, I'm not living alone. And the only reason you're being a featherheaded jackass about Falco is because you want to court Selena and don't know how to do it."

"I never said I wanted to court Selena!"

"But you do want to, don't you?"

"Yes, I want to, but I never said it!" He crossed his arms and muttered, "Stone-headed female."

Breanna crossed her arms in exactly the same way and muttered, "Featherheaded jackass."

Finally remembering they had an audience, he looked at the Crone sitting in a chair across from them. Her lips were pressed together and she was shaking with the effort not to laugh.

Breanna hunched further into the sofa. "You wanted to talk to me, Grandmother?"

The Crone laughed, shook her head, and rose. "There's no need. I've already learned what I needed to know. But remember, Breanna, I *am* your elder now. If you need my help—for anything—you must come to me . . . or ask me to come to you." She walked over to Liam and took his face between her hands. "And you, Grandson. A witch enjoys being courted the same way as any other woman."

Liam looked sulky. "I refuse to spend my evenings writing bad poetry."

The Crone sighed. "That's too bad. It would give her something to laugh over when she's my age."

They sat side by side for a long time after the Crone walked out of the room.

"Truce?" Liam finally said. "I won't nag you about Falco, and you won't nag me about Selena."

"Truce." Breanna smiled. "Besides, there are plenty of other things I can nag you about. Rhyann made up a list for me."

Chapter 54

new moon

L iam hovered in the doorway, watching Selena pack her saddlebags. "You don't have to go."

"This is your mother's room, and she's coming back to live here with you and Brooke."

"There are plenty of other rooms. You don't have to go."

"Yes, I do."

It wasn't fair. From the moment she'd arrived at Willowsbrook, they'd been caught up in the fight to survive. Now, when they could finally spend a little time getting to know each other better, she was leaving. "Why?"

He found the color suddenly flooding her cheeks intriguing.

"Because my father would disapprove," she said, stuffing garments into the saddlebags with more speed than care.

So her father had gentry sensibilities when it came to his daughter. *That* he understood.

"Where are you going?"

"Not far. Across the brook, actually." The color in her cheeks deepened. "Breanna said they have plenty of room, and since her handfast to Falco was witnessed by the Bard, the Muse, *and* her family's elder, it would be proper to stay with them. And— And she mentioned that it wouldn't be that far for a . . . friend . . . to ride to come visit."

To hide his own delight, he muttered, "She's been spending too much time with Rhyann."

"Oh, Rhyann's going to live there, too." Selena looked up, her eyes filled with amusement.

"Mother's tits."

She laughed. "Rhyann does tend to produce that reaction." Picking up her saddlebags, she walked to the door, stopping when he didn't move aside. "Thank you for your hospitality, Baron Liam."

"It was my pleasure, Lady Selena." He took the saddlebags from her and smiled. "I'll see you to your horse. It's the least a friend can do."

Chapter 55

waning moon

A fter glancing at Lyrra, who nodded, Aiden reined in. "Ashk?"

She turned the dark horse and walked it back to them.

He understood her keeping the dark horse. She'd lost her horse, he'd lost his rider, and since there were two other dark horses at Bretonwood, he'd also be among his own kind.

But he didn't understand about the puppy.

When they'd stopped at that inn on their way back through the Mother's Hills, it had broken his heart when the innkeeper asked about Morag, explaining that he was keeping a bitch puppy for her—a shadow hound mix. Lyrra had burst into tears. Ashk had simply walked away. But the next morning, when they were getting ready to leave, she came out of the inn wearing an odd kind of sling with the puppy tucked inside.

She wouldn't talk about it, had actually said very little during the journey back to the west.

"What is it, Aiden?"

He didn't want to voice his thoughts. Everyone else had already parted from them. The Fae who lived closest to the western bay were escorting Mihail's wife and daughter to a harbor town where a ship would take them to Sealand. The Fae from other Clans had split off, taking other routes to return home. The handful of huntsmen from Bretonwood were the only ones left except for him and Lyrra. But this was the place—and it was time.

"This is where we part ways," he said gently.

"You're welcome to stay with the Bretonwood Clan."

"We know. But we've been talking, doing a lot of thinking. We don't really want to live with the Clans anymore. We've lived in the same world and remained strangers—the Fae, humans, and witches. Since Lyrra and I have more experience living outside the Clans . . . Well, there's a place we'd like to go if they'll accept us."

Ashk looked puzzled. Then she studied the unmarked road that forked off the main road—and smiled for the first time in days. "Oh, I think they'll welcome the Muse and the Bard and his dancing horse. You'll let me hear from you when you're settled in."

"And we'll come to Bretonwood for a visit before the Winter Solstice." Because the thought had been weighing on him more heavily the closer they got to this spot, he finally said what he'd wanted to say since they left Willowsbrook. "She only wanted to go home."

Ashk looked away. "She couldn't. She dreamed of it, Aiden. That's what haunted her. She dreamed of an enemy she couldn't find fast enough, couldn't stop. But she saw what it did. She saw it kill the people she loved. That's why she asked for the promise. If she couldn't stop it, I had to." Her eyes filled with tears. "But she will come home."

"You think she'll come back to one of the western Clans this time? Maybe even Bretonwood?"

"No, I don't think she'll come back to the Clans. I think, not too many years from now, Ari will look into her baby daughter's eyes and recognize the spirit looking back at her. And when that day comes, Morag will be home." Turning the dark horse, she added, "Blessings of the day to you," and rode away.

He stared after her.

"The dark horse," Lyrra whispered. "The puppy."

Aiden nodded. "From the moment she decided to take the dark horse, she's been preparing for that day, whenever it will come." He wiped the tears from his eyes and took a deep breath to steady himself. "Come along, wife. Let's see if we can find our own place in the world."

Backtracking a few steps, they headed down the unmarked road.

Wiccandale was still the prettiest village Aiden had ever seen. The first time they'd ridden down this main street, he and Lyrra had been traveling to Bretonwood, still searching for the Hunter, and the people's wariness of strangers had provided a cold welcome—until Minstrel changed the tune. This time, when they rode to the tavern, men nudged each other and smiled. Women pointed at Minstrel and whispered something to their children that made the children laugh.

"So you've come back," the tavern owner said, coming out to stand in his doorway. "And in good time as well. Come along, then. I'll show you the cottage and you can decide if it suits you." He turned his head and shouted, "Kellie! The Bard, the Muse, and the dancing horse have come. I'll be showing them old Nara's cottage."

"Tell them to come back for supper!" a woman shouted in reply. "They'll not be wanting to cook their own supper their first night."

"Done and done. I'm Gavin, by the way. Come along. It isn't far." He set off at a brisk walk.

Bewildered, Aiden and Lyrra urged the horses to follow him.

He was right. The cottage wasn't far, but it was set off by itself.

"It was the women in Nara's family who first walked the boundaries of Wiccandale and gave the wiccanfae a place to call their own that wasn't quite Clan, wasn't quite a human village but a bit of both, do you see? And so it's been with us. There's more witches among us than in times past, but there's still plenty of us who are wiccanfae."

"I'm wiccanfae," Lyrra murmured.

"Are you, now? Well, then."

The cottage was lovely, warm and welcoming, but Gavin didn't give them time to linger before herding them back outside.

"That bit of a barn there has plenty of room for a couple of horses, a ponycart, tack and feed," Gavin said, pointing. "On that side of the stone fence is common pasture, but this here is part of the land in Nara's keeping. Those fruit trees and berry bushes, too, along with the hayfield. Now. Over the past few years, Nara had a bargain with a few of us about the hayfield. We'd tend it and harvest it. She received enough hay to see her animals through the seasons and we split the rest between us. Worked well for everyone. If you're agreeable, we'll keep doing the same. Since I've got the tavern and have use for them, Nara gave me and Kellie her cow and chickens, with the understanding that whoever took the cottage would get the milk and eggs they needed." When he finally paused, Aiden just nodded, not sure what else to do. Cows? Chickens? Hayfields?

"What happened to Nara?" Lyrra asked.

"She packed up. Said she was needed in the world, what with all the troubles going on in the east. Now that it's settled, she said witches were needed to touch the land again, wake up the magic in the Old Places. A few of the youngsters went with her, those of an age to have restless feet and a desire to see what's beyond the home fields. So she said I was to find someone to care for the place while she was gone. She's got nieces and nephews—I should know, I'm one of them—but we've all got our own places and we're happy where we are."

"Why us?" Aiden asked.

Gavin gave him a long look. "Well, I'll tell you, Bard. The day Nara packed up her ponycart, she took me aside and told me she'd had a dream the night before about the right people for this land. She told me she dreamed she walked her land just like she always did, but she heard music in the air around the fruit trees and stories bloomed among her flowers. When I heard you were coming into the village, it just seemed . . . It was like she knew you were coming. So, what do you think, Bard?"

His head was spinning, and he wasn't sure what he thought. But now that Gavin had finally stopped talking, he realized the man was fidgety, nervous—and he understood why. Gavin wanted them to stay. Whether it was because of Nara's dream or for some other reason, he and Lyrra were wanted here, welcome here.

He looked around again at the cottage, at the small barn that would be a snug shelter for the horses, at the flower and vegetable gardens. He could see himself sitting under the fruit trees with his harp, working on a song. He could picture Lyrra sitting on that bench near the flowers, working on a story or just sitting peacefully and letting her gift flow into the world. He could see them in the tavern on winter evenings, entertaining friends and neighbors. He could see it—and the picture warmed his heart.

"So, what do you think?" Gavin asked again.

Feeling Lyrra's hand slip into his, Aiden smiled. "I think we've come home."

THE TIR ALAINN TRILOGY

by

Anne Bishop

The *New York Times* bestselling Black Jewels Series

by Anne Bishop

"Darkly mesmerizing...fascinatingly different."
—*Locus*

This is the story of the heir to a dark throne, a magic more powerful than that of the High Lord of Hell, and an ancient prophecy. These books tell of a ruthless game of politics and intrigue, magic and betrayal, love and sacrifice, destiny and fulfillment.

Daughter of the Blood
Heir to the Shadows
Queen of the Darkness
The Invisible Ring
Dreams Made Flesh
Tangled Webs
The Shadow Queen
Shalador's Lady

R420